Even the Darkest Night

A Terra Alta Investigation

When Melchor Marín goes to investigate the horrific double-murder of a rich printer and his wife in rural Cataluña nothing quite adds up. The young cop from the big city, hero of a foiled terrorist attack, has been sent to Terra Alta till things quieten down. Observant, streetwise and circumspect, Melchor is also an outsider.

The son of a Barcelona prostitute who never knew his father, Melchor rapidly fell into trouble and was jailed at 19, convicted of driving for a Colombian drug cartel. While he was behind bars, he read Hugo's Les Misérables, and then his mother was murdered. Admiring of both Jean Valjean and Javert – but mostly the relentless Javert – he decided to become a policeman.

Now he is out for revenge, but he can wait, and meanwhile he has discovered happiness with his wife, the local librarian, and their daughter, who is, of course, called Cossette.

Slowly at first, and then more rapidly once ordered to abandon the case, he tracks the clues that will reveal the larger truth behind what appears at first to be a cold-blooded, professional killing.

JAVIER CERCAS

Even the Darkest Night

A Terra Alta Investigation

Translated from the Spanish by
Anne McLean

MACLEHOSE PRESS
A Bill Swainson Book
QUERCUS · LONDON

First published in the Spanish language as *Terra Alta*
by Editorial Planeta, S.A., in 2019

First published in Great Britain in 2021 as A Bill Swainson Book by

MacLehose Press
An imprint of Quercus Publishing Ltd
Carmelite House
50 Victoria Embankment
London EC4Y 0DZ

An Hachette UK company

A CIP catalogue record for this book is available from the British Library.

ISBN (HB) 978 1 52941 000 6
ISBN (TPB) 978 1 52941 001 3
ISBN (Ebook) 978 1 52941 003 7

1   3   5   7   9   10   8   6   4   2

Designed and typeset in Sabon by Patty Rennie
Printed and bound by CPI Group (UK) Ltd, Croydon, CR0 4YY

Papers used by MacLehose Press are from well-managed
forests and other responsible sources.

*For Raül Cercas and Mercè Mas,
my Terra Alta*

Part One

1

Melchor is still in his office, simmering on the low flame of his own impatience waiting for the night shift to end, when the phone rings. It's the duty officer at the front desk. Two dead at the Adell country house, he announces.

"The printing company Adells?" Melchor says.

"That's right," the officer says. "Do you know where they live?"

"Out on the Vilalba dels Arcs Road, no?"

"Exactly."

"Have we got anyone there?"

"Ruiz and Mayol. They just phoned in."

"I'm on my way."

Until that moment, the night had been as calm as usual. In the hours before dawn there is hardly anyone left in the station and, as Melchor turns off the lights, closes his office door and runs down the deserted stairs, pulling on his jacket as he goes, the silence is so intense that it reminds him of those first days in Terra Alta, when he was still addicted to the roar of the city and the silence of the countryside kept him awake, condemning him to sleepless nights he fought with novels and sleeping pills. That memory brings back the forgotten image of the man he was four years earlier, when he arrived in Terra Alta; it also brings back an obvious fact: that he and that individual are two different people, as distinct as a criminal and a law-abiding man, as Jean Valjean and Monsieur Madeleine, the split and contradictory protagonist of *Les Misérables*, his favourite novel.

When he reaches the ground floor, Melchor checks out his Walther P99 and a box of ammunition from the armoury, telling himself it's been too long since he last read *Les Misérables* and that he'll have to resign himself to missing breakfast with his wife and daughter that morning.

He gets into his Opel Corsa and, while he pulls out of the station garage, he phones Sergeant Blai.

"You better pray that whatever you have to tell me is important, *españolazo*," the sergeant grunts, his voice still drenched in sleep. "Or I'll string you up by your balls."

"There are two dead at the Adells' house," Melchor says.

"The Adells? Which Adells?"

"The printing Adells."

"You're joking."

"I'm not joking," Melchor says. "A patrol car just called it in. Ruiz and Mayol are already there. I'm on my way."

Suddenly awake, Blai begins to give him instructions.

"Don't tell me what I have to do," Melchor interrupts him. "Just one thing: should I call Salom and the forensics team?"

"No, I'll make the calls," Blai says. "We've got to tell everyone and their dog. You take care of preserving the scene, sealing off the house—"

"Don't worry, Sergeant," Melchor cuts him off again. "I'll be there in five."

"Give me half an hour," Blai says and, as if no longer talking to Melchor but to himself, grumbles: "The Adells, for Christ's sake. What a shitstorm this is going to be."

4

Without turning on the siren or his flashing lights, Melchor drives full speed through the streets of Gandesa, which at that hour are almost as deserted as the stairs and corridors of the police station. Occasionally he passes a cyclist in cycling gear, or a runner in running gear, or a car that might be returning from a long Saturday night or just beginning a long Sunday. Dawn is breaking in Terra Alta. An ashen sky heralds a morning without sun and, when he reaches the Piqué Hotel, Melchor turns left and leaves Gandesa on the road to Vilalba dels Arcs. He accelerates there, and a few minutes later turns off, taking a hundred-metre-long dirt track that leads to a country house. It is surrounded by a high stone wall crowned with broken glass and almost completely covered in ivy. The brown metal gate is open and, parked in front of it is a patrol car, its blue lights blinking in the dawn; beside it, Ruiz seems to be consoling a middle-aged woman, who sits on a stone bench, crying.

Melchor gets out of his car and says: "What's happened here?"

"I don't know," the patrolman says, pointing to the woman. "This lady is the cook here. She's the one who phoned. She says there are two dead people inside."

The woman is trembling from head to foot, sobbing and wringing her hands, her face bathed in tears. Melchor tries to calm her and asks her the same question he asked Ruiz, but the only response he gets is a look of terror and an unintelligible stammer.

"And Mayol?" Melchor says.

"Inside," Ruiz says.

Melchor tells him to tape off the entrance and stay with the woman until the others arrive. Under the gaze of two closed-circuit cameras, he goes through the gate and walks briskly along a path through a well-tended garden – past mulberry and cherry trees that dot the lush lawns, and beds of geraniums, peonies, lilies and roses, jasmine climbing the walls – until around a corner the facade of the old three-storey farmhouse you can see from the crossroads appears in front of him, with its big wooden door, its trellised balconies and open attic windows. Mayol is leaning against one of the door jambs, with his legs slightly bent and both hands holding his pistol. The dark blue of his uniform stands out starkly against the dark ochre of the facade. When he sees Melchor he beckons him over.

Melchor pulls out his pistol while he studies the baroque pattern of a tyre track in the earthen drive that widens out into a parking area in front of the half-open front door.

"Have you been in?" he asks Mayol.

"No," Mayol says.

"Is there anyone inside?"

"I don't know."

Melchor notices that the lock on the door is undamaged. Then he sees that Mayol is pouring with sweat and has fear written all over his face.

"Stay behind me," he tells him.

Melchor kicks open the big door and enters the house, followed by Mayol. Cautiously, he inspects the ground floor, which is in semi-darkness: a front hall with a coat stand, a large chest, armchairs and glass cases of books, a lift, a bathroom, two bedrooms with wardrobes, made-up beds and ceramic water jugs, a well-stocked larder. Then he goes up to the first floor by a stone staircase that leads to a large living room lit only by a ceiling lamp. What he sees there plunges him, for long drawn-out seconds, into an overwhelming sense of unreality, which he is only yanked out of by Mayol's agonised groan as he throws up on the floor.

"My God!" the patrolman splutters as he spits out a disgusting mush of bile and bits of food. "What's happened here?"

It is the first murder scene Melchor has encountered since he arrived in Terra Alta, but he saw many before that and he doesn't remember anything like this.

Two bloody masses of red and violet flesh face each other on a sofa and armchair soaked in a lumpy liquid – a mixture of blood, entrails, cartilage and skin – which has spattered the walls, the floor and even as far as the fireplace. Floating in the air is a violent smell of blood, of tormented flesh, of supplication, and a strange sensation, as if those four walls had preserved the howls of agony they'd witnessed; at the same time, Melchor believes he senses in the room – and this is perhaps what disturbs him most – a certain aroma of exultation or euphoria, something he doesn't have words to define but that, if he did have them, he might describe as the festive slipstream of a macabre carnival, or a demented ritual, or a joyful human sacrifice.

Fascinated, Melchor moves towards that double horrifying mess, trying not to step on any evidence (on the floor are two pieces of torn cloth drenched in blood that had almost certainly been used as gags), and, when he reaches the sofa, he can tell that the two blood-soaked shapes are the meticulously tortured and mutilated bodies of a man and a woman. Their eyes have been gouged out, their fingernails torn off, their teeth pulled out, their ears cut off, their nipples also, their bellies have been sliced open and their guts have been ripped out and scattered around them. He has only to see their whitish grey hair and their bare, flaccid limbs (or what's left of them) to realise that these were two very elderly people.

Melchor feels as though he could contemplate that spectacle for hours under the weak glow of the ceiling light.

"Is it the Adells?" he says.

Mayol, who has stayed a few metres away, approaches, and he repeats the question.

"I think so," the patrolman says.

Melchor has occasionally seen the Adells in photographs in the local papers and regional publications, but never met them in person, and beneath the butchery he's not able to recognise what he remembers.

"Stay here and don't let anyone touch anything," he tells Mayol. "Sergeant Blai should be here any minute. I'm going to take a look around."

The house is enormous, and seems to be full of bedrooms. It has been renovated in a way that Melchor thinks comes straight out of an architectural journal, preserving the old structure and modernising everything else. Between the first and second floor, in a small room that might once have been a storeroom, Melchor finds a panel with several blank monitors; it's the security room, and all the alarms and cameras have been switched off.

On the second floor he comes into a vast rectangular hall with six doors, two of which are wide open. Beyond the first is a master bedroom where chaos reigns: the bed has been stripped of sheets, pillows, duvet and mattress, which lie piled up and torn in a corner; the bedside tables, chests of drawers and wardrobes have been searched and the contents dumped on the floor; chairs, stools and armchairs have been thrown all over the place, bedclothes, shirts, trousers, dresses, underwear and bits of plastic, glass and metal that – Melchor verifies after examining them – are the remains of destroyed mobile phones, SIM cards removed; there are medicine bottles, lotions, creams, shoes, slippers, magazines, newspapers, printed papers, smashed cups and glasses, empty jewellery cases; a beautiful wood-and-ivory crucifix, an oil painting of the Sacred Heart of Jesus and several silver-framed family photographs have been torn off the walls and smashed against the elaborate floor tiles. It is clear that this is the old couple's bedroom and, as he observes the disorder, Melchor wonders if the murderers were simply thieves, or if they were looking for something that they may have found, or may not have.

In the next room he discovers another corpse, a big-boned woman with straw-coloured hair and very white skin, sitting on the floor beside the unmade bed. Her back leans against a partition wall and her head has fallen against her shoulder. She is wearing a cream-coloured nightdress and a blue dressing-gown, and her eyes are wide open as if she's seen the devil. A perpendicular trail of dry blood runs to her nose and mouth from a hole in her forehead the size of a ten-cent piece.

Melchor inspects the other four rooms – a living room and three more bedrooms – but he finds nothing out of the ordinary. On the top floor he realises almost immediately that the intruders did not get that far and looks out of a window. Seeing that five cars are now parked outside the gate, he decides to go back downstairs.

Blai and Salom are contemplating the corpses of the old couple when Melchor joins them. Three forensics officers, their backs turned, are silently preparing their equipment and instruments. Blai asks: "Are there any more dead?"

The sergeant is forty-five years old, but looks younger. He's wearing tight jeans and a striped T-shirt that shows off his biceps and pectoral muscles and, beneath his bald pate, his direct, clear blue eyes observe the carnage with a mixture of incredulity and disgust.

"One," Melchor says. "A woman. They shot her, but didn't torture her."

"That must be the Romanian maid," Blai surmises. "The cook says she lived in."

"The old folks' room has been ransacked," Melchor goes on. "Well, I think it's their room. There are bits of mobiles on the floor, deliberately destroyed. Have you seen the tyre tracks in the garden?"

Blai nods without taking his eyes off the Adells.

"It's the only strange thing," Melchor says. "Everything else reeks of professionals."

"Or psychopaths," Blai suggests. "If not demonic possession. Who else could come up with something like this?"

"That's what I thought when I first saw it," Melchor says. "A ritual. But I don't think so anymore."

"Why?" Blai says.

Melchor shrugs.

"The door hasn't been forced," he says. "The security cameras and alarms were switched off. They've smashed the mobiles and taken the SIM cards so we can't see what calls the old folks made. And they've tortured them expertly. It might be a robbery, they may have taken jewellery and money, although I haven't come across a safe. But does this butchery fit with a robbery? Maybe they were looking for something and that's why they tortured them."

"Maybe," Blai says. "Anyway, being professionals doesn't mean they aren't psychopaths. Or that this wasn't a ritual. What do you think Salom?"

The corporal seems hypnotised by the corpses of the two elderly people, apparently unable to believe his eyes. The impact has robbed him of his usual serenity: he is a little pale, a little shaken, breathing through his mouth; a tiny tremor quivers on his upper lip. He's a little overweight, with a bushy beard and somewhat old-fashioned glasses, all of which makes him

10

appear much older than Blai, even though there's barely a couple of years between them.

"I wouldn't say straight off that it's the work of professionals either," he says. "Maybe you're right, it could have been a couple of whack jobs."

"Did you know them?" Blai says.

"The old folks?" Salom says, pointing vaguely at the mutilated bodies. "Of course. Their daughter and son-in-law are friends of mine. Life-long friends." Turning to Melchor, he adds: "Your wife knows them too."

There is a silence, during which Salom finally manages to control his trembling lip. Blai lets out a resigned sigh before announcing: "Well, I'm going to call Tortosa. We can't deal with all this on our own."

While the sergeant speaks to the Territorial Investigations Unit in Tortosa, Melchor and Salom stand contemplating the slaughter a moment longer.

"Do you know what I'm thinking?" Melchor says.

Salom is gradually pulling himself together. Or that's the impression he gives.

"What?"

"About what you said the day I arrived here."

"What did I say?"

"That nothing ever happens in Terra Alta."

With the help of two colleagues on the investigation team, Melchor has just discovered that all the house's alarms and security cameras have been off for a day and a half, disconnected at 10.48 on Friday night. A patrolman leans his head into the converted security room.

"Deputy Inspector Gomà has arrived from Tortosa," he tells

Melchor. "Deputy Inspector Barrera and Sergeant Blai want you to come down."

It's nine o'clock in the morning and the entire Terra Alta Investigations Unit, which Sergeant Blai leads, in fact half of the whole police force, including its chief, Deputy Inspector Barrera, is in the Adells' house. A silent frenzy has reigned over the sealed-off house for the last couple of hours: uniformed and plain-clothes officers coming and going, exchanging information, taking notes, taking photographs, filming, looking for fingerprints or putting numbered cards in places where they find – or think they've found – evidence, trying to keep the crime scene intact and to isolate useful clues. At the gate, two uniformed officers have been keeping the ever-increasing crowd of journalists and onlookers at bay. The morning will be hot and humid; the grey dawn sky has given way to pot-bellied clouds, threatening rain.

In the first-floor living room, Barrera and Blai are talking to a man who, Melchor deduces, must be Deputy Inspector Gomà, the new chief of the Territorial Investigation Unit at Tortosa. To his left is a skinny woman in her thirties, tough-looking with short, curly brown hair, holding an iPad in her hands and with a red heart pierced by an arrow tattooed on her collar bone; this is Sergeant Pires. Melchor knows her from the odd meeting in Tortosa, but he's never noticed her tattoo before, or maybe she's just had it done. The four senior officers observe the tortured bodies of the old couple while several forensics officers, in white coveralls and gloves, blue overshoes and green masks, bustle around them, speaking only in whispers, engrossed in their work. Melchor stays a few steps away from them, sure that Barrera and Blai are giving the recent arrivals time to process that macabre scene, and he wonders if they too could spend hours contemplating the dead bodies. Blai is itemising the tortures the Adells appear to have been subjected to, as if they weren't in everyone's plain sight, until he suddenly notices Melchor's presence. Blai introduces him to Deputy Inspector Gomà, who shakes his hand with a mixture of curiosity and suspicion.

"You were the first detective on the scene?"

"Yes," Melchor says. "I was on the night shift."

"Tell me what you know."

They both turn their backs on the corpses and walk towards the centre of the room, followed by the others. Beside them, Pires takes notes on her iPad and Blai qualifies or adds to Melchor's recitation occasionally, but does not contradict him. When Melchor finishes speaking, Gomà reflects for a moment and asks Barrera and Blai to post a couple of men at the gate and gather the rest of the team on the ground floor.

Five minutes later a band of police has formed around Gomà and Barrera. Gomà addresses them all, but especially the forensics team. He promises he'll be brief. He says it's impossible to exaggerate the importance of the case and the repercussions it will surely have in the media. He says there's a lot at stake. He says they have a day of hard work ahead of them, that they will not be able to handle it on their own and that in the course of the morning reinforcements from Tortosa will continue to arrive. He says it is essential to preserve the crime scene as well as they can and for that reason, apart from the forensic officers, the fewer officers who go to the upper floors the better. He says that the forensics team should divide the house into zones and examine it millimetre by millimetre, down to the last detail, no matter how insignificant something might seem. He points to Pires and says that she will be in charge of the investigation and writing up the report and that he needs an officer from the Terra Alta forensics team to collate all the evidence

13

in order to pass it on to her. Gomà looks questioningly at Blai.

"Sirvent?" Blai says, pointing to an officer whose oval face and beady eyes peek out of the facial opening of his coveralls. "Will you take charge?"

Sirvent nods. Satisfied, Deputy Inspector Gomà looks around, as if he wants to scan all of his subordinates. He is a man of average height, with cold eyes and grey hair impeccably combed and parted on the left; he's wearing a beige suit, a white shirt and a brown tie, and his glasses, small, square and unframed, give him a slightly academic look.

"That's all," the deputy inspector says, wrapping up. "Remember, every detail counts. If you have any doubts, ask. Is that clear?" Everybody nods. "Let's get started."

The group disperses throughout the house, but Gomà orders Melchor to remain.

"Tell me something," he says, once the two of them are alone with Barrera, Pires and Blai. "Why do you think this is the work of professionals?"

"Because they haven't made any mistakes," Melchor says. "At least at first glance. Except the tyre tracks."

"They're Continentals," Blai says. "But I don't think that'll tell us the make of car."

"Maybe it's not a mistake," Gomà suggests. "I mean –" he rushes to clarify – "it seems like too obvious a mistake to be a mistake. Maybe they did it on purpose, to mislead us."

The deputy inspector's observation is met with silence. Blai breaks it.

"I'm not so sure it was a professional job," he says.

"Me neither," Barrera backs him up. "Besides, there are prints all over the place."

"I bet most of them belong to the victims," Melchor says. "Or to their relatives—"

"Speaking of relatives," Gomà interrupts, "have we informed them?"

"Not yet," says Blai.

"What are we waiting for?" Gomà says. "As soon as you've told them, take their fingerprints. And those of everyone who's been in this house over the last two days. Then we can distinguish them from those of the murderers. If we find any, that is."

Pires takes down the deputy inspector's orders on her iPad, and Blai turns from one side to the other, looking for someone he doesn't find before leaving the room. Gomà heads for the first floor, asking Melchor to come with him; behind them Barrera and Pires climb the stairs. When they get to the room where the corpses are, Gomà stops for a moment, looking at them, and then points to a mushy puddle on the floor.

"Can someone explain what this is?" he says.

"The patrolman who was with me threw up," Melchor says.

"He's not the only one," Barrera tells them. "The rest of us were more discreet, though."

Gomà observes his colleague with a hint of irony, until Barrera looks away, unhappily.

"You should have warned me," Barrera complains, stroking his belly. "I just had breakfast and I chucked up every last bit of it."

The chief of the Terra Alta police orders the puddle cleaned up, but then corrects himself before Gomà can remind him that nothing must be touched until the forensic agents finish their work. Blai joins them again.

"I'm going to set up an investigation team," Gomà announces. "We'll supply five men, plus the sergeant. I need you to lend me two more."

"As many as you need," Barrera says.

Gomà points to Melchor.

"One is this kid," he says. "And I want another who knows the area well. And lives here."

"I've got your man," Blai says. "He's a friend of the family."

"Of the Adells?"

"Yes."

"Tell him to come here."

"I've just sent him to give them the news."

"Call him back."

Blai steps away from the group to speak briefly on his mobile. A short time later Salom appears. Gomà points to the corpses and asks if he knows them.

"Everyone in Terra Alta knows them," Salom says. "This is a small place."

"Personally, I mean."

"Yes." Salom nods. "I was born in Gandesa and I've almost always lived here, same as them. Well, same as him; she was born elsewhere, though she's spent her whole life in Terra Alta. But the ones I know best are their daughter, and their son-in-law. Especially the son-in-law. We're good friends."

"They don't have any other children?"

"No. No other immediate family. As far as I know."

Gomà asks if it's true that the Adells are the richest family in the region. Salom nods again.

"The old man was a high-flying entrepreneur," he says. "Half of Gandesa belongs to him. And Gráficas Adell, of course."

"They manufacture paper products," Barrera chimes in. "Packaging for cakes and biscuits, pastry trays, chocolate boxes, cards, egg boxes. Things like that. It's the biggest business in Terra Alta."

"They have their main factory on La Plana industrial estate, on the outskirts of Gandesa," Salom adds. "And subsidiaries in Eastern Europe and Latin America."

"Who ran all that?" Gomà asks.

"Who was in charge?" Salom asks in turn. Gomà nods. "The old man," he says. "There's a manager who's been with him for ever who oversees everything. And the son-in-law is the managing director."

"The son-in-law your friend," Gomà says.

"Yes," Salom says. "His name is Albert Ferrer. But the old man was the one in charge. He was still making all the important decisions."

"How old was he?" Gomà says.

"I don't know," Salom says. "He had to have been at least ninety."

The deputy inspector raises his eyebrows, curls his lip and shakes his head a little, surprised by the information. Then he turns towards the bodies, as if to be sure they are still there. Pires does the same; she has stopped taking notes and is watching Gomà expectantly. A little away from the group, Barrera and Blai are talking to each other. Melchor stares at the tattoo on Sergeant Pires' clavicle and realises there is something written on it, but he can't read it.

"I want a complete report on the family's companies," Gomà suddenly says; he is speaking to Pires, who starts tapping on her iPad again. "For this afternoon's meeting. What time have you scheduled it?"

"At five," she says without raising her eyes.

"Do you think that'll be enough time?" Gomà says. Pires nods and the deputy inspector adds, pointing to Melchor and Salom: "I want you two there, as well. At the station, I mean."

Melchor and Salom nod.

"Tell me something," Gomà goes on, now speaking to Salom. "The Adells must have had a lot of enemies, no?" The question seems to disconcert the corporal; the deputy inspector clarifies: "People who disliked them. People who hated them."

"I don't think so," Salom says. "Why do you say that?"

"Because rich people tend to have enemies," Gomà explains. "The richer you are, the more enemies you have."

"I doubt that was the case for the Adells," Salom says sceptically. "At least here, in Terra Alta. They provided jobs for many people, half the region worked for them. Besides, they were very religious people. They'd joined Opus Dei, though they were very discreet about it. That's what they were like: discreet. And austere. And they mixed with everybody. And they helped people. No, I think that people liked them around here. And their family as well."

Barrera and Blai support the corporal's opinion with facts and personal impressions that Pires seems to be noting down or summarising on her iPad. When the exchange of information flags, Salom says: "Well, I'd better go and tell the family."

"Yes, go," Gomà says. "And don't forget to take their fingerprints. Sergeant Blai, have you called the judge?"

"Right after calling you," Blai says. "He told me to let him know when we're ready."

"Well you can do that."

Blai walks to a corner already examined by the forensic agents to speak on the phone, and says something to a patrolman looking for Barrera, who, after hearing his message, excuses himself and leaves the room. For his part, Gomà starts giving Pires instructions, at which point Melchor decides he will go and get on with his own work. But before he can do so, Gomà stops him again.

"Wait," he says. "I haven't finished with you."

Melchor waits. Meanwhile, two members of the Tortosa forensics team, cases in hand, burst into the room and freeze

18

for a few seconds before the corpses of the Adells, then they walk over to Sirvent and speak to him while they finish putting on their coveralls, gloves, overshoes and masks. Very near Melchor, a colleague from the forensics unit has been dusting a sideboard for fingerprints for several minutes. When Pires' mobile rings, Gomà nods to her to answer it.

"One moment," the sergeant apologises, raising her index finger. "It's Lopez, from the press office."

Gomà takes Melchor by the arm and steers him to a corner of the room, near the stairway that leads to the second floor.

"Barrera and Blai have told me who you are," he says, switching to the informal *tú*.

Gomà has let go of his arm; behind the lenses of his glasses his cold eyes have turned icy, inquisitive. Melchor guesses what the deputy inspector is referring to, but simply returns his stare.

"I'd heard a lot of talk about you," Gomà admits. "How long has it been since the attacks? Four years, five?"

Melchor tells him four.

"That was good," the deputy inspector goes on, shaking his head again. "It takes balls to do a thing like that. Well done." He takes his glasses off, exhales on the lenses and, using the corner of a handkerchief to clean them, qualifies his praise: "But not everything they say about you is so complimentary. You know that, don't you?"

Melchor knows, of course, because he knows that many stories have circulated about him, especially since he arrived in Terra Alta, and most of them false. For a moment he thinks about the true ones and is about to tell Gomà that yes, he knows, though only to add that he is not who he used to be, that in those four years he's changed, that now he has a wife and a daughter and a different life. But, because he's sure that he wouldn't be able to explain this to the deputy inspector in the right way, and because he doesn't want any trouble, he says nothing.

Gomà lets a few seconds go by then puts his glasses back on.

"What I mean to say is, don't confuse things," he explains, looking Melchor in the eye. "There are people who forget that this is teamwork. I don't. I am always aware of it. I hope you will be too, at least as long as you're working with me. You've already seen that I chose you to help me in this matter. That means I trust you. I've been told I can; I hope you won't disappoint me. In any case, on my team, you're just one member. That's all. One of the team. Got that?"

Melchor nods.

"It's important you understand," Gomà insists. "If you don't understand, tell me. I'll take you off the case and no hard feelings. It would be for the best. For you and for me. And for the case."

Melchor nods again. A satisfied smile reveals the deputy inspector's teeth.

"Wonderful," he says. "I'm glad we understand each other."

Pires' phone call ended a few seconds earlier and, since then, she has been waiting at a discreet distance for the two men to finish their private discussion. Now she approaches, but before she reaches them, Gomà switches from his brief familiarity back to the formal *usted*, aware that the sergeant can hear them again.

"If you were on the night shift, you won't have slept," he says.

"No," Melchor says.

"Wait until the judge arrives," the deputy inspector says. "I want you to tell him what you told me. Then go and get something to eat and rest for a while. I need you to be fresh this evening."

The judicial retinue appears at the house shortly before eleven o'clock. Advised of their presence by a patrolman, Deputy Inspectors Gomà and Barrera receive the group in the garden, accompanied by Sergeants Blai and Pires. Melchor and Salom watch them from a distance, from the front door of the house. The retinue comprises the coroner, the judicial secretary and the judge, an obese, chubby-cheeked and almost bald man whose trousers are held up with braces and who, after talking to Gomà for a few minutes, walks at the head of the group towards the scene of the crime. As they pass Melchor and Salom, Gomà orders them with a gesture to join the group. They obey, and can therefore see the recent arrivals' differing reactions as they enter the room where the two dead bodies are: the judge – still panting from the effort of walking up the stairs and wiping sweat off his brow with a white handkerchief – freezes and stares wide-eyed, his mouth hanging open, more or less like the judicial secretary, while the coroner, possessed of a professional calm, prepares to get down to work, scrutinising that bestiality as if he were not a coroner but a mathematician and what he had in front of him was not two slaughtered human bodies but a double quadratic equation.

"Good God," the judge finally exclaims. "What the fuck is this?"

A short time later, the magistrate and secretary having barely recovered from the shock, the process of removing the bodies begins. Protected by a pair of blue gloves and a grey apron, the coroner starts to examine the remains of the Adells, and the judge, still mopping his brow with his handkerchief, asks Deputy Inspector Gomà to explain in detail what his team knows so far.

"He should tell you." Gomà points to Melchor. "He was the first to arrive."

The judge looks at Melchor. The two men see each other often enough in court, but Melchor is not sure the judge knows him by name.

"Tell me, son," the judge says. "I'm all ears."

As soon as the key turns in the lock, Melchor hears a squeal from inside the house. Seconds later his daughter is in his arms, hanging off his neck, kissing him and panting as if she's just run a hundred-metre dash. Without even saying hello, Cosette is trying to explain something that Melchor does not understand; finally he realises she's asking if she can go and play at a friend's house.

"Please, Papá!"

They've just reached the kitchen. Melchor questions his wife with a look.

"We ran into Elisa Climent in the plaza," Olga tells him. "She and her mother have invited her over to her house to play."

Melchor pretends to be surprised.

"Seriously?" he says.

"Yes!" Cosette shouts. "Can I go, Papá?"

Now Melchor pretends to have doubts.

"Well, I don't know what to say, young lady," he says.

"Please, Papá!" Cosette implores, squirming in his arms. "Please, please, please!"

Melchor lets out a laugh.

"OK," he finally says, and in an outburst of gratitude, Cosette plants a kiss on his cheek. "But on one condition."

Cosette pulls her face back from his, looking worried.

"What?" she says.

"That you give me a kiss."

Cosette smiles: a radiant smile that lights up her face.

"But I already have!"

"Another."

Cosette kisses him.

"A bigger one," Melchor says.

Cosette crushes her lips against her father's cheek as hard as she can.

"Harder," says Melchor.

Irritated, Cosette pouts.

"Mamá, look at Papá!" she protests.

Melchor puts his daughter down and pats her bottom. On the table are two plates with the remains of pasta, an empty glass, a half-full glass of red wine and a half-bottle of water.

"You've already eaten?" Melchor says.

"Yes," Olga says. "We didn't know when you'd be back, and Elisa and her mother will be here any minute. But we saved you some."

"Thank goodness," Melchor says. "If there wasn't any food –" he crouches down and growls while baring his teeth and reaching out threatening arms towards Cosette, turning his fingers into claws – ". . . I'd have to eat you two."

Cosette squeals and, laughing, runs to hide behind her mother. Melchor laughs too, delighted by the fright he's just given his daughter, who peeks watchfully from behind her mother's legs.

"You must be dead on your feet and starving," Olga says.

"More or less," Melchor says, standing up. "Let me take a quick shower."

While he's in the shower, the doorbell rings and, when he comes back to the kitchen in pyjamas, Cosette has left and on the table a steaming plate of pasta with Bolognese sauce and a cold can of Coca-Cola await him.

"How awful about the Adells!" Olga exclaims.

"How did you hear?" Melchor says.

"How could I not hear? The town's buzzing with the news. There hasn't been this much talk in Terra Alta since the Battle of the Ebro. Do you know who might have done it?"

"No idea."

"Don't you have any clues?"

"None. But don't worry. We'll catch them."

Sitting sideways in front of him, with her back leaning against the wall and legs crossed at the knee, Olga tells him what she's heard that morning on the radio while she sips her glass of wine. She's wearing a white shirt and a pair of well-worn jeans, and her straight black hair is held at the nape of her neck by a clip. Melchor listens to her, gulping down his Coca-Cola between mouthfuls of pasta, enjoying how well she expresses herself, amazed at having a woman like her all to himself: good-looking, smart, kind.

Almost thirty, Melchor often feels that, since he met Olga, his life is not what it was destined to be, that his mother had given birth to him to lead the sordid existence he'd led until he arrived in Terra Alta and that, since then, he's been using up someone else's luminous life, an infinitely better life than the one he's meant to have. Sometimes he suffers from nightmares about his other life, he wakes up drenched in sweat in the middle of the night, and, after an instant of dazed panic, realises with enormous relief that he is there, in his house in Gandesa, with his wife sleeping beside him and their daughter a little further away, on the other side of the hall. Back in reality, he caresses Olga's body, gets out of bed, goes into Cosette's room, watches her sleep for a few seconds, goes to the dining room, closes the doors and paces back and forth gesturing like a madman, shouting at himself in silence, in the total quiet of the early morning, that he is the luckiest man on earth.

Melchor lets Olga talk, nodding every once in a while, sometimes trying to sweeten, lessen or mask the gruesomeness of what has happened in the country house, or what some journalists have been saying happened, and at some point he asks her if she knew the Adells.

"Of course," Olga says. She is holding her wine glass by the stem, and spinning it slowly back and forth, concentrating. "Especially their daughter, Rosa. She's much older than you. My age. We went to school together as children, we were almost neighbours. I know her husband too."

"He's friends with Salom," Melchor says.

"Yes, good friends." Olga looks up to agree with Melchor and her glass stops spinning. "They're like night and day, but they were roommates in Barcelona when they were students, then they became friends. I had more to do with her. My father and her father were friends as well. Well, they were friends for a time, when we were little, then they stopped speaking. My father told me Adell was an orphan, it seems his father was killed in the war, and he had to scrape by on his own." Olga raises her glass to her lips and takes a sip. "As a kid he made a living collecting scrap metal in the hills, as my father did and so many other people around here – after the war the countryside was full of shrapnel. Then Adell became a scrap dealer, and in the sixties or seventies he bought a bankrupt printing company for a song. He started to make his fortune there. But, of course, it wasn't an overnight thing. He worked like a madman, night and day, Saturdays, Sundays and holidays; he was a very ambitious man, he wanted to prosper, to amount to something, be someone, that's what my father said. He was also very smart. That's how he turned Gráficas Adell into the leading business in the region. Nobody gave him a free ride."

"Why did he and your father stop speaking?"

Olga shrugs.

"I don't know, my father never told me. What I do know is that he was a strange guy. You'll have heard that he was very Catholic." Melchor nods and spears some pasta with his fork. "Well, it's true, but my father always used to say to me that, when they were friends, Adell told him: 'Look, Miquel, any day I don't screw someone over is a day I'm not happy.'"

Olga smiles, at Adell's phrase or at the memory of her father, and a fine mesh of lines appears at the edge of her mouth. While he's chewing, Melchor remembers how he met his wife, when he first arrived in Terra Alta, and a cold thread like a twinge of desire runs up his back.

"But people here liked them, didn't they?" he says. "The Adells, I mean."

"Who told you that?"

"Salom."

Olga tilts her head and half-closes her eyes, looking doubtful.

"Well, at least they provide jobs for lots of people," Melchor insists.

"Yes, but what kind of jobs?" Olga says, uncrossing her legs, looking straight at Melchor and moving her glass to one side, so that there is nothing between them. "The wages they pay are very low, because they have a pact with the rest of the business-owners in the region, and their factories don't even have works councils. Anyone who wants to stay in Terra Alta has to make do with the paltry money they offer. You know that better than I do. How many foreign workers must there be in Terra Alta for each local one?"

"Three or four," Melchor says. "Most of them Romanian and lots of illegal ones."

"In other words," Olga explains, "poor people ready to work for three times less than people here."

"And, in spite of that, those from here don't leave."

"Of course not, because in Terra Alta we are conservative, I've told you a thousand times. Those who were born here don't want to leave, we want to keep living here. And, if we do leave, we come back, like Salom, or like me. Or like the Adells, who could live anywhere they wanted, but here they stay. Of course, the Adells are rich. But it doesn't matter, the rest of us are like them. This is a poor place, we don't need much to get by."

Olga stands up, pours herself more wine and downs it in one, leaning against the refrigerator door.

"Look, Melchor," she goes on. "The Adells are like a tree that gives a lot of shade, but doesn't let anything grow around it. They control everything. They own property all over Terra Alta, and half of Gandesa belongs to them, so they give people work in their factories, sell them the houses they live in and even the tables and chairs to furnish them with – who do you think owns Terra Alta Furniture? Anyway, the truth is that Adell was a despot. That's not speaking ill of him, it's just describing him."

"Are you saying that more than one will be pleased by what happened?"

"No, I'm saying what I'm saying. And what I'm saying is the truth. Salom knows it as well as I do. Speak to the workers at Gráficas Adell and you'll see. I'm sure they won't tell you he was a nasty piece of work, or that he mistreated them personally, because I'm sure he didn't. Quite the contrary, everyone says he was a very kind old man. But I bet they'll end up admitting that he exploited them." Olga points her empty glass at Melchor's empty plate. "Do you want more pasta?"

Melchor shakes his head and Olga asks if she should make him a coffee. Melchor says no again.

"What I want is to sleep for a while," he says, pointing at the clock on the wall shaped like an apple, showing half past two. "At five I have to be at the station."

They both clear the table and leave the dishes in the sink. Olga bends down to put the Coke can in a bag that already has an empty tetrapak and a couple of plastic bottles in it. When she stands up, Melchor puts his arm around her waist, kisses her neck, looks for her mouth, finds it. Pulling away, Olga says:

"To bed with you, don't be a pain, go to sleep."

Melchor smiles, takes her hand and pulls it down between his legs.

"I'd sleep much better after a good screw."

"Fuck, *poli*." Olga laughs. "You're always ready to shoot."

2

His name was Melchor because the first time his mother saw him, just emerged from her womb and covered in blood, she exclaimed between sobs of joy that he looked like one of the Magi. His mother's name was Rosario and she was a prostitute. As a young woman she worked in brothels on the outskirts of Barcelona, like the Riviera, the Sinaloa or the Saratoga in Castelldefels, or the Calipso in Cabrera de Mar. She had once been a beautiful woman, with a wild, intense, working-class beauty, but her charms did not survive the ravages of her profession and the corrosion of age and, by the time Melchor reached adolescence, she was selling herself at knock-down prices, outdoors. She was ashamed of earning a living by sleeping with men, but she never hid it from Melchor, who would have preferred it if she had. Sometimes she brought clients home and, although he never saw them, because she took care to prevent it, as a boy he would play at guessing which one of them was his father. The game consisted of trying to identify the nocturnal sounds that reached his room while he pretended to sleep, and speculating about them: was the man who strode down the hall with confident proprietorial steps his father, or was it the one who walked on tiptoe, trying to pass unnoticed? Was it the old man who coughed and sputtered late into the night like a hardened smoker or someone terminally ill? Was it the man whose sobs came one night through the partition wall that separated his room from his mother's, or was it the one he once heard, from behind the half-open door to the dining room, tell a ghost story? Maybe it was the man he saw briefly several times, from behind, wearing a long leather jacket, and always leaving at dawn? Melchor often amused himself during sleepless nights with these impossible riddles, and for many years he couldn't pass a man in the street without wondering if he was the one who had unknowingly contributed to bringing him into the world.

Melchor lived with his mother in a tiny apartment in Sant Roc, Badalona, a working-class district on the northern edge of Barcelona. The building stood within a recreation zone, so the clearest memory Melchor had of his childhood and adolescence was noise, noise so ubiquitous and persistent that he found it indistinguishable from the ordinary sound of reality, as if reality had no right to exist without the roar of car, motorbike and bus exhaust pipes and horns, without drunken shouts and bellicose insults, or the quarrels of vandals, and without the seismic pulse of music from the bars and nightclubs. Melchor's mother knew that Sant Roc was a toxic neighbourhood for her son, but she also knew it was *her* neighbourhood and she didn't want to live anywhere else (or maybe she couldn't imagine living anywhere else); that's why she paid for him to go to a school in another neighbourhood: a Marist Brothers' School. She was determined that Melchor should study, and the phrase she repeated most often during his childhood and adolescence was: "If you want to end up as miserable as me, don't study."

Melchor seemed to mistake this sarcastic warning for actual advice. At first he was an obedient and timid pupil and earned decent grades, but from the age of twelve or thirteen, around the same time that his mother abandoned the precarious protection of the strip joints and risked plying her trade wherever she could, Melchor turned into a tough and unruly student who got into fights (or provoked them) and often skipped class. He never became completely integrated into the school, never stopped living his life in Sant Roc.

At thirteen he began to drink, smoke cigarettes and use drugs. At fourteen he was expelled from school for punching one of his teachers in the middle of a lesson. At fifteen he appeared before a judge for the first time. The judge was a magistrate of the Juvenile Court, a patient man in his sixties, subdued by decades of dealing with juvenile delinquents. Melchor's mother and a legal-aid lawyer tried to convince him not to punish the young teenager, using the false argument that it was the first offence he'd committed and the double promise that he was going to stop consuming and selling cocaine and take a professional development course that would turn him into a ceramicist.

Resolved to grant this young tyro a second chance the judge allowed himself to be taken in. But Melchor, however, did not honour either promise, and over the next two years appeared twice more before the same court, once for a fight with the bouncer of a nightclub in Sant Boi (in which he gave at least as good as he got) and once for stealing a woman's handbag on the Rambla in Barcelona. The first misdemeanour cost him barely three weeks in a juvenile unit in L'Hospitalet, but for the second he had to serve five months in prison. His mother visited him every day, and the afternoon he was released she was waiting for him at the gate. That night, when they finished having dinner alone at home, his mother wanted to know what his plans were. Melchor shrugged: "Why?"

His mother answered at once: "Because, if you're going to carry on living the way you were living before, I don't want you in this house."

His mother was fifty-four years old and had been born in a village in Jaén that Melchor had often heard her talk about but had only once visited. It was called Escañuela. There, among that handful of snow-white little houses surrounded by orderly rows of olive trees, Melchor had seen, for the one and only time in his life, two old people – as wrinkled as raisins – who turned out to be his grandparents. He remembered them now, a decade after spending a few days in their house, while he observed his mother wrapped in a frayed towelling robe and now looking like an old lady herself – flabby flesh, dry, wilted skin, her eyes dimmed – and felt for her the same pity and lack of affection he'd felt for his grandparents. That feeling enraged him for an instant. Then, without a word, he stood up from the table and went to his room and began to fill the suitcase his mother had just unpacked. When he finished, she was waiting for him in the hallway. She said: "You're leaving?"

"No," Melchor said. "You're kicking me out."

His mother nodded several times, weakly; as she did so she burst into tears. They both stood there for a few seconds, mere centimetres apart, she crying and he watching her cry. He had never seen tears in his mother's eyes, and the silence felt eternal.

"Don't go, Melchor," she said at last, choking back her tears. "You're all I have."

He didn't leave, but he didn't change his life. Quite the opposite. Thanks to a Panamanian he'd met in the juvenile detention centre, Melchor began to work for a Colombian cartel that imported cocaine through the port of Barcelona. At first he took care of low-level jobs, chiefly distributing drugs in Badalona, Santa Coloma, Sant Andreu and other towns and neighbourhoods on the downtrodden outskirts of Barcelona; he also supervised the dealers who sold the drugs. Gradually he became indispensable and won over his bosses, who began to trust him with less routine jobs. At that time he was earning more money than he could spend, staying out every night, sleeping with lots of women, and drinking whisky and snorting cocaine like there was no tomorrow. He also learned to shoot. He was instructed, on the orders of the Colombians, by an old German mercenary who was called or called himself Hans. Under his orders he practised for several weeks in a row at a gun club in Montjuïc. They didn't speak much, but they forged a certain friendship.

"You shoot well," Hans congratulated him in his perfect guttural Spanish when they were having a farewell drink in a nearby bar. "But you're going to get paid for shooting at men, not at targets. And shooting a man is not the same as shooting a target."

Melchor asked if it was harder.

"It's different," Hans said. "Depending on how you look at it, you might say it's easier. To shoot a man you don't need to have perfect aim: you just need to be cold-blooded enough to get as close as possible."

Shortly after finishing his training as a marksman, Melchor travelled to Marseilles, Genoa and Algeciras as a bodyguard for two of the cartel bosses. He didn't need to apply the mercenary's last lesson, but he got a clearer idea of the volume and reach of a business that not only had affiliates in several Latin American countries but also in several European cities. It was after returning from this trip that Melchor was involved in an incident that shattered the total confidence he had inspired in the Colombians up until that moment.

It happened one morning in February on the outskirts of

Barcelona. Melchor had gone to El Prat airport to pick up one of his bosses, a man called Nelson, who was arriving very early from Cali by way of Paris, to take him to his house in Cerdanyola. Nelson was returning from visiting his Colombian family, and just before leaving had had a screaming fight with his wife. He'd been unable to close his eyes at all on the transatlantic flight and when it landed he was tense, drunk and achy, but fell fast asleep as soon as he sank into the back seat of the Audi Melchor was driving. Melchor turned off the music and tried to drive as smoothly as possible among the tight columns of cars that were entering and leaving Barcelona at rush hour. It was bitterly cold outside, and a ridge of clouds hung over the city in the shape of a brain.

Suddenly, near Rubí, or perhaps Sant Cugat, Melchor glimpsed through the shreds of morning mist a group of women standing at a stoplight. Four prostitutes. They were keeping warm by huddling round an oil drum from which flickered the red and blue intermittent flames of a fire. From the distance, Melchor thought he recognised one of them: she was in profile, wearing a blond wig (or that's what he thought), thigh-length white boots, tight shorts and a black top; it was hard to tell how old any of them were. Melchor found his throat seizing up and, with fear turning his legs to jelly, he calculated that the light would turn red as his car reached the intersection, that he would have to brake and spend hair-raising seconds beside the women. He did not think: he accelerated brutally, flinging Nelson against the window, snaked through the lanes of cars at full speed, crossed the intersection on an amber light and drove rapidly away from the group of freezing prostitutes while the Colombian, astounded, bewildered and shaken, shouted and insulted him, demanding explanations that Melchor improvised and which the other man did not believe.

That was it: just an incident; but, for the pathologically suspicious Colombians, that incident could not fail to have an alarming significance. Melchor never found out if the prostitute he'd thought he recognised was his mother, and he never asked her, but the Colombian's incredulity, added to the paranoia that the cartel believed protected it from the lethal poison of informants and infiltrators, as well as the recklessness, laziness and carelessness of its men, squandered in an instant all the faith his bosses had invested in him till then, and it might have cost him his life.

At the beginning of March, however, the police took down the cartel. Melchor was arrested at the very beginning of the operation, which was carried out simultaneously and with mathematical precision in various locations. He was captured in the small hours in a place in the Free-Trade Zone which the organisation used as a drug depot and which became a rat trap when a horde of heavily armed National Police officers surrounded it. Minutes later a shootout began during which Melchor tried to get two of the Colombians out of the trap the police had set for them, but all he achieved was for one of them – the biggest of them all: a former National Liberation Army guerrilla called Óscar Puente – to get shot in the eye, and killed instantly, at which point the other Colombian, paralysed with terror, spattered with his dead colleague's blood and shouting hysterically, forced Melchor to surrender with him. And thus ended his attempted escape.

The next day all the newspapers and radio and television news programmes described how the National Police had inter-cepted shipments of more than a ton of cocaine at the ports of Barcelona and Algeciras, and that the drugs, coming from Pan-ama, Colombia and Bolivia, had arrived in Spain inside three containers, hidden among legal cargo; they also stated that

35

twenty-six arrests had been made in four different cities, among them the director of the Cargo Terminal at the port of Barcelona, the deputy director of the port of Algeciras and the owner of a group of transport and logistics companies that operated out of several Mediterranean ports, who was accused of using his business to give legal cover to the narcotics entering the country.

Melchor was transferred immediately to Madrid, as were the rest of his companions in misfortune. He spent several nights in the police station on calle Leganitos, where he was interrogated by a national court judge who then ordered that he be detained as a precautionary measure in the Soto del Real prison. He spent some months there awaiting trial. The day he arrived he was brutally beaten up on the orders of the Colombians or their henchmen. Melchor never knew for certain why, but always thought it was a sort of cautionary beating: in case the blow to the cartel had anything to do with the suspicions they had about him (Melchor knew that, if the suspicions had been any more than suspicions, he wouldn't have got a beating: they would have killed him). When his mother first visited him in prison, he had just come out of the infirmary. His face was covered in bruises, he had a patch over one eye and needed a crutch to walk, or rather to limp. When she saw him come into the visiting room, Rosario thought that he was still a child; then she thought he was broken. Since she knew her son would lie to her, she didn't ask what had happened, only how he felt. Melchor lied to her all the same: he said he felt fine.

"Great," replied his mother, who over the years had perfected a sarcastic rhetoric, because she was convinced that, at least between the two of them, it was all her son understood. "That's what I like to hear. Always look for the silver lining."

"I didn't know prison had a silver lining," Melchor said, with all the ironic disdain he could muster.

"Of course it does," his mother said. "At least you're not going to get shot in the head. Not to mention that you'll stop drinking and taking drugs."

"Don't be so sure," Melchor corrected her. "From what I've seen, they've got everything in here."

"Great," his mother said again and at that moment realised that both impressions she'd just had of her son had been mistaken: he was no longer a child, but the interrogations, prison and beatings hadn't destroyed him either. "Keep this up and you'll be dead within a couple of years. Maybe less."

They spoke of other things. At some point his mother told him she'd hired a lawyer to defend him. Melchor had just refused the one the Colombians wanted to saddle him with, in theory to help him, in practice to control him and to pin as many of the charges on him as they possibly could.

"And who's going to pay him?" he said. "I don't have a cent. They've frozen all my accounts."

"I'll pay him," his mother said.

The lawyer was called Domingo Vivales and as soon as Melchor saw him two days later – on the other side of the bars and double-strength glass of the same visiting room with rat-coloured walls and a whiff of disinfectant where he'd heard his name for the first time – he thought his mother had gone crazy or was playing a joke on him. This so-called Vivales turned out to be a big man with a stony face and the body of a truck driver, unshaven, hair uncombed, wearing a grey raincoat, a wrinkled suit and a shirt covered in stains, with the knot of his tie loose. Despite the mistrust inspired by his appearance, Melchor decided to listen to him.

"I don't like wasting time or my clients' time," Vivales warned him. "So let's get straight to the point."

The lawyer began by saying that, of course, the outcome of

Melchor's trial was uncertain. Then he reminded him of the charges the prosecutor was bringing against him, and he told him that at the end of the trial he could get between twelve and fifteen years in prison. Up till now, nothing had surprised Melchor; the surprise came later. Vivales told him that he'd studied his case in depth and that, supposing he accepted him as his lawyer and followed his instructions to the letter, he would promise to get the judge to reduce by half the sentence demanded by the prosecutor, perhaps by more than half. And if he added penitentiary privileges – that is, the reductions of sentence which, once in prison, he could earn through work and good behaviour – Melchor could be free in two or three years.

"No more," Vivales concluded. "I have it all figured out. But, of course, you have to trust me. If not, you should look for another lawyer."

"I want you to find me another lawyer," Melchor told his mother the next time he saw her. "This one talks a lot of nonsense. He's taking you for a ride."

"That's not true," his mother answered with conviction. "He's a good lawyer. And a good person. I guarantee it. He's not taking me for anything."

Melchor scrutinised his mother, and read in her eyes two complementary certainties. The first was that Vivales was not going to charge for defending him. He wondered why the lawyer was doing that, wondered what kind of relationship he had or had had with his mother and if he was or had been her client. In a flash he remembered the man who strode down the hallway of their apartment with an assured proprietorial tread, the one who tiptoed trying not to be heard, the one who coughed and spat like a terminal patient or an impenitent smoker, the man who sobbed inconsolably behind the partition wall, the one who told ghost stories, the one who left at day-break in his long leather jacket and all those intruders who had troubled the sleepless nights of his childhood, but none of them seemed to have the face of the shyster who – this was the other certainty he saw in his mother's eyes – he had no choice but to accept as his defence lawyer, because Rosario did not have enough money to pay for a passable lawyer. For the rest of the visit, Melchor did not ask his mother out loud any of the questions he was asking himself in silence, but when they said goodbye he asked her to tell Vivales that he was prepared to put his fate in his hands.

The trial (or megatrial, as the sector of the press most inclined to hyperbole termed it: only thirty-six people were tried) was held much sooner than expected. The prosecutor accused Melchor of criminal association, trafficking narcotics and illegal possession of weapons, and, during the weeks leading up to the hearing, Vivales came to the prison almost daily to prepare his client's defence down to the last detail. That was when, little by little, he began to win Melchor's trust, and the truth is that he more than fulfilled the promise he'd made at their first meeting: the prosecutor had demanded a sentence of twenty-two years, but in the end Melchor received four, less than any of the other defendants. Vivales also arranged for Melchor to serve his sentence in Quatre Camins prison, close to Barcelona.

At the end of the trial, Melchor thanked the lawyer unreservedly for his work.

"I told you I had everything under control," Vivales replied dryly, seemingly no more satisfied than if he'd lost. "But don't thank me. Thank your mother." And, trying to take advantage of that moment of victory, he added, no less grumpily: "Will you let me give you some advice?"

39

Melchor answered with a half-smile and a single syllable: "Nope."

The Quatre Camins prison was older and smaller than Soto del Real, and Melchor went in determined to do whatever he could to get out of there as soon as possible. His mother visited him every week, sometimes more than once a week; Vivales also paid regular visits to him, as well as to the two or three other clients he had in Quatre Camins. That was the limit of his contact with the outside world, among other reasons because he'd lost track of his old friends from his neighbourhood some time ago. As for inside, he soon understood that the long arm of the Colombians did not extend to that prison, or his old bosses had ended up absolving him of their suspicions. Despite this, his first days in Quatre Camins were not exempt from brushes with the rest of the inmates.

Soon after his arrival, two guys eating opposite him in the dining hall began to interrogate him. One was very skinny, with an inflamed scar running across his face from cheekbone to chin; the other was short, tough-looking, with almond-shaped eyes. At first, Melchor responded to their questions politely, but, as soon as he realised they were trying to provoke him, he decided to ignore them. Then the two guys pretended to be annoyed by his silence, complained about his lack of courtesy, his lack of solidarity, his arrogance, started talking about him as if he weren't sitting across from them, tried to ridicule him in a veiled way. Until, all of a sudden, an indifferent and fatigued voice cut short their insidious duet.

"Julián, Manolito," it said – a French accent – "if you don't shut the fuck up, I'll cut your balls off."

The voice belonged to the man eating to Melchor's left. He looked to be in his fifties and was albino and almost bald. He was wearing tracksuit trousers and an undershirt that emphasised his Buddha's belly and his almost feminine breasts and left his enormous, flabby arms on display. He had very white skin and an alarming resemblance to a sperm whale. Falling quiet, the two guys turned to the interloper, who didn't even look up from his plate; then they laughed uncomfortably among themselves, made a conciliatory comment, hurried through the rest of their meal and left the table.

"You didn't have to defend me," Melchor said once they'd left. "I can look out for myself."

"I wasn't defending you, kid," the man answered, concentrating on peeling his tangerine. "I just like to eat in peace. One who dines in peace, sleeps in peace. And I'm very fond of sleeping."

The Frenchman finished eating his fruit and, without introducing himself or shaking hands, he left. His name was Gilles, although everyone in the prison called him Frenchie, except for the guards, who knew him as Guille. He'd been in Quatre Camins for five years and, although he had no friends inside, he commanded universal respect. He played no sports, nor did he spend any time in the workshops or participate in almost any of the activities the prison offered its inmates, but he was well known, notorious even, for having the best of relations with the penitentiary surveillance judge, with the governors, with the prison guards and with the instructors. He also enjoyed certain privileges: he slept in an individual cell, had the use of a computer and his only known job was to look after the library. He read a lot. One morning, while he was sitting on a bench in the sun in the main yard with a book in his hands, Melchor heard someone shout to him: "Frenchie, stop reading, your brain's going to dry up!"

The comment provoked agreement among others in the yard. Raising his eyes from the book, the Frenchman identified the joker and said: "Do you know why I read so much, Quesada?"

"Why?" the other challenged him, high on his success.

"To lose sight of this shithole, and of you, dickhead."

Days later something happened that reminded Melchor of this exchange of insults. That afternoon there was to be a talk by a writer in the prison; the inmates' routine allowed for very few distractions, so, even though, like many others, Melchor had no interest in books, he attended the event.

It took place in the library. The advertised writer appeared with the prison governor, a guard, several instructors and a woman. They all sat in a row of folding chairs, facing several similar rows occupied by the inmates. Melchor was sitting in the second row. The writer was called Arturo Ventosa and, although he was more than fifty, he dressed like he was in his twenties: a striped T-shirt, jeans ripped at the knees and sagging at the back, trainers, backwards baseball cap. The woman was thin with red hair, much younger than him, and wearing a tight blue dress and stiletto heels. The governor was the first to speak. He assured them that it was an honour to welcome this guest, in his opinion one of the greatest contemporary novelists in Spain, and he emphasised that he was an intellectual committed to the problems of his time, "not one of those who live in an ivory tower". That said, he introduced the woman – she was a professor and literary critic, he said – and ceded the floor to her. The professor, who had been whispering with the novelist while the governor was speaking, thanked him, unfolded some sheets of paper and began to read them.

She was an attractive woman, so, although nobody understood a word she said, all the inmates listened attentively. Then it was the novelist's turn; he thanked the governor for the invitation and the critic for her words, tried out a joke that only the governor and critic laughed at and then declared that all novelists have a duty to stand in solidarity with the disenfranchised and persecuted, and that was the reason he was there. He said that, for him, a writer was a person like any other, no better and no worse, who had to be aware of the limitations of literature and had to banish the narcissistic and outmoded presumption that it might be useful in some way, because literature was basically nothing more than an intellectual game, an entertainment incapable of teaching anybody anything or changing anything. He concluded that he had much more to learn from them than they had to learn from him.

"That's also why I've come here," he added. "I've come to learn, not to teach. To listen, not to speak."

These last words pricked Melchor's curiosity, who heard in them a blatantly false note, as he'd so often heard from the mouths of shabby dealers who were trying to rip him off. Next to the novelist, the literary critic forced a complicit smile. Melchor looked around at his companions, but didn't perceive confusion, sarcasm or reticence, just a ton of bored looks converging on the writer's expression of false modesty, who concluded his talk with an invitation: "You guys tell me."

Only then did Melchor notice the Frenchman, who was watching the scene with a sullen look, his body sprawled across his librarian's desk, one cheek squashed against his right hand. Just behind him, a prisoner called Morales did his best to catch the literary critic's eye by simulating fellatio with his hand and mouth. The governor tried to get out of the tight spot the novelist had landed him in by organising a dialogue between the guest and the inmates with the help of the instructors. The improvisation failed, and the only thing the governor achieved was that the inmates used the presence of the novelist as a shield to renew in public, with a series of intertwined and unconnected interventions, amid a growing clamour, the protests about their personal situation that they'd expressed in private a thousand times.

43

The event was on the point of disintegrating when the Frenchman raised a polite hand and the governor hastened to hush the racket.

"Well, well," he said, relieved and out of breath, his shirt darkened by large circles of sweat. "Finally, we're going to talk about literature." Turning to the novelist and pointing to the Frenchman, he said: "Guille is our librarian. A voracious reader. And also a writer. He's just published a memoir with an important French publisher, haven't you, Guille?"

"Can I speak or not?" the Frenchman said.

"Of course," the governor answered unctuously.

The Frenchman looked around the library until there was a reasonable silence. Then he began: "First of all, I'd like to thank the gentleman novelist for coming to visit us." The writer received the welcome with an ironically elaborate bow. "And then I'd like to say that I agree with him."

"In what sense, Guille?" the governor encouraged him.

The Frenchman ignored the question.

"This week I read both novels your publisher was kind enough to send us," he continued, speaking exclusively to the writer. "And I'm going to give you my opinion. The first . . . *The Respite of the Gods*, that's the title, isn't it?"

"Exactly," the governor said.

"Well, it's a piece of shit," the Frenchman pronounced.

The verdict provoked a ripple of laughter from the inmates. On the novelist's right the literary critic stiffened, but didn't lose her smile. The governor interrupted again:

"Guille, please."

"No, no," the novelist said, holding the governor's arm with a magnanimous hand, as if wanting to prevent him from denying the Frenchman the chance to speak. "Freedom of expression, first and foremost."

44

The Frenchman waited patiently for the room to calm down.

"Real shit," he repeated, spelling it out. "That's the first novel. And the second? What's the second called?" Wary now, the novelist didn't help him with an answer, nor did the literary critic or the governor. "It doesn't matter, the second is even worse. So you're right: your books don't have anything to teach anybody. Nothing at all. But that's not because you're just like everyone else. No, it's because you're as bad as your books. You, mister novelist, are nothing but a fucking fraud."

The governor snorted and turned around in his chair, but he seemed to have exhausted his bag of diplomatic tricks, and he said nothing; the guard stood expressionless, as if this was nothing to do with him; the instructors looked at each other without knowing how to react; and the literary critic had developed a tic in her upper lip and occasionally winked her left eye while Morales continued to besiege her from behind the Frenchman. As for the rest of the inmates, after the first moment of hilarity had passed, they seemed to be waiting with genuine curiosity for their fellow inmate to continue.

"And do you know why you're a fraud?" he insisted. "Because you speak only lies. You haven' come here to listen to us or support us or any of that shit you were spouting. You've come to look at us as if this were a zoo and we were animals, and then go home feeling happy, with your good left-wing virtue-signalling conscience as clean as a whistle. Can one say that . . . ?" Before anyone could answer his philological query, he specified: "Oh, and to have your wicked way with the young lady."

Morales reappeared behind the Frenchman, nodding approvingly and grinning from ear to ear. Humiliated, the governor did not look up from the floor. The novelist had taken the literary critic by the hand and whispered something in her ear, trying to console and calm her. The Frenchman added: "Please accept my condolences, Miss."

The governor could take no more.

"Guille, enough."

A chorus of protests interrupted the governor's interruption, while Morales, his lascivious smile still plastered on his face, shook his head behind the Frenchman, even though it was impossible to tell if his disapproval was directed at the governor, the Frenchman, the novelist or the literary critic, whose tic and left-eye winking were now out of control. The instructors stifled the protests.

"Just one last thing, sir," the Frenchman went on undeterred. "If you'll allow me." With a disdainful gesture of surrender, the governor encouraged him to say whatever he wanted. "It's just to agree with the novelist about something else. Look, six years ago, before coming here, I was the owner of a company with a staff of a hundred and fifty workers. You heard right: a hundred and fifty. What do you think? Incredible, right? Well, it's true. And do you know why you think it incredible? Well, because now you see me as a monster, as an animal, as someone who has nothing in common with yourself, and you find it incredible that six years ago I was like you. What do I mean, like you? I was twenty times better than you, who aren't even capable of writing a decent novel, while a hundred and fifty people's lives depended on me, a hundred and fifty families! You can't even imagine what that's like! You can't believe that six years ago I had a wife and family, and a life like any other, better than many lives . . . You can't believe it, can you? But it's true." The Frenchman paused, and for two or three seconds the silence in the library seemed to petrify. "Until one day I lost my head and, bam, I sent it all to hell," he continued. "So, here I am, locked up till I rot. And, do you know something? The worst is that you, who think you're so smart and original, are no exception. You're the norm. What I mean is that what you think is what everybody on the outside thinks, in other words that we, the ones who are here, are different from you, that we're from a different race, worse than you. But that's not true. We're like you, you could just as easily be in my place and I could be in yours. So I congratulate you, you were right about that too: we have much more to teach you than you have to teach us."

The last sentence provoked such an outburst of mirth that they had to declare the event over while the novelist slipped out of the room with the literary critic and the inmates crowded around the governor, the guard and the instructors to continue pressing their complaints or requests. In the midst of the tumult, Melchor watched the Frenchman, who began to straighten up the books on his desk as if nothing had happened, alone and indifferent to the uproar he'd unleashed.

The episode left Melchor with a vague aftertaste of victory and the sense of a bond with the Frenchman.

Two days later he returned to the library. Seeing him come in, the Frenchman raised his eyes from the book he was reading under the fluorescent ceiling lights and looked at him, but immediately reimmersed himself in his reading. On that occasion there was nobody else in the room apart from the librarian. Melchor cast a lost look around the shelves, many of them half-empty, and approached the Frenchman's desk.

"I'd like to read your book," he said.

It was the second time they'd spoken, but the phrase sounded like they'd known each other all their lives. The Frenchman looked at him again, huge and distrustful.

"What book?" he said.

"The book you wrote. Your memoir. The governor said the day before yesterday . . ."

"Why do you want to read it?"

Melchor shrugged. In the Frenchman's eyes, the distrust had turned into curiosity. He brusquely opened a drawer, took out a book and put it on the desk. Melchor read the title, leafed through it.

"It's in French," he said.

"What did you think it'd be in?"

"It's just that I don't speak French."

"You don't need to," the Frenchman said. "Read it with attention and you'll understand. Deep down, French and Spanish are the same language: badly spoken Latin."

Melchor didn't get the joke, supposing it was a joke, but he started to read the book that same day. He soon discovered that the Frenchman was not entirely right; but nor was he altogether mistaken: Melchor didn't get the meaning of all the words, but he did get some of them, and the others he deduced from the context. He liked the game and, although it wasn't enough to understand the whole book, it did enable him to get an approximate idea of the Frenchman's biography, and especially the moment when, as he'd told the novelist, he'd lost his head, when he'd caught his wife cheating on him with an acquaintance and killed them both with a hammer, an episode narrated over and over again in the book with a delirious brutality that left the reader with the feeling that the Frenchman had not stopped reliving it for a single second since it happened.

Melchor tried to return the book to the Frenchman as soon as he finished it.

"It's yours," the Frenchman said. "Keep it."

Melchor accepted the gift and asked: "Is it all true?"

"All what?"

"What you say in the book."

"All of it," the Frenchman said. "I have no imagination."

Melchor nodded. He would have liked to say that he'd enjoyed the book, or at least that he'd enjoyed what he'd understood, but the Frenchman did not seem interested in his opinion and Melchor thought that any comment would be out of place.

"I want another book," he said.

"With imagination or without?"

Melchor thought the librarian was making fun of him, but he didn't mind. After a second, the Frenchman gestured vaguely at the whole library.

"Take your pick."

He randomly chose a couple of short books, which bored him and which he didn't finish. The day he took them back to the library, the Frenchman was checking in a very thick two-volume book called *Les Misérables*. Inevitably, Melchor remembered his mother's repeated warning: "If you want to end up as miserable as me, don't study."

"Have you read it?" he said.

"Of course," the Frenchman said. "It's a very famous novel."

"Is it good?"

"That depends."

"Depends on what?"

"Depends on you," the Frenchman said. "The writer supplies half of a book, the other half comes from you."

That same morning he began to read the novel. He did so with an utter lack of conviction, but, influenced by the Frenchman's comment, he also did so as if it wasn't him reading the novel but the novel that was reading him, and after a hundred pages, when he got to the episode when Jean Valjean was wandering through the city of D— in search of shelter, which no one would offer him, having recently left prison hungry, stiff with cold, exhausted and ragged, Melchor noticed that tears were spilling down his cheeks. Confused, not knowing what was happening to him, he stopped reading and dried them. Then he went on reading:

And then, human society had done him nothing but injury; never had he seen anything of her, but this wrathful face which she calls justice, and which she shows to those whom she strikes down. No man had ever touched him but to bruise him. All his contact with men had been by blows. Never, since his infancy, since his mother, since his sister, never had he been greeted with a friendly word or a kind regard. Through suffering on suffering he came little by little to the conviction that life was a war; and that in that war he was the vanquished. He had no weapon but his hate. He resolved to sharpen it in the galleys and to take it with him when he went out.

This passage exasperated him, roused him, electrified him, and ended with him empathising with Jean Valjean, the convict who never laughed – surly, unfortunate, sombre and lost in thought – who "seemed to be continually absorbed in looking upon something terrible". He identified with him completely: Jean Valjean's fury was his fury, his pain was his pain, his hatred was his hatred. The fellow feeling, however, was short-lived. Just a few pages later, Jean Valjean changed his name and became Monsieur Madeleine, the industrious and virtuous and saintly and wise and respected Monsieur Madeleine, and Melchor felt that he'd become a distant, tiresome character. It was just then that, luckily (luckily for him, at least), Javert showed up in the novel, a police inspector with the eyes of a raptor, a heart of wood and the face of a dog descended from a wolf, a rootless man without hope or future, son of a prisoner of the galleys and a fortune-teller, who finds his roots, his hope and his future in intransigent devotion to the cause of the law and becomes the relentless pursuer of Jean Valjean, his deadly enemy, his nemesis.

Javert bewildered him. What Melchor felt for that marginal and marginalised being was much more complicated and more subtle than what he'd felt for Jean Valjean. Javert was the bad guy of the novel, the author had created him to attract the reader's scorn with his flinty antipathy, his legalistic vehemence and his at times diabolical fanaticism. That was clear. But Melchor also felt that, perhaps in spite of the author, Javert had another face, and he felt that, in his stubborn defence of the rules, in his inflexible insistence on fighting against evil and bringing about justice, there was a generosity and adamantine purity, an idealistic, gentlemanly and single-minded zeal to protect those who lacked any other protection than the law, a heroic awareness that someone should sacrifice his reputation and personal well-being to preserve the well-being of all. Against Monsieur Madeleine's cloying public virtue, Javert personified virtue disguised as vice, secret virtue, genuine virtue.

He was moved when he finished the novel, certain that he was no longer the same person who began to read it, and that he never would be that person again. This time, when he returned the book to the library, the Frenchman asked him what he'd thought of it. Still unsettled by his reading, Melchor could only manage a response that came straight from his guts:

"It's fucking awesome."

The Frenchman responded with a beastly laugh: it was the first time Melchor had seen him laugh, and his cavernous mouth with the yellow teeth of a predator made a big impression. Since he felt unable to add anything about the novel, Melchor added: "I'd like to read another book like this."

"There is no other book like it," the Frenchman replied.

Then, however, he began talking about novels. The French-man assured him that the nineteenth-century ones were the best and almost everything written since then didn't matter, and in the end he gave Melchor a novel by Balzac, *Lost Illusions*, and one by Dickens, *A Tale of Two Cities*. Melchor read them in a couple of weeks.

"They're good," he told the Frenchman when he took them back. "But they're not like *Les Misérables*."

"I already told you there is no other novel like *Les Misé-rables*," the Frenchman reminded him. "Actually, no two novels are alike and no two people have read the same novel. Not even *Les Misérables* is the same as *Les Misérables*. Read it again and you'll see."

Melchor wanted to find out if the Frenchman was right and immersed himself in the novel again. He had started the second volume when, one afternoon, while he was reading in his cell, a guard interrupted to say the governor wanted to speak to him and was waiting in his office. Surprised, Melchor asked why; the guard answered truthfully that he didn't know. As Melchor followed the guard through the corridors, he had a bad feeling and, when he went into the office and saw Vivales standing there beside the governor, looking shaken, he knew something bad had happened.

It was Vivales who gave him the news that his mother had died. At first, Melchor did not react, didn't ask any questions at all, didn't open his mouth and, as the lawyer and governor commented later, at that moment they both felt that some fuse had blown in his head, that he was mentally gone. In spite of that, Vivales told Melchor what he knew: at dawn the lifeless body of his mother had been found on some waste ground near La Sagrada, in Sant Andreu; everything indicated that she had died that same night; for now the police didn't know much more, they had opened several lines of investigation, though not many, because it seemed there were few clues. Vivales had not yet finished his explanations when Melchor's face contracted into an uncharacteristic grimace, as if he'd been stung by an insect or as if a tremor was running through his whole body from head to foot, almost at the same time as he exhaled a mixture of howl, snort and sob and immediately began kicking and punching everything in the office, including the lawyer and governor, who only managed to restrain his outbreak of fury with the help of three guards and an injection of haloperidol that laid him out in the infirmary.

What happened over the next forty-eight hours was always wrapped, for Melchor, in an excruciating chemical fog. The little he remembered he remembered in a confused way: he remembered one of his hands being put in a cast in the infirmary and that, outside the prison, he'd been watched over day and night by Vivales and two police officers; he remembered Vivales had tried to prevent him from seeing his mother's corpse, that he had seen it and that, in spite of the efforts made by the embalmers at the funeral parlour who had washed and cleaned and made her up, death had reduced his mother to an unrecognisable ghost, with her nose and skull broken and her body covered in bruises; he remembered that, apart from the two policemen and Vivales, nobody had come to the funeral except a handful of her fellow sex-workers and a handful of neighbours from Sant Roc, most of whom he didn't know or only knew by sight; he remembered that, on the night of the burial, after everything was over and he went back to prison, the inmates he passed in the corridors gave him their condolences, and that the Frenchman came to his cell for the first time, told him he was sorry about his mother's death and sat in silence with him for a while.

"Now you're a man, son," he said when he left. "Welcome to the club."

As a result of his mother's murder, Melchor stopped going to the workshops he used to frequent and gave up playing sports. He withdrew into himself. He gained weight. He couldn't control his thoughts, so his thoughts controlled him, morbid and unalterable thoughts, obsessed with what had happened to his mother, or with what he imagined had happened to her. The only two activities that appeared to alleviate his fixation were those that most fed it: talking to Vivales and reading *Les Misérables*, which in those days of mourning stopped being a novel and was transformed into something else, something without a name or with many names, a vital or philosophical guide, an oracular or wise book, an object of reflection to twist and turn like an infinitely intelligent kaleidoscope, a mirror and an axe. Melchor often thought of Monsieur Myriel, the bishop who converts Jean Valjean into Monsieur Madeleine, the saint persuaded that the universe was an immense illness the only cure for which was the love of God, he thought of the bishop and told himself it was true that the universe was an illness as the bishop believed, but, unlike the bishop, he lived in a world without God, and in this world the illness of the universe had no cure. Of course he thought of Jean Valjean and of his certainty that life was a war and in this war he was one of the vanquished, that he had no weapons or fuel aside from his rancour and hatred, and he felt that Jean Valjean was him, or that there was no essential difference between the two. But most of all he thought of Javert, of Javert's hallucinatory rectitude, of Javert's integrity and his scorn for evil, of Javert's sense of justice, and that Javert would never allow his mother's murder to go unpunished.

That was how he saw *Les Misérables*. As for Vivales, after

Melchor's mother's death the lawyer began to visit him more often, but the topics of conversation between the two of them, which over time had diversified and become more personal, became more restricted until they were almost reduced to a single one: his mother's murder; or, more precisely, what the police were discovering about his mother's murder. In this respect, Vivales seemed to be sparing with the information he supplied to Melchor, as if he didn't think he'd be able to handle the blow or as if he wanted to keep his attention over time or as if he himself was only being dripfed by his contacts in the police and the court. One afternoon he told him that he'd been able to read the forensic report, according to which his mother had been stoned to death but had not been raped. Another day he told him that on the night of her murder his mother had been working around the Barça ground, as it seemed she had frequently been doing lately. Another afternoon he assured him that the detectives had identified three eyewitnesses from that night, two women and a man, and that, thanks to their testimony, they had begun to reconstruct what had happened: it seemed his mother had indeed been hanging around the Barça ground that night, without picking up a single client, when around one-thirty in the morning she got into a car with four men in it with whom she'd earlier been negotiating a price for her services, and after that no-one had seen her again until she was found dead hours later. Another day he told him that, unfortunately, none of the three witnesses to his mother's disappearance remembered the licence plate of the car, and that among them there was a complete difference of opinion about the make and colour of the vehicle: one woman remembered a brown BMW and the other a dark Volkswagen, while the man remembered a black Skoda. Another afternoon he explained that the police had discovered that, while his mother was negotiating with the suspicious-looking clients and when she got into their car, there was another woman with her, but that she had also disappeared the same night and nobody had seen or heard of her since. This dribble of information went on for weeks, until one afternoon Vivales arrived at the visiting room with no news, or with news that was no news, because it wasn't new. Days later he admitted that there were no solid clues about the murderers; after a while, that the investigation had hit a dead end and the police were going to mothball the case.

For Melchor it was a shock, and for several weeks he refused to speak to Vivales. He didn't hold him responsible for anything, didn't blame him for anything: he simply did not want to see him. In fact, he didn't want to see anyone. During that time, he left his cell only when forced to, and spent the days sitting on the floor, naked, with his back against the wall, like a fakir, rereading *Les Misérables*.

A month and a half later he requested a meeting with the lawyer. Vivales showed up the next day, and the first thing Melchor did when he walked into the visiting room and saw him sitting there waiting for him, with his disgruntled face and his shabby clothes, his conman's air and his absurd patience, was to announce an irrevocable decision.

"I want to study," he said. "I'm going to be a police officer."

3

"Good afternoon, I think we all know each other, more or less," Deputy Inspector Gomà begins, cleaning the lenses of his glasses with his handkerchief. "So we can skip the introductions. And do me a favour, put your mobiles on silent and don't take any calls unless absolutely necessary."

Sitting to the left of Gomà, who is at the head of the table, Melchor watches him put his glasses back on and his handkerchief away. They are sitting around a rectangular table in the meeting room at the Terra Alta police station with nine other people. Apart from Deputy Inspector Barrera and Sergeant Blai, all of them – three women and six men – are members of the team created that morning by Deputy Inspector Gomà to investigate the Adell murders. Of that improvised team, the only two who don't belong to the Territorial Investigations Unit of Tortosa are Corporal Salom and Melchor, both from the Terra Alta Investigations Unit, under the command of Sergeant Blai. Melchor, who that afternoon had tried to make up for a night shift with a far too brief siesta, has never worked with most of these officers before, and barely knows them. Everyone present switches their mobiles to silent. It is quarter past five on Sunday afternoon: the meeting is starting late because Deputy Inspector

Gomà and Sergeant Pires have only now arrived at the station.

"I don't think it's necessary to remind you of the importance of the case we have in hand," Gomà says, with his well-modulated voice and professional tone. He has not taken off his jacket, his tie looks freshly knotted and his hair newly combed; he has before him a blue cardboard file and a Moleskine notebook open at a page on which are some scribbled notes. Sergeant Pires is sitting beside him, with her mobile on top of a pile of papers next to her iPad. "I imagine by now you have all realised the repercussions the murders have had and the social alarm they have caused. Our bosses are concerned, the commissioner has just called me to ask that we spare no efforts and keep him informed . . . We're all aware how journalists work, we all know these things sink as fast as they surface and, depending on what news there might be over the next few days, next week nobody's going to remember these murders. But for the moment we're going to be on every television and radio programme and in all the papers. Every single one of them." The deputy inspector pauses, before going on: "As you also know, it has got out that the Adells were tortured, and there are stories circulating that, as far as I can see, are pretty close to the truth. I suppose it was inevitable. I don't know who's been talking, nor am I going to try to find out. All that matters is that we isolate ourselves from all the media noise. I don't want us confirming or denying those stories, I don't want us paying attention to what's said or not said on TV, to whether there's been a leak that affects us and how it affects us, to the alleged witness statements the journalists collect and to all the verbal diarrhoea that this is going to generate. I want us to focus solely and exclusively on what concerns us, and to share information with no-one – and when I say no-one I mean absolutely no-one, not even our own families. I hope that's clear."

The deputy inspector looks around severely, trying to measure the effect of his words. With the exception of Deputy Inspector Barrera, all those present are under fifty, and several are not yet thirty, Melchor among them. Also, with the exception of Deputy Inspector Barrera, who's wearing his uniform, all those present are in very informal civilian clothes: jeans, summer shirts or blouses, T-shirts, trainers. Behind Gomà, the leaden afternoon light comes in through a large picture window overlooking a deserted playground and, further on, a weed-infested plot and a string of recently built semi-detached houses. Even though summer is about to begin, the day dawned grey and is still grey, but the clouds have not released a drop of rain and for the last few hours a gusty wind has been blowing, fluttering both flags – one Spanish, one Catalan – atop the two flagpoles at the station entrance, and raising little swirls of dust every once in a while in the playground.

"I suppose you all also know that the judge has issued an NDA," Gomà went on. "That will help us avoid leaks. Sergeant Pires and I will collate all the information. I shall be in permanent contact with the judge, she will run the investigation and write up the report, so she needs to receive all the information we manage to get hold of, beginning with what the forensic officers have collected at the Adells' house since this morning. Sergeant López, who has stayed in Tortosa dealing with the media, will be in charge of press relations. Corporal Salom will keep the Adell family informed. He's a friend of the managing director of Gráficas Adell, the husband of Rosa Adell, the only child of the murdered couple – have I got that right, Corporal?" Deputy Inspector Gomà says looking at Salom, who nods. "Tell us, how did they take the news?"

"Badly," Salom says. "Especially Rosa. The family is in shock."

"Have you taken a DNA sample from Rosa Adell?" Deputy Inspector Gomà says.

"I didn't know that was necessary," Salom says.

"It might not be," Deputy Inspector Gomà says. "But we may need it to identify the bodies."

"I'll take it this evening, when Melchor and I go to interview them."

Gomà agrees, and, while he adds that Rosa Adell and her husband should be taken to see the house as soon as possible, Melchor hears a mobile phone vibrate on his left; Viñas, in her thirties and noticeably pregnant, gives her phone a sidelong glance and declines the incoming call.

"You don't need me to tell you that the first days are crucial," the deputy inspector says. "And that we have to go all out now because what we don't do now we'll have a hard time doing later. So please make yourselves available twenty-four hours a day. I've already asked the forensic team – they're still working at the house and will carry on doing so over the next few days, and I've ordered that it remain sealed until further notice – and I'm asking it of you now, beginning with Corporal Salom and Agent Marín, who are our men in Terra Alta." The deputy inspector points to them both while continuing to talk to the rest of them. "These two are going to be vital to the investigation. They will be our eyes and ears in Terra Alta. Please keep that in mind. And speaking of requests –" Gomà now focuses on Deputy Inspector Barrera and Sergeant Blai, who are sitting opposite him – "I also have to ask you to do something."

"We are at your disposal," Barrera assures him. "It's your investigation."

"Thank you, Tomás," Gomà says. "What I have to ask you to do is leave the room."

Barrera and Blai look at him without understanding, the deputy inspector with his mouth hanging open, the sergeant not even hiding his annoyance. Apart from Pires, the rest of those present look at each other, as perplexed as the commanding officers.

"I'm sorry," Deputy Inspector Gomà assures them. "I did warn you there would be sacrifices. But it's for the good of the investigation. Please understand. It's not that I don't trust you; it's that I want to be rigorous in respecting the rules I've imposed. Nobody who's not on the investigative team should know anything about its process. And you two are not on the team, so it's best that you don't know any more than you know already."

The two commanders of the Terra Alta station exchange a brief glance, without shaking off their bewilderment. Melchor, who has been working under Blai's direct orders for four years, knows the sergeant can only interpret this decision as an insult. Barrera says: "Are you sure, Miquel?"

"Completely," Deputy Inspector Gomà says. "Right now I'd prefer not to have to explain why. We have no time to spare. If you want, we can talk later."

"Excuse me, Deputy Inspector," the sergeant protests, doing his utmost to keep from drilling Gomà with an incandescent stare, "I don't agree."

Before Blai can outline his objections, Barrera cuts him off: "Be quiet, Sergeant."

Blai's body tenses – his fists clench, his forearms tremble, his jaw looks as if it's about to dislocate itself – but he obeys without another word. Barrera stands up and orders the sergeant: "Let's go." Then he turns to Deputy Inspector Gomà and says, "If you need me, I'll be in my office."

Gomà thanks his colleague as Blai, head hanging, leaves the

meeting room behind his boss; Pires relieves the uncomfortable silence by handing out some stapled computer printouts to each of those present. Gomà takes a similar set of pages out of his briefcase and studies the notes he has made in his Moleskine.

"OK," he says, "let's get to the point: what do we know so far?" Consulting his notebook every once in a while, he recapitulates: "This morning, at about quarter past six, the Adells' cook found the bodies of Señor and Señora Adell in the living room of their house. The cook is from Ecuador and her name is María Fernanda Zambrano. She says she left the house last night at about half past eight, having prepared their supper. She also says she didn't see or hear anything strange, that everything was as it always was, that the Adells were alone except for a maid, the woman who we found shot dead in her room. Her name was Jenica Arba. Señora Zambrano has worked for the Adells for eight years and lives in Gandesa with her husband and son. Señora Arba was Romanian, had been working for the Adells for a year and a half and lived alone in El Pinell de Brai, but it seems she has a daughter in her own country, at her parents' house, and that she periodically sent her money. Do these women have anything to do with the murders? Was either of them associated with the killers?" The deputy inspector is silent for a moment, looking for something in his notebook, then goes on: "All the alarms and security cameras were switched off at 10.48 on Friday night. At that moment the house was full of people, because, every Friday evening, Francisco Adell had dinner there with his wife and his daughter and the senior management of Gráficas Adell. They hired a catering service for that dinner, with chefs, waiters and the rest. We'll have to speak to them, all of them, and especially with the guests. But the Adells' two employees were also there, knew the house very well, moved around it freely and could have taken advantage of the occasion when there were more people in the house to switch off the alarms, so that suspicions would be spread among everyone who was present and wouldn't fall directly on them." The deputy inspector stares at an agent with a pockmarked face, long hair and sideburns, dressed in a brightly coloured T-shirt, sitting at the end of the table to his left. "What can you tell me, Ramos?"

"I'd rule out the Ecuadorian," he says. "Viñas and I interrogated her at midday, her and her husband. They're scared to death, wouldn't kill a fly."

"Never," Viñas agrees, looking at her partner and caressing her pregnant belly.

"I wouldn't rule out the Romanian, though," says Claver, a man with a military-style haircut whose face is hidden by three days' stubble, and who moves his head back and forth as he doodles mechanically on the papers Pires had handed out. "I haven't managed to locate her parents, who apparently live in a tiny village near Timisoara, but I have spoken to her neighbours in El Pinell de Brai. They say she was a nice person, that she didn't do anything strange, didn't even bring men home, but . . ."

"But what?" Gomà presses him.

"She was fed up with living here," Claver explains, and stops doodling. "She wanted to go home to Romania, and needed money. People who need money can be tempted by good offers, no matter who they come from or how risky they are. I repeat, I wouldn't rule her out."

"We'll rule out the cook, but not the maid," Deputy Inspector Gomà agrees. "It could have been her who let the murderers in, the doors weren't forced, and neither was the gate. But if that's what happened, if the Romanian maid helped the murderers, why did they kill her? Because they didn't want to leave any witnesses who could identify them? And why did they kill her in her bedroom and not in the living room, where they killed the old folks? But what if it wasn't her but one of the Adells who opened the door to the murderers? What if they knew the people who killed them? That would explain the unforced doors, but not the disconnected alarms and cameras, don't you think?"

Melchor thinks Gomà is right, but he doesn't say anything; nobody else says anything either. Unmoved by the tacit approval that meets his words, Gomà looks thoughtful and turns the pages of his notebook as if looking through them for an explicit answer to his question or waiting for some comment or some objection. Or as if he doesn't know how to continue. Everyone in the room is looking at him, except for Salom, who, sitting next to Melchor, sneaks a look at his mobile.

Breaking the silence, the corporal says, "I'm getting a call from my friend, Albert Ferrer, the son-in-law."

Emerging from his abstraction, the deputy inspector motions for him to take the call and the corporal leaves the room.

"Let's press on," Gomà says. "What do we know about the Adell family?" He looks at his notes again, and this time seems to find what he's looking for straight away. "We know that the two victims, Francisco and Rosa, were the proprietors and sole shareholders of Gráficas Adell, the most important business in Terra Alta. They have two factories in Spain, both in Terra Alta, and four abroad: one in Poland, one in Romania, one in Mexico and one in Argentina. The Spanish factories employ just under six hundred workers, and the foreign ones more than four hundred. We're talking about a business that turns over some sixty million euros a year. And that's only a part of the Adells' holdings. All in all, they own half the region. They have other smaller companies, an infinite number of properties, shops, farms, houses, flats. In short, an empire." The deputy inspector brandishes a fistful of pages he has pulled out of his briefcase, identical to the ones that Pires has just handed out, and says: "Here you have a provisional report on the matter. Study it thoroughly. And I want two of you to go over the Adells' accounts with a fine-toothed comb, *and* those of their businesses."

Pires suggests that Rius, an athletic-looking guy in his thirties, with a shaved head and a harelip, and Gómez, a small woman with rounded breasts, bulging eyes and black-framed glasses, should take charge. They both have experience investigating financial crimes, so Gomà has no objections, and, turning to them, orders them to find out whether there have been any large deposits or payments into any of the Adells' accounts, any unusual transactions or anomalous operations.

"We already have judicial authorisation," he informs them. "So you can start on that first thing tomorrow, as soon as the banks open. I'm saying this to all of you: be meticulous; there's no such thing as a trivial detail, any detail might be important."

Sitting almost facing each other, Rius and Gómez nod, first looking at the deputy inspector and then at each other. Gomà glances uneasily towards the glass door through which he can see an unusually busy corridor in which, however, he cannot make out Salom.

"Let's wait a moment," he says. "And see if the corporal comes back."

Several minutes go by, during which Melchor immerses himself in the papers they've been given. Some colleagues do the same; others go off to the bathroom or stretch their legs or whisper to each other; Deputy Inspector Gomà goes over the notes in his Moleskine and Pires writes on her iPad. Eventually Salom reappears.

"Rosa Adell is not well," he declares, responding to the deputy inspector's silent question. "My friend is begging us to leave the interview until tomorrow afternoon, after they've been to the house." The corporal sits down across from Melchor, beside Pires. "I said yes. I think it's better not to overwhelm the family."

The deputy inspector confines himself to narrowing his eyes in resignation. Sergeant Pires sums up what was said while the corporal was out of the room and, when she finishes, Deputy Inspector Gomà starts talking about the Adells again, first asking Salom to correct him if he's mistaken.

"They have just one daughter," he says. "Her name is Rosa, she is married and has four children. She lives near Corbera d'Ebre, a fifteen-minute drive from her parents. Everything indicates she is their sole heir, although she is not a shareholder in any of their companies. As for her husband's position as managing director of Gráficas Adell, it is a largely decorative role, isn't that right, Salom?"

"In theory no," the corporal says. "But in practice the one who made the key decisions was the old man. Señor Adell, I mean. And the one who runs the business day to day is the manager."

"Josep Grau," Deputy Inspector Gomà prompts.

"That's right," Salom says. "I don't know him personally, but I've heard a lot about him. Grau's spent his whole life at the factory. Albert only began working there when he married Rosa. He's an economist. We'll speak to Grau tomorrow, too."

"I want you to talk to all of the company's executives as well," Gomà says. "And to the workers, if needs be. The Adells were austere, very religious people, who kept pretty much to themselves, but the husband was born in Bot, he must have had a friend in his hometown."

"As far as I know, very few," Salom says. "In his hometown or anywhere else. And the few friends he had have died. The closest was Grau. But, if he had any others left, we'll find them and speak to them."

"Good," Deputy Inspector Gomà says. "What about Señora Adell?"

"I don't know much about her," Salom says. "She wasn't from Terra Alta, she was from Reus. But she lived here all her life. In any case, I'll get on it."

The deputy inspector nods.

"For the moment, I want you and Marín to concentrate on the family and the senior management," he says to Salom. "As for you three –" the deputy inspector points to Ramos, Viñas and Claver – "there's something else I want you to do. Sergeant Pires."

Pires smooths her curly hair while clearing her throat, eyes fixed on her iPad. From his seat, Melchor glimpses a fragment of the tattoo over her collarbone, almost hidden by her polo shirt.

"As you all know, we have no leads so far," she says, looking up from her iPad. "Apart from the tread marks on the way in, if indeed they are a clue. We have verified that they are Continentals, but, of course, thousands of cars have those tyres. The Adells' nearest neighbours are a couple of kilometres away. The parents are both doctors; they have two children." She turns to Rius, who is sitting on her right, between Salom and Claver. "You spoke to them. Were you able to get anything useful from them?"

"Nothing whatsoever," Rius says, shaking his head. "They slept at home last night, but they didn't hear or see anything out of the ordinary. They are quite scared now, though."

Pires raises her eyebrows and for a second her features soften, then immediately recover their cool professionalism.

"There are any number of fingerprints all over the house," she says. "Naturally, most of them belong to the Adells, the maid and the cook."

"Have you taken Rosa Adell's and her family's?" Gomà says.

"I did," Salom says.

"We took the cook's as well," Viñas says.

"They've all been entered into the case file," Pires informs them.

"You said most of the fingerprints," Gómez says. "What about the rest?"

"We have to look into those," Pires says. "So far there aren't that many. They may belong to family members, to the senior management who had dinner at the house on Friday, the catering staff . . . It seems that most of them are clear, but there are some that are smudged, and we may not be able to identify those." Turning to Deputy Inspector Gomà, she says: "I've already mentioned that the forensics team is overwhelmed with work."

"I can go and help them when we finish here," Salom offers. "I worked in forensics for years."

"OK," Gomà says. "Give them a hand. Who is in charge of collecting the evidence?"

"Sirvent," Pires says.

"Speak to him," Deputy Inspector Gomà orders Salom. "Tell him tomorrow we can send more people from Tortosa. And that, if necessary, we'll request reinforcements from Barcelona."

After a pause, he motions to Pires to continue, and she turns her attention back to her iPad, sliding her finger across its screen.

"As the deputy inspector mentioned just now," she goes on,

looking up at her colleagues, "the security cameras and alarms in the house were disconnected on Friday night. Someone switched them off. They weren't working at the time of the murders. And another thing: the next closest security camera to the house is in Gandesa, so it's no use to us at all. That means we have only one way of finding out who was in the vicinity that night."

"Mobiles," Viñas says.

"Exactly," Pires says, with a quick look at her colleague, who still has her hand resting on her belly. "They've promised that by this evening I'll have the complete list of phones that connected last night to the two masts closest to the house. Including any that weren't used. As soon as we have the list, we can ask the service providers for the coordinates of their owners."

"We'll have to request the judge's authorisation, as well," Ramos says.

"No," Pires corrects him. "We only need judicial authorisation to access the content of the calls and messages, not to request this information. If all goes well, it's possible we'll start receiving the names and addresses of the owners tomorrow."

"In that case, tomorrow you can start to interrogate them," Deputy Inspector Gomà says, turning back to Ramos, Viñas and Claver. "One by one."

"There could be hundreds," Viñas warns, widening her eyes and lifting her hand from her belly, a little shocked.

"Even if there are thousands," the deputy inspector says, implacably. "One by one. Then, when we've identified the suspects, we'll request authorisation from the judge to go through the content. One thing is certain: the murderer is the owner of one of those phones. Or the murderers. Assuming, of course, that they didn't take the precaution of going into the Adells' house without their mobiles. And that would reinforce the theory that they're professionals."

"I wouldn't be surprised if they were," Rius says.

"Me neither," Gómez says. "And if they are professionals, it complicates things."

Several of those present agree with the professionals hypothesis; others question it. Deputy Inspector Gomà looks at Melchor, perhaps wondering whether he's going to share his opinion on the matter with his colleagues, but Melchor simply goes on listening. At some point Claver brings up the issue of mobiles again.

"It's clear that the murderers knew that mobile phones were a danger to them, which is why they destroyed the Adells' and the maid's," he observes.

"True," Deputy Inspector Gomà concedes. "But there are amateurs who know that too. Besides, professionals make mistakes, don't they? Anyway, let's go step by step and not assume the worst for now."

Gomà falls quiet and seems to hesitate; Pires leans towards him, shows him her iPad and points to the screen, allowing Melchor to get a fleeting glimpse of the red heart pierced by a black arrow the sergeant has tattooed over her collarbone, though he doesn't manage to read what is written on it.

"Yes,"Deputy Inspector Gomà goes on. "One more thing. The coroner has promised us a complete report by the day after tomorrow, Wednesday at the latest, but there are already a couple of important details we know for sure. The first is that the Adells died between ten at night and five in the morning. We could have deduced this, of course. If the cook, Señora Zambrano, left the house around eight-thirty and came back at six-thirty, the crimes had to have been committed within that time period. The coroner says he may be able to pinpoint the time more precisely when he's finished the autopsy, but not by much. The second thing we know, and this may be more pertinent, is that the Adells did not die straight away. I mean, the murderers did not kill them and then mutilate their bodies. No, they tortured them first and then they killed them. The coroner says it seems likely they tortured them for a long time, that they kept them alive for as long as possible, so they would suffer as much as possible. You will all be wondering the same thing as I am: who would want to make a couple of old people suffer like that? And why? Out of sadism? Were they just burglars who lost their heads for whatever reason and ended up torturing the old folks out of pure evil, fury or simply for their own amusement? We know they turned the Adells' bedroom upside down, but we don't know what they took, if indeed they took anything. We hope their daughter and son-in-law will help clear that up. Or were the murderers looking for something specific and tortured the old couple to get them to say where it was? If that's the case, what were they looking for? Did the Adells tell them what they wanted to know? Did they find what they were looking for and take it away? Or did they not find it and leave empty-handed? Was what they were looking for within the house or outside? And, indeed, did they torture the old couple at the same time or one after the other? Did they torture one in front of the other and then, once the first was dead, torture the second? The fact of the torture is horrifying. And disconcerting."

"Why disconcerting?" Ramos asks. "If the murderers were looking for something and the Adells didn't want to give it to them, torture was a method to get them to give in. At least the murderers might think so."

"I'm not saying it wasn't," Deputy Inspector Gomà says. "But remember the way in which they were tortured. Those people suffered unspeakably before dying. Does that kind of brutality square with a mere interrogation?"

Looking at Gomà, Ramos shrugs and narrows his eyes in a doubtful gesture meaning: why not?

"That is not taking into account one more thing," Gomà insists. "As far as we know, the Adells were well liked in Terra Alta, they don't seem to have had enemies. Of course, they may have been killed by people from somewhere else, but –"

"Maybe they weren't so well liked," Melchor interrupts. "Especially Señor Adell."

It is the first time he has spoken, and even though he has done no more than murmur it, as if the words were intended only for the deputy inspector, all eyes converge on him. Deputy Inspector Gomà encourages him to explain. Melchor repeats what he said, louder this time.

"There are those who think Adell behaved like a despot," he says. "That he monopolised everything. And there are those who think he exploited his workers and that his shadow was so big nothing could grow around him."

"The monopoly thing is true," Rius says, flourishing the report on the Adells' properties and dropping it on the table.

"Who thinks that Adell was a despot?" Gomà asks. "People who work for him?"

"I've heard people from the region say it," Melchor says, reluctant to put his wife's name forward. "People born and raised here. But I don't think it's an isolated opinion."

Undoubtedly remembering what Salom had said at the Adells' house a few hours earlier ("I think that people liked them around here"), Deputy Inspector Gomà wordlessly consults the corporal, who has been listening to them while scratching his beard and who, before giving his opinion, leans back in his chair and pushes his glasses up the bridge of his nose.

72

"What Melchor says is true," Salom agrees, looking at Gomà. "Certainly more than one or two in Terra Alta think that of Adell. It's natural, after all. You said yourself this morning, Deputy Inspector: rich people tend to have enemies. And Adell was very rich. Success always breeds envy, the more so in the case of a man who came from practically nothing and had been orphaned as a child. I think his father was a day labourer . . . Adell was what they call a self-made man. That kind of person is admired in other countries, but not in ours. This is how it is, why kid ourselves? But although it's impossible to amass a fortune like Adell's without making the odd enemy – some humiliated competitor or disgruntled sacked employee – here in Terra Alta what predominates is regard and gratitude for a man who, at the end of the day, has brought prosperity to the area and provided work for a great many families. But I could be wrong."

"That's what we have to find out," Gomà says, speaking for all of them. "Whether the Adells had enemies, and what kind of enemies they were. Did the Adells have enemies who would torture and slaughter them like that? Were they barefaced enemies, or enemies who posed as friends and accumulated resentment for years, in secret, until they spied their opportunity? Is that why the Adells opened their door to their killers, supposing that they did open it, because they thought they were friends? Did they murder the Adells themselves, or did they hire someone to do the job? Whoever it was who killed the Adells or ordered they be killed, did they kill them to steal from them? Did they kill them because they wanted to get something out of them? Or did they kill them for revenge? These are the possibilities that occur to me at the moment. Well, there is one more that occurs to me . . ."

Gomà pauses in a strategic, even slightly theatrical way.

73

Sitting next to him, Melchor believes he guesses what he's thinking, but doesn't say; around him, everyone is intrigued and waits in silence. Melchor sees that, on the other side of the window, a timid sun is emerging from behind the clouds; and the wind seems to have died down: the Spanish and Catalan flags hang limply from their poles, barely stirring. He has just noticed this when a gust of wind lifts them again, shaking them violently and raising a whirlwind of dust in the playground.

"A ritual murder," Gomà finally reveals. "To be honest, it was the first thing I thought when I walked into that house and saw those tortured bodies. I'm sure more than one of you thought the same. Of course, ritual makes it sound like a film, but we all know reality can sometimes be filmic. And there are people who love to imitate films. The thing is, the Adells were very religious, both were members of Opus Dei. That doesn't mean anything, of course, but . . ." He stares off into the distance, and his features relax into something resembling a smile. "I don't know who it was who said that God and the devil were two sides of the same coin, and that whoever has a strong connection to God will eventually be connected to the devil . . . Anyway," he adds, perhaps uncomfortable with his own words – any remnants of a smile have vanished from his lips, "it's just one more hypothesis. But one we'll have to rule out. Or confirm."

Deputy Inspector Gomà's conjecture is received in silence during which the members of the team exchange glances that Melchor doesn't know how to interpret. After a few seconds, the deputy inspector looks at his notes again, turning the pages of his Moleskine, and asks: "What else, Sergeant?"

Pires' only reply is to raise her eyebrows and hold her hands and arms open in a simultaneous double gesture, which Melchor translates as "nothing else, as far as I'm concerned".

Gomà then addresses the whole room: "Any questions? Any comments?" He looks around expectantly, before saying: "Very good. Just remember the essential thing. We have to be permanently available. We have to talk to each other a lot. We have to share information. It's fundamental that we exchange data. Remember, two heads are better than one, and three are better than two. Most of all, remember that we're a team. Let's take advantage of these first hours, these first days. Let's concentrate on the finances, on interviewing the owners of mobiles who were driving near the country house around the time of the crime, on the Adell family and their associates. I know we can't get properly down to work until tomorrow, but let's use this evening and tonight to steep ourselves in the Adells: besides the papers the sergeant handed out, there's plenty of information on the internet. And don't talk to anybody outside the team, please. The whole country is watching us, and the force's prestige is at stake. That's all. Let's get to work."

Melchor and Salom stand in the corridor for a few minutes, commenting on the meeting and dividing up the work. Around them there is unusual excitement, especially for a Sunday evening. The triple murder at the Adell country house has not only put their Investigations Unit and that of Tortosa on a war footing, it has stirred up the whole station. Melchor does not remember the building ever being in such commotion.

"Well," Salom says. "I'd better get over to the Adells' house."

"Do you want me to go with you?"

"No. You don't have any experience in forensics. Besides, if we're going to interview the managers of Gráficas Adell tomorrow, you'd be better off getting up to speed on the family business."

They say goodbye on the stairs and, while Salom goes down to the underground car park to get his car, Melchor heads for the office he shares with the corporal and the nine other members of the Terra Alta Investigations Unit (Sergeant Blai has an office of his own), a vast room with five desks, five computers and a bank of filing cabinets. He finds Corominas and Feliu there, two colleagues from forensics who are chatting and drinking coffee, who ask him if there is any news. Melchor tells them no, and since he knows that they should be at the Adells' house, collecting clues, he asks them the same thing. Corominas, a big man with a round head and a boxer's nose who's on the heavy side, tells him there's no news from there either and adds that they've come to the station to deposit the evidence they've collected so far.

"We're taking a break," Feliu says, raising her coffee cup: she is blond and looks a bit tarty, with very tight clothes, her hair combed into an almost punk-like crest. "This is going to take a while."

Corominas supports his partner's prediction and asks Melchor if he too thinks the Adells could have been the victims of a ritual murder.

"I don't know," Melchor says, sitting down at his desk. "Why do you ask?"

"Because that's the rumour going round. They say the victims were very religious. The two old people, I mean."

"That's what they say," Melchor admits.

"Well, I'll tell you one thing," Corominas announces, speaking to Feliu now. "If that's true, I wouldn't be a bit surprised if it were a ritual murder. Do you know why?"

"Tell us," she says.

"Because religion has been driving people crazy lately," Corominas says. "Take it from me."

76

He then goes on to tell the story of a friend of his, a gardener in Amposta who went to the Holy Land last summer. Melchor wonders for a moment if he should go down to the cafeteria and get a coffee, but remembering the foul taste of his last cup of dishwater from the machine there decides to give it a miss and, as he turns on his computer, he listens distractedly to the anecdote Corominas is telling.

"He wasn't a religious guy," his colleague explains, leaning back in his chair and crossing his feet on his desk. "The opposite, in fact. He'd gone to a Catholic school, but he was anticlerical. He took the trip out of curiosity, as a tourist."

Corominas explains that, when he got to Jerusalem, his friend took a room in a cheap hotel in the city centre, and one night, after he'd been there for three days, a couple of police officers arrested him for wandering around the old city wrapped in a sheet from the hotel, reciting fragments of Moses' second speech from the Book of Deuteronomy. Fortunately, they let him out straight away, because he led the authorities to believe he was a seminarian on a study trip and that it had just been a meaningless joke, but the next day he hired a bicycle and disappeared, and a week later he was found sitting on a rock in the Negev Desert, convinced he was the prophet Elijah and that a chariot of fire pulled by horses of fire was about to take him up to heaven in a whirlwind. He was admitted to the Kfar Shaul psychiatric hospital in Jerusalem, and spent the rest of his holiday lying in a bed next to an American tourist who thought he was Samson and had tried to pull down the Wailing Wall, and near a Polish tourist who was sure she was in labour and about to deliver the Messiah. And then, at the end of his holiday, the gardener went home.

"And there he remains as if nothing happened," Corominas concludes. "Come to Amposta some time and I'll introduce you to him, he'll tell you the story himself. Of course, whatever happens was not as he tells it, because he doesn't remember a thing, just what he was told happened. As I was saying: religion drives people crazy."

Feliu is still doubled up with laughter at the story of the gardener from Amposta ("The funny thing is I'd always thought he looked a bit like a prophet, with his gaunt face and little beard and stuff," Corominas has just said, really trying to milk his success) when Sergeant Blai bursts into the room. Feliu stops laughing instantly and Corominas takes his feet off the desk, but Blai doesn't ask what's going on: upset and anxious, he just asks Melchor if the meeting with Deputy Inspector Gomà has finished. Melchor says yes and then Blai asks him where the corporal is.

"He just left for the Adells' house," Melchor says. "He's gone to lend a hand."

"We can certainly use it," Feliu says, throwing her empty paper cup into the waste bin. "There's a week's worth of work there. Back to the grindstone, Coro?"

"Let's go," Corominas says, standing up with a crunching of joints. "Looks like nobody's getting any fucking sleep tonight."

Ignoring Feliu and Corominas, Blai asks Melchor to come into his office. Only a glass wall separates it from the investigators' room and when Melchor comes in Blai is already leaning on the edge of his desk, which is buried in paper, waiting for him and looking really pissed off.

"That guy is a son of a bitch," the sergeant says, once Melchor has closed the door behind him.

"Which guy?" Melchor says, even though he knows the answer.

"Gomà. Who else?" Blai says. "Didn't you see? He threw me and Barrera out on our arses. In front of everybody. He didn't even have the decency to tell us in private. Fucking son of a bitch."

Breathing heavily, enraged and edgy as a caged animal, Blai stalks around his desk, sits down and signals for Melchor to take a seat.

"Barrera is soft, he's got a few months before he retires and he doesn't want to get into trouble," Blai says, without noticing that Melchor is still on his feet. "If it were just me, I would have stayed and stood up to him. I've been warned about him, you know. 'Watch out for Gomà,' they told me when he came to Tortosa. 'He's a climber. He comes from a good family and wants to make commissioner no matter how.' Fucking bastard. A proper case falls to us in Terra Alta and I'm not on it because this little piece of shit wants all the glory for himself. Damn it. And have you seen that two-faced Pires? Seems like Gomà's lapdog. I bet they're screwing."

While remembering the sergeant's tattoo and wondering if Blai just wants to blow off some steam, Melchor resolves to be patient and listen to him rant and rave against Deputy Inspector Gomà, against Pires, against his bad luck. On the other side of the glass, he can see the deserted investigators' room; only his computer is still on. In front of him, behind the sergeant, a big window gives onto a suburban landscape that, in the early evening desolation of that June Sunday, doesn't seem much different from the one he was looking at earlier from the meeting room (semi-detached houses, buildings under construction, vacant lots where the north wind is raising thick dust clouds), and, further away, he can see the sky severed by the abrupt outline of the mountains, whose slopes wave like a sea of trees, tremulous and green, dotted with wind turbines that, from a distance, look like giant metal insects, their blades spinning at full speed. To his right, a multi-coloured cork panel fastened to the wall displays notes, photographs, reminders and announcements; at one edge, very visible, a sticker with a starred flag proclaims in English: "Catalonia is not Spain". Melchor is wondering how he can contain the tirade of venting and grievances the sergeant is subjecting him to when, unexpectedly, Blai focuses on him again.

"You have to do me a favour," he says.

Right at this moment Melchor's phone chimes in the silence of the office.

"It's from Salom," he explains.

The message contains two telephone numbers, a landline and a mobile:

these are josep grau's phone numbers, the general manager of graficas adell. you call him, I'm tied up, ask him for an interview tomorrow morning, wherever he wants, as long as it's first thing. later I can't. ok?

Melchor writes back:

OK

"What's he say?" Blai asks.

"Nothing."

"See? This is precisely what I want to ask you."

"What?"

"Keep me up to date on the Adell case."

"Impossible. You heard Deputy Inspector Gomà: outside the team, total silence."

Blai moves around in his chair, gestures in desperation, shakes his head.

"Don't fuck with me, *españolazo*," he says. "You too? What

80

can be wrong with you telling me what you find out? You know I keep my mouth shut."

"I'm sorry, Sergeant, I can't do that. Talk to Gomà."

"Fuck Gomà!" Blai shouts, slamming his hand onto the mess of papers on his desk. "I'm telling you. You know me, you know that I know Terra Alta like the back of my hand and that I can help. You also know that bastard has played a cathedral-sized dirty trick on me. Do me a favour, for fuck's sake. How many favours have I done you since you came here, eh? How many?"

Melchor remembers a few favours Blai has done him over the years, but none of the scale or nature of the one he's asking of him. Though, nor can he deny that, at least in part, he's right: Blai is not incompetent, knows Terra Alta better than almost anybody and has accumulated many years of experience, so it is arbitrarily prejudicial to the deputy inspector's case to exclude him from the investigation, because sooner or later he might be useful. And then they'll regret not having involved him. As for the rest, no-one's more interested in discretion than the sergeant, at least in this matter.

"Alright." Melchor gives in. "Let me think it over."

Blai's expression changes instantly.

"Thanks, *españolazo*," he says, touched: he stands up and walks over to Melchor with open arms. "I knew I could rely on you."

"I only said I'd think about it," he warns, trying to contain his boss' elation.

"OK, OK." Blai backs off. But, sure of his triumph now, he clasps Melchor's shoulder with his left hand while vigorously shaking his right; he looks him in the eye and says: "You scratch my back, I'll scratch yours."

In his office, Melchor calls the mobile number that Salom has

81

sent him, but it's switched off; then he calls the landline, which rings for several seconds without anyone answering. Sitting in front of his computer, he checks his email and, just as he sees he has no new messages, Blai raps on the glass that separates the two offices and waves goodbye, making circles with his index finger to signal they'll talk tomorrow and then giving him a thumb's up. Not without wondering if he was right to give in to the sergeant's pressure, Melchor immerses himself in the report on the Adells' businesses that Pires had given them, and spends the rest of the evening reading about the family and their companies, searching the internet for supplementary information and, every once in a while, calling the two numbers Salom gave him, always in vain. Until, around half past nine when his stomach is starting to grumble and he's struggling to keep his eyes open, because he's barely slept in the last two days, someone answers the mobile he has been calling for hours.

Melchor asks for Señor Josep Grau, manager of Gráficas Adell. The voice, old, faint and rough, answers that he is Señor Grau, and Melchor introduces himself and asks if they can talk to him first thing tomorrow.

"It's about the death of the Adells."

"So I imagined," Grau says. "Yes, that's not a problem. Come and see me at my office."

"I'll be coming with another officer."

"Bring whoever you want. My office is in the company building, beside the factory, on the La Plana industrial estate. You can't miss it. I'll be there from eight o'clock."

"Will the factory be open tomorrow?" Melchor asks.

"Of course," Grau says. "Would it do any good if we didn't open?"

Melchor feels that this question has not been asked for him to answer, and is about to say goodbye when Grau speaks again.

"Tell me, have you any leads on the murderers?"

"None," Melchor says. "And, if we did, I couldn't tell you."

"At least tell me if the things they're saying on the radio and television are true."

"What do you mean?"

"That the Adells were tortured before they were killed."

Melchor understands that it makes no sense to lie or feign ignorance on this specific point, to this old man or to anyone else.

"More or less," he says.

At the other end of the line there is a sudden heavy silence, and for a second Melchor thinks that Grau has hung up on him; then he hears a sound that at first resembles a sob and then the screeching of a chair being dragged across a floor.

"I understand," the man says, with a hard, unemotional voice. "Well, come and see me tomorrow. I'll do what I can to help."

Melchor hangs up, then dials Salom, who answers immediately.

"Perfect," the corporal says when Melchor relays his conversation with Grau. "Let's meet at the entrance to the offices at nine tomorrow morning."

"OK. How're things going over there?"

"Good. But we've got a lot more to do tonight."

Melchor again offers to help, and Salom again turns down his offer.

"Go home to bed," he says. "You must be dead on your feet."

"I had a siesta."

"Doesn't matter. Listen to me. Go and get some sleep. See you tomorrow morning at Gráficas Adell. And give my regards to your girls."

Melchor remains at his computer for a moment, rubbing his exhausted eyes and listening to the silence now reigning once more over the almost deserted station. Then he switches off his computer, turns out the lights in the office and, on his way out of the building, waves to the patrolman on the night shift, who wishes him good night. As he walks towards the centre of town through the badly lit streets of the outskirts, the wind is still blowing strongly.

4

Some months after the murder of his mother, Melchor had announced to Domingo Vivales in a visiting room in the Quatre Camines prison that he intended to join the police. The lawyer made a face that meant he supposed he was joking. He looked at Melchor: he wasn't joking.

"I've researched it and I can do it," Melchor said, reading the perplexed look on his face. "First I'll finish school. I can do that from in here: I've talked to an instructor and she said she'd help me. When I get out I'll have to wait two or three years to get my criminal record expunged, and then I can take the entrance exams. They're not hard. I'll pass."

Vivales listened, astonished.

"What do you think?" Melchor asked.

"Good." The lawyer blinked several times. "Great."

"I'm glad you think so because I need you to pay my enrolment fees," said Melchor, who seemed to want to make up for the ecstatic passivity of recent months with an iron determination. "I also need a computer. How much more time do you think I have to spend in prison?"

"If everything carries on as it has till now, a year and a half," Vivales calculated. "Maybe a little less."

"As soon as I get out I'll look for a job," Melchor promised. "I'll pay you back every last cent."

Although they had used up the allotted visiting time, Vivales had not yet asked Melchor why he'd taken that unlikely decision, but he already knew him well enough to know he was not going to change his mind. For his part, Melchor didn't even mention *Les Misérables*. That same week a laptop computer was delivered to his cell, and he registered with the IOC, Catalonia's Open Institute, to complete the second stage of his Compulsory Secondary Education, and began his online studies. He was surprised to discover he enjoyed the subjects, he liked studying, and he liked that solitary way of learning. He gave up the occupational workshops to devote himself exclusively to his new task. After three months, with the agreement of both the prison instructor and his IOC tutor, he enrolled in the third stage of the CSE course as well, with the aim of finishing his whole secondary education in a single year and leaving prison with a high school diploma in his hand. To Vivales' astonishment, but not his instructor's or his tutor's, he managed it. He received his marks the evening before his twenty-first birthday. Vivales went to see him.

"Your mother would be proud of you," he said.

Melchor's lips stretched into a minimal smile.

"My mother's dead," he said. "And I'm going to find the sons of bitches who killed her."

He spent his last months in prison reading nineteenth-century novels and playing sports and exercising as hard as he could. Vivales continued to visit him regularly. Since his mother's death, Vivales was the only person who did. In spite of how often they saw each other, Melchor knew almost nothing about the lawyer. He barely ever talked about himself and Melchor never asked. All he knew was that he was an expert in criminal law with the confirmed reputation of a sweet-talker (it was a long time before he found out that his surname was not Vivales but Perales, because everyone called him Vivales; he himself often signed with his nickname, which facilitated some of his judicial dodges). He also knew he lived in the Eixample neighbourhood, on calle Mallorca at the corner of Cartagena, that he liked Havana cigars and Irish whiskey, that he'd been divorced three times and had no children as far as he knew. Melchor was grateful for his proven efficiency and his habit of offering only what he could accomplish, but he was exasperated by his propensity to meddle in his affairs and was still perturbed by not knowing the exact nature of the relationship that had linked the lawyer to his mother: he didn't know if he'd been one of her clients, he didn't want to think he'd been one of her lovers, he wasn't sure that she had paid him to take charge of his legal defence (although nor was he sure she hadn't), and he didn't understand why, once she was dead, he continued looking after his defence, nor why he came to see him so often. One day, during one of those claustrophobic conversations in the visiting room, Melchor asked him straight out.

"Do you want the truth or would you rather have a lie?" Vivales said. "I should warn you that you're not going to like the truth."

Melchor immediately regretted his imprudence, but was not brave enough to retract it, or didn't know how. While noticing the cold foam churning in his stomach, he lied: he said he'd prefer the truth. Vivales looked at him with a disdain tinged with profound compassion.

"Because you're a loser, Melchor," he answered. "And if I don't lend you a hand, tell me who will."

Shortly after inflicting this indisputable truth without anaesthetic – which Melchor took as proof of integrity and not as an intention to wound him – Vivales arranged for him to be transferred to the Modelo Prison in central Barcelona, where he began to enjoy third-stage incarceration, meaning he only had to sleep in the prison; he also found him a job at a print shop on calle Riera de Sant Miquel, in the Gràcia neighbourhood. So, from then on, he left the prison in the morning and returned at night, having spent the day making photocopies. This regime of semi-liberty did not last long. In view of Melchor's irreproachable conduct, after three and a half months the supervising judge granted him unconditional release.

The day he left prison, Vivales was waiting for him at the gate on calle Entença, leaning against the building across the street, smoking a Partagás Series D No. 4. He had just been to the barber and carried his raincoat over his arm. He wore a clean and pressed suit, a new shirt and a tight, well-knotted tie.

"Shall I drive you home?" he said with a triumphant smile. Melchor put his bags down on the ground and shook his hand. "I've prepared a welcome gift for you," he added.

In Vivales' car, the two men crossed Barcelona from one side to the other in silence, while Melchor savoured his first minutes of unrestricted freedom. The Sant Roc neighbourhood, in Badalona, had not changed much in his absence, nor had the street or apartment block where his flat was. The flat, however, did seem different, or that's what Melchor thought as, with a lump in his throat, he walked around the rooms inhabited by the triple ghost of his dead mother, his fatherless childhood and his angry adolescence, and discovered that Vivales had bought new furniture, had the walls painted and filled the refrigerator.

When he finished his inspection, Melchor gestured around the flat, tidied up and ready for him to live in. "Is this the gift?"

In reply Vivales took a folded piece of paper out of his jacket pocket and handed it to him. Melchor unfolded it and began to read.

"It's the certificate of cancellation of your criminal record," the lawyer explained. "You're clean."

Disconcerted, Melchor looked up from the paper. Vivales took a puff on his Partagás and exhaled a thick cloud of smoke. Melchor looked back at the paper: this document implied that he didn't have to wait the three obligatory years that, legally, he should wait between leaving prison and applying to join a police force.

"Is it legit?"

"Sure," Vivales said. "And I'm Saint Joseph of Calasanz. But don't worry: it's all under control. Nobody's going to discover that it's a fake. Besides, your record has disappeared from police archives. So, as far as they're concerned, you've never been in jail."

Stupefied, Melchor waved the document: "Where . . . ?"

Vivales didn't let him finish.

"There's something else," he went on. "The Catalan government has just announced thirty vacancies for the Mossos d'Esquadra. The exams are three months from now. If I were you, I'd start studying today."

Melchor stared at Vivales, not knowing what to say. The lawyer took another puff on his cigar and blew out the smoke.

"Well, I think that's all, kid," he said. "Welcome to freedom."

At last on his own, Melchor wondered for the first time in his life whether Vivales might be his father.

During the following three months he studied for the entrance exams to the Institut de Seguretat Pública, the police academy. He steeped himself in basic legislation, the highway code, the civil code and the penal code, the statute of Catalan autonomy and the Spanish Constitution; he also did things he'd never done before, such as read the newspapers every day, because he'd been told that the exams might include questions about current affairs. He passed the exams unspectacularly, was admitted to the academy and spent the next nine months attending classes at their headquarters in Mollet del Vallès, near Barcelona. Many of his classmates came from far away places and lived in the academy residence or in shared flats nearby; he came and went from his home every day, a little over half an hour by car. The daytime schedule of his classes obliged him to give up the job at the print shop, but he soon found a place at a nightclub in Badalona called Scorpio's, where he worked the door four nights a week. He didn't get much sleep, but he still enjoyed his classes a lot. He spent all his free time studying. Partly because most of his classmates were younger than him and he didn't have time off to share with them, and partly because of his reserved character, Melchor did not make friends at the academy. He didn't stand out for anything either, apart from his elegant reports and his skill at target practice. At the end of the first round of these, the instructor had a chat with him.

"Where did you learn to shoot?" he asked.

"Around."

"Are you a hunter?"

"More or less."

"What do you want to specialise in?"

"Investigation."

"If you like, I could recommend you for the Special Intervention Group. It's riskier, but you won't be bored. And it's well paid."

Melchor didn't even weigh up the offer.

"Thanks. But I'd rather be a detective."

Nine months later, during the graduation ceremony that concluded his training, the marksmanship instructor reiterated his proposal and Melchor turned it down again.

"Up to you, Marín," the instructor said regretfully. "In any case, do me a favour and look after that aim of yours. It's priceless."

A little while later Melchor began his practice patrols in Cornellà de Llobregat, another working-class district on the outskirts of Barcelona. The police station was on calle Travessera, and the partner they assigned him as guide or adviser as he took his first professional steps was a former *guardia civil* transformed into a *mosso d'esquadra*. His name was Vicente Bigara. He was thirty years older than Melchor, didn't believe in his job and mocked regulations; he also drank heavily, smoked like a chimney and womanised prodigiously.

Live and let live, was the motto he repeated at the slightest excuse, applying it across the board not only to his superiors and comrades, but especially to criminals and delinquents. "If you don't piss them off," he told Melchor on the first day, "they won't piss you off. And if they piss you off, a couple of whacks round the head and into the cells. Got it?"

Melchor said yes to everything. Bigara laughed his head off at Melchor's adherence to the law and never called him by his name: he called him *"pardillo"*, as if he were a gullible young fool. In spite of the fact that they were different in every way (or precisely because of that), they got along really well, made a good professional team and never fell out. So Melchor was unhappy when, once his practical training was finished, he wasn't allowed to stay in Cornellà and was stationed in Nou Barris, an immigrant area north of Barcelona. He made up for the disappointment by immediately applying to sit an exam to become a criminal investigator; he passed without any trouble, and for three months went back to attending classes at the police academy. This time he was very conscientious, trying to learn as much as he could, and, as soon as the course finished, he arranged to meet Bigara and announced that he needed to ask him a favour.

"Name it," the old civil guard said.

"Have you got any friends at the Sant Andreu station?"

"I've got friends everywhere, kid."

"I need you to get me a copy of a file on a murder case. It was committed four years ago in Sant Andreu."

"And why don't you ask your superior officers?"

"Because I can't. Nobody can know anything about this, especially not my superiors. I'm going to investigate the case on my own."

Bigara scrutinised him through his cigarette smoke. They were sitting at the bar in the Bacarrà, a strip joint the old civil guard frequented, near Turó Parc. Bigara was drinking whisky and Melchor Coca-Cola. They'd just caught up on each other's lives and Bigara had just congratulated him on his promotion to detective. That's why he said: "Has your success gone to your head, or what?"

Melchor then told Bigara something he'd never told anybody: he told him about his mother's murder, told him where, how and when it had happened and that the file he needed was for that case. When Melchor finished talking, the old civil guard spun all the way around on his barstool and, without a word, sat watching the naked or half-naked girls dancing along the wide, illuminated catwalk in the middle of the club. After a few seconds, during which he seemed to be following the dancers' moves with complete attention, he turned back to the bar, drank his whisky down in one and ordered another.

"You can count on it," he said to Melchor.

A week later they arranged to meet in the same place and Bigara handed him a folder containing five pages of computer printout, marked with the stamp of the Sant Andreu police station.

"They didn't bust a gut," Bigara said, whisky in hand, while Melchor examined the file avidly. "What do you think you'll do?"

"Find my mother's murderers," Melchor said without looking at him.

"And then?"

"Then we'll see."

The old civil guard nodded, his lower lip over his upper lip and his glass of whisky resting on his protruding belly. More than obese, he was swollen, and, under the blue and red strobe lights, his whitish face and cardinal's double chin made him look like a toad.

"Be careful, *pardillo*."

Melchor began to investigate his mother's murder in his free time, unbeknownst to his colleagues and commanders. He was aware that investigating a case he hadn't been assigned, and, on top of that, one to do with a member of his own family, was acting in an irregular way ("Watch out, kid," Bigara warned him more than once. "If they catch you, you'll be in shit up to your neck."). The file Bigara had given him contained the coroner's report, and the first thing Melchor realised when he read it was that, when Vivales told him about it during their talks in Quatre Camins, after his mother's death, the lawyer had deceived him by softening its contents. Although the report registered that his mother had died due to cranio-encephalic trauma, as Vivales had indeed told him, it also showed something that he had hidden from him, and that was that death had occurred after the victim had been raped several times, anally and vaginally, which had caused tearing to both orifices. Furthermore, apart from the aforesaid report, the file contained the statements of just three witnesses and not much more, and Melchor was shocked that, years earlier, those four poorly stitched morsels of information had been enough to fuel so many conversations with Vivales in the visiting room, and to allow him to conceive of so many unfounded hopes.

After reading the file, Melchor interviewed the coroner and the three witnesses. The coroner had forgotten the case, but he remembered it when he reread his report, to which he could only add that it was a flagrant case of extreme cruelty to the victim. As for the witnesses, they were two prostitutes and a pimp, and all three repeated so invariably what they'd said in the long-ago statements collected in the file that Melchor understood their memories had fossilised, and that what they told him was not what they remembered, but what they remembered having previously recited. Even so, the two women added one decisive detail, which to Melchor's astonishment was not in the file: the prostitute who was with his mother when she was negotiating with her last ever clients was called Carmen Lucas.

That discovery changed everything. Once he had made it, Melchor devoted one hundred per cent of his free time to the search for Carmen Lucas, convinced that the woman must know some crucial detail about his mother's death and had, for that very reason, vanished after her murder.

He found not the slightest trace of her in the police archives, or on the internet, but he was not prepared to let himself be defeated by this first setback. He resolved to speak to all the prostitutes who had worked around the Barça ground at the same time as his mother, with all the pimps, all the owners of singles clubs and the women who had lived off prostitution, or around prostitution, in those times; in fact, with all Barcelona's nighthawks, including his own colleagues, who could have had relations with his mother or might have some idea of Carmen Lucas' whereabouts.

While he was engaged in that impossible enterprise, he had lunch from time to time with Vivales, who was aware of his informal investigations and whom he occasionally asked for information and help, despite the fact that the lawyer had categorically refused to let him repay his defence fees or the money he'd lent him until he could support himself. Also at that time he began to gain a reputation around the Nou Barris station as an intellectual bully. His colleagues knew him for three things. The first two were public and everyone congratulated him for them: his talent for writing clear, succinct and precise reports, and his astuteness as an interrogator able to break even those detainees most armour-plated against the relief of confession ("It's not a matter of astuteness," Melchor said. "It's a matter of putting yourself in their shoes."). The third thing was never discussed. Nobody congratulated him for it. They all looked the other way, starting with his immediate superiors: they all knew that, after every complaint filed by a woman for domestic abuse, the abuser would get a beating, and everyone knew, though no complaint was ever filed against Melchor, that he was the one responsible.

Very late one Friday night, as he drove home after spending the evening asking in vain about Carmen Lucas in several nightclubs in Gavà, he got a call to say that Vicente Bigara had just been found dead in the Montcada Night Club, on the other side of town. When Melchor arrived, there were two patrol cars at the entrance, all the lights were on and the music off, and a group of girls were murmuring at the untended bar. Bigara's body was in one of the rooms, lying face-up on an unmade bed, in an unnatural position, with his mouth and eyes still open and his naked body uncovered; in the hallway and inside the room were various people, among them a very young girl crumpled in the arms of an older woman, three patrolmen and the coroner, who was still examining the corpse.

"His heart gave out," the doctor stated once he had finished. "Too old, too much coke and too much whisky."

Melchor stayed in the room until the magistrate ordered the corpse to be removed, unable to abandon the lifeless body of his old friend. The next day he understood why it had occurred to someone to call him when Bigara died: his wife, from whom he had been separated for many years, was never seen at the funeral home, nor were his children, who nobody could find because he never saw them; so Melchor realised that, if he hadn't looked after the bureaucracy of death, nobody would have. There was no funeral worthy of the name, and, apart from Melchor, only three plainclothes police officers attended the cremation, one of whom arrived by bus from Medinaceli, in the province of Soria, just in time to be present at that shadow of a ceremony and to ask Melchor what his friend had died of. When Melchor repeated the coroner's diagnosis, with the trio of abuses that had finally stopped the heart of the old civil guard, the policeman from Soria pronounced the only words Melchor's memory retained from those hours.

"Yeah," he said. "And too much solitude."

A short time after Vicente Bigara's death, Melchor received a visit at the station from a sergeant from Internal Affairs. He was one of those guys who looked as old as they were, tall and pale, with a long face, who said his name was Isaías Cabrera and asked Melchor if they could speak alone, somewhere discreet.

They were in the office of the investigative team, surrounded by officers who swiftly understood or suspected or imagined who the intruder was, though not what he was doing there. Melchor took him to an interrogation room and, as soon as they sat down across from each other, with the table between them, the sergeant began to ramble. Melchor listened to him for a while, before interrupting him to ask the purpose of his visit. Cabrera smiled uncomfortably. As if he needed to ponder his response, or as if he were looking for it in his surroundings, the sergeant glanced around the spartan room, with its bare walls, and no furniture apart from the table and three chairs. From the floor rose a slight smell of ammonia.

"We've received some information about you," Cabrera explained with his hands in his lap, invisible to Melchor. "Things people are saying."

"Oh yeah?" Melchor said. "And what kind of things are they saying?"

"For example, that you're going around asking questions about things that are none of your concern." Cabrera paused and added: "But it's not true, is it?"

Melchor held his gaze for a moment: the sergeant had pale, narrow, inquiring eyes.

"No," he lied.

"Of course not," Cabrera said, with a relieved expression. "I was sure it wasn't. Because if it was true, it would be very serious. You know that, don't you?"

Melchor nodded.

"So serious that we might have to open an investigation on you," Cabrera continued. "And when a file gets opened, you never know what you're going to find. The past is full of surprises. You understand what I mean?"

Carried along by some sort of inertia, Melchor kept nodding.

Until Cabrera smiled again, took his hands out of his lap and revealed them.

"Great," he said. "I'm glad we understand each other so well. I'll be frank with you: I wish it were like this with everyone."

Apparently satisfied, the sergeant stood up, shook his hand and said goodbye, but before leaving the room he stood still for a second, with the door ajar; he closed it and turned back to Melchor.

"Speaking of the past," he said. His expression had changed again: now it was one of annoyance, almost pain. "You spent some years in prison, did you not?"

Melchor sat bolted to his chair, feeling that the floor beneath his feet had opened up and he was about to fall into the void. Cabrera smiled again; for the first time his smile seemed sincere.

"Don't look so glum!" he said cheerfully. "The criminal records check you submitted when you sat your entrance exams for the police academy was forged. A good forgery, I have to admit. But a forgery nonetheless. Your dossier disappeared from our archives, but not from the court's. It's still there. Perhaps you didn't know that."

Cabrera waited in vain for Melchor's reaction; in his eyes there was more curiosity than reproach: it was obvious, now, that he was enjoying himself.

"You see how full of surprises the past is?" he said before changing his tone. "But don't worry. How would you like us to keep this a secret? You and me, I mean."

Melchor assessed the offer for a couple of seconds. He was still in his chair, so he was looking up at Cabrera from below, making no attempt to hide his mistrust.

"In exchange for what?"

This time Cabrera laughed out loud.

"Don't be so suspicious, man," he answered, opening the door again and settling the matter. "In exchange for nothing."

After Cabrera had left, Melchor stayed in the interrogation room for a few minutes. He was perplexed and concerned. He wasn't surprised there had been complaints about him looking for his mother's killers in his own time: after all, he had talked to too many people for news of his investigations not to have reached the wrong ears; what surprised him was that they knew he'd been in prison and had submitted a forged certificate when he applied to take the police academy entrance exam. How had they found out? Who had told them, if he'd never told anybody and, as far as he knew, the only ones who knew were Vivales and whoever had helped Vivales forge the document? Or had they found out purely by accident? As for his concern, it didn't stem so much from any disciplinary action they might take against him and the consequences that could have for him as much as the obvious fact that, from then on, his future depended on Internal Affairs keeping silent. It was equally obvious that if that original deception came to light, the most probable result would be his immediate dismissal from the force. He was at the mercy of Internal Affairs – or rather at the whim of that sinister individual who had just threatened him in a veiled way – and this left him in a delicate and uncomfortable position, especially if he wanted to continue investigating his mother's murder.

At his next weekly lunch with Vivales, Melchor told him about Cabrera's visit, and the lawyer, who had no idea who could be the source of the leak of the fraud he had engineered years earlier, exhorted him to stick to the letter of the law when it came to his professional obligations, at least for the time being, and to stop investigating what he wasn't supposed to be investigating and await developments. Melchor followed his advice, although for much less time than Vivales advised. After a month and a half without news from Cabrera or Internal Affairs, he began his haphazard investigative rounds again.

From the start Vivales had tried to dissuade him from his determination to find the trail of his mother's murderers, because he considered it a waste of time that could end up turning into a self-destructive obsession, but Melchor never lost hope; nevertheless, more than one night – while he wandered through bars, nightclubs, massage parlours, brothels, escort clubs and dance halls, as well as streets, intersections, roads and tracks lined with prostitutes of all classes and conditions, where he occasionally spoke to someone who remembered his mother, but never anyone who had heard of Carmen Lucas – he thought that the saying "looking for a needle in a haystack" had been coined for him, and that he would only find some trace of that evanescent woman if fate made him the gift of a small miracle.

Eventually, the gift was given – or he thought it was given.

It was the middle of August 2017, when Melchor was a couple of days away from a week's holiday. Early that evening he decided to walk around the outskirts of Montjuïc cemetery, where three or four dozen prostitutes congregated every night. The cemetery spreads down the slope of the mountain facing the sea, at the eastern end of the city. It is far from Nou Barris, but Melchor knew the place because, years before, when he worked for the Colombian cartel, the dealers who distributed their drugs used to tell him nostalgically about the early years of the century when the biggest drug supermarket in Spain, and possibly in Europe, was still functioning in the last cheap houses of the Zona Franca. In fact, the prostitutes who remained around the cemetery, all or almost all of them addicts, were the last trace of that narcotics emporium, and also the most degraded: fellatio was practised there for four or five euros at any hour of the day or night, or for a couple of cigarettes, a few hits on a spliff.

Melchor stopped in front of the first woman he met on the way up to the cemetery and questioned her without getting out of the car. The woman stuck her whole torso through the open window. She made every kind of sexual offer before, convinced he wasn't going to accept any of them, she withdrew. Melchor then decided to get out of the car, and a moment later, not knowing how, he found himself surrounded by an agitated group of loud-mouthed, half-naked painted women displaying their undesirable, exhausted and beaten bodies, adorned with pendants and beads as if they were trophies from a lost war. In the midst of that cacophony, while one or another questioned him and questioned each other, Melchor saw another woman and her client come down a little slope that led to some railway tracks that were used only to transport merchandise from the Zona Franca and the port. The man kept his head down and hurried off towards his car, but the woman came towards the group when she reached the road and, when she got close, said: "What's up with Carmen Lucas?"

She was unashamedly fat, with black eyes and hair, large-framed glasses, big earrings in the shape of anchors and a medallion nestling in her cleavage. The whole group turned towards her, while Melchor felt with a shudder of joy that he'd just found the proverbial needle.

"Do you know who she is?" asked one of the women, quite obviously transsexual.

"This handsome fellow here is looking for her," said another, with a strong Andalusian accent: she was the youngest of all and was wearing nothing but very high heels and a pair of cycling shorts.

The woman had just reached the group and she stared at Melchor.

"What are you, kiddo," she asked. "A cop?"

Melchor said yes, but added that he wasn't looking for Carmen Lucas for professional reasons, but rather personal ones: she'd been a friend of his mother's.

"Do you know her?" he asked, meaning Carmen Lucas.

The women's attitude didn't change when they found out Melchor was a police officer, which maybe meant they had all known or suspected as much from the start.

"I knew her," the woman answered. "But I haven't seen her for a long time. They called her Babyface."

"Do you know where I could find her? Have you got an address or a phone number?"

The woman kept looking at him, reticently, and, without forcing his imagination, Melchor guessed that, beneath that ravaged flesh, in her day she had been a beautiful creature.

"I don't know," the woman said. "But if you want I'll give you a blowjob you won't believe."

The offer unleashed a torrent of counter-offers, shouts, special prices, insults, laughter and shoves, and for a moment Melchor had the impression of having accidentally got himself involved in the private squabble of a unisexual, scruffy and viscerally eccentric (but not alien to him) family. He was about to repeat his questions to the woman when she said very loudly that she was done for the day and asked Melchor if he'd drive her home.

The woman, who said her name was Sara, asked him to make for calle Parlamento and, as Melchor drove there, told him without his having asked that she'd been working the cemetery hill for five years, after having worked around the Barça ground and the alleyways of the Raval neighbourhood.

She said she took two buses to get there for the early hours and another two to get home in the late afternoon. She told him she'd been addicted to crack but hadn't taken drugs for quite a while thanks to a foundation that helped addicts; that she went there every week to stock up on condoms, get check-ups and chat with the staff.

"Park there." She pointed to a space on the avenida del Parelelo, which a car was pulling out of at that moment. "My place isn't far."

He parked and, without asking questions, followed her. They went up the dark and smelly staircase of an old building and Melchor was surprised at the cleanliness and order that reigned in the room Sara rented there, on the third floor, a room with no bathroom but with a kitchen and views and a balcony overlooking the street. Melchor didn't know why she'd made him come with her, though he started to suspect when the woman began leafing through a stack of papers piled up in one corner of the room, beside a neatly made bed. From the balcony came the light of the setting sun and the noise of the street.

"Here it is," Sara said after a while, waving an envelope. "I knew I had it."

She took a letter out of the envelope and read it.

"Of course, she wrote to send some money she owed me," she said. She handed the envelope to Melchor and added, looking at him with a sort of class pride: "Carmen was like that."

Melchor took the envelope. No longer astonished he saw the return address was, in fact, Carmen Lucas, calle la Vereda, 95, El Llano de Molina.

"Is that any use to you?"

Melchor nodded: the letter burned in his hands like a treasure. He memorised the address and handed it back to Sara.

Then he took out his wallet and gave her twenty euros; the woman didn't turn them down.

"You're sure you don't want a blowjob, kiddo?" she said, with a maternal smile. "If you're not satisfied, I'll give you your money back."

El Llano de Molina is a district of Molina de Segura, fifteen kilometres from Murcia and a six-hour drive from Barcelona. Melchor drove along the Mediterranean Motorway, leaving behind Tarragona, Castellón and Valencia, encountering a drier landscape as he went south. He left the motorway not far from Molina de Segura, and as he approached the city, near the banks of the Segura the green of vegetable gardens began to dominate the view. Melchor arrived at half past six in the evening, when the August sun was still a ball of fire in the sky, and soon found his way to El Llano, where, after wandering through the town for a few minutes, up and down little streets where nobody had yet emerged from their siestas, he found the address he was looking for, almost where the countryside began, beside a sign: CAMINO DEL CASERÍO. Melchor got out of his car and rang the doorbell of a modest, recently built, single-storey house, with freshly whitewashed walls. A woman opened the door. Melchor asked for Carmen Lucas.

"That's me."

She was dark-haired, with tanned skin and calm eyes, and she was wearing flip-flops and a blue striped smock that hid her shape. Melchor wouldn't have known her age just by looking at her. Incredulous, he asked her again if she was really Carmen Lucas; the woman said again that she was, this time with less conviction. He introduced himself, mentioning his mother's name. As soon as she heard it, she became more guarded and her eyes changed from calm to suspicious.

"You have nothing to fear," Melchor said. "I've come from Barcelona. I just want to talk to you for a moment."

The woman stared at him for a second in silence, and he had the immediate feeling that, just as he had been looking for her for a long time, she had been waiting for him for a long time, privately convinced that for her that past had not passed, and that sooner or later it would come back. In the end, after that first moment of suspicion, the woman invited him in. Melchor followed her through a dark hallway and a dining room, until they came out in a courtyard full of plants shaded by a canopy of leafy foliage; the tiles had been recently rinsed and were exhaling a humid breath. The woman indicated a woven rush chair and asked him if he'd like something to drink; Melchor accepted her offer but remained standing. Seconds later, after disappearing through a door into the house, the woman returned with a glass of water. Melchor drank it in one go. It was cold.

"How did you find me?" she said.

When he finished telling her, Carmen Lucas took the empty glass from his hand and asked if he wanted another. Melchor said no. There was silence.

"You don't know how sorry I was about your mother," Carmen Lucas said then. "We were good friends."

Melchor nodded.

"I don't want to be a nuisance to you," he told her. "If I've spent so much time looking for you, it's because you were the last person I know of to see my mother alive and I want to know if you have any idea who killed her, or any suspicion, if you can give me any clues. Whatever it might be. Anything could be useful."

The woman sat down in the chair she had offered to Melchor, and he sat in another, facing her. Further on, under the still powerful evening sun, a farmyard spread out; in one corner there was a chicken coop behind wire netting, where, alongside a cockerel, seven or eight hens pecked at the ground.

"I've gone over that night so many times," Carmen Lucas said, setting the empty glass down on the still gleaming wet tiles. "Sometimes I've told myself that I could have prevented it, because I had a bad feeling and didn't pay any attention to it. But other times I think it's not true, that I made up the foreboding later, to make myself feel guilty. I don't know."

The woman told Melchor what she remembered of the night his mother died. According to her, it started like so many others, with the only difference being that his mother, who tended to pick up clients quite easily, hadn't attracted any.

"She was pissed off," Carmen Lucas said. "Otherwise, she wouldn't have got into that car."

"Do you remember the make? Did you see any of the occupants?"

She didn't remember anything, Carmen Lucas said, except that it was a dark-coloured, high-end car with tinted windows, and there were several men inside. They had a rule – never to get into a car unless there wasn't the slightest sign of risk or it was someone they knew – and Carmen Lucas knew that her friend hesitated for a long time before getting into that one, in fact, she'd refused an offer from them earlier the same night; but when they came back, at around three-thirty or four in the morning, with her working day nearing its end, it seemed the offer was more tempting or his mother was desperate enough to accept it. Carmen Lucas remembered what his mother had said to her after rejecting her future murderers, the first time they'd approached her that night.

"When she came back from talking to them I asked her who they were," Carmen Lucas said. "'Nobody,' she told me. 'A gang of rich kids out for a good time in papá's car. I don't trust them.' That's what she told me. With those words: I remember as if she just said them. That's why I was so surprised when she got into the car later. And I think that's why I had the bad feeling."

That was all the woman remembered about the night of the murder. Melchor made her repeat it several times, interrogating her about his mother, about herself and the other working girls and their clients back in those days around the Barça ground. And then they heard the front door open.

"It's Pepe," the woman said. "My husband."

Carmen Lucas' husband turned out to be shorter and younger than her, a robust man, almost bald, but with bushy hair at his temples; he was wearing Terylene trousers and a shirt with circles of sweat under the arms; he shook Melchor's hand firmly, after Carmen Lucas introduced him as the son of an old friend from Barcelona. Melchor looked at his watch: it was nine o'clock.

"You're not leaving yet, are you, lad?" Pepe said.

They insisted he stay for dinner and spend the night in their house, an invitation Melchor accepted without hesitation because he was sure he still had lots of things to talk about with Carmen Lucas. But, since he imagined that Pepe couldn't have known how his wife had earned her living a decade earlier in Barcelona, he preferred not to return to the subject until he was alone with her again. During the meal he found out that Carmen and Pepe had been living together for almost four years and didn't have any children, that Pepe worked in the maintenance department of a transport company with its headquarters in La Segura industrial estate in Molina de Segura, and that Carmen looked after the house and nearby vegetable plot and orchard.

"I'll show it to you tomorrow," Carmen promised.

Though what they mostly talked about that night was Melchor. Because as soon as Pepe discovered he was in the police and worked as a detective in Barcelona, it was as if he wanted to return the treatment his wife had been given, and he began to bombard Melchor with questions, devoured by a natural curiosity nourished by TV series. The evening went on until midnight, but Melchor took for ever to get to sleep: first, because just a thin partition wall separated the guestroom from Carmen and Pepe's bedroom, and for a time that seemed interminable he heard them making love, talking and laughing, as if his being in the room next door didn't matter or as if they didn't imagine he could be listening; and second because, once his hosts' activity subsided, he was kept awake by the small-town silence.

He fell asleep at dawn, just when Pepe got up to go to work, and he didn't wake again till noon. By then Carmen had gone out to do her errands, but first she left him breakfast prepared and served in the kitchen. Melchor drank a cup of coffee and waited for her, snooping around the house, the courtyard and farmyard.

The woman came back at two, weighed down with several shopping bags, and asked Melchor to help her make lunch. The two of them ate alone – as Carmen explained, Pepe had gone to Murcia and wouldn't be home until nightfall – and after lunch they went back to talking about Melchor's mother and he asked her to tell him again everything that happened on the night of the murder. Carmen told him again; she also told him about the friendship she'd had with Rosario since they'd met in a brothel in the Barrio Chino in Barcelona, and about her long years in the city, where she'd arrived following a man she'd met as a teenager in a nightclub in Molina de Segura. Melchor asked her why she had disappeared after his mother's death.

"I told you," Carmen said. "Because I got scared. It's not that anyone threatened me. I just thought that, if it had happened to her, it could happen to me." After a pause, she added: "Well, and because I was fed up. I'd spent more than half my life doing something that disgusted me and that I was ashamed of, but that I didn't know how to stop doing. Your mother's death persuaded me to leave it."

They looked at each other in the shadows of the dining room, where the closed venetian blinds blocked the pitiless heat of the sun. Melchor had his hands crossed on the table; Carmen stretched out one of hers to touch his.

"Your mother saved my life, Melchor," she said, without looking away. "If it hadn't been for her, I'd still be there."

Melchor knew that Carmen was lying, but he liked this lie, and couldn't help thinking of Sara and the other women around the Montjuïc cemetery, nor could he help the flood of overwhelming gratitude he felt towards them, as if those irredeemable losers were all that survived of his mother.

Carmen Lucas went on talking, although Melchor stopped listening to her until, after a few seconds, his mother's friend stood up and said: "Well, it's time to show you my garden."

They went out under the roasting afternoon sun, turned right on camino del Casería and, leaving the village behind, found themselves among allotments, orange groves and irrigation channels. A short time later, just past a poplar grove, they reached Carmen's patch of ground. It was small, square and at one end had a wooden shed that held her gardening tools; it didn't take an expert eye to see that that piece of land was looked after with a fondness and sensitivity inherited from generations of market gardeners.

Almost without Melchor noticing, Carmen began to work, and as she went along, showing him plants heavy with tomatoes, cucumbers, aubergines, peppers and courgettes, he gradually forgot the reason he was there, six hundred kilometres from Barcelona, and let himself be overtaken by the almost physical pleasure of watching Carmen work. Without interrupting her tasks, she told him that she'd been born in El Llano, told him about her parents, who had made a living cultivating silkworms, and about her life with Pepe in the town, surrounded by young couples with children who had settled there for a calm rural life.

They walked back to town when the light began to wane. On the way, both carrying wicker baskets brimming with vegetables, Carmen talked about Melchor's mother again and her time in Barcelona, and Melchor deduced that, contrary to what he'd assumed the night before, Pepe was aware of how his wife had earned her living during her years in the city.

"Of course he knows." Carmen laughed when Melchor asked her. "Pepe knows everything about me."

She told him that Pepe had also been born in El Llano, that their parents were neighbours and friends and that they had known each other for as long as they could remember, that they'd practically grown up together. She told him that Pepe had been after her since they were children and that she'd always avoided a relationship, among other reasons because she was six years older than him, and she said that when she left Barcelona and returned to the village, after more than twenty years working as a prostitute, broken, frightened and defeated, there he was, waiting for her.

"How strange everything is, don't you think?" Carmen said, smiling with melancholy. "I followed the love of my life to the other end of Spain, and didn't notice that he was right here at my side."

110

When they got back to the house, Melchor discovered he had five missed calls on his mobile, all from the Nou Barris police station. He called back.

"What do you mean, what's up?" came the answer. "You must be the last person in this country who doesn't know."

That afternoon there had been an Islamist attack in Barcelona, there were several dead, and a police operation to capture the terrorists had been under way for several hours.

"Where are you?"

Melchor said where he was.

"Get in your car right now and get back here."

He said goodbye to Carmen and asked her to say goodbye to Pepe for him. Carmen wrote her phone number down for him.

"Call us," she said as she handed it to him. "Come and visit. Pepe would like that."

Melchor drove the first part of the trip listening to the radio. News about the attack was still sparse and contradictory: it had happened on the Rambla, just before five in the afternoon, when a van had driven at great speed down the promenade, running over everyone in its path; they spoke of about a dozen killed and several injured, though the numbers of both kept going up; those responsible for the massacre had not yet been arrested, but one of them seemed to be holed up, with several hostages, in a restaurant in the old quarter and the police had reinforced the city, setting up roadblocks on the way in and out, which were causing tailbacks many kilometres long. This was the basic information. As night fell the newscasters began to repeat almost identical bulletins, and Melchor got tired of hearing the same thing over and over again and turned off the radio.

Then he thought of Carmen Lucas and of his mother and, gradually, began to feel bad. He understood it was all over. He understood that, in spite of having found Carmen Lucas, he had

111

no more idea of who had murdered his mother than before, and that now he never would. He understood that Carmen Lucas had been his last hope and that now he'd lost it. He understood that his search had always been condemned to failure, that deep down he'd known it from the start and that, in spite of knowing it, he'd carried on. He understood he would never find his mother's murderers. He understood he was not going to get justice for her. He thought of Javert and felt hatred, cold, indiscriminate hatred, only comparable to Jean Valjean's hatred of the world. He also felt a furious, abstract desire to do damage. And he felt like he was suffocating, that the hatred and fury and appetite for destruction were asphyxiating him. He drove for many kilometres, with his throat blocked by anguish, gasping for air inside the car, barely able to breathe.

Just after one in the morning they called him again from the station and asked him where he was: he told them he was twenty kilometres from Tarragona.

"Perfect," they said. "Make a detour through Cambrils. Seems like there might be another terrorist attack."

"Should I go to the station?"

"There's no time. Go straight to avenida Diputació. You'll find it easily, it runs parallel to the beach. They're going to set up a roadblock there: see if you can lend them a hand. It looks like half their people are on holiday."

From that moment on everything happened very quickly. Overcome, still gasping for breath, Melchor left the motorway at the Cambrils exit. When he got to avenida Diputació they were still setting up the roadblock; he introduced himself to the uniformed sergeant who was organising it, and she asked him to help put out the rumble strips, spike barrier and cones. He hadn't yet finished this task when, out of nowhere, an Audi smashed into one of the two patrol cars directing the traffic, knocked down the sergeant and drove at full speed towards the esplanade. In the midst of the commotion, Melchor ran over to the officer, checked she had no broken bones or bleeding and, with adrenalin pumping and his heart in his mouth, took off running after the Audi while gesturing with his unholstered pistol and shouting at everyone to take cover or get down on the ground.

He saw the Audi mow down two pedestrians, and then he saw it flip over at a roundabout, beside the Yacht Club. As he got closer, the occupants started to scramble out of the vehicle. Two of them made for some people who had seen the accident and who started shouting and running, but another one ran towards him. Melchor saw it was a youngster, almost a boy, holding a butcher's knife in one hand and, around his waist, something that looked like an explosive belt; at that instant, a phrase pierced his brain like a bolt of lightning ("To shoot a man you don't need to have perfect aim: you just need to be cold-blooded enough to get as close as possible to him") and, instead of moving back, he walked steadily towards the kid. When he was a few metres away he stopped, anchored his feet on the tarmac, aimed at his head and fired. The noise of the shot multiplied the shouting and attracted the attention of the other two terrorists, who ran towards him, brandishing knives and shouting war cries, their chests wrapped with explosive belts as well. Melchor advanced towards them, stopped after a few metres, anchored his feet on the tarmac once more, aimed at the first terrorist's head and fired, then he aimed at the second, who was now very close to him – he had time to see that he too was just a teenager – and fired again. He still had his knees bent when he noticed that a fourth boy, who had just climbed out of the Audi, was rushing at him, screaming, and he barely had time to aim and fire before he was on top of him.

That was the end of it all.

For a few seconds he stood still on the road, gasping for air, with the bodies of the terrorists lying on the asphalt around him, the roundabout and the esplanade immersed in such a silence as he had never heard, a deafening silence, saturated with panicked screams, howls of police sirens, the noise of helicopter blades threshing above his head. He felt as if his heart was about to explode, but at last he could breathe.

Melchor lived through the days following the terrorist attacks in a swirl of total confusion. The toll of the attacks was shocking: sixteen dead and a hundred injured in Barcelona; one dead and six injured in Cambrils. In total, six terrorists brought down, four of them by Melchor. (The rest of the terrorists in the cell that organised and took part in the attacks, twelve of them, also ended up dead or arrested.) For Melchor, however, the toll was different. In spite of the attempt from the first moment to keep his identity secret, not least to avoid possible Islamist reprisals, from one day to the next he became the force's unofficial hero: his colleagues' congratulations rained down on him, as did those of his commanding officers and their political overseers, who immediately looked for a way to exploit his feat. In their own way, the press too tried to exploit it. They christened him "the hero of Cambrils", and rumours soon began to circulate about him: they said he was a woman; they said he'd been in the foreign legion and that's why he was an expert marksman and had reacted the way he did; it was assumed that he was assigned to the Cambrils police station.

Melchor did not feel particularly proud of what he'd done, and endured the situation with increasing unease, paralysed by that disturbance that kept him from thinking while a sentence from *Les Misérables* hammered away in his head: "He is a man who does kindness by musket shots." So it was Vivales who had to step in and demand that the police union write a formal letter of protest to the Ministry of the Interior regretting the fact that the Catalan government had leaked some of Melchor's personal information to the press, together with a photo, from the back and almost in profile, receiving the applause of his comrades, his commanders and even the president of the Generalitat, Carles Puigdemont, which was a flagrant breach of the theoretical intention of protecting him from the terrorists' followers; likewise, the union's missive urged the ministry to put into action the necessary measures to guarantee Melchor's anonymity and safety.

The letter had an effect. Days after receiving it, the leadership of the Mossos d'Esquadra summoned Melchor to a meeting at central headquarters, in the Egara complex, near Sabadell. A commissioner from the Information division named Enric Fuster, and two of his adjuncts, an inspector and a deputy inspector, attended the meeting. After congratulating him on what he called his feat, Fuster – cordial, strong, red-headed, forty-something with a rectangular face and a goatee – explained that he had become an essential figure to the force, that the leadership was resolved to ensure his safety and boost his career, and, for that reason, the best plan was to transfer him, send him to a tranquil, isolated area far from the capital, where only a very few people would know who he was and why he had been posted there. Fuster emphasised that it was a provisional solution that would last only as long as it took for things to return to normal and everything to calm down, at which point Melchor could return to his current posting in Barcelona and take up the career he had been forced to set aside, or choose with the strongest guarantees whatever posting might suit him best.

"We think this is best for you," Fuster said, adding: "But we won't do anything without your consent. Take as long as you need to think about your answer."

Melchor had gone to the meeting in a mood of pure distrust. The proposal that Fuster made (or that the leadership of the corps made through Fuster) caught him off-guard and struck him at first as nonsensical. But he soon realised that recovering his anonymity was preferable to going on spinning inside that whirlwind, transformed into the focal point of everyone's attention and the object (or victim) of all their flattery. He had never lived outside the metropolis and, although he had just witnessed Carmen and Pepe's bucolic happiness, he thought he knew that the countryside was not made for him or he for it, and he was sure that he would feel out of place there; but he told himself – as Fuster had assured him – that it was only a temporary solution, that in any case what they were proposing was better than what he had, and that, after the final failure of all his investigations into his mother's death, his life had lost both its direction and the goal that had ruled it for the last few years, and he concluded that a short-lived change of scenery, which he imagined as a kind of long vacation, couldn't do him any harm.

"I don't have anything to think over," he said. "When do I leave?"

At that very meeting they suggested various destinations. Blindly, having never been there, having never even heard of the place, he chose Terra Alta.

The next day he went to the station to tell his commanding officers and colleagues that he was leaving and asked them to transfer his pending cases. He was collecting his things from his desk when Isaías Cabrera appeared. It was almost nine in the evening, and in the Investigations Unit office there were only a couple of other agents left. Melchor looked at the sergeant from Internal Affairs coldly.

"Don't worry, I've just come to say goodbye," Cabrera tried to reassure him. "You're leaving tomorrow, aren't you?"

Melchor nodded, then went back to collecting his belongings. Without anyone's permission, Cabrera sat in a chair, crossed his legs and added, after watching him in silence for a while:

"They told me you're going to Terra Alta." Melchor said nothing and carried on putting his things in a box. "A good place. For some time now they've been making splendid wine, and in the summer they re-enact the Battle of the Ebro, with the river crossing and everything. They put on a good show, you'll like it. Although, now that I think of it, you only drink Coca-Cola, and you don't give a shit about history. Truth is, Marín: I don't know what the fuck you see in novels."

Cabrera went on watching him, with a bored look on his face, saying no more, until Melchor picked up the box of his stuff, ready to leave. Then the sergeant uncrossed his legs, stood up, took a piece of paper from the inside pocket of his jacket and held it out to him. Melchor looked at it as if it were radioactive.

"What's that?"

"Your criminal record," Cabrera said, waving the paper. "The one from the court, I mean. You're clean."

Still not understanding, Melchor put the box back down on the desk and took the paper, read it, saw that the sergeant wasn't lying and searched his face for an explanation.

"What do they call you in the newspapers?" Cabrera said; a shrewd smile narrowed his eyes. "'The hero of Cambrils', no?" He shrugged. "There you go."

Melchor nodded several times, but took a while to say thank you.

"Don't thank me," Cabrera said, when he finally did. "If it had been up to me, I'd have thrown the book at you. But orders are orders. Anyway, a leopard doesn't change his spots, and I've got the feeling we'll meet again. What do you think?"

Melchor put the folded document in the cardboard box and, without shaking Cabrera's hand, said goodbye to the sergeant in three words.

"Go to hell."

5

There are still parking spaces available in front of Gráficas Adell, but Melchor decides to park his car on the street. As Grau had told him on the phone the night before, it's at the end of La Plana Parc industrial estate; beyond it is open country, and in the distance rise the first foothills of the sierra, crowned by a string of wind turbines with still blades under the brilliant morning sun.

The factory's offices are near the entrance to the courtyard, just the other side of a metal gate, in a grey octagonal building. Behind it stretch the windowless white warehouses. To the left of the stairs leading up to the offices a sort of monolith, also painted white, displays the company logo, a black eagle with wings outspread, and in red and black letters: GRÁFICAS ADELL.

A Catalan television van parks behind him as he gets out of the car, and reporters and camera crew start climbing out of it. At the desk inside there are two receptionists. Melchor tells one of them who he is and asks for the manager; the receptionist – thickset and attractive, heavily made-up, with her hair dyed mahogany blond – looks at him with curiosity, and answers that Señor Grau is waiting for him in his office and hands him a laminated visitor's pass with which to open the automatic barrier. Melchor thanks her, saying he'll go up as soon as his partner arrives, and starts killing time by looking through the lobby windows. Once the cameras and microphones are set up, the Catalan TV crew heads towards the groups of workers that have gathered in the courtyard. Apart from that, nothing betrays the fact that the proprietors of the business were murdered only a little more than twenty-four hours ago: just as on a normal weekday, people, cars, motorcycles, a few vans and a lorry go in and out of the factory gate. From professional habit, Melchor notices that the security measures on the premises are sparse – he doesn't see cameras anywhere, or alarms, and even the fence around the complex is human height – and he says to himself that if someone wanted to break in, it wouldn't be hard.

Salom doesn't arrive until half past nine.

"Sorry to be late," he says to Melchor, a little bit agitated, as they go up the stairs from the lobby. "I didn't leave the station until way past midnight. I'm not going to be able to stay long. I've arranged to see Rosa Adell and Albert at eleven-thirty. I have to get a DNA sample from Rosa, and then I'll go to her parents' house with them. Gomà will be waiting for us there."

"Do you want me to go with you?"

"No, I'd rather you stayed here, see who you can talk to. We can meet for lunch in the Terra Alta later and you can bring me up to speed then."

When they get to the first floor they take a left, following the receptionist's instructions, until, as the hallway widens out into a waiting room, they see two open doors. Through the first they glimpse a woman crying, accompanied by two men, one of whom is bent over as if he were trying to console her; through the second, an older woman, dressed entirely in grey and looking like a nun. She turns out to be the manager's secretary, who, once they have identified themselves, asks them to wait outside for a moment.

The word "moment" is not hyperbole. No sooner had they crossed the threshold of the manager's outer office than his secretary calls them to go through.

"You're late," Grau greets them, shaking their hands and offering them seats. "You might agree that arriving late shows a lack of respect, the kind of thing that people of no interest resort to, in order to seem interesting. But don't apologise, please, in this country everyone arrives late. It's the custom, isn't it? Would you like some coffee?"

Grau asks his secretary to bring three coffees and the two policemen sit down on a black leather sofa on one side of his office, a spacious rectangular room where modern and antique furniture seem mixed together without rhyme or reason, as if in a faulty palimpsest, chandeliers and ultramodern lamps, fine hardwood, old leather and shiny metal, all illuminated by the morning sun pouring in through a large window open onto the factory courtyard.

"What horrible news about Paco and Rosa!" Grau says, in an imperious tone in which Melchor detects no horror, and none in the small steely and incisive eyes behind the metal-framed glasses either. "I still haven't got used to the idea. One knows at a certain age the end is near, but to die like that? How awful! Do you people know how long I've been working for Paco Adell? More than fifty years. More than fifty! Easier said than done, eh? An entire lifetime." The old man sighs, leaning back in his chair, crosses his legs, which are as thin as sticks, and says: "Well, tell me what you know."

Salom does not give in to the temptation to compensate Grau for the wait by telling him more than he should, so he tells him only what the newspapers, radio and television stations have been broadcasting for the last twenty-four hours. While the corporal speaks, Melchor observes the manager. He is a minuscule old man with stooped shoulders and pale wrinkled skin, held up by a frame of bones that looks very fragile. He is dressed in strict mourning, though all his clothes are too loose: the suit trousers, the waistcoat, the tie, the white shirt, the shiny black shoes. Around his neck hangs a cord, at the end of which hang the two halves of another pair of glasses, these with red plastic frames. Melchor has not yet finished his examination of the manager when the secretary returns to the office, sets down on the glass table in front of them a tray bearing a nickel silver coffee service, pours the coffee into floral-patterned china cups, and then leaves the room.

"That's more or less what I'd heard," Grau says when Salom finishes his improvised summary, still stirring his coffee. "Anyway, tell me how I can help you."

At that moment, Melchor's phone vibrates; he sees it is Domingo Vivales and decides not to answer.

"Do you want to know where I was the night of the murder, as they say in the movies? Well, I'll tell you: in my house, listening to opera. Do you want to know which opera it was? *Twilight of the Gods* by the maestro Wagner. Good gracious, now that I think of it, it seems like a premonition, doesn't it? Unfortunately, I don't have anyone who can confirm my alibi, so you won't be able to cross me off your list of suspects. But ask away, ask whatever you want. I will tell you for a start that I have no idea who could be responsible for such barbarity."

"Did Señor Adell have any enemies?" Melchor says, a little disconcerted by Grau's ironic self-confidence. "People who hated him. Competitors, for example. Businessmen who felt they lost out due to his success, people who had done badly because he had done well—"

122

"Yes, of course he had enemies!" the manager interrupts him, setting his teaspoon down on the saucer, taking a sip of coffee before continuing. "A man's worth is measured by the number of enemies he has. And Paco Adell was worth a great deal, of that you can be sure. We Catalans make very bad politicians, but magnificent businessmen. He was an example of that. Now, if you mean enemies here in Terra Alta . . ."

Grau seems to be reflecting as he passes a hand over the crest of smooth hair that begins almost at his forehead and, meticulously combed back, widens over his skull down to the nape of his neck. Observing him, Melchor remembers what he read about him the night before, which wasn't much as the manager seems even more jealous of his privacy than the Adells, or maybe nobody has ever taken an interest because he's always lived in the shadow of his boss: in fact, everything Melchor knows about Grau is connected to his relationship with Adell, whose fixer and right-hand man he is considered to be, some emphasising his canine fidelity and others his intelligence, perspicacity and lack of scruples.

The manager empties his coffee cup in one gulp and leaves it on the table. Suddenly he smiles.

"Do you two remember General Narváez?" he says.

Neither Melchor nor Salom replies. Grau shakes his head a little, as if disappointed by the ignorance of the police.

"He has a bad reputation, but he was a good officer and a good politician," he says. "He died in 1868, on April 23, of pneumonia, if I'm not mistaken. When he was on his deathbed, his chaplain asked him to forgive his enemies. 'I cannot, sir,' the general replied. 'I've killed them all.'" The manager's croak of laughter sounds like a smoker's terminal cough; the two policemen exchange sidelong glances. "Well, had he been in the same situation as Narváez, Paco could have given the same answer.

When he founded this company, there were several more or less similar ones in Terra Alta. Now those that are left are insignificant, so small compared to us that they can't even hate us. It would be like an ant hating an elephant."

"And beyond Terra Alta?" Salom says.

"Oh, that's different," Grau says. "But the problem is, in our business, everyone hates everyone, and everyone's right. I suppose other businesses work the same way, that's what capitalism is, right? It's dog eat dog and only the strongest survive. So, if you're looking for enemies of Gráficas Adell, you have to start with the leading Spanish businesses in the sector and continue with those in all the countries where we have affiliates. We've played dirty tricks on all of them, and they've all done the same to us. Start there, and then go on."

"Did any of these companies hate Señor Adell enough to kill him?" Melchor says.

"I don't know." Grau shrugs and remains silent for a few moments before repeating: "I don't know. Frankly, I have the impression that the older I get the less I understand human beings." He uncrosses his legs, leans towards the table, and says: "More coffee?"

Grau refills the three cups.

"If I understand you correctly," Salom says, "what you mean to say is that, beyond Terra Alta, Señor Adell had so many enemies that you find it hard to single out one in particular."

"You understand perfectly. When one has so many enemies, it's like not having any."

"But he could also have some here in Terra Alta, couldn't he?" Melchor insists. The old man's fingers go back to stirring the spoon in his coffee: thin and arthritic fingers with carefully manicured nails. "There are those who say that Gráficas Adell is like a tree so big that nothing can grow in its shadow."

He hesitates a moment and then adds: "And that Señor Adell exploited his workers."

"The same thing is said of all companies, isn't it?" Salom interrupts, trying to soften the harshness of the statement. "And of all businessmen."

"And it's true," Grau says. "It's what I was trying to explain: that's how capitalism works." The manager replaces the spoon on his saucer, picks up his cup and looks at Melchor with curiosity: behind the lenses of his glasses, his eyelids, pale and wrinkled, half close and his eyes narrow almost to slits. "You're not from here, are you?"

"No," Melchor says.

"No." Grau nods, turning towards Salom with a complicit, slightly malevolent smile. "He doesn't speak with a local accent."

Salom doesn't react, and for an instant Melchor is about to explain that, although he wasn't born in Terra Alta, he's been living here for four years, but he says nothing. Grau takes a sip of coffee, tastes it, puts the cup down on the saucer and the saucer on the table. The increasingly strong morning sun is pouring in through the window, heating up the office.

"Look," the old man says to Melchor didactically, "this is an inhospitable, very poor land. It always has been. A land people passed through and the only ones who stayed were the ones with no other choice, the ones with nowhere else to go. A land of losers. Nobody loves this region, that's the truth, and the proof is that they only ever remember us in order to bomb us. What are we known for outside the region? For the Battle of the Ebro, the most ferocious battle that's ever been waged in this country, a plague of fire like biblical retribution, an apocalypse that killed boys from across half the world. Of course, we had no part in it, but they left this land even more barren than it already was, a place where eighty years later you can still find shrapnel in the hills, and if you don't find a lot more it's because for years we took charge of collecting and selling it, to keep from starving to death. That's Terra Alta. And, in a place like this, a company like ours is a blessing, almost a miracle." He falls silent for a moment, staring at Melchor. "Were there lots of people who didn't like Paco and cursed him? Sure there were. Of course! People always complain about those in charge, and rightly so. That's what the man in charge is for, so those who aren't in charge can complain about him. But I dare you to try an experiment. Tell anyone you meet in the street in Gandesa today that Gráficas Adell is leaving Terra Alta. You'll see what they say. Do you know how many direct or indirect jobs we've created here? Do you know how many families earn a living thanks to us?" He pauses again; the smile has gradually disappeared from his wrinkled mouth, replaced by a vindictive sneer. "Believe me, if it weren't for Paco Adell, Terra Alta would be dead. That is the unvarnished truth. Everything else is a fairytale."

As he listens to Grau, Melchor can't help wondering where the scrawny old man gets so much energy; he also wonders what kind of relationship he had with Adell, and if the murder hasn't affected him much more than his pride allows him to show. When Grau finishes his apologia, Salom asks him how he met Adell, how he came to work for him.

"Oh, that's an interesting story," Grau says, crossing his legs and smiling again. "Let me tell you."

Grau explains that in the mid-sixties, not long after finishing his Economics degree in Barcelona, he was working at Gráficas Sintes, at that time the largest graphic arts company in Terra Alta. Adell had just bought at a knock-down price a bankrupt company called Gráficas Puig, which he immediately

126

renamed Gráficas Adell. He didn't know anything about the business, but in a short time he'd restructured the company and got it competing on an equal footing with all the others in the region, except for Gráficas Sintes. One day Adell found out that Grau had clashed with his boss and went to see him in his office. Both men had been born in Terra Alta – Adell in Bot, Grau in Arnes – but they didn't know each other. Adell, who was eleven years older than Grau, spoke to him as if they'd known each other their whole lives. "This business isn't worthy of you," he told him at the outset. "Besides, it's going down. Sink with it or swim with me: you choose." Grau had heard a lot about Adell, but he was impressed by his solid self-assurance and the air of authority he gave off; in spite of that, he thanked him for his offer and told him he would not take him up on it. Adell raised the stakes. "I'll pay you double what you're earning here." Knowing the accounts at Gráficas Adell, Grau called his bluff. "You can't pay me that." "It's true," Adell admitted. "I'll pay you double what I earn. Now and as long as you work for me." Grau laughed out loud, but, thanking Adell again for his offer, turned it down. Unable to accept the refusal, over the following weeks and months Adell insisted over and over, calling him on the telephone, visiting him and contriving to bump into him, until Grau had another falling-out with his boss and ended up going to work with him.

"I never found out if Paco provoked that row with Señor Sintes," Grau laughed. "But I have to admit that he kept his promise to the letter: even now I still get paid double what he pays himself. And that's not even the funniest part," he adds. "The funniest thing, as he told me later, is that when he came to see me at my office in Gráficas Sintes, Paco didn't know the business was in trouble. But it was. The proof is that it ceased trading four years later. That's another thing you have to have in business and Paco had it in spades: luck."

Grau illustrates Adell's good fortune by telling a second story, this one to do with the affiliate of his company in Córdoba, Argentina, and, when he starts telling a third, he interrupts his tale.

"Don't misinterpret me," he says. "I'm not saying Paco did all he did only because he was a lucky man. I'm saying that without luck he wouldn't have been able to do it. Without luck and audacity. And without his overwhelming self-confidence."

Grau falls silent. For a moment he twists to look to his left, where his desk and computer float in a lake of golden light, and his face empties of expression. Melchor and Salom look at each other fleetingly again.

"Yesterday I spent the whole day watching television, listening to the radio and reading the newspapers in Rosita Adell's house," Grau says, back from his reverie. "And do you know something? What most surprised me was that so many people were surprised that a poor, uneducated man like Paco Adell had created Gráficas Adell and everything else almost from nothing." His gaze leaps nervously back and forth from Melchor to Salom and from Salom to Melchor while he uncrosses his legs, sits up in his armchair and leans his forearms on his thighs. "Why surprising? Paco did what he did precisely because he was poor and had never been to school. Poor people are stronger than the rich, especially if they have the misfortune to be orphans as well and to survive a war in childhood, as happened to Paco. The rich are too spoiled, have too much to lose; that makes them soft, vulnerable. Poor people aren't like that. Paco knew what misery was, what hunger and cold felt like, because he had experienced them. He wasn't afraid of them. Actually, I've never known anyone with less fear, and a

128

man without fear is capable of anything. Besides, Paco worked fifteen-hour days every day of the week, including holidays, for his whole life. Have you come across anyone like that? As for schooling, I don't know about you, but I have dealt with many good-for-nothings festooned with top marks. And I can assure you of one thing: Paco Adell was the exact opposite."

Melchor and Salom accept Grau's opinion without argument, and perhaps for that reason he willingly volunteers to answer their questions about Gráficas Adell's finances. The manager tells them about investments, income statements, foreign affiliates, Gráficas Adell's relationship to the rest of the family's companies. He does so with passionate and rigorous precision, as if he had a computer in his head, but after a while he seems to tire or get bored of the topic and asks them to change the subject, taking cover behind the argument that the figures for all their companies are public and that, if Melchor and Salom want to know them, they can find all they want in the Commercial Registry.

"Besides," he adds after looking at his watch, a heavy gold thing with a leather strap that for a second looks to Melchor like a strange parasite on his childish wrist, "in a few minutes you're going to have to excuse me. I've promised to speak to the press. See what happens when you arrive late? Come, come, ask your questions."

"This afternoon we'll speak to Señor Adell's daughter," Melchor says. "I'd like to know what kind of relationship Señor Adell had with his family."

"Normal. Fine," Grau says.

"And you?" Melchor says.

"With Paco's family?"

Melchor nods.

"Also fine," Grau assures them. "Rosa was a simpleton,

poor thing, but she didn't harm anyone and we got along well. Deep down she was never anything but a snobbish little miss from Reus; her father was a notary, I think that's why Paco fell in love with her, supposing he did actually fall in love, of course, and didn't just marry her because at fifty, when he was most buried in business, he got it into his head that he needed descendants and found himself a woman from a good family, fifteen years younger than him . . . Their daughter, Rosita, is better, she was a charming little girl. And very clever. To be honest, I always thought she'd be the one to take over the business. But she married that idiot Ferrer, started having children and things fell apart. Marriage is a mistake, people aren't made for it, don't you think? Look at me: still a bachelor and happy as can be."

"Do you think Albert Ferrer is an idiot?" Melchor says.

"There is not the slightest doubt about it," Grau says. "A useless idiot. Naturally, like all useless idiots, he has a very elevated opinion of himself, but that's what he is."

"He's also the managing director of Gráficas Adell," Salom reminds him, coming out in defence of his friend.

"As if he were captain general," Grau says. "How many idiots with inflated job titles do you know? Paco named him that to make Rosita happy and keep him quiet, but in this company he's nobody. He spends his days playing golf, strutting his stuff and swanning around with girls who could be his daughters."

"Did Señor Adell know that?" Melchor says.

"That he went around with young ladies?" Grau says. "Of course."

"And what did he think?"

"What was he going to think?" The old man shrugs again. "Once he spoke to him, even tried to threaten him, but Ferrer didn't care. What could Paco do? Break his legs. He would have done, believe me, but Ferrer was his granddaughter's father and his daughter's husband, and Paco adored Rosita. Anyway, if the company ends up in the hands of that fool, we can say goodbye to Gráficas Adell."

"Do you think that's what's going to happen?" Salom says.

"What?"

"That Albert Ferrer will take over the management of the company."

Grau composes an expression that blends scepticism with indifference.

"I don't know," he says. "And to be frank, I couldn't give a damn. If it were up to me I'd be retired by now. So, if Rosita asks me to leave, I'll go and that'll be that. Actually, she won't even have to ask me: at the first sign I'm not needed, I'll be gone. But I don't know if she'll do that, I told you she's not stupid, even though she married a stupid man. There are those who think that a business like Gráficas Adell, with its history, its portfolio of clients and its infrastructure, runs itself. They're mistaken. It's very difficult to build a company like this one, and very easy to destroy it. But, anyway, if it gets destroyed, it won't be the end of the world, businesses are like empires: they appear and disappear, just like people. That's life. And, like it or not, it will go on like that." Grau looks at his watch again. "Well, I think we've talked for long enough. You're going to have to excuse me—"

"Could we speak to the other managers?" Melchor prevents him from finishing. "There are only two below you, as I understand it? I've seen that the structure of the company is very simple."

"The secret of efficiency," Grau says, standing up. "Simplicity is efficient, complexity is inefficient. You want to talk to both of them? When?"

"If it's up to me, right now," Melchor says, also standing up.

While Grau sits at his desk and dials a number, Melchor and Salom walk over to a wall almost completely covered in framed photographs, beside an old oak sideboard transformed into a drinks cabinet and stuffed with books. Melchor recognises Grau in almost every image, sometimes much younger but never looking very different from his present appearance (as if he'd always been old, he thinks, or as if he'd always tried to look old), often with Francisco Adell, other times with different people, including the entire Adell family; in one with the president of the Generalitat of Catalonia, Jordi Pujol; in another with the king of Spain, Don Juan Carlos de Bourbon; in another, Adell and his wife pose beside Pope Benedict XVI.

"All set," Grau announces. "You can go and talk to them right now. My secretary will show you where to find them." When he joins the two policemen, he points to the photograph of the pope. "That was at the tenth anniversary of the canonisation of Escrivá de Balaguer."

Grau leans towards the picture, takes off the glasses he's wearing, clicks the magnetic connection of the two halves of the plastic framed glasses that hang from his neck, puts them on and concentrates for a few seconds on the image; then, smiling and barely moving his head from side to side, leans back from it while taking off one pair of glasses and putting on the other.

"Who would have imagined he'd end up so sanctimonious?"

"You mean Señor Adell?" Melchor asks, knowing the answer.

"He wasn't when I met him," Grau explains. "Rather the opposite. Rosa yes, she always was, but not him. The thing is, a few years ago he had a health problem. The doctors didn't get the diagnosis right and they admitted him to hospital in Barcelona to do all sorts of tests. In the end it turned out to be nothing, but while he was there, I don't know how, he met a priest who won him over."

"Is that when they joined Opus Dei?" Salom asks.

"Seems like it," Grau says. "The truth is it took me a while to find out, because in practice nothing changed. Paco managed it very discreetly. Sometimes he said strange things, talked about sanctifying work and nonsense like that, or he'd disappear for a week and then I'd find out he'd been on a spiritual retreat. Paco Adell on a retreat, good God! At first I laughed at him, until I realised it was better not to. Besides, as I said, it didn't translate into anything practical, he was still the same as he'd always been and kept doing the same things he'd always done." All of a sudden a sardonic spark shines in Grau's eyes. "Do you know why I think Paco converted?"

Melchor and Salom don't answer. Just at that moment the door opens: it is Grau's secretary; the journalists have arrived. The manager assures her he'll be right out and the secretary closes the door again.

"Out of fear," Grau says, answering his own question. "He converted out of fear."

"Before you said Señor Adell had no fear," Salom reminds him.

"And it's true," Grau says; his smile has been infected by the sharpness of his eyes. "But that was when he was young. In old age he did, like everyone. I think he really was afraid. And that's why he converted. Have you read Pascal?"

Grau clicks his tongue against the roof of his mouth at the predictable silence of his two visitors.

"I was afraid not," he said, with a twinge of ironic reprimand. "You should. Pascal says that believing in God is a safe bet: if you lose you lose nothing; if you win, you win it all . . . There you have it: that was Paco's language. He hadn't read

Pascal, but he was Pascalian. He always reasoned like that. I don't know if I've explained myself."

Without waiting for a reply, Grau opens the door for the two policemen and walks out with them into the lobby, where a group of journalists is already waiting. Grau waves to them and asks them to wait a minute. Then he shakes the officers by the hand.

"Come back and see me whenever you want," he says in parting. "I am at your service. But do me a favour: catch the people who killed Paco as soon as possible."

"We will," Salom promises. "But allow me one last question."

"The last one," Grau agrees.

"Did you consider yourself a friend of Señor Adell?"

The question surprises Melchor, striking him as superfluous or impertinent; he also has the impression that it surprises Grau, who sighs and, glancing quickly at the journalists, grabs both men by the arm and pulls them towards him until he can whisper in their ears:

"Paco Adell did not have friends, Corporal," he says. "Men like him do not have friends." Without letting go of their arms, he leans back from them a little, looks them in the eyes and adds: "You understand me, I trust."

Melchor walks past the counter of the Terra Alta, says hello to a group of domino players, by the entrance to the restaurant, spies an empty table by a window and sits at it. The owner comes over straight away. He is a knock-kneed, easygoing man, with a belly that strains the buttons of his shirt to their limit.

"What a mess, no?"

Melchor doesn't ask what the owner is referring to: for the last day and a half, the only thing Terra Alta has talked about is the Adells' murder.

"Imagine."

"Do you know anything?"

"No. And, if we did, I wouldn't tell you."

The owner laughs.

"You eating alone?"

"No. Salom should be here any minute."

"The usual to drink?"

Melchor nods. In spite of being located in Corbera d'Ebre, almost five kilometres from Gandesa, the Terra Alta is a regular meeting place for people from the station, but at that moment, during the lunchtime rush, Melchor doesn't spot any of his colleagues. A murmur of conversation and cutlery reigns over the restaurant and, although there are only three men sitting on stools at the counter, behind it the activity is intense: the owner and waiters go in and out through the swing door to the kitchen, pour glasses of draught beer, take ready-prepared dishes of ice cream from the freezer, busy themselves with the coffee maker. Just above the domino players, on a TV screen, a handful of football players celebrate a goal in a stadium whose stands seethe with ecstatic fans. Above the screen, a wall clock shows twenty-five past two. A severe midday glare shines through the window, and on the other side of the glass a farmyard extends towards some houses, beyond which he sees a succession of vineyards and, beyond them, the mountains and the sky.

The owner brings Melchor a Coca-Cola and lays two paper place mats with two napkins in front of him, places two glasses and two sets of cutlery on top of them and hands him the menu – a couple of typed pages. He hasn't finished reading it when Salom sits down across from him.

"How did it go?" Melchor asks.

Salom glances over the menu with a demoralised expression.

"Rosa Adell is not well," he says. "She fainted when we came out of her parents' house. She's stuffed with tranquillisers, but if she goes on like this they're going to have to admit her to hospital."

The owner greets Salom and takes their order. Salom asks for a beer, fideuà with alioli and stuffed squid; Melchor, a green salad and steak with potatoes.

"The beer is urgent," the corporal says.

"It's on its way," the owner assures him, as he collects the menus and heads to the bar.

Salom takes off his glasses, rubs his eyes and the bridge of his nose with his thumb and index finger, then puts his glasses back on.

"I was wondering about giving this afternoon's session a miss," he says, thinking out loud.

"You mean questioning Rosa Adell and your friend?" Melchor says.

"Yeah," Salom says. "I've already talked to them. We should leave them alone. They are shattered and don't have anything to do with this."

"No-one says they have anything to do with it," Melchor says. "But I'm sure they can tell us useful things."

"They've already told them to Gomà and me."

The owner puts Salom's beer down in front of him. "Fastest beer in Terra Alta," he boasts. Melchor waits for his partner to take his first sip, a long and savoured swallow that seems to perk him up a bit, if not reconcile him with reality, and leaves a trace of foam in his moustache and beard.

"What did they tell you?" Melchor asks.

Salom sets the glass down on the place mat.

"There's money missing from the Adells' house," he says, wiping the foam from his face with an expert finger. "Not much, a thousand, fifteen hundred euros maybe. There's also jewellery missing."

"Do they think it could have been a robbery?"

"It's a possibility," Salom admits, picking up his glass, which leaves a wet circle on the place mat. "But there are others."

The corporal takes a second sip. Melchor watches him impatiently.

"What others?" he asks.

Salom looks at him and, although it's impossible that anyone might hear him in the hubbub around them, he lowers his voice to say: "Grau."

They haven't said another word when the owner serves their first course. While Salom jokes with him, Melchor looks out of the window: above the mountains a few cottony clouds have appeared, dirty white, or whitish grey, threatening rain. When the owner leaves, he picks up the subject again.

"Your friend thinks it was Grau's doing?"

"He didn't put it like that," Salom says, stirring the alioli into the noodles and seafood with his fork. "And much less in front of Rosa: Grau's like an uncle to her, he's been coming to her house since she was a little girl. He doesn't say it, but he thinks it. What kind of impression did the old man make on you this morning?"

Melchor considers this, while Salom brings the fork laden with fideuà to his mouth.

"He seemed like an intelligent guy," he says. "And he seemed to talk about Adell as if he were Napoleon. That's why I didn't understand why at the end you asked him if he considered himself his friend."

"I asked him so he'd answer the way he answered," Salom

says. "In other words, as if Adell really was Napoleon and his murder was an assassination. And especially so he would confirm what we were both thinking, that Grau did not feel himself to be his friend, even though he'd been working with him for fifty years."

"Fifty years working with him and seeing him every day and having an almost familial relationship with him."

"Exactly. I don't know what you think, Melchor, but I don't trust that man. Do you know what really made me suspicious?"

Melchor enquires in silence, raising his eyebrows while chewing.

"All that about him not caring what happens to Gráficas Adell in the future," Salom says. "That he has no aspirations and that he'll just go home when he sees he's not needed. That's what the most ambitious people say, especially if they're old; the screen of unselfishness behind which they want to hide their ambition, the typical trap for the unwary. How is he not going to care about a business he practically built from the bottom up and which he's been running for fifty years? I'll bet you whatever you like that he is sure that Rosa will put him in charge of Gráficas Adell, because he believes that right now he's the only one capable of managing it."

"Is that what she thinks?"

"I don't know, but I'm sure it's what Grau thinks. He couldn't have said it more clearly. Don't you see? Adell's death leaves him in the best situation possible."

"True, he didn't seem too broken up. Or maybe he didn't want to show it."

"He didn't show it or have a reason to feel it. That death benefits him, Melchor. That's what he thinks. Not to mention that he's spent his whole life under Adell's thumb, who was

138

a brute by all accounts and according to Albert treated Grau very badly."

"Him too? The other two managers say the person he treated the worst was your friend."

"Albert?"

"That's what they say. That he wouldn't let him do anything, that he ridiculed him at meetings, that he laughed at him. Maybe that's why he spent so little time at the factory."

"Adell must have treated everyone badly."

"Probably. Olga says that as a young man he had a slogan: 'The day I don't screw anyone over, is a day I'm not happy.'"

"Olga knew him?"

"He and her father were friends. The thing is, the workers didn't speak so badly of Adell. I talked to a bunch of them and, if you draw them out, they all say the factory exploited them and they grumble about it, but they also insist that Adell was a great guy, kind and affectionate, that he went to their company dinners and lunches and made all kinds of nice gestures. I think they were sincere. I came to the conclusion that Adell was tough with his closest collaborators and soft on everyone else."

The owner comes over for their empty plates a moment later. Salom scratches his beard gently and says:

"There's one thing I haven't told you."

"What's that?"

"Do you know what kind of tyres Grau has on his car?"

Melchor stares at him. Salom nods while still scratching.

"How do you know?" Melchor asks.

"His car was in the factory car park."

"Is there a way to find out if it's the one we're looking for?"

"No, but . . ."

The owner brings their main course and asks if they want anything else to drink. They say no in unison and start to dig in without looking up from their plates, pondering. They've been working together daily since Melchor arrived in Terra Alta, and they're used to this mutual silence that no longer makes either of them uncomfortable. At first, as well as being Melchor's corporal, Salom was his guide, but for a long time now he's been the colleague he talks with about everything, who he consults on everything, with whom he discusses everything and tests out all his theories about whatever cases they happen to be investigating. Although Salom's almost old enough to be his father, Melchor has a blind faith in him, as well as being personally in tune with him, he thinks, as he's never been with anyone else, not even Vicente Bigara, not even Domingo Vivales. Thinking of the lawyer reminds him of his call that morning; and also that he has to return it. When he finishes his steak, Melchor wipes his mouth and says: "Do you really think it was the old man?"

"I don't know," Salom says, crossing his knife and fork on the empty plate. "It's a possibility."

Melchor nods.

"Silva and Botet are also possibilities," he says.

Salom looks at him without understanding.

"That's what the other two managers are called," Melchor clarifies. "Or assistant managers. Grau's subordinates. They also talk about Adell as if he were Napoleon, and they also lived under his thumb. And they're young and ambitious besides. If we're speculating, even Ferrer would be a possibility, no?"

"Albert?" Salom smiles, perplexed. "You don't know him. He's a nice, inoffensive slacker. A bit scatterbrained. He was smart when he was young, got a degree in business studies and could have done important things, I'm sure. But he got together with the local rich girl, understood he wouldn't have to worry about anything and gave himself over to the good life. That's

140

what Grau said this morning: when you get things too easily, it's over. The old man was right about that." He pauses then adds: "And you're right to want to meet Albert. We'll go see him as we arranged. If we can't talk to Rosa, we'll just talk to him. He'll tell us about Grau and Silva and Botet. He knows them well."

"And you? How do you know Ferrer?"

"The way we all know each other in Terra Alta: our whole lives. His family and mine were friends. But I'm a bit older than him, and we only became real friends in Barcelona, when we were students. We shared a flat for two years. He was at university and I was at the Police Academy and then at Nou Barris for a year of training. That's where he started dating Rosa. Olga can tell you as well. Ask her."

While they have dessert and coffee, Salom tells Melchor about his relationship with Albert Ferrer and Rosa Adell, then Melchor gives Salom a summary of his interviews with the Gráficas Adell assistant managers Silva and Botet that morning.

It is pouring with rain when they stop in front of the big iron gate and Salom phones Albert Ferrer, who is waiting for them inside the house. It is just after five in the afternoon. They're not coming straight from lunch at the Terra Alta, but from the station, where Melchor has left his car and had time to write up a hurried report on his morning's meetings at Gráficas Adell and send it to Pires so she can add it to the investigation. Meanwhile, Salom has talked to his colleagues in forensics who he helped the previous night at the Adells' house; he has also talked on the phone to Albert Ferrer and, a couple of times to Deputy Inspector Gomà and to Sergeant Pires. On the way to the late afternoon meeting, Salom has told him that the mobile phone service providers have begun to supply the names and numbers of their clients who were close to the Adells' house on Saturday night. Pires and Gomà have urged them to start interviewing as soon as possible, because Ramos, Viñas and Claver won't be able to cope with all that over the next few days.

The iron gate opens and they advance slowly up a gravel drive that crunches under the car's tyres into a leafy garden peppered with rain, skirting an old three-storey farmhouse until they reach a sort of hunting lodge. There, waiting for them with the door ajar, is Ferrer, who gestures them to park beside a red Porsche Panamera. They do so and, although they sprint the few metres separating them from the lodge, they are soaked and swearing by the time they come through the door.

"What a downpour!" Ferrer says. "Do you want a towel?"

The officers turn down the offer and, when they've composed themselves a little, Ferrer holds out a hand to Melchor.

"Finally!" he says, smiling widely. "You don't know how much I've been wanting to meet you. Ernest has told me a lot about you, but he seems to want you all to himself. He's always been very selfish."

They shake hands. Ferrer is only a year younger than Salom, but he seems much younger due to his good looks, his trim physique and his tight and youthful attire: green polo shirt, white trousers, Nike trainers. His hair is short and black, parted on the right, and his eyes focus with the intensity of a born seducer.

"I'm just sorry we had to meet in such tragic circumstances," he adds. "But sit down, please. Make yourself at home: I take very seriously the saying that any friend of a friend is also a friend of mine."

What at first glance appears to be a sort of hunting lodge is actually a sort of studio with a huge window looking out onto the garden, its wood-lined walls and shelves overflowing with compact discs and vinyl records. In the middle is a solid wooden table with a laptop computer on top of it and, behind it, a stereo system flanked by two towering speakers and two amplifiers. The afternoon has darkened and the room seems shrouded in a bluish, underwater light. At Ferrer's suggestion, Melchor and Salom take a seat on the threadbare sofa, and their host turns on a standard lamp with a golden shade to dispel the gloom as he offers them coffee, liqueurs or water. Melchor and Salom opt for coffee, and Ferrer goes over to a sideboard where there is a coffee maker and a drinks cabinet.

"This is my secret refuge," Ferrer explains to Melchor, placing a Nespresso capsule in the coffee maker and closing the lid. "Although it's not very secret, is it, Ernest?"

The corporal agrees and asks after Ferrer's wife; his friend says that Rosa Adell is asleep, that he didn't want to disturb her and that he's left word at the house that if she wakes up they should let her know that the two of them have arrived. While he listens to Ferrer and Salom talk, Melchor remembers how Olga described the two of them the night before ("They're like night and day") and wonders how it is possible for two men who appear to be so different to be such good friends.

"You shouldn't have done that," Salom scolds Ferrer. "Rosa needs to sleep, not to be bothered by us."

"It's no bother," Ferrer says. "She wants to help. It's just that –" he turns to Melchor – "she's devastated. She loved her parents very much, especially her father. This is going to kill her."

"I've already told him," Salom says.

"My daughters are also very upset," Ferrer continues. "The two older ones arrived from Barcelona yesterday, although I want them to go back soon. Tomorrow, if possible, after the funeral. Life has to go on for everyone, but especially for them, don't you think?"

The question is directed at Melchor, who doesn't answer. Salom stands up, takes the two cups of coffee, hands one to his partner and holds on to the other.

"With your permission I'll have a whisky," Ferrer says, as he drops two ice cubes into a square, heavy crystal glass. "It's unbearable without one."

As he pours himself a generous shot of Lagavulin and collapses into his armchair, Ferrer tells them that he and his wife have been weighing up the idea of hiring a lawyer to act as the family's spokesperson.

"That's a good idea," Salom says. He has sat back down beside Melchor. "That way nobody will bother you."

"But then it occurred to me that the spokesperson could be you, Ernest." Ferrer takes a sip of his whisky and sets the glass down on the table. "And Rosa thought it was a great idea."

Ferrer is explaining why Salom is the ideal choice to carry out this task when the corporal interrupts him.

"If that's what you two want, I'd be happy to do it." Then he adds: "It's a bit unusual, but I don't think there'd be any objection. Anyway, let me ask Deputy Inspector Gomà about it."

"Ask him, please," Ferrer says. "Let's hope he thinks it's appropriate. It would be best for us. And I'm sure Rosa would find it reassuring."

"Salom told me you realised some things were missing," Melchor says. "From your wife's parents' house, I mean. Jewellery and money."

"Yes." Ferrer picks up his whisky glass again, though without taking a sip; behind him, on the other side of the window, the rain keeps battering the flowers and trees in the garden,

144

which is increasingly drenched and hazy. "They didn't usually keep a lot of money at home, but on Friday night it happens that Rosa saw an envelope of cash in her mother's bedroom. I don't know, they must have had to pay for something . . ."

"Was that the last time you two were in the house?" Melchor asks.

"Yes," Ferrer says, and Melchor notices his fingernails are tiny, bitten down to the quick. "My father-in-law was in the habit of having his staff to dinner every Friday, to take stock of the week."

"Silva and Botet told me about it. Arjona was also at that dinner, wasn't he? And Grau, as well."

"Arjona is the factory supervisor?" Salom asks.

"Yes," Ferrer says. "He's been coming to the dinners too, at least lately. My mother-in-law and my wife, too, even though, as I said, they're mainly work meetings. The only exceptions were Christmas Day and Saint Rosa's Day, when we celebrated my wife and mother-in-law's saint's day with the managers' families, and the suppers would turn into a party."

Ferrer goes on for a few minutes about the weekly meetings at the Adells' house and, while he is doing so, Melchor notices that every once in a while he makes a sudden almost imperceptible movement of his head, as if he had a nervous spasm or as if one of his ears was blocked with water and he wanted to shake it clear. He asks again about the jewellery.

"According to Rosa, the best of it was in a safety deposit box at the bank," Ferrer says. "But the pieces at home were not trinkets. And they've all disappeared."

"Do you know if your in-laws kept anything of value there, something someone might have been very interested in, an object, a password, or something like that, something that might explain why they'd torture them before killing them?"

"I don't know." Ferrer crosses his right ankle over his left knee, revealing fine, pure white socks. "Of course, if they did have something like that, I wouldn't have known about it. Rosa might have, but not me. Anyway, Rosa has no idea either."

"How did you get along with your in-laws?"

Ferrer appears not to understand the question and, biting the inside of his cheek, turns towards Salom, who just then gets up to take his empty cup to the sideboard.

"Tell him the truth, Albert," the corporal encourages him. "You've got nothing to hide."

Ferrer uncrosses his legs and swirls his whisky glass, making the ice cubes clink together.

"With her, fine," he says, his eyes fixed on Melchor and jaw clenched. "Very well, in fact. She was a good woman, and she loved me like a son. With him it was different." For a couple of seconds he looks at Melchor, who feels that Ferrer is not seeing him, that he's seeing another person, or perhaps he sees himself. But then he takes another sip of his whisky and smiles again. "Well, we don't have to over-analyse it. I don't suppose he could ever bear me sleeping with his daughter. It's that simple, and deep down that vulgar, isn't it? Maybe the same thing will happen to me, except for me it'll be quadrupled."

Ferrer lets out a short and fake chuckle, but nobody joins in and it sounds hollow against the constant rain battering the window. The storm intensifies for a few seconds, but soon calms down. Salom has poured himself a glass of water, and now observes his friend with it in his hand, leaning against a bookshelf. Melchor has let his coffee get cold, and no longer feels like drinking it.

"Paco Adell was a tough guy," Ferrer continues. "I believe he looked down on me. Well, I know he did."

"Paco Adell looked down on everybody," Salom says.

"It's possible." Ferrer downs his whisky and stands up. "That said, he was my wife's father and the grandfather of my daughters, and I'm not at all happy about what happened to him. I'm not sure everyone can say the same."

"Are you thinking of Grau?" Melchor asks.

Ferrer bites the inside of his cheek again and looks at Salom again, who nods.

"I've told him," he says.

Ferrer puts another ice cube in his glass.

"Who else would I be thinking of?" he asks, pouring another shot of whisky into his glass. "The relationship between those two men . . ." He takes a sip and sits back down in his armchair, across from Melchor. "Well, somebody ought to write a book about them. In a way they were the perfect couple: one was a sadist and the other a masochist. That's why they lasted so long together, I guess. That and because they were both mentally unbalanced and lived only to work, as if they were two monks, or two crusaders. I've never seen anybody exploit themselves to such an extent. And all for what? My father-in-law at least had a family, but Grau didn't even have that. I can't understand why he wants so much money when he doesn't ever have time to spend it."

"Melchor says that Grau talks about Adell as if he were Napoleon," the corporal says.

"Or Jesus Christ!" Ferrer exclaims. "You can't imagine the level of devotion he had for him, the extremes of servility he'd go to. It was disgusting, to tell you the truth. And I don't have to remind you who sold out Christ."

"Are you saying that Grau might've had something to do with the murder?"

"I'm saying that it's only a short step from devotion to

147

hatred. And that, after fifty years of daily torture, Grau could have taken it. At least, I wouldn't be surprised if he had. Didn't you find the tyre tracks of his car in my in-laws' garden?"

"We're not sure they were from his car," Salom stresses. "The brand of tyres is the same as his, Continental, but it's impossible to prove they were made by Grau's car." Suddenly uncomfortable, the corporal moves away from the shelves, leaves his half-empty glass of water by the drinks cabinet, and says: "Well, I think we'd better get going."

At that moment Melchor notices that it has practically stopped raining and that, above the exuberance of the dripping garden, the blanket of clouds that was covering the sun has been torn and behind it a scrap of shiny, luminous, vividly blue sky peaks out.

"Shouldn't we wait for Señora Adell?" Melchor says.

"She's not going to come," the corporal says. "And what we should be doing is questioning the people whose mobile phones were in the vicinity as soon as possible."

"I don't know if Rosa is up to answering many questions," Ferrer says. "But why don't you have a drink before you leave? The thing about police not drinking while they're on duty only happens in films, right?"

Neither of them accepts the offer, but Melchor takes the chance to ask him about his job at Gráficas Adell. Ferrer says that it has changed over time and that, in recent years, especially since Adell and Grau stopped travelling due to their age and named him managing director, he has mainly taken care of liaising with the foreign affiliates, which has meant frequent trips to Eastern Europe and Latin America. Listening to Ferrer, Melchor thinks this must have been what Grau meant by "strutting his stuff".

"We could say that for the past few years I've been the

148

visible face of the company for many," Ferrer summarises. "It's not work I dislike, because I love to travel and because I'm a sociable person. I can be accused of many things, but not of being unpleasant, right, Ernest? However, I'm not going to lie to you: I would have liked to work more inside the business, with executive duties and so on."

"And why didn't you?" Melchor asks.

Ferrer laughs again, this time for real, and shakes his head abruptly, victim once again of a spasmodic movement or a problem with his ear.

"You can tell you really didn't know the old man!" he says after another swallow, his mouth twisted into a bitter sneer. "He was incapable of teamwork, didn't know how to delegate; he had to control everything and everything had to be done his way. What's known as a tyrant. Being under his orders was a nightmare."

"But the company works well," Melchor says.

"Worked!" Ferrer corrects him, waving his whisky glass where now only two ice cubes survive. "It has become obsolete. It operates on twentieth-century methods. No, not twentieth: nineteenth! Adell had no idea about the new ways of managing a business, and no interest in them. On top of that, he didn't trust anybody, not even Grau."

While Ferrer strings out an anecdote intended to exemplify Adell's ecumenical distrust and his devious relationship with Grau, Melchor sees through the window, behind his host, a woman come out of the door of the main house and walk towards the studio along a waterlogged path. The rain has stopped, but the woman has an umbrella up.

"Here comes Rosa," Salom says, going to the door.

Ferrer and Melchor stand up. Salom greets Rosa Adell with a kiss on the cheek as she closes her umbrella and leaves it in an umbrella stand by the door. Ferrer introduces her to Melchor and they shake hands.

"We were just about to leave," Salom says.

"Please, sit down," Rosa Adell says.

She sits down too. Although she looks haggard and is dressed haphazardly – long grey skirt, black shirt and a cardigan, also grey – Melchor is impressed by her serene, clear beauty, which he doesn't recall from the photographs he has seen of her: oval-shaped face, large deep-set eyes with slightly swollen lids, full lips, straight nose, dark, silky skin. It's obvious that she's been crying, but also that she's trying to hide it. Sitting on the sofa beside her, Ferrer wraps one arm around her shoulders and points to Salom with the other.

"Ernest has agreed to be the family's spokesperson," he announces.

"You'll do it?" Rosa Adell says.

"Of course," Salom says. "If Deputy Inspector Gomà authorises it, I have no objection. Quite the contrary."

"You don't know how grateful I am, Ernest," Rosa Adell tells him. "We'd thought about a lawyer, but it's much better if you do it instead of a stranger." After a long silence, which all three men respect, she murmurs: "I just don't understand what's happened. I can't understand it. My parents . . ." She seems to be about to burst into tears, but she presses her lips together and does not cry. "I don't know what to say, Ernest."

"You don't have to say anything."

Rosa nods, cowers a little, pulling her cardigan around her and crossing her arms, as if she were cold. Then she reconsiders and carries on:

"Yes, of course I have to say something." She looks at Melchor. "I imagine you have a lot of questions. Ask me whatever you want, please."

150

"We don't want to bother you, Rosa," Salom insists. "Besides, we're in a hurry."

"If you're worried about what happened this morning, you're making a mistake," Rosa Adell says. "I'm much better. Besides, you two have to do your work. The problem is I don't know how to help you, I can't think of anyone who could be responsible for this horror. The only thing I am certain of is that neither María Fernanda nor Jenica had anything to do with it. Poor Jenica."

"Since you insist," Salom concedes, "there is something I didn't ask you this morning."

"What's that?" she asks.

"Do you remember when you last spoke to your mother?"

"It would have been Saturday evening. I don't know. We spoke constantly. She called me at all hours. That night we had an early dinner and then Irene and Ana went to their rooms and we watched a TV series."

"*Mad Men*," Ferrer specifies.

"I fell asleep while we were watching it, and then I went to bed and Albert came over here to listen to music. It was just a normal Saturday night. On Sunday we were supposed to have dinner with them. With my parents, I mean."

"Are you sure you didn't speak to them after dinner?" Salom asks.

"No. I don't think so. But I'm not sure. If you want, I can check. The call would be listed on my mobile."

"Check it, please," Salom says. "Tell me something else. Did you notice anything odd about your parents in recent days? As if they had some worry or anything like that."

"No." Turning towards her husband, she says: "Did you notice anything?"

Ferrer shakes his head.

151

"They lived a very quiet life," Rosa Adell says. "My father still went to work every day. My mother almost never left the house anymore, not even to do the gardening, which she used to really enjoy. They were both very old, especially my father, though neither of them had any serious health problems."

"We've heard that they didn't have many friends, either," Melchor says. "That they didn't socialise."

"They never did," Rosa Adell says, focusing her gaze on him. "And, at their age, even less. My father lost his parents very young. They were from Bot. His father was killed in the war. I don't know anything about his mother, I never met her and my father never spoke of her. We had a lot more contact with my mother's family. They were from Reus. When I was little we would go and see my grandparents and my aunt there. Then all three of them died and we stopped going. We were my parents' social life, Albert, me and our daughters."

"And Josep Grau," Melchor says.

"That's true." Rosa Adell nods. "Señor Grau is also one of the family. Have you spoken to him? He spent the whole day here yesterday. He didn't shed a single tear but I know inside he's shattered."

Rosa Adell stops talking, her eyes wander and a solid silence takes over the studio, while the three men watch her. It is Melchor who breaks the silence.

"Have you thought about what is going to happen to the company?"

Coming around, Rosa Adell scrutinises the silence with a furrowed brow.

"He asked if you've thought about what you're going to do with Gráficas Adell," Ferrer says.

She relaxes her expression and shrugs.

"You mean who's going to take my father's place?" she

152

says, not taking her eyes off Melchor. "I don't know. I hadn't thought about it. To tell you the truth, right now I couldn't care less."

"There'll be plenty of time to think about that," Ferrer says, squeezing her close again. "Now is not the time. But sooner or later you will have to make a decision, if only for your father's sake."

Rosa Adell responds with a vague gesture, denoting inability or anguish (or both), and her husband offers her a drink, an offer she declines. Just then, Melchor's mobile vibrates: for the third time that day, it is Vivales. He doesn't answer this time either, and Salom, making as if to stand up, says that they had better get going. Rosa Adell looks at him with fatigue that resembles disappointment but is probably relief.

"You don't want to know anything else?" she asks.

"I told you we were in a hurry, Rosa," Salom says. "We'll come back another day."

"I'd like to know something," Melchor says. "Are you two also members of Opus Dei?"

Again the woman gives him a surprised look, and Melchor is afraid she has not understood him. Beside her Ferrer says no with a shake of the head.

"No," Rosa Adell says. "That was my parents' thing. They didn't even try to convince us to join them."

"Were you two already married when your parents joined Opus?"

"Of course," she says. "It was only ten or twelve years ago."

"Señor Grau told us your father's life didn't change in any significant way when he joined," Melchor says.

"It's true," Rosa says. "My mother's didn't either. She was always religious, Sundays and holy days we always went to

Mass, but that was it. We never prayed at home, for example. Now they did, although it was just the two of them, each night before bed, they never mixed us up with any of that. Sometimes they went on retreats with other older couples. That sort of thing. But nothing else."

"Did you know any of those couples?"

"None of them. In fact, it was different couples each time. And I don't think they made friends with any of them. My mother would have told me. Although the truth is that my mother talked to me about everything except that. And I accepted her silence."

"Do you think she was embarrassed by being in Opus?"

"I think she thought it was a very private, very personal thing. And that she didn't have to involve anyone else in it, not even me. And I also think . . ." she takes a deep breath, hardens her expression and continues: "I think Opus was their way of preparing for death. For what they couldn't imagine . . ."

This time she's not able to contain herself: her lips tremble and contract, her eyes flood and she bursts into tears. Ferrer grips her shoulder again and pulls her close while she takes a tissue out of her cardigan pocket, dries her tears with it and stammers an apology. Salom says that she has nothing to apologise for and, when she stops crying, stands up.

"Well, this time we really are going," he says. "We've troubled you long enough."

Melchor stands up with him and they both say goodbye to Rosa Adell.

"I'll see you out," Ferrer says.

The three walk into the garden and towards the police car, which is parked next to Ferrer's Porsche. Melchor breathes in the intense aroma of wet earth, trees and flowers drenched by the downpour; a turbulent, rust-coloured light varnishes

154

everything. Ferrer shakes his hand and grips his arm with his other hand.

"I'm sorry, I told you Rosa's not feeling well," he apologises. "Let's hope this is all over soon and we can meet up for dinner and a few drinks. My treat. Agreed?"

While Ferrer and Salom are saying goodbye, Melchor looks back at the studio and, through the window, sees Rosa Adell still sitting on the sofa, head down, her back to him. Then his eyes focus on the Panamera's tyres: they're not Continentals but Pirellis.

"Cosette was waiting for you," Olga says. "But she finally fell asleep."

"I couldn't get away any earlier," Melchor apologises. "I think you two are going to have to forget about me for the next little while."

"Why didn't you tell Salom to come up for something to eat? I made supper for him as well."

"I did. But he was tired and wanted to go home."

Melchor devours a plain omelette and a salad of finely chopped tomatoes and lettuce, topped with chicken, cheese, nuts and avocado, dressed with olive oil and balsamic vinegar. Olga watches him eat, while caressing the stem of her glass, half full of red wine. They are sitting at the kitchen table under a lamp that throws a bright circle of light over the checked tablecloth; a homely half-light prevails in the rest of the room.

His wife asks about the investigation.

"Let's talk about something else," Melchor says, chewing with a can of Coke in hand. "The judge has issued a nondisclosure order. The less I tell you about it, the better. How was your day?"

"Good," Olga says. "Vivales called."

"Oh shit, I forgot. He's been calling me all day. What does he want?"

"What else would he want?" She smiles. "The usual: just to know that everything's under control. And to have a chat with Cosette, who adores him. I talked to him a little bit too. About the Adells, of course. And about you: he says he hasn't spoken to you in two weeks."

"I'll call him later."

Olga starts to tell him how her day has gone and Melchor tries to concentrate on what she's saying, but he is soon distracted – unwillingly his thoughts have strayed to the Adells, to Grau, to Ferrer, to Silva and Botet – until at a certain moment he thinks he hears a name he recognises.

"Who?" he asks.

"Arturo Ventosa," Olga repeats. "The writer. The councillor for culture is a fan. He's been chasing me for ages to invite him to talk about one of his books at the library, and he finally got his way. Have you read him?"

"No."

"So why are you smiling?"

Melchor wonders for a moment whether or not he should tell Olga about Ventosa's visit to the Quatre Camins prison, in what now seems like a previous life.

"No reason," he says. "Can you manage without me at the library? I don't think I'm going to be able to help you set up for the book launch. Like I said, unless we have a lucky break, I don't think I'm going to be around for anything this week."

"Don't worry," Olga says. "Anyway, I don't know yet when we'll be able to host the book launch. Not before autumn."

Olga talks about Ventosa or Ventosa's book launch, or maybe about the councillor who's a big admirer of Ventosa, while Melchor finishes his salad, preoccupied again. Then he stands up and opens the fridge.

"Do you know Ferrer?" he suddenly says.

Olga looks at him, unsurprised, as if deep down she knew Melchor wasn't listening to what she was saying.

"You mean Albert Ferrer? Rosa Adell's husband? Yes, a little. The one who really knows him is Salom. They're really good friends, as I told you yesterday, he will have told you as well. I know his wife better, though it's ages since I last saw her. Didn't I tell you that? We were at school together. Her best friend since forever was Helena, Salom's wife. I suppose that's partly how Salom and Ferrer became such good friends."

The alarm in the fridge begins to go off; Melchor takes out a yoghurt, closes the door and the alarm stops. He gets a spoon out of the drawer and sits back down.

"What do you know about him?"

"About Ferrer?"

Melchor nods.

"What everyone knows."

Olga holds her glass against her lip, but doesn't drink, as if she needs to think about her reply.

"Salom says he's scatterbrained," Melchor says.

"If he says so . . ." She finally takes a sip of wine. "I told you I don't know him very well. Lots of people speak badly of him, it's true, but you know what people are like, and much more so in small towns. I suppose people are envious of him, and that's why that legend has grown up around him."

"What legend?"

"The legend that he never lifts a finger, spends a fortune gambling, cheats on his wife with every passing woman . . . What do I know?" Olga finishes her wine; now she's the one who smiles, perhaps a little tipsy. "He was three years older than

157

us, and one thing I will tell you: at school we were all crazy about him. He was handsome, cheerful, nice . . . and then he goes and marries the richest girl in town. How could people not be envious?"

"The manager of Gráficas Adell says that the thing about his skirt-chasing is true."

"Have you been talking to Señor Grau? That man has a legend too, and a very dark one."

"Him too?"

"Him too. This is Terra Alta, Melchor, everyone here has their legend."

"Including Rosa Adell?"

"Of course, except in her case it's a good one. And rightly so. At school she was a great girl and, as far as I know, she still is. I remember when my father talked about her, he always said: 'Luckily that girl takes after her mother.' Anyway, I don't know why, but I get the impression that you didn't really warm to Ferrer."

"Or Grau."

"And Rosa?"

"I talked to her and Ferrer this evening." Melchor scrapes out the last of the yoghurt. "That woman is having a hard time. They've stuffed her with tranquillisers."

"When she was young she was very beautiful."

"She still is."

Olga stares at Melchor, who is savouring the last spoonful of yoghurt.

"Should I be jealous?" she asks.

Melchor doesn't answer. Olga keeps her eyes fixed on him, until her husband notices the silence.

"Sorry," he says as if he's just woken up. "What did you say?"

158

"Should I be jealous of Rosa Adell?"

Melchor explores her gaze, trying to understand; he swiftly understands and, in slow motion, a naughty smile spreads across his face.

"Depends how you behave yourself tonight."

Olga shakes her head very seriously and bangs her empty glass gently on the table.

"This is not a decent house." She laughs. "It's a bordello."

Part Two

1

Melchor and Salom walk into Deputy Inspector Gomà's office and he stands up just long enough to shake hands and point to two chairs. The two officers sit down opposite him, in front of a desk where a computer cohabits with several piles of cardboard folders and a tin in the Barça colours, over-flowing with pencils and pens.

"I've had you come here to give you some news," he says, pushing aside the keyboard of his computer. "I could have told you over the phone or by e-mail, but I preferred to tell you in person."

Deputy Inspector Gomà leans his elbows on the desk and intertwines his fingers at the level of his mouth, as if he wants to hide the still red nick his morning shave has made in his otherwise smooth chin. In spite of the air conditioning that cools the office, he has his shirtsleeves rolled up, his top button undone and the knot of his tie loose; behind the lenses of his glasses, his eyes examine the two policemen without affection. A rectangular window behind him frames a path bordered by a row of dusty plane trees that withstand the red-hot midday July sun undaunted.

"The judge and I have decided by mutual consent to close

the Adell case," he says. "Needless to say, this is a provisional closure. If a clue shows up one day, and we do hope one soon does, we'll open it again. Meanwhile, it's best to shelve it and devote our efforts to other matters that are urgently demanding our attention. It seems the most sensible thing to us after six weeks on this, full time, with no tangible results." He pauses and adds: "Incidentally, we should tell the family as soon as possible."

"I'll do that," Salom says.

"That would be best," Deputy Inspector Gomà says. "After all, you've been the one keeping them informed all this time."

"Don't worry. I'll go and see them this afternoon. Should I also inform the press?"

"Not necessary. Why inform them if they're not asking? Besides, they've forgotten all about it recently, you know how the media are, with that case of the child from Riumar in the spotlight now . . . Anyway, I regret that the investigation hasn't turned out the way we'd have liked, but at least nobody can reproach us for not having done everything possible." The deputy inspector untwines his fingers and opens his hands in a gesture of resignation. "Well, I think that's all I had to tell you. That, and thank you for your help: it's been a pleasure working with you both."

He is about to shake their hands goodbye, when Melchor interrupts.

"I'm sorry," he says. "I think we're making a mistake."

Gomà blinks several times.

"Excuse me?" he says.

"I mean it seems to me a bad idea to close the case. I think we should keep investigating."

Now his superior raises his eyebrows and smiles vaguely, with an air of mild annoyance.

164

"I don't know why, but this doesn't entirely surprise me." He turns to Salom. "Do you agree, Corporal?"

Salom strokes his beard without answering, and Melchor understands he is looking for a way to square the circle: an honest reply that won't harm his partner, or at least not leave him stranded.

"The corporal and I have been working together for four years and have disagreed many times," Melchor says, jumping in to get Salom out of his difficulty. "This is just one more."

Salom's silence supports his partner, and Gomà nods, looks at his watch and back at Melchor.

"So you think we should keep investigating?"

Melchor nods.

"Investigating what?" the deputy inspector asks. "The what, who, how and where?"

Melchor meets his gaze. When he is about to reply, Gomà turns to Salom, then looks at Melchor again and continues: "Listen, Marín. You know we've done everything possible. Do I need to remind you?" He grasps the little finger of his left hand with the index finger and thumb of his right. "We have examined the Adells' house millimetre by millimetre and we have found tons of fingerprints, but not a single useful one, and not even the famous Continental tyre tracks help: they could be from any car." He lets go of his little finger and clutches his ring finger. "We have sent people to Gdansk and Timisoara, to Córdoba and Puebla, to speak to the heads of the Gráficas Adell affiliates there, and we have gone over the accounts of all the family's holdings front to back and back to front and we haven't found anything or anybody suspicious, not a single strange financial transfer, not a euro out of place." He lets go of the ring finger and grabs his middle finger, with emphasis. "We have interrogated, without the least result, all the visitors to the Adells' house in the days preceding the murders, and also almost two hundred people who, according to their mobile phone records, were in the vicinity of the house that night, and that has only turned up one kid who thought he saw a car pulling into the Adells' house from the main road, but who doesn't remember either the colour or the make of the car or what time it was when he thought he saw it." He lets go of the middle finger and clutches his index finger with even more emphasis. "We have spoken to the representatives of the Opus Dei centre in Reus with which the Adells were connected and have deduced absolutely nothing apart from the fact that the old couple were signed-up members of Opus and that Opus treated them like royalty." He lets go of his index finger, grabs his thumb, waves it around with a dramatic flourish, raises his voice and adds, his eyes wide open, and each word separated for emphasis. "We have tapped the telephones for almost four weeks of all the executives of Gráficas Adell, including Francisco Adell's son-in-law. And what have we concluded?" Gomà lets go of his thumb, opens his hands again and shows his empty palms to Melchor. "Nothing at all. Do you want me to go on?"

Melchor does not answer. After a moment of silence, Deputy Inspector Gomà takes a deep breath and stares at the metal canister in Barça colours, then pulls out a very sharp pencil and, holding it by both ends, starts twirling it on its axis.

"Look, your first impression was right," he says, in a conciliatory tone. "Everything points to the Adells' murderers being professionals. Also, we have a pretty rough idea of what happened that night. Señora Adell's last phone call to her daughter was just after ten, and the coroner estimates that the crimes occurred between midnight and four in the morning. The murderers must have arrived at the house when everyone was asleep, or at least once they were all in bed. Someone must have let them in. It's not likely to have been the Romanian maid, because she was killed in her bedroom. Of course, it's not impossible that it was her all the same: maybe they killed her there precisely so we wouldn't think she was the one who'd let them in. Then again it might have been the Adells who opened the door to the murderers because they knew them. Or perhaps the murderers had keys to the house, even though we believe that, apart from them and the cook, only their daughter had a set. Whatever the case, it's most likely that the murderers were looking for valuable items, money, jewellery, things like that, maybe someone had told them that the Adells kept something in their house, or maybe they were looking for something that wasn't in the house, we just don't know what that might have been. Maybe they found it, because the old couple told them where it was, or maybe they didn't, because the couple withstood the torture or because there was nothing to find and the murderers tortured them in revenge, or to let off steam or amuse themselves. In short, that's what must have happened, or something very much like it."

"It doesn't sound very credible to me," Melchor says.

The deputy inspector stops twirling the pencil and, behind his glasses, his initial cold gaze returns. At that moment, someone knocks on the door and, when Gomà sees that it is Sergeant Pires, his expression changes again: it becomes warm, welcoming, almost sweet.

"Are they here?" he says.

"They've had some trouble," Pires says, through the half-open door. "Nothing serious. They'll be here in five minutes."

Deputy Inspector Gomà tries to look annoyed, to harden his expression again, but he barely manages it. For an instant he seems to hesitate.

"Come in, Pires, please, don't stand there," he says, overcoming his indecision; the sergeant obeys. "You've come just in time. The 'Hero of Cambrils' here doesn't think we should close the Adell case. And I've just decided that he has won the lottery: let's give him five minutes to convince us that we're wrong. What do you think?"

"I think that's an excellent idea, Deputy Inspector," Pires says.

Melchor detects curiosity rather than irritation in the sarcastic tone in which Deputy Inspector Gomà uses the nickname, which the press bestowed on him four years earlier, after the Islamist attacks, a sobriquet he hasn't heard once since arriving in Terra Alta, although during this time word has got around that he was the one who brought down the four terrorists in Cambrils.

"Go ahead then, Marín," Gomà encourages him. "You've got five minutes."

Melchor points to Pires, who has taken a seat beside the deputy inspector.

"I would have preferred for the rest of us to be here as well," he says. "I mean—"

"I know who you mean," the commander cuts him off. "Are you kidding? This is the police, Marín. Decisions are not made by committee. I make them."

"Of course. I simply said that because maybe some of them might also think the case shouldn't be closed."

"All your colleagues know we're going to close the case, and none has protested. I'm warning you: the clock is ticking."

Deputy Inspector Gomà returns the pencil to the metal canister and leans back in his chair while, at his side, Pires folds her arms across her chest. Melchor notices for a second the red heart pierced by a black arrow she has tattooed over her collarbone and, as he looks up, realises that she has seen him noticing it; a teasing smile plays on her lips. Sitting beside Melchor, Salom tries to hide his discomfort by pretending to be less interested in what's going on inside the office than in what's going on outside the window, on the esplanade lined with plane trees, where nothing is going on.

"I, too, think the murderers were professionals," Melchor begins. "What doesn't convince me is the theory that they were merely burglars."

"Why not?" Deputy Inspector Gomà asks.

"Because it seems implausible that thieves would spend so much time torturing an elderly couple that way."

"I agree," Pires says. "The problem is that reality is full of implausibilities. It's a bit different from novels that way, isn't it?"

Melchor is accustomed to his commanding officers and colleagues making ironic comments about his reading habits. He's not bothered by sarcasm and doesn't rise to it often.

"Not good ones, no," he says. "But bad ones are, yes."

"Then you should read bad novels, Marín," Deputy Inspector Gomà says. "You'd learn more. You'd learn for example that reality is a place where you find all sorts, including a whole bunch of nuts and psychopaths who don't follow any rules. Much less the ones in novels."

"Novels don't have rules," Melchor says gently. "That's their charm. But it doesn't matter. Not even in a terrible novel would mere burglars have tortured the Adells. It makes no sense. If they wanted to drag some secret out of them, there would have been no need to torture them: they would have told them straight away. They were elderly people, don't you see? Besides, what secret are we talking about? What did the Adells know that could have been of such interest? As far as we know,

169

nothing. And, if it wasn't about extracting a secret from them, it makes even less sense to torture them. One thing is clear: they both suffered enormously, and people make others suffer like that because they hate them. The other thing that is clear is that those who had most reason to hate Francisco Adell weren't his competitors but his collaborators, the people who were closest to him."

"That's why we requested their mobiles," Pires says. "To find out where they were that night. And that's why we asked the judge for permission to tap their phones. And what did we conclude from all that?"

"Not much," Melchor concedes.

"No, not 'not much'," she says. "Nothing."

"OK," Melchor admits. "But even so, that's the only lead we have. We should have continued the phone taps, we should exhaust the lines of investigation."

"What lines?" Pires asks. "Four weeks of monitoring isn't enough to convince you they have nothing to do with it?"

"No," Melchor says, and at that moment some words of Blai's cross his mind: "And have you seen that two-faced Pires? Seems like Gomà's lapdog. I bet they're screwing." In recent weeks Melchor has spoken frequently with Gomà and with Pires, mostly by phone, and, although he's only seen them together three or four times, he has never asked himself whether Blai was right about them and if their mutual understanding reflects some degree of sentimental, or at least sexual, involvement. Nor does he ask himself now that Pires has taken it upon herself to reply to him with Gomà's implicit consent. "Maybe they think we're listening," Melchor goes on. "If any of them had anything to do with the murders, they surely took all possible precautions and will continue to do so. Besides, Botet and Arjona can explain where they were that night and their phones confirm it, but Grau's and Silva's were switched off. They have no alibis. And Ferrer's isn't watertight."

"I think it is," Pires says.

"Well, I don't," Melchor says. "It's true that he was at home that Saturday night with his wife and two of his daughters. But the girls went to their rooms after dinner, his wife also went to bed after watching a TV programme and he went to a studio he has behind the house, in the garden. That must have happened around eleven, maybe eleven-thirty. We don't know what time Ferrer went to bed, but we know that from his house to the Adells' is no more than a fifteen-minute drive. So he could perfectly easily have left his house and driven to his in-laws' and back in three quarters of an hour or an hour without his wife or daughters knowing. At twelve-thirty or one he could have been in his bed as if nothing had happened."

"The tyres on Ferrer's car are not Continentals," Pires reminds him.

"Yes, but he could have taken a different car that day," Melchor says, and carries on before Pires tries to stop him again. "Don't get me wrong. I'm not saying that Ferrer was the murderer, or that he helped the murderer. I'm saying he could have helped them. In other words, I'm saying that we don't know enough to be able entirely to rule out that he might have helped them. And the same goes for Grau and for Silva, except even more so. I mean Grau and Silva had it even easier than Ferrer. In fact, I wouldn't even rule out Botet and Arjona. After all, the five of them were in the Adells' house on Friday night, and any one of them could have switched off the security system."

"OK, we can't entirely rule them out," Pires relents. "But we don't have a single even slightly solid clue that points to any of them. And our resources are not unlimited, so—"

"I'm not asking for anything out of this world. I'm just requesting another couple of weeks of work and a judicial order to search their offices and computers, and, if necessary, their houses. That's all."

Pires gives up arguing with him: it's obvious that Melchor's protest has left the dispute up for judgment, awaiting Deputy Inspector Gomà's verdict. He has been listening to his subordinates attentively, although now, suddenly, he seems uninterested or fatigued or irritated, as if it bores him that he has to be the one to settle the controversy, or as if it were an illusory controversy and had been settled long before it started. But he soon recovers his composure, clears his throat, exchanges a fleeting glance with Pires and leans his elbows on the desk again, once again intertwining his fingers to hide his shaving cut.

"Get that idea out of your head," he admonishes Melchor. "The judge is not going to authorise what you want, and I'm not going to ask him to. I had a hard enough time getting permission to tap the phones, so forget about doing it again, and especially about bothering the Adells again. Those people have been hounded from all sides, and I have no intention of making them suffer any more. Because that is the question," Deputy Inspector Gomà goes on, looking for a moment at Salom and then back at Melchor, who thinks that what is going to make Rosa Adell suffer is not continuing the investigation, but closing it and her parents' murderers not being made to pay for what they did. "It's not only that there isn't a single clue pointing to Adell's subordinates. It's that, deep down, that hypothesis makes no sense. At first, I confess, it was mine as well, but it no longer is. Look, everyone, more or less, hates their boss, but they don't end up killing them, do they, Pires?" Delighted, the sergeant smiles, and Gomà smiles back, before continuing: "Was Adell a tyrant with his co-workers, especially his closest collaborators? Did some of them, including Grau spend their whole lives putting up with humiliations and scorn from him? Yes, but so what? Tell me, what would Silva or Botet or Arjona stand to gain from Adell's death? Risk losing a job that many rightly envied them? Because that's what might happen to them now. And do you think people like that would get themselves mixed up in such a serious matter simply for revenge? I don't. And I don't see Grau as capable of doing it either. That old man is nobody without Adell! He's spent half his life by his side and he admired him much more than he hated him, supposing he really did hate him! As for Ferrer, I regret even having tapped his phone. Because he had less reason than any of them to want Adell dead. It's true he was his father-in-law as well as his boss, and he did bully him relentlessly. But, as badly as he got along with him, he knew the old man was over ninety and not immortal, and that his wife would inherit everything when he died. Why would he risk losing it all by getting mixed up in a murder when, with a little patience, he could have it all without doing anything? Ferrer might be a shallow, cheating bullshitter, but he's not a fucking idiot or a nutcase. Am I right or not, Corporal?"

Salom half-closes his eyes and presses his lips together in an expression of forbearance, as if he is sorry to find himself forced to admit that Gomà is right.

"It makes no sense whatsoever," Deputy Inspector Gomà says, looking at Melchor again. "I'm not saying that, if we had enough time and resources, it wouldn't be worthwhile continuing with the investigation. But, as Sergeant Pires was saying, time and resources are exactly what we don't have, at least here in Tortosa. I know that in Terra Alta things are different, there you've got more than enough time for everything, even for reading novels, but here things are the way they are, and this investigation is being run from Tortosa. Believe me, I'm sorry too." Before Melchor can react, the deputy inspector stands up and turns to Pires. "Well, the five minutes are up. They must be here by now."

They drive out of Tortosa without a word, and without saying a word they drive the first kilometres towards Gandesa, until, not far from Xerta, Salom decides to break the silence.

"Stop going over and over it once and for all, would you?" he says. "Gomà's right."

In the passenger seat, Melchor stares straight ahead, as if bewitched by the asphalt, where the reflection of the sun creates illusory puddles of trembling water. On each side of the road rows and rows of orange trees jut out of the thirsty ground. Salom drives with his right hand on the steering wheel and left forearm on the edge of the window. They aren't in Terra Alta yet.

"I don't know why you're getting so worked up," he goes on. "We could see this coming from the start. We knew only too well: if solid clues don't show up in the first days, you start to kiss the case goodbye. At the end of the first week we were already drawing blanks, and ever since then it's all been stabs in the dark. Gomà's done well to hold on. Normally a case like this would have been closed earlier. Think it through, it's what anyone would have done."

"This is not a normal case," Melchor says.

"Why not? Because it made the news? Rubbish. All cases are basically the same, at least for us. The only difference is that some we solve and some we don't. And this one we aren't going to solve. Don't take it so personally, you can't let the vigilante inside you come out every time something like this happens. What does Olga call him?"

Melchor doesn't answer, lost in thought, staring at the road. Salom lets a few seconds go by before rephrasing the question.

"Javert," Melchor says. "The police inspector in *Les Misérables*."

"That's the one," Salom says. "If you let him take over, you're going to ruin your life. Yours and your family's."

Once again in silence, they pass Xerta, whose houses seem to be dozing beside the road, in the searing early afternoon heat, and, when they are almost at Benifallet, Melchor's mobile rings. It's Sergeant Blai, impatient to know what happened at the meeting with Gomà. Melchor tells him, making a huge effort to maintain his composure.

"So it's over?" Blai finally asks. "Has he shelved it for good?"

"Not definitively," Melchor says. "Or that's what he says. But, yeah, for the moment it's closed."

"Son of a bitch!" the sergeant exclaims. "Anyway, you can't say I didn't warn you, eh? When they found the body of that child in Riumar, I told you: get ready, this'll be the end of your case. And that's what's happened. The journalists rushed off to that case, and now who remembers the Adell murders? As soon as it stopped showing up on television, Gomà lost interest. So there goes our favourite deputy inspector riding off with the cavalry to Riumar, desperate to smile for the cameras and put a lid on his failure in a noisy case with another even noisier one. For fuck's sake."

"He doesn't have enough resources to work on both cases," Melchor says, playing devil's advocate. "That's what he meant. Though he didn't breathe a word about the Riumar thing."

"Bollocks!" Blai fumed. "The Territorial Investigations Unit of Tortosa doesn't have resources? Ha! They've got all they want. And, if they don't, they can request them from Barcelona. It's what I just said: the thing with Gomà is that he has no bloody idea where to turn with the Adell case and he's left himself no choice but to hide this fiasco behind whatever he can. Even if it's a child's corpse."

"That's another reason he gives for closing the case," Melchor says. "That he didn't know which way to turn."

"He's fucked us over!" the sergeant complains, even more furious. "If he hadn't shoved us aside from the start, he'd be singing a different tune. But, of course, he had to steal the show, nobody could be involved in the case who might steal his lime-light, and anyway, everyone knows that the Terra Alta force is second-rate, I told Barrera so he would tell him, that Gomà needed more people on the ground, people with a thorough knowledge of Terra Alta to give you and Salom a hand, that sending two guys to Argentina and another two to Romania or wherever it was looked great on the TV news but was only good for spending money and wasting precious time; but you know what Barrera's like, he just does what he's told, that man doesn't want any hassles with anybody, least of all with Tor-tosa. Especially when he's on the brink of retiring. And I'll tell you something else, Marín. I'll bet you anything you want that now Gomà will open the case to me, from now on, for sure, he won't restrict my access to the information and he'll enable my password to allow me to review what you guys have investi-gated, as if saying: 'Here's the shit-heap I've left you, see if you can figure it out, see if you, who railed against me so much, can find anything, that's right, without any resources or people or shit, now that it's all resolved and there's nowhere left to dig.' If he can, he'll try to leave the killings on my books. I bet you anything."

While Sergeant Blai goes on venting, Melchor holds the phone away from his ear a little. As he does so he remembers something that happened a few minutes ago, just after the

176

meeting in Deputy Inspector Gomà's office had finished, and it's this: while he was saying goodbye to Sergeant Pires, she had got close enough to him that for the first time Melchor could read the words of the tattoo on her collarbone: ETERNAL LOVE. Melchor read them over again once, twice, and, when he looked up from the tattoo, he had the impression that the sergeant winked at him.

"Melchor, are you there?" Blai says.

"Yeah," he says, not entirely sure of having experienced the scene he's just recalled.

"Ah, I thought we'd been cut off. Anyway, as I was saying, don't get pissed off. Suck it up, *españolazo*: like it or fucking lump it. Are you still with Salom?" Melchor says yes again. "I'm meeting Corominas and Feliu for lunch. See you in the Terra Alta?"

"I'd rather eat at home. If you don't mind."

"I don't mind," Blai says. "See you tomorrow at the station. And say hi to Olga for me."

Melchor finds a spot in the car park, leaves the car there and walks briskly towards the courthouse, a two-storey building with cream-coloured walls on avenida Joan Perucho, on the outskirts of Gandesa. He bounds up the steps two at a time, between the flowerbeds, and goes in through the front door, under two poles from which wave two flags, one Spanish and one Catalan. It is almost 10 a.m. and in the courthouse lobby, outside the door to the courtroom, a large group of people has gathered, most of them travellers. Melchor waves to a couple of uniformed colleagues, goes up the stairs to the first floor and knocks on the office door of the judge, who hasn't arrived yet. He learns this from the judge's secretary, a woman in her forties – tall and commanding, with a square face and a tenor voice – who knows him well.

"Bad day for surprises, my love," she tells him when Melchor asks if he can speak to her boss. "He's got a case at ten: if you don't catch him before it starts, you can forget about it for the rest of the day."

Melchor thanks her and goes back down to the lobby, where the crowd outside the courtroom has grown; his uniformed colleagues, however, appear to have vanished. After looking for them in vain, he goes outside and waits for the judge, leaning against one of the faux classical columns that hold up the entrance portico, under the flags. He is sure about what he's going to do. Last night, while tossing and turning in bed beside Olga, he still had doubts; this morning, after dropping off Cosette at nursery, he made up his mind while having a coffee at the Pastelería Pujol. "One last try," he thinks. "Nothing to lose," he thinks. "I've already been told no," he also thinks. There are people going into the courthouse, but nobody coming out; the mother of a baby-faced dealer he arrested a few months ago – a young, thin, good-looking woman wearing a print suit – greets him with an arrogant glare. Once in a while, a car drives past along the avenue. Closer to him, in the flowerbeds that run down towards the road, are parallel rows of cypress trees underplanted with the green stems and violet flowers of lavender. To his left, a screen of pines protects a sports field; to his right he can see Gandesa bus station. A few threads of clouds add a white brushstroke to the blue of the sky.

Barely a quarter of an hour has gone by when the judge's black Citroën pulls up into the parking space reserved for courthouse staff and Melchor rushes to open the door for him.

"Thank you, son," says the judge, as he struggles out of his car with Melchor's help. "I'm late, aren't I?"

Without answering the magistrate's question, Melchor says good morning, asks him if he has a moment to spare, reminds him who he is and, while the two of them climb the courthouse steps, tells him as fast as he can that he thinks they're making a mistake with the Adell case, explains that they should keep investigating, asks for his authorisation to search the offices and computers of the Gráficas Adell executives.

The judge stops on the porch; he is panting, and a heavy drop of sweat drips from his temple towards his recently shaved, moisturised and scented cheek.

"Who did you say you are?" he asks Melchor.

Melchor repeats his name and rank. While he catches his breath and mops the sweat off his face with a handkerchief, the judge seems finally to recognise him, and his surprise becomes stern.

"You know that you shouldn't be speaking to me about this, don't you?" he says. "And much less here, at the entrance to the courthouse."

"You're right, your honour," Melchor admits. "I'm sorry. But—"

"No buts about it," the other man stops him, calmly. "What you're doing is totally irregular, and you know it: if your superiors found out, you could be in trouble." Waving the handkerchief towards him, he hurries to put him at ease: "Don't worry, they're not going to find out." Then he goes on: "I am going to close the case, though. It was my decision, not Deputy Inspector Gomà's, although he does agree with me. In any case, if you think I'm wrong, if you think I shouldn't be closing it, follow the proper channels and tell your commanding officer. He's the one who should be speaking to me, not you. You understand, don't you?"

Melchor opens his mouth as if to say something, then shuts it and nods with his gaze fixed on the judge's shoes, shiny and black. At that moment the door opens and the judge's secretary leans out, bearing a sheaf of documents.

"We're running late, your honour," she says. "They're waiting for you."

The judge puts the handkerchief in his trouser pocket and makes as if to follow his secretary. But he does not follow her. Although he is a head shorter than Melchor, he must weigh almost twice as much; he's wearing a well-made dark blue suit with black braces and a neatly pressed white shirt.

"Look, son," he admonishes Melchor, taking hold of his braces with his plump hands. "In our line of work we have to learn to live with frustration. In yours, and in mine and in anyone's. As one of my teachers used to say, that's what civilisation consists of: learning to coexist in a reasonable way with frustration. As for the Adell case, believe me, we're not getting anywhere, so it's reasonable to close it. Later on, who knows, maybe we'll get a lucky break when we least expect it. It wouldn't be the first time. But now the sensible thing is what we've done. No doubt about it. So pay attention, forget about this matter and enjoy your youth. It's not as short as we old guys say it is, but almost."

The secretary leans out of the door again and, with an expression of exasperated disbelief, looks daggers at the judge, mumbling something Melchor can't quite hear. This time the magistrate does follow her.

"I'm coming, I'm coming," he grumbles, walking behind her. "But let's not start the day with a scolding, eh?"

Melchor tries to follow the judge's advice, to forget about the Adell murders as soon as he can and get back to his normal life in Terra Alta. He does not manage it. The case has disappeared from the television, the radio, the newspapers and social media since, a week earlier, a couple of Norwegian tourists found the dismembered body of a five-year-old child on the beach at Riumar in the Ebro delta, not far from Terra Alta, and, although Melchor never fails to show up at the station, works on the cases assigned to him and goes back to writing up reports and taking part in the day-to-day briefings, in group meetings and daily or almost daily patrols with Salom, he is unable to get the deaths of the elderly couple and their Romanian maid out of his head. Luckily, nobody around him notices his obsession, except Olga, who, every time she catches him with a lost look and absent expression on his face, brings him back to reality with their private joke: "How's it going, Javert?"

Until, after a while, Melchor gives in to his own obsession and, despite the case being officially closed, decides to immerse himself in it again, which means immersing himself in an ocean of files and documents that Deputy Inspector Gomà's investigative team gathered during the six weeks of intensive work, a team in which almost forty people collaborated at one time or another, as Sergeant Pires records at the beginning of the report.

Melchor works in his spare time and behind his colleagues' backs. He's aware that these surreptitious incursions leave electronic fingerprints and that any of his superiors could detect that he has continued investigating out of hours and under nobody's orders, which could get him into trouble; but he does not even ask himself whether he is willing to run the risks he's running and deal with the consequences: he simply runs them. He is prudent enough not to phone or visit Ferrer, because he's sure that he would tell Salom. Nor does he return to Gráficas Adell to interview Grau, Silva, Botet or Arjona, but one night he makes a rash phone call to the old manager to ask him two questions. The first is vague: what does he remember about the dinner on the Friday evening before the Adells were murdered? The second is concrete, and it is whether he thinks any of the managers of Gráficas Adell might be involved in the crime. Grau replies to the first question that he doesn't remember anything in particular, that it was in every way a normal dinner, like so many they'd had over the years on Friday nights at the Adells' house, without anything exceptional happening to distinguish it from any of the others. He receives the second question with a harsh and crafty guffaw.

"If they could have killed Paco without anyone finding out, pushing a button, for example, any of them would have done it," he says. "You can be sure of that. But, since it's impossible, the answer is that none of them has what it would take to do something like that. Well, not none. There's one who would have been capable of doing it."

"Who?"

"Me."

That night Melchor hangs up the phone convinced that it is impossible that Grau is implicated in the murder of Adell, because no murderer would point himself out as a murderer, much less to a police officer. The conviction does not last long, because he immediately understands that pointing to oneself as the murderer, and especially to a police officer, could be the safest protection against suspicion, the best way to remove any suspicion.

Days later, a chance encounter confirms his intuition. It happens at nine in the morning, just after he's dropped Cosette off at the nursery and is heading to the Terra Alta where he's arranged to meet Salom for coffee on their way to the Móra d'Ebre police station. As he drives past the bus station, he recognises Albert Ferrer's Porsche Panamera in the car park.

Indecisive, he doesn't stop, but when he gets to the Hotel Piqué he turns around, goes back and parks next to the sports car. He walks into the station café and immediately sees Rosa Adell sitting beside a big window that overlooks the road, typing on a mobile phone. In front of her are a cup of tea and a glass vase with a plastic fuchsia wrapped in a piece of tulle. Melchor goes over to her; she stops typing and looks up from the screen. At first she doesn't seem to recognise him, but then she smiles weakly and says hello.

"May I sit down?" Melchor asks.

"Please do," Rosa Adell says, gesturing towards a chair opposite her. "I was just about to leave."

Melchor orders a coffee while Rosa finishes typing on her mobile.

"I hope I'm not bothering you, ma'am," he says.

"You're not bothering me," she says as she pours the rest of the tea in the teapot into her cup. "As long as you stop calling me 'ma'am'. I'm not even that old."

"I wasn't calling you 'ma'am' because you're older than me," he hurries to apologise. "It's just a habit."

"A bad habit." While she sips her tea, she watches him over the rim of her cup and Melchor catches an ironic glint in her large oval eyes. "Albert told me you're married to Olga Ribera. Did you know she and I were friends?" Melchor says yes; Rosa lowers her cup and looks straight at him, all irony gone. "We went to school together. We got along really well. Then . . . anyway, you know how these things go: you grow up, live your life, lose sight of people. I haven't seen Olga for ages. Is she well? I heard the two of you have a son."

"A daughter," says Melchor. "Her name's Cosette."

"Cosette? That's a French name, isn't it?"

Melchor nods but doesn't enlarge on the origin of the name

because the waitress arrives with his coffee. While Rosa speaks with her for a moment, Melchor observes the Adells' daughter. She barely seems to be the same person he met almost two months ago in her husband's studio, and Melchor thinks that this new look, fresher, younger and more cheerful than before, is not just the work of the time that has passed since the murder of her parents; now colour enhances her lips, her eyelashes, her cheeks, and her attire no longer consists of greys and mourning black: she's wearing a white, short-sleeved, silk blouse, marked only by a small black brooch like a last splinter of mourning. A light summer jacket and a handbag hang on the back of her chair; in her ears are two natural pearls.

"Your husband's not here?" Melchor asks, once the two of them are alone again. "I saw his car outside."

"I'm picking him up in Barcelona," Rosa says. "He's arriving tonight from Mexico. I'm going to run a few errands while I'm there and have lunch with my daughters." She points to her mobile phone on the table, motionless like a sleeping reptile. "I was just writing to my youngest when you came in. Anyway, I'm trying to distract myself a little."

"I understand." He is assailed by a sudden urge to let her know he's not just saying that, he truly understands, that he thinks he knows how she feels or something very similar to how she feels, that his mother was also murdered and her murderers went unpunished. But the urge vanishes almost immediately, or maybe Melchor stifles it. He hears himself ask: "Can I ask you a question?"

She looks at him with interest.

"It's about the last time you saw your parents," he says. "About dinner that Friday at their house, with your husband and Señor Grau and the rest of them. I'd like to know how you remember that night. Señor Grau says it was just like any

184

other Friday night and he doesn't remember anything out of the ordinary, and none of the other senior staff told me anything about it, though I didn't really insist either. It's just that recently I've been thinking that maybe we didn't take it as seriously as we should have. Do you remember anything that made it stand out?"

Rosa Adell studies him, no longer with interest but with disappointment. She looks away and then around the room, a space full of white tables surrounded by white and fuchsia chairs where tourists are sitting in couples wearing shorts and summer T-shirts. On the back wall, a screen announces the departures of buses to Barcelona, Tarragona, Tortosa and the towns of Terra Alta; under the screen there is a display case full of bottles of Terra Alta wine and a sketch of Audrey Hepburn. When she looks at him again, the disappointment in her eyes has turned to sorrow.

"I thought you'd closed the investigation," she says.

"It is closed," Melchor admits. "But we shouldn't have closed it. I think that—"

"Salom told us you couldn't go any further, that you'd hit a brick wall," she stops him, looking down at the vase with the plastic fuchsia. "He said you didn't know how to continue, and that you were going to leave it. And do you know what?" She looks up at him again. "Maybe it's for the best. The longer the investigation is open, the longer the suffering. Now at least the journalists have left us alone, and as a family we're starting to recover our peace of mind. We've earned that at least."

"I would have preferred justice to be done."

"And you think I wouldn't?" she says, leaning her face close to Melchor's, who only then notices a detail: the black brooch that mars the immaculate white of her blouse is a miniature eagle with outstretched wings, the Gráficas Adell logo. "But, what do you want me to do? Demand you carry on when you don't know where to look? Hire a private detective? Don't think I haven't thought of that, but Salom convinced me it would be no use. If you lot haven't got anywhere, no private detective is going to: after all, you people know Terra Alta better than anyone and you've got more resources than anyone. Besides, justice is not going to bring back my parents. Or save them from . . .”

She does not finish the phrase, but purses her lips and leans away from the table, lowering her gaze again to the plastic flower. Fearing she might burst into tears, Melchor feels a temptation to take her hand, but he does not give in to it.

“Sorry,” Rosa Adell apologises, forcing a smile.

“No, I'm sorry,” says Melchor.

This double apology generates an unexpectedly comfortable silence, during which the Gráficas Adell logo pinned to the company heiress' blouse hooks his attention again.

“There is one thing that intrigues me,” Melchor says, when she seems to have regained her composure. “Don't worry, it's nothing to do with your parents.”

The smile has not disappeared from Rosa's lips.

“Why didn't you want to work at Gráficas Adell? You've known the business for ever, your father would have liked it if you ran it, you're an economist, like your husband . . .”

“That's precisely why I didn't want to,” she says. “Too many economists in the house, too many people working at the company. I didn't want to work with my father and Albert. Besides, I wanted to raise my family. I realise there are people who don't understand that, but I don't care. I've known since I was a little girl that I'm privileged, and as an adult I've wanted my daughters to enjoy that privilege. I don't regret it. Although maybe from here on in things need to change.”

“In what way?”

186

"I'll probably have to get more involved in the company's affairs, now that my father's not here and my daughters don't need me as much as they did. I don't know. We'll see."

Rosa Adell is silent for a moment. Melchor watches her, wondering how it's possible that a woman like her could have fallen in love with a man like Albert Ferrer, and noticing a knot in his stomach as he remembers that Ferrer fools around behind her back; since he married Olga he has stopped covertly beating up men who mistreat women, but he wonders nevertheless if Ferrer has ever beaten his wife. The woman sighs after looking at her watch: "Well, I have to get going."

Melchor stands up too, lets her pay for his coffee and the two of them walk outside, where a dry and windless morning announces a stifling day in Terra Alta. Standing beside her husband's Porsche, with her jacket under her arm, Rosa Adell digs around in her handbag while a bus parks behind her, in one of the station bays, and he senses that she is not done with their encounter. Finally, she pulls out the car keys and a pair of very large sunglasses with white frames; she puts the glasses on, as if sheltering behind them, and, when she looks back at Melchor, he recognises himself in the black of the lenses.

"Señor Grau is right: it was a regular Friday night dinner," Rosa Adell says, answering the postponed question. "It was my father's custom, I suppose you've been told. We always had dinner at their house on Fridays, he and his closest associates, my mother and me. But I was not included in those meetings until I turned fifteen: before that I wasn't allowed, and I longed to know what they talked about there." She falls silent; her fingers toy with the automatic car key. "I don't know, the only difference between that dinner and the rest of them was that Albert and I were the first to leave."

"That wasn't normal?"

"No. We usually stayed until everyone except Señor Grau had left, chatting for a while with my parents, commenting on the dinner, having a whisky, talking about the girls, whatever. I don't know what happened that night to make us leave so early. Maybe Albert was feeling nervous; before my parents' death he went through a rough patch."

"Do you know why?"

"No. Work, I guess."

"I was told that these dinners served to take stock of the week," Melchor says, trying to spur her memory. "Is that what you talked about that day?"

"More or less. But it was they who did the stock-taking, the ones who had important positions in the company – my mother and I barely took part. But yes, that's what they did, the same thing every Friday. Talk and argue."

"What did they argue about? Who argued?"

"All of them, but most of all my father and Señor Grau. They were always the ones who ruled the roost. You'll have heard this too. They'd known each other their whole lives and every time I saw them together they were arguing. Always. Sometimes, if things got too heated, someone might try to mediate between them. I remember Albert trying a few times when he first started working at the company. I told him not to, that it was the way my father and Señor Grau related to each other, that's how they worked. In the end he stopped as it was impossible, everyone eventually gave it up as impossible. It was like trying to mediate in a cockfight."

"Do you mean they were violent arguments?"

"Violent?" Her lips stretched into a tenuous smile again. "No! They were fantastic. When I started to go to those dinners, as a teenager, I believed those arguments weren't serious, that my father and Señor Grau argued to amuse themselves, or rather to amuse the rest of us. And it's probably true, but that's how they always made important decisions: arguing till they were exhausted."

"What were they arguing about that night?"

"Lots of things, especially what they were always arguing about at around that time, I think: the Mexican subsidiary. My father had been toying with the idea of closing it for months, it had started to lose money recently, but Señor Grau thought it would be a mistake and had managed to convince everyone else that it would be a mistake and that they had to carry on . . ." She pauses. "Well," she corrects herself, "all except Albert."

"Is that unusual?" Melchor asks.

Rosa Adell takes a few seconds to answer; the station's public address system announces the departure of a bus for Tarragona.

"No," she says. "I don't think so. It's just that, on that subject Albert had always been on Señor Grau's side, and had always opposed closing the factory in Puebla, in fact Señor Grau relied on Albert because he travels there often and knows it well . . . But that night Albert took my father's side against Señor Grau. I think it was the first time, and that's why I was surprised. Of course, Albert had just been in Mexico and had surely realised that my father was right and that it would be best to close the factory. I don't know. You should ask him."

"Do you think that argument had something to do with your husband's nervousness, I mean the rough time he was going through before your parents' deaths, or with your leaving early that night? Do you remember if Albert was angry when you left? Did he say anything on the way home?"

"No. I don't know. To be honest, I don't remember. Is it important?"

"It might be. But let me ask you something else: do you remember if anyone left the table during dinner and was out of the dining room for longer than usual? To speak on the phone, go to the bathroom . . ."

Before Melchor runs out of conjectures, Rosa Adell stops playing with the car keys, takes off her sunglasses and breaks into a bright smile.

"OK, that question I certainly can answer," she says. "I don't know anyone who goes to the bathroom as often as Señor Grau."

"I didn't notice that when I was at his office with him."

"That's because he wasn't drinking. As soon as he starts, the parade begins. As long as I can remember he's had trouble with his prostate, my father always made fun of him, said that's why he was still a bachelor: because all the women he took out to dinner ended up thinking he had something wrong with him. He was always mocking Señor Grau, but he loved him dearly, he was his life-long pal . . . Hey, why did we end up talking about this? Oh, yeah." Rosa puts her sunglasses back on and Melchor again sees a dark reflection of himself in the opacity of the lenses. "Anyway, you're going to have to excuse me. It really is time for me to get going. I'm very glad to have seen you again. Will you say hello to Olga for me?"

"I have to ask you something, Salom," Melchor says.

"What's that?" Salom says.

"I need you to get me a key to the Gráficas Adell offices. I'm going in."

They've just left Gandesa and are driving along the El Pinell de Brai road, with the green and brown massif of the Cavalls Sierra on their left, covered in wind turbines, their blades spinning in a calm rhythm. It is nine in the morning, the sun is shining and the sky is an intense, almost metallic blue. The car's air conditioning is not working, so Salom has rolled down his window and a breeze that has not yet entirely lost its night-time coolness ruffles his hair and even stirs his beard a little. The corporal exchanges a look with Melchor.

"Have you gone crazy or what?"

"I just want to have a look around. Nothing more."

"You're an idiot," Salom blurts out, turning back to watch the road. "Do you know what could happen if they catch you? Disciplinary proceedings, at the very least. You might get sacked."

"They're not going to catch me," he says. "There are no security cameras in the offices. No alarms. I saw the day we were there. To get in I just need one key."

"Not from me, Melchor."

"I'm not asking you to come with me," he says. "Just get me a key. A master key would be best. Ferrer must have one."

Salom shakes his head as they meet a truck carrying household appliances, followed very closely by a delivery van, and the corporal is forced to move over, because the road is narrow and has no hard shoulder.

"Damn it," he says, once he's completed the manoeuvre, pounding the steering wheel with an irritated fist. "Why this bullshit now? When are you going to get your head together? You have a wife and a daughter. You're almost thirty. You can't go around being a smart-arse. Christ, you're not a kid anymore. Have you told Olga what you're thinking of doing?"

Salom closes the window, as if the wind were bothering him, and the racket in the moving car is suddenly reduced to a background buzz.

"Are you going to help me or not?"

"The case is closed," Salom says. "Why do you want to keep sticking your nose in?"

"Because it's not closed. You and I know when a case is closed, and this one is not. That's why I want to keep going. Because of that and because I don't want to carry this inside me."

"What?"

"This feeling that I didn't do all that I could to solve it," Melchor says, his fist clenched over the pit of his stomach. Then he explains: "A few days ago I ran into Rosa Adell. We were talking about the last night she saw her parents, dinner on the Friday with the company people. Apparently her father and Grau were arguing."

"Those two old guys spent their whole lives arguing," Salom says. "You're only just discovering this?"

"They were arguing about the Mexican subsidiary," Melchor says, paying no attention to the corporal. "They were talking about possibly closing it. It seems that was a long-standing issue. Grau was in favour of keeping it open. Adell was against it. Everyone else supported Grau, except Ferrer, who that evening had changed his mind."

"And?"

"I don't know," Melchor admits. "But it was an important matter, it's possible it was making Ferrer very anxious. Don't you think it's strange that nobody told us about it? I do. I want to know what it's about, why nobody mentioned it. Call it a hunch. And don't forget the fact that someone who was at that dinner could have switched off the security cameras and alarms. Grau, for instance. He knows the house very well and that night he got up to go to the bathroom a lot. He's got prostate trouble."

"Anyone could have switched off the security cameras and alarms, starting with the Romanian maid. What was her name?"

192

"Arba. Jenica Arba."

"That's it. As for Grau, I'm not saying you couldn't be right. If we rule out the robbery hypothesis, he would still be my prime suspect. The problem is we don't have a single piece of evidence against him. Not one. Hunches don't count."

"That's why I want to get into his office, to find the proof we need. If I don't find it, I'll look in the other offices."

"And if you don't find it there either?"

"Then it's over. Full stop. I'll leave it. This is my final attempt: if it doesn't work, I'll forget about it for good. I promise. What do you say, are you going to help me or not?"

"No way."

"Please, Salom. Think it over."

"There's nothing to think over."

"I'm begging you. You don't have to answer now. But think about it, OK? That's all I'm asking."

"Here it is," Salom says, a few days later, handing him a small, silver-plated key with a rectangular head and smooth blade. "This opens all the doors in Gráficas Adell, except for the one to the courtyard."

"Don't worry," Melchor says. "The fence is low. I won't have any trouble getting over it."

Salom also gives him a laminated card with Albert Ferrer's name on it with a passport-sized photograph of its owner and two words – MANAGING DIRECTOR – stamped on it.

"And this gets you through the entrance barrier, the lobby and into the computers," Salom says. "It works for all of them: as soon as they boot up they're connected to the company's network. I don't have the passwords for the emails, but it doesn't matter, these people are so obsessed with online piracy they change their passwords every week, so they must have them written down somewhere, because it's impossible to remember them. I'm sure you'll find them on a Post-it or something like that. What else?"

"How did you get all this?" Melchor asks.

"It's better you don't know. Oh yeah, one more thing. You were right: there are no alarms or cameras. Although there is a security guard. He's more concerned with the factory than the offices, but you should be careful anyway, especially on your way in. I think that's all. Well, not all. If you get caught, I don't know anything about this crazy plan of yours. I guess you understand that."

"Of course," Melchor says, "but don't worry: nothing will happen."

"I hope not," says Salom. "You owe me another one. How many's that now?"

Melchor parks several blocks away from Gráficas Adell, between two transport trailers, and walks swiftly towards the factory. It is the dead of night, and La Plana Parc industrial estate is deserted and almost completely dark, because, even though a moon like a big silver coin is shining in the sky, its brilliance doesn't make up for the lack of street lighting. The air is warm and heavy – velvety – and every once in a while a breath of wind brings a pungent scent of shrubs and dry earth.

Melchor walks up a long, paved avenue lined with pine trees and, when the premises of Gráficas Adell appear on his left, crouches behind the stone wall that surrounds it, outside the metal fence. He hasn't seen anybody up till then, but for a few seconds he inspects the surrounding area in the midst of a silence broken only by a distant and unidentifiable thrumming,

194

like a generator. When he's made sure there's nobody in sight, he clears the wall and then the fence, lands in the paved courtyard and runs bent over to the wall of a warehouse. Right up against it, protected from the moonlight by its shadow, he makes for the octagonal building where the offices are, passing close to the monolith on which the company logo and name are engraved in stone. Leaving the car park to his right (the metallic structure of which in the dark for a second reminds him of a hollow dinosaur skeleton), he walks up the front steps and with no difficulty at all opens the door with the master key. He crosses the dark lobby, opens the automatic barrier with Albert Ferrer's laminated card, goes through and, when he arrives at the dense darkness of the stairwell, activates the torch on his phone. Shining the cone of light ahead of him, he climbs the stairs to the first floor, turns to the left and carries on down the hallway to where it widens out. In front of him are the two doors. He opens the one to Grau's reception area, also with the master key, then goes into the office and locks himself in.

Flooded by the grey moonlight that filters in through the large windows, Grau's office seems smaller and more crowded than he remembered, conjuring up the subaqueous gloom of an aquarium. Melchor takes a few deep breaths and, spurred on by the adrenalin of his clandestine adventure, gets down to work.

First he looks through the papers on the desk, around the computer and in the drawers; next he explores the contents of the two filing cabinets he doesn't remember from his first visit, perhaps because they weren't there then or more probably because he didn't see them, tucked away in a corner. He proceeds unhurriedly, with extreme care, turning on his phone's torch only when it's essential and making sure he can't be seen through the windows. This initial search reveals nothing – none of the files that he sees refer to the overseas affiliates of Gráficas

Adell, or to the one in Puebla, the one he's most interested in – except for a small notebook with a brown cover where a list of passwords has been written in extremely small handwriting, all crossed out except for the last, which Melchor deduces must be the current one.

To check, he sits back down at the desk, in front of the computer, a new iMac, and turns it on by sliding Albert Ferrer's card into the slot on the side. A second later the company's homepage appears on the screen, with the name in black and red letters, and, in close-up, an image of two little cakes topped with walnuts, almonds, raisins and crystallised fruit, both packed in brown cardboard containers, one in the shape of a tray and the other like a doily. PACKAGING TO SERVE MODERN INDUSTRY, runs the slogan across the page in large letters. At the top of the screen are several tabs. He clicks on the one that says DIRECTORY; once in the directory he clicks on IDENTIFICATION, and instantly at the centre of the screen appears a password prompt. Melchor shines his torch onto the last password in the brown notebook, types it in and Grau's email in-box immediately appears.

It contains a thousand messages, the last one from just a few hours earlier, the first from four months ago. Wondering if he could do in a single night all that he's set out to do, he selects the messages originating in Mexico, which are the ones ending in the letters *mx*; to his relief, there are only forty-six. He begins to read them, starting with the latest, but he hasn't even read five of them when he thinks he hears a noise. He stops reading, stays perfectly still and listens attentively. After a few seconds, during which he hears nothing or hears only silence, he goes back to reading the messages, sure that he has heard no sound, that he just imagined it. They are mostly messages from the manager to the administrator of the Puebla factory, although

196

there are also some from the personnel manager and a couple from section chiefs, the majority of them conventional or anodyne messages or responses to very specific questions from Grau. He reads some of them from top to bottom, others he skims, others he barely reads and dismisses in an instant.

He still has a few messages to go when again he thinks he hears a noise, this time more clearly, a noise like the scrape of a hinge in need of oiling or like a deep creak of wood or bones. Melchor stops reading, holds his breath and listens, but soon convinces himself that his imagination is playing tricks on him and goes back to the emails. Minutes later, after finishing the last message, he switches off the computer by taking the card out of the slot and closes it. He is about to stand up when the office door suddenly opens and, almost at the same moment, he is dazzled by the beams of several ceiling spots, like a multiple searchlight pointing at him. The doorway does not frame Josep Grau, but Albert Ferrer.

"What are you doing here?" he asks.

2

Two weeks after the Islamist attacks in Barcelona and Cambrils, Melchor arrived at the Terra Alta police station after driving down the Mediterranean Motorway, then a main road which snaked between mountains and forests and finally along a back road that went down to the Ebro, crossed the river at Móra d'Ebre and entered Terra Alta, between rocky hills, deep ravines, bare cliffs and vineyards, plantations of almonds, olives, pines and fruit trees. It was his first time in the region, and, although it was just a two and a half hours' drive from Barcelona, the abrupt, barren, inhospitable, wild and isolated territory that spread out in the south of Catalonia, right at the border with Aragon, seemed to him like the ends of the earth. He did know that eighty years earlier, towards the end of the Civil War, it had been the site of the bloodiest battle in the history of Spain. He didn't regret his decision. He had always been an urbanite, allergic to the countryside, but the idea of getting away from the city until the turmoil around him and his role in the terrorist attacks died down appealed to him, and he had arrived at the conclusion that some time away from Barcelona was necessary, if not for his personal safety (as everyone seemed to think), then at least to preserve his sanity. As for the rest, his brain kept repeating the same sentence from *Les Misérables* that had been running through his head since he had killed four terrorists on the Cambrils boardwalk: "He is a man who does kindness by musket shots."

The station building was a brand-new, two-storey cube, with solid grey walls interrupted by large picture windows, that stood in the middle of an open space, on the outskirts of Gandesa. The duty officer observed Melchor with curiosity from behind the bullet-proof screen of the front desk and asked him if he was the new guy. He nodded.

"They're expecting you."

Following the man's instructions, he walked up a corridor with wood panelling on the walls until the left wall became an enormous window overlooking an interior courtyard, illuminating the entire building with bright daylight. At the end of the corridor he climbed some stairs, knocked on a door and waited. To his right was another door, which led to a small room, not much bigger than a phone booth; on his left he saw a more spacious office, occupied at that moment by two men and a woman. It was unusually quiet and still, unusual at least for Melchor, accustomed to the boisterous hustle and bustle of the Nou Barris station. A sign fixed to the wall declared: SGT BLAI. CHIEF OF THE INVESTIGATIONS UNIT. He knocked again and this time heard:

"Come in!"

Sergeant Blai made no move to stand up when Melchor opened the door: he merely raised his eyebrows without hiding his displeasure as the newcomer introduced himself. Until, suddenly, it dawned on him.

"Damn it!" he exclaimed. "Melchor Marín? Shit, of course, come in, come in."

Sergeant Blai shook his hand firmly, offered him a chair and sat back down while clearing away some of the chaos of papers on his desk, then picked up a yellow cardboard cup, half full of coffee.

"Sorry," he said. "Commissioner Fuster called me the day before yesterday to tell me you'd be arriving this morning, but it slipped my mind." Once the first moment of confusion had passed, the sergeant sprawled back in his armchair, smiled showing a healthy set of teeth and, almost as if he and Melchor were old friends, said: "So, tell me, how does it feel to be a hero?"

Melchor stared at him, not knowing what to say.

"Come on, come on, kid," Blai encouraged him. "Don't be modest. We're all proud of you, the truth is I still don't know how you managed to bring down four guys all in one go. And four of those . . . Do you know how many lives you may have saved?"

The sergeant went on and on about what he called his heroic deed. As soon as he got a chance, Melchor asked how many people in the station knew who he was and why he'd been posted there.

"Only me and Deputy Inspector Barrera," Blai assured him. "The deputy inspector is the boss. Fuster wanted him to be the only one who knew, but since he's on holiday he decided to tell me as well. Nobody else is going to find out, if that's what you're worried about. I only told your workmates that you're being sent as reinforcement for a few months, because of the pro-independence process and stuff. You worked at the Nou Barris station, didn't you?"

Melchor nodded.

"I'll tell you first off that this place is as much like Nou Barris as an egg is like a chestnut. A thousand times better here, of course, starting with the women. You're not married, are you?

200

Much better. I'll just tell you that I arrived a bachelor and now I'm married. It's a shame we can't say who you are, because you'd drive them all crazy."

The sun was pouring in through a window that overlooked a patch of wasteland where the town ended, and beyond which the Pàndols mountains stood out against the immaculate morning sky, bristling with white metal wind turbines, their blades spinning. To the left of the sergeant, a corkboard on the wall displayed notes, reminders and announcements; in one corner, a very prominently displayed, a sticker of the Catalan independence flag proclaimed: CATALONIA IS NOT SPAIN. Sergeant Blai stopped talking, turned to look at the sticker and then back at Melchor.

"What are you looking at?" he asked with a mischievous smile. "The flag?"

Melchor didn't answer. The sergeant's voice filled with irony.

"You wouldn't be an *españolazo*, would you?"

This time Melchor felt obliged to answer.

"I don't understand politics," he said.

"Yeah," Sergeant Blai said, slightly sarcastically. "Well, I have a theory, you know? And I think anyone who says they're neither pro-independence nor pro-Spain is pro-Spain. And that anyone who says they don't understand politics is a fucking *españolazo*. What do you reckon?"

Melchor shrugged. Blai scrutinised his reaction without his smile fading and, after rubbing his hand over his shaved head, he rapped the desk with his knuckles and gulped down the rest of his coffee.

"Come with me," he said, standing up. "I'm going to introduce you to the gang."

They walked into the office next door. The three people

Melchor had seen from the corridor while waiting to go into the sergeant's office were still there. The sergeant made the introductions, presenting Melchor as a new member of the group and Feliu and Corominas as forensics officers.

"Though here we all do everything," Blai warned him. "Like I said, this isn't Nou Barris."

"You've come from Nou Barris?" the third officer asked.

"You were there, weren't you?" Sergeant Blai said.

"Centuries ago," he answered. "I'm sure there's nobody left from my days."

He mentioned a couple of names, which Melchor had never heard, and Sergeant Blai took him by the shoulder.

"And this is Ernest Salom," he said. "Your corporal. He'll tell you how we work. There are two more guys in your unit: Martínez and Sirvent. Then there's another unit . . . Hey, Salom, why don't you tell him and show him around the station at the same time?"

It was an order disguised as a question. Before the corporal could answer, Sergeant Blai claimed he had something he had to do and said as he left:

"Welcome to Terra Alta, kid."

"Did you catch him sleeping?" Feliu asked, as soon as the sergeant left the office.

"Don't worry," Corominas said. "Blai spends his mornings dozing."

"And his nights screwing," Feliu said.

"As soon as the daily briefing's over, he's out like a light. Exhausted from so much sex."

"Mind you," Feliu clarified. "He only screws his wife."

"Ugh!" Corominas exclaimed, his face contorted in disgust.

202

"Has he no shame? Isn't incest a crime? Someone should arrest those two for incest."

"Don't pay any attention to these brainless morons," Salom interrupted. "Blai is a first-class professional and a great guy."

"As you see, our dear corporal is a creep," Corominas said. "In any case, he's right about one thing: Blai's a good guy. Not like us."

"That's the most sensible thing I've heard you say all year," Salom said. "And, by the way, shouldn't you two be at the cooperative by now?"

Salom, Feliu and Corominas talked for a couple of minutes about the report from a wine-making cooperative in El Pinell de Brai. Before they left, Corominas advised Melchor to look for a flat in Gandesa.

"Listen to what Coro says," Feliu agreed. "If I could, I'd move right now. I've had it up to here driving back and forth from Tortosa every day."

"They're right," Salom said, once he and Melchor were on their own. "I don't know how long you're going to stay here, but in Gandesa everything will be more convenient for you. Do you have somewhere to sleep tonight? If you want, you can stay at my place. I live alone."

"Thanks," Melchor answered. "I reserved a room in the Hotel Piqué."

"Well, whatever you like." The corporal wrote something down on a piece of paper and handed it to him. "That's the address of an estate agent. Tell them I sent you. They know me there."

He told him he'd been born in Gandesa and his whole family was from there, and then he expanded on details Melchor already knew because Commissioner Fuster had beaten him to it: that the station did not just take care of the region of Terra

Alta, for example, but also that of Ribera d'Ebre, that there was a precinct station in Móra d'Ebre and that theirs was in turn subordinate to the regional station, with its headquarters in Tortosa. He also told him things he didn't know: that the Investigations Unit, under the command of Sergeant Blai, had a total of eleven officers at its disposal, and was divided into two teams, each under the command of a corporal.

"We work shifts," he explained. "This week we're on mornings, from seven to three. Next week we'll do evenings, from three to eleven. And everyone has to take a turn on the night shift, of course."

Melchor asked a few questions: very few and all of them succinct; Salom answered with equal brevity. Then he assigned him one of the desks and told him he'd have to share it with another officer; he'd also have to share the computer.

"I don't know what things are like in Nou Barris, but out here we're dirt poor," he said. "Both inside the station and outside. Especially outside. Anyway, let's take a walk around. I'll show you what there is."

Salom showed him the rooms and offices upstairs and introduced him to any officers, commanders and clerks whose paths they crossed. On the ground floor, he opened the meeting room, the cloakroom and, while they were in the lunchroom – a space with tables, several vending machines, two fridges, a sink and a microwave – he warned him: "Start getting used to the idea that this isn't Barcelona. How many detectives did you work with in Nou Barris? Fifty, sixty?"

"Something like that," Melchor said.

"That's how many work here in the whole station. Tell me something else: how many people would you usually arrest on a weekend? Fifteen, twenty?"

"More or less," Melchor said.

"Well, that is more or less the number of people we arrest in a whole year. And I'm sure in Nou Barris you had ten or twelve violent robberies every day, if not more, while here we don't even get that many in a very bad year. I bet you can't guess how many people with criminal records we know the whereabouts of in all of Terra Alta?" Melchor remained silent. "Not even a hundred. How many do you have there? Two thousand?" Salom started walking again. "Anyway, this is no spa, though it does seem quite a bit like one. We also have fewer resources than other places, of course, but . . ."

The conjunction hung in the air, resonating in the empty stairwell they were taking to the basement.

"The fact of the matter is that we live pretty well here," the corporal continued. "Our salaries go a bit further. Of course, that doesn't mean we're not poor, especially if you're like me, with two daughters at university. Then you realise what it means to work for the police in this country. How badly they treat us, how they grind us down. Yeah, of course, when things get ugly they turn to us to protect them and expect us to risk our lives for them. Meanwhile, they consider us scum, pay us a pittance, humiliate us. If they could, they'd keep us hidden, because they're ashamed of us. God, it makes me sick. When I think about these things it makes me want to quit the force, it really does. But, anyway, at least here in Terra Alta you'll be a bit better off than in Barcelona, especially if you live alone."

They had a look at the storeroom where they kept anti-riot gear and evidence for cases currently under investigation; they also went into the garage, which was empty of patrol cars at that moment.

"Tell me," Salom said, opening the metal door, "where have you seen a station with natural light even in the cells?"

There were five cells – one for minors or women and four for men – and they were indeed lit with sunlight, just like the entrance and the custody suite, where people they arrested were searched and identified ("Don't tell me that, compared to Nou Barris, this isn't a fucking luxury hotel," Salom said). There was not a single prisoner in any of the cells or the review area, and everything smelled of disinfectant.

They went back up to the ground floor.

"Take a couple of days to settle in," Salom said. "And when you fancy it I'll invite you over for dinner. I'm a good cook."

While he walked him to the exit, the corporal told him where he'd been posted after he'd worked at Nou Barris – Palamós, la Seu d'Urgell – and mentioned that for years he'd worked in forensics. In the end he had returned to Terra Alta.

"Blai told us you're here temporarily," he said to Melchor as he shook his hand in the foyer. "Doesn't matter, you'll have time to get bored, you'll see. Nothing ever happens here."

That first night, in his room at the Hotel Piqué, Melchor didn't sleep a wink. Nor did he sleep the next night, in a rented flat on the outskirts of Gandesa on the road to Bot. That was where he realised, as he tossed and turned in bed, exasperated by a second consecutive sleepless night, that what was preventing him from sleeping was the same thing that kept him from sleeping when he stayed with Carmen Lucas, in El Llano de Molina: the silence, that absence of noise. Except on windy nights, when gusts from the north furiously lashed the region and alleviated that supernatural quiet (allowing him to get to sleep), during the following weeks Melchor fought the insomnia with some heavy sleeping pills that left him at times in an almost catatonic state, aggravated by a certain sensation of unreality. It was not an unjustified sensation: after all, everything in Terra Alta was new and strange to him. This didn't trouble him; or maybe it did, but, since he knew the troublesome feeling was temporary, he tried to enjoy it.

He found it hard to adapt to some things. In Barcelona none of his neighbours knew he was a policeman, and he barely nodded to most of them; as soon as he moved to Terra Alta, however, everyone started saying good morning, good afternoon and good evening, and after a few weeks, every single one of his neighbours knew what he did for a living. In Barcelona he went everywhere with his standard-issue pistol, a 9 mm Walter P99, in his shoulder holster; in Terra Alta, however, the pistol seemed superfluous, and he also soon realised it was very difficult to go unnoticed with it, that no matter how he tried to hide it, it caught people's attention everywhere he went, so he decided to imitate his colleagues and only carry his pistol when he was on duty. Of course, he felt observed, insecure and vulnerable without the protection of his anonymity and his weapon, but, as soon as he got used to doing without them both, he understood that this time away from Barcelona could be more than the conventional holiday he'd imagined, more of a holiday from himself, and he believed he understood Jean Valjean's fleeting happiness when, at the beginning of *Les Misérables*, he changed his place of residence, left behind his ignominious convict past and began a new life as a new man, endowed with a new identity: Monsieur Madeleine. He only kept in touch with two people from his former life: Domingo Vivales, who called him every once in a while to make sure everything was under control, and Carmen Lucas, who e-mailed him about his mother and about her life with Pepe in El Llano de Molina.

Nevertheless, what chiefly transformed his life once he arrived in Terra Alta was that he'd never had so much time to himself. He only worked in the mornings or the afternoons and since he no longer had to spend his spare time investigating his mother's murder, the rest of the day was his own. He had no trouble filling the hours of leisure time that opened up before him each day. When he worked on the afternoon shift, he woke up early and went for a run at sunrise, following a trail that zigzagged gently up a hillside, passing isolated farmhouses, stands of pines and oaks, rosemary and lavender bushes, until it reached a summit that overlooked Gandesa, with its houses crowded round the church steeple and the jagged profile of the Pàndols mountain range behind it, dotted with wind turbines. At this spot he turned around and followed the same trail back down. When he got home, he took a shower, had breakfast and stretched out on the sofa to read. He usually stayed there until noon. Around about then he went to the plaza and sat on the patio of the bar, where he'd order a Coca-Cola and drink it while he went on reading – always a book, never the newspaper: he wasn't interested in newspapers. At one or one-thirty he'd order another Coke and something to eat, normally a steak and salad, and, after drinking two consecutive coffees, he paid and went to the station, where he arrived punctually at three.

That was his morning routine when he worked the late shift. When he worked the morning shift, he kept up the routine, but with slight variations: since he couldn't run at dawn, he ran at dusk (but the route was always the same); since he couldn't have lunch in the bar in the town plaza, he had dinner there (but the menu was always the same); since he couldn't read in the morning, he read in the evening, but his reading didn't change – the novels he'd brought with him from Barcelona. Melchor also adapted to the habits of the station without any trouble, after all they weren't much different from any other station: the daily briefing, team meetings, writing up reports, going out on patrol. Thanks to driving back and forth among the villages of the region – from Arnes to Vilalba dels Arcs, from Bot to Prat de Comte, from Corbera d'Ebre to Horta de Sant Joan – he began to familiarise himself with the geography of Terra Alta and with the informers, crooks, dealers and scammers who lived there.

As for his co-workers, he almost immediately felt that they formed a more compact nucleus than those in Nou Barris, where everyone pretty much kept to themselves. The feeling proved to be correct, as was demonstrated by the fact that the team didn't even split in the days before and after the independence referendum of October 1, shortly after his arrival in Terra Alta, when the Constitutional Tribunal halted the referendum, the judges ordered the Mossos d'Esquadra to prevent the voting and, pressured by the pro-independence politicians in the Catalan government who had called the illegal plebiscite, the force's commanders gave their officers veiled instructions not to obey the judges, or not too much, or not entirely. This discrepancy between the judiciary's explicit orders and the commanders' implicit orders caused tension in almost every station of the corps; Terra Alta was no exception. The one who suffered most in the Investigations Unit was Sergeant Blai, who got involved in several verbal altercations with colleagues from Public Safety who were in favour of facilitating the holding of the referendum, or at least not preventing it. Melchor and Salom witnessed one of those confrontations while they were having coffee one morning in the station; later, when the three of them were alone, the corporal tried to pacify the sergeant by making light of the dispute and joking about his pro-independence stance. The joke infuriated Blai even more.

"For Christ's sake, Salom," he said, grabbing the corporal by the lapels. "I've been pro-independence since I was born, not like this gang of converts governing us, who'll leave us in the lurch as soon as they can. But I'm a policeman first, and the police have to obey the law, in other words we have to do what the judges say, not what we fucking well feel like. And if the goddamn judges order me to close the polling stations, I stand and salute, I shove my pro-independence up my arse and close the polling stations, and that's that. Is that clear?"

Salom held up the palms of his hands as a sign of acquiescence. Not content with that, Blai turned towards Melchor.

"Is that clear, yes or no?"

Melchor assumed an apathetic expression. The sergeant let go of Salom and, still furious, seemed for a moment about to pounce on Melchor, though he did not. His eyes still on him, his breathing gradually slowing, Blai shook his head from left to right, until he smiled as if he were giving up. Before leaving he spat out: "Go fuck yourself, *españolazo*."

This happened at the end of September. By then, the four weeks that Melchor had spent in his new post had woven a tight and asymmetrical complicity between him and Salom. For eight hours a day, they were barely apart, but it was always or almost always – while they were working in the shared office or driving along the regional roads or having breakfast or drinking coffee or having lunch or dinner at the Terra Alta – Salom who talked and Melchor who listened or pretended to listen. This verbal diet did not differ essentially from the one he'd had with Vicente Bigara, but, unlike the old civil guard who had loved Melchor's almost perpetual silence, Salom tolerated it with less patience, especially at first. Later, when he understood that his new colleague's muteness was not a form of disrespect but simply an aspect of his temperament, he learned to counteract his silences with monologues, and even stopped getting annoyed when Melchor pretended not to hear or put him off each time Salom invited him to his home for dinner, or didn't answer or answered vaguely when he asked him if it was true, as Sergeant Blai had explained, without anyone believing him, that he'd been posted to Terra Alta for political reasons.

Salom had an assortment of talking points, but they always led in one of two directions: his family or money (or, rather, a lack of money). That's how Melchor found out that, five years earlier, Salom had been left a widower, that his wife had been a teacher and, like him, from Gandesa, and that she'd died of breast cancer after a lengthy illness; he found out he had two daughters, Claudia and Mireia, that they both lived in Barcelona and only came back to Gandesa for the holidays, that Claudia was in her second year of a Physics degree and Mireia was in her first, studying Aerospace Engineering; and he found out how difficult it was to support two daughters in Barcelona on a corporal's salary. Aside from that, Melchor very soon understood that Salom had not exaggerated in the slightest when he predicted that he'd have time to get bored in Terra Alta, because nothing ever happened there.

At least during the first month he spent in the region, that's how it was. In fact, he and Salom only investigated two formal complaints in all that time: one to do with the theft of some jewellery from a farmhouse near La Fatarella and the other after a man got a nasty beating outside a nightclub at the end of a confusing brawl. They solved the La Fatarella robbery in less than a week, thanks to Salom knowing the victims and almost immediately realising that the theft had been committed by the youngest of their four children, a cocaine addict who lived most of the time in Reus and only showed up at his parents' house to scrounge off them. It took them longer to solve the incident at the nightclub, an old farm converted into ultramodern premises in the middle of a field between Corbera and Móra d'Ebre, and the focus of the province's nightlife. Even so, after carrying out some inquiries and taking statements from the victim and several protagonists and witnesses of the fight, they concluded that the perpetrator of the aggression could only be a young man in his twenties with no priors who they'd already interrogated once, a guy called Riu Clar who worked for a courier firm with headquarters on an industrial estate in Amposta. They interrogated him again, this time at the station, or rather Salom interrogated him for almost three hours, bombarding him with questions in vain. Discouraged, the corporal stepped out of the interrogation room with Melchor.

"It's incredible," he snorted, trying to let off steam. "That son of a bitch is a rock. At this rate he'll get away with it."

"He won't," Melchor said. "He's a good kid. He wants to confess."

Salom stopped and looked him in the eye. Melchor repeated what he'd just said.

"The problem is he doesn't know how."

But for the two of them, the first-floor corridor was deserted. It was past eleven at night and silence reigned in the station.

"Let me try," Melchor said. "Take a walk around town, have some dinner and then come back. An hour should do it."

An hour later, when Salom returned, Melchor was sitting in the shared office, waiting for him, mobile in hand, downcast.

"I told you he was a rock," the corporal said, confused by his colleague's air of defeat. "Where have you put our little friend?"

Melchor put his mobile away and picked up a paper recently spewed out by the printer.

"Sleeping in the cells." He handed the page to Salom. "Here's his confession."

The corporal began to read.

"How did you do it?" he asked, in astonishment. "You didn't hit him?"

Moving his head vaguely towards the basement, Melchor said: "Go down and see him if you want."

"So then?"

"I told you he wanted to confess. It's just that . . . Well, I think he was embarrassed to admit to you what he did. And why he did it."

"And what did he do?"

Melchor pointed at the paper.

"Read the rest."

Salom finished reading and looked up.

"He was on the verge of killing that guy because he'd spent the night telling misogynist jokes?" he asked.

"Seems like it," Melchor said.

Salom sat down in a chair, scratching his beard.

"And why wasn't he embarrassed to tell you?"

Melchor shrugged.

"I don't know," he said. "I suppose because I convinced him that, if I'd been in his place, I would have done the same thing."

Salom stopped scratching his beard and looked doubtful. They stared at each other for a couple of seconds, during which Melchor saw a shadow of concern darken the corporal's eyes.

"You tricked him, right?"

Melchor gave an enigmatic smile.

"What do you think?" He sighed. "It's my turn to eat now. Will you write it up?"

By the middle of October, a month and a half after his arrival in Terra Alta, Melchor had finished all the novels he'd brought with him from Barcelona. One day he went into the only bookshop in Gandesa. It was small and not very well stocked and, after looking around for a while, he didn't find a single book he felt like reading; he couldn't be bothered to ask the bookseller either. A little while later he heard that the best bookshop in Terra Alta was not actually in Terra Alta but in a village called Valderrobres or Vall-de-roures, on the Aragón side of the line, but in the end he didn't go because it was more than an hour's drive from Gandesa.

One morning he decided to visit the public library. It was not quite nine-thirty and he found it closed. He drank a coffee in the Café Pujol and went back shortly after ten. This time he found it open, but empty. A librarian came through a door, noticed him there, standing at the entrance, and gestured for him to come in. The library was a big bright space, with exposed brick walls and a very high ceiling, illuminated by a broad glass facade that let the autumn sunshine in. Melchor walked between the rows of shelves and stopped in the fiction section. After a while, he came out empty-handed, and was about to leave when he decided to approach the librarian's desk.

"Can I help you?" she asked.

"Yes," Melchor said. "I'm looking for a book."

"Which book?"

"I don't know."

The librarian looked up from the book she was checking in and observed him over the top of her reading glasses.

"You don't know what book you're looking for?"

"No," Melchor said. "But I like novels."

"What kind of novels?"

"Ones from the nineteenth century. You haven't got many. And the ones you do have I've already read."

The librarian took off her glasses. She was dark-haired and very thin, with a nice face and dark eyes beneath which were

214

signs of sadness or fatigue; she was wearing her hair up in a chignon and had on a white camisole that highlighted her small breasts. Melchor had the impression she recognised him.

"You only read novels from the nineteenth century?"

"Yes," Melchor said. "A friend told me the ones written since weren't worth bothering with."

The librarian frowned, as if afraid Melchor was trying to pull her leg. When she realised that wasn't the case, she said: "Wait a moment."

With short, hurried steps that reminded Melchor of a bird or a little girl, she walked over to the shelves and came back with a book.

"It's really short," Melchor said, holding it in his hands.

"Really short but really good," she said. "Let's see if you like it."

Melchor read the title: *The Stranger*.

"Does it come with hidden intentions?" he asked.

The librarian smiled. She had full, well-defined lips, and when she smiled a fine mesh of creases formed at the corners of her mouth. Melchor didn't know how old she might be.

"No," she said. "Although I do know you're new here. I've seen you reading in the bar in the plaza. You work with Ernest Salom, don't you?"

"You know him?"

"We all know each other here. His wife was a friend of mine."

Melchor nodded as he flipped through the book. "Mother died today," the first sentence went. He didn't like it, but he said: "I love how it starts."

He spent the rest of the morning reading in a corner of the library, beside a big window that overlooked a gravel-covered courtyard. Shortly after midday he returned the book to the librarian.

"How did you like it?" she asked.

"It's the second-best book I've ever read," he lied.

The librarian smiled again.

"And what's the first?"

"*Les Misérables*," Melchor said. "Have you read it?"

"No," the librarian said. "But I've heard a lot about it."

Melchor asked what she'd heard and the librarian told him an anecdote. Apparently, Victor Hugo was in exile in Belgium when *Les Misérables* was published and, keen to know how his novel had been received, he wrote his editor a letter that consisted of a question mark; the editor wrote back to Hugo by return of post, also with a letter consisting of a single punctuation mark: an exclamation point. The novel had been a resounding success. Melchor laughed: it was the first time he had laughed since his mother's death.

"They say it's the briefest correspondence in history," the librarian said.

On her advice, Melchor took Boris Pasternak's *Doctor Zhivago* home with him, and that afternoon, while on patrol with Salom on the road that links Prat de Comte with El Pinell de Brai, he told the corporal that he'd met a friend of his wife's.

"What friend?"

"I don't know her name," Melchor said. "She works at the library."

"Oh, that's Olga Ribera," Salom said. "And it's true: she and Helena were friends."

Instead of asking any questions, Melchor went back to looking out of the car window, pretending to be satisfied with their frugal exchange. It was dusk. The setting sun turned vines weighed down with grapes and the skeleton of a ruined farmhouse a pale red; beyond that was a shadowy grove of trees and then the steep slope of a hill on the crest of which wind turbines turned. Melchor was confident that Salom, resigned to his monologues on the road, would carry on talking about the librarian as soon as he was convinced that Melchor was going to remain cocooned in his usual laconic state. He was not wrong.

"Very good friends," the corporal began, hands on the steering wheel and eyes on the road. "They went to school together. Then my wife went to study in Tarragona and Olga went to Barcelona. Librarianship, or whatever it's called that librarians study. After that my wife and I got married and we lived away from here for years. Olga got married too, but they separated after a short time. Later she lived with some other guys. The last one was called Barón. Luciano Barón. They lived in Tortosa. We went to their place three or four times. He was a nasty piece of work, that guy. One to watch out for. He didn't lift a finger, lived off her salary. He hit her. He gave her some awful bruises. My wife told Olga many times she should report him, and so did I, but she never listened. A classic case. That Barón was an idiot, but he'd crushed her self-esteem. Luckily he left her for another woman, because she wouldn't have been able to leave him."

Salom stopped talking. Melchor kept on looking out of the window: the sky over Terra Alta was a virginal blue, without a single cloud. They were driving very slowly. Every once in a while they met another car; occasionally, another car overtook them. Melchor turned back towards the corporal, who noticed him looking and took up the thread again.

"She moved back to Gandesa more or less when my wife got sick. She was living with her father, and going back and forth to Tortosa every day, until they opened the library here. Her father died not long after that. And so did my wife. Now I hardly ever see her, I don't even know how she's doing."

Melchor did not answer the question – supposing it was a question – and they both kept quiet for a time. As they drove out of El Pinell de Brai it started to get dark, and the lights of the Opel Corsa switched on automatically.

"What did you say that guy's name was?" Melchor said.

"What guy?" Salom asked.

"The one who lived with your librarian friend," Melchor said. "The one who beat her."

"Barón," the corporal answered. "Luciano Barón. Why do you ask?"

"No reason."

He didn't go back to the library until he'd finished reading *Doctor Zhivago*. Olga was sitting behind the counter: he called her by her name, returned the book, told her he'd liked it a lot.

"It's like a nineteenth-century novel written in the twentieth," he said.

"How do you know my name?" she asked.

"I'm a policeman, remember? Also, we have friends in common. I'd like to read more novels by Pasternak."

"That's going to be difficult," Olga said. "He only wrote one and you've just read it."

"Really?"

"Really."

Melchor looked disappointed.

"These things didn't happen in the nineteenth century," he said.

Olga smiled, and Melchor again noticed the lattice of lines that appeared beside her lips. Like the previous week, the library had just opened; like the previous week, they were alone.

"Pasternak was a poet," Olga said. "Do you like poetry?"

"Not really," Melchor said; he had read barely any poetry. "I think poets are lazy novelists."

218

Olga looked pensive.

"You might be right," she said. "Although most novelists seem to me to be poets who write too much."

They talked for a while about Pasternak's novel. Melchor realised that, not counting the telegraphic conversations he'd had with the Frenchman in the library of the Quatre Camins prison, it was the first time he'd ever talked to anyone about his reading. That morning Olga was wearing a blue blouse and had her hair down; the dark circles under her eyes had disappeared, or some invisible make-up had hidden them. While they were talking, Melchor thought he'd like to sleep with her, and at a certain moment, fearing the conversation was lagging, he mentioned a film based on *Doctor Zhivago*, which he'd heard something about somewhere.

"It's right over there," Olga said, pointing at a shelf full of DVDs. "But I wouldn't advise you to watch it."

"Don't you like films?" Melchor asked. He almost never went to the cinema.

"I love them. But I don't like seeing films based on novels I've read." She touched her forehead with her index finger and explained: "What for, if I've already made my own film of it up here."

"That's what a friend of mine used to say," he replied. "Half of a novel comes from the one who writes it, and the other half from the one who reads it."

"That was an intelligent friend," Olga said. "Not the one who said there hadn't been any good novels written since the nineteenth century."

"Bingo: two different friends," Melchor lied again. "You should be a fortune-teller."

"Fortune-teller, my foot." Olga laughed. "If that were true I'd know your name. They'll have told you that everyone in this town knows everything about everybody, but now you see it's not true."

Melchor told her his name.

"Well, Melchor," Olga said, coming out from behind the counter and walking over to the shelves. "I'm going to give you another novel you're going to like."

She came back with a book with a blue cover.

"Here you go," she said. "Another nineteenth-century novel written in the twentieth century."

Melchor read the title and the author: *The Leopard* by Giuseppe Tomasi di Lampedusa.

"Is this also the only novel this guy wrote?"

"Afraid so."

"What a bunch of slackers."

Olga laughed again; Melchor felt like kissing her and was about to ask her what time she got off work, to ask her out for a drink, when Olga gave him the news.

"By the way," she said. "Yesterday I started reading *Les Misérables*."

Melchor decided to delay the invitation, but from that day on, he dropped into the library almost daily.

"How's *Les Misérables*?"

"Give me time," Olga said. "It's really long."

"It always feels short to me," Melchor said. "Where are you in it?"

Olga told him and Melchor asked again, anxiously, if she was enjoying it.

"Yes," she said. "But it's odd."

"Odd?" Melchor seemed worried, or pretended to seem worried.

"Let me finish it and then we'll talk."

*

220

It was a little after ten-thirty at night when he parked in front of a three-storey building on the outskirts of Tortosa. On the other side of the badly lit street, beyond a line of spectral trees, the wide Ebro flowed silver in the moonlight.

He got out of his car, walked up to the front door of the building and pressed the intercom. Nobody answered. He rang again: still no answer. He looked left and right. As well as being badly lit, the street was deserted. He returned to the car, turned on the radio, looked for a station playing music, found one and listened to it briefly, then turned off the radio. He leaned back in the driver's seat and waited.

On the other side of the river the city lights shone. The silence was dense, almost total. After a while a man and a dog walked past his car, an old Labrador, on a leash. A few metres further on, the animal stopped, approached a tree, sniffed the trunk and the area around it, crouched and defecated. When he finished, the dog and the man walked on. Two cars came from the far end of the street, one after the other, driving at full speed, and their two pairs of headlights shone inside his car, blinding Melchor for a moment. Then the silence and darkness returned. Until suddenly, as if out of nowhere or from the depths of the night, a man appeared, walking towards the door of the building.

Melchor jumped out of the car, walked towards the man and said:

"Hey, Luciano."

The man turned and looked at Melchor, who said: "Are you Luciano Barón?"

The man only had time to say yes, because he immediately received a direct kick to the testicles and fell to the ground, doubled over in pain. He twisted like a worm, groaning: "What are you doing, man? Have you lost your mind or what?"

221

One knee on the ground, Melchor gave him three slaps and forced him to stand up.

"Don't shout," he said, his face a centimetre from the other man's nose. "If you shout again, I'll kill you."

Barón protected his testicles with both hands.

"I don't know who you are, man," he said, in a terrified sliver of a voice. "You've made a mistake. I haven't done anything."

Melchor grabbed him by the neck with his left hand and punched him in the stomach with the right, and when Barón instinctively tried to protect that part of his body, he kicked him again in the testicles, even harder than the first time, leaving him writhing on the ground again, groaning in pain. Then Melchor grabbed him by the shirt and the hair and dragged him fifteen metres down the pavement and threw him into a vacant lot, where he hit him again in the testicles, in the stomach, in the face. By the time he got tired of hitting him, Barón looked like a sack of throbbing flesh. Grabbing him again by the front of his shirt, Melchor pulled him upright and sat him on the ground with his back leaning against the wall of a shed, one of those improvised huts construction workers use to store their tools. He crouched down in front of him. The guy was panting and sobbing: one of his eyes was swollen half-shut and his eyebrow, nose and lower lip were bleeding.

"Listen to me, you piece of shit," Melchor said. He slapped him again and forced him to turn his face towards his. "Take a good look at me, you piece of shit. Do you hear me?"

Barón grimaced, weakly. A small bubble of saliva appeared at the corner of his mouth and immediately popped.

"Do you know why this is happening to you?" Melchor asked. He didn't wait for an answer. "Because you're a fucking coward and you like to hit women. Don't you? You get off on hitting women, isn't that right?"

On Barón's face tears mixed with the blood. Before speaking, he felt around in his mouth with his tongue and spat something out, a chunk of flesh or a tooth.

"I haven't done anything."

Melchor brought his face right up to his again, almost brushing up against it.

"Don't lie to me," he whispered. "Lie to me one more time and I'll beat the shit out of you. Tell me, does hitting women get you hard, yes or no?"

Still whimpering, Barón nodded.

"That's better," Melchor said. "With the truth out in the open. Now listen carefully again, because I don't plan on repeating this: if I hear that you've laid a hand on a woman again, what just happened to you here will seem like a joke. Is that clear?"

Barón nodded again.

"Very good," said Melchor. "Any questions?"

Barón shook his head. Melchor patted his bleeding face and stood up.

"That's great," he said. As he brushed the dust off his trousers he added: "By the way, this is best kept between just the two of us, on account of what people might say. Understand?"

Barón nodded one last time. Melchor left him in the vacant lot, went back to his car and drove away.

The next morning, while Melchor was reading *The Leopard* at home, Sergeant Blai phoned to say that an old lady had reported a scam. He gave him an address in Corbera and told him he should go there that afternoon with Sirvent to take her statement. Melchor called Sirvent and they arranged to meet at the Terra Alta at four to go to Corbera together.

Melchor arrived punctually at the bar, ordered a coffee and sat near a group of old-age pensioners who were playing dominoes. The lunchtime rush had died down; in fact, there was just one couple drinking coffee. He'd finished his when a message from Sirvent reached his mobile: he'd had a problem with his son and was going to be a bit late. He answered the message and ordered a second cup of coffee. The pensioners finished their game and, while one of them mixed the dominoes for the next round, they chatted. Someone mentioned a man from El Pinell De Brai who'd been more than a hundred years old and who'd just died. Apparently he was or had been a shepherd, and several of the old men had known him; two of them were wondering at his profound knowledge of the Pàndols mountain range.

"He knew the sierra so well that during the Battle of the Ebro he was Líster's liaison officer," the old man who was mixing the dominoes said. Then, as if he'd just remembered something, he stopped mixing them. His eyes were very blue, his skin was weathered by the sun, and he looked like the oldest of the group, or the one with the most authority; in any case, they all fell silent as he spoke. "One day I was with him at the Santa Magdalena chapel and he told me a story."

The pensioner said that it had all started at Líster's command post, in the village of Miravet, in the middle of the Battle of the Ebro. According to him, at dusk that day the Republican general, who was by then the commander of the Fifth Corps of the Army of the Ebro, ordered his liaison officer to go up to the chapel of Santa Magdalena in Pinell, where one of his companies had been fighting since dawn, trying to hold on to a position on a nearby hill. "Find out what's happened," Líster ordered his liaison officer. "If they've lost the position, tell the officer in command to retake it by whatever means necessary."

And, so there would not be any doubt, the general gave him a piece of paper on which he'd written out the order in his own hand. The liaison officer obeyed, hiked up the mountain, arrived at the chapel. The spectacle waiting for him there was desolate: collapsed against the trunk of a cypress tree, a Republican captain was panting with his face blackened and his uniform in tatters, stained with gunpowder and blood; scattered around him were fifteen or twenty soldiers shattered by combat, hidden among the trees. Líster's liaison officer asked the captain where the rest of his unit was and the captain gave him to understand they were all dead or gone, in spite of which the liaison officer relayed Líster's order and handed him the paper on which the general had written it down. The captain read the order. Once he'd read it, he seemed to go blank for a moment, absent, and then he began to shake his head from side to side, as if silently refusing to comply, or as if he were about to go mad. Then, after a time the liaison officer didn't know whether to measure in minutes or seconds, the captain stood up and, like a sleepwalker, walked over to the few men he had left, gathered them together and said: "I've just received an order to recover the position." An incredulous silence greeted the news; the captain paused so that his soldiers could take it in, perhaps to finish taking it in himself, until finally adding: "I am going to obey it. Anyone who wants to follow me should come with me. Anyone who doesn't should get lost out there." According to the pensioner (or according to the tale the liaison officer told the pensioner), the captain said this last line with an indifferent gesture that seemed to want to take in the whole mountain range, and, once he'd said it, he took his pistol out of its holster and started walking up the mountain towards the position occupied by the Francoists, without looking back or taking any precautions, without knowing if he was going up alone or if any of his soldiers were walking behind him. The liaison officer then saw how, one by one, that handful of exhausted, famished, dusty soldiers stood up and followed their captain, he saw how they all spread out across the unprotected slope, climbing towards the summit in the midst of a deadly silence, like a cortège of ghosts wandering the sierra at dusk, certain they were offering easy targets and that they were all going to die. And at that moment a miracle happened or something that the liaison officer, paralysed with terror among the cypress trees of the chapel, trembling from head to foot but unable to tear his eyes away from the butchery he was about to witness, could only interpret as a miracle, and it was that the Francoists who were occupying the summit did not fire on that ragged band they'd been killing since the sun came up, they did not massacre them, but instead retreated without offering resistance, as if they were surrendering in the face of that collective suicide or as if they were as fed up with the war as their enemies were and no longer had the spirit to keep on killing.

"So the fifteen or twenty Republican soldiers took the position without firing a single shot," the old man finished.

The end of the story was greeted with a series of hesitant and melancholy comments, which Melchor took advantage of to send a message to Sirvent, who answered immediately that he would be there at any minute and asked him to wait for him outside the door of the Terra Alta. While the pensioners went back to playing dominoes, Melchor paid for his two coffees and sat in a chair at the entrance to the bar, on the side of the road, until Sirvent's car stopped in front of him.

"Sorry, man," Sirvent said. "My son broke his finger playing handball."

"Don't worry," Melchor said, buckling his seatbelt. "I've

been kept entertained listening to some old guys telling stories in the bar."

"I bet you any money they were talking about the war."

Melchor turned to face him.

"How did you know?"

"Don't be daft," Sirvent said. "Because the old folks don't talk about anything else around here. Apparently nothing's happened in Terra Alta for the last eighty years. So, where are we going?"

3

"Do you realise what you've done?" Deputy Inspector Barrera says. "We could have opened disciplinary proceedings against you. You could have lost your job and ruined your career. The Adells could have prosecuted you for breaking and entering. What on earth did you think you were doing?"

Melchor doesn't reply to this question either. Like the first, it hadn't been asked in order to be answered but to hang in the air as a reproach.

They are in the deputy inspector's office standing face to face, Barrera looking him up and down and Melchor staring into space, above the almost hairless skull of his superior. Also standing, Sergeant Blai and Corporal Salom are silent and grim-faced witnesses to the scene. Of the four of them, only Barrera is in uniform, a uniform that, due to his weight problem, is a little tight.

"You are very fortunate when it comes to your superior officers," he continues, without mentioning Sergeant Blai and Corporal Salom. "They have defended you staunchly. They've even persuaded the Adell family not to press charges. I don't know if I would have been so generous. Even Commissioner Fuster has called from headquarters, someone must have told him, apparently you still mean something to the force . . . Anyway, I do not like what you've done one bit, but this time I'll look the other way. On the condition, that is, that you never act on your own authority again. And that you forget about the Adells. Until further orders, that case is well and truly closed. Understood?"

"Don't worry, Deputy Inspector," Blai hurries to assure him. "This time Marín has learned his lesson."

"I would prefer to hear it from him," the deputy inspector says.

Barrera doesn't take his eyes off Melchor, who takes a few seconds to answer.

"Understood."

Apparently satisfied, Deputy Inspector Barrera takes his hands from behind his back and shows them as if he'd just performed a magic trick and needed to prove he wasn't hiding anything in them.

"Very well," he says. "You can go. That was all I had to say."

Barrera turns his back on them and walks around his desk while Sergeant Blai, Corporal Salom and Melchor make for the door. They're still on their way out when the deputy inspector speaks again.

"Marín," he says.

All three turn towards him. Barrera has sat down in his office chair, behind his computer and the piles of folders and papers that cover his desk. He is stroking his moustache.

"Do you know how long I've been on the police force?" he says. "Forty years. And do you know one thing I've learned in that time?" He looks up at Melchor and fixes him with an aged, somewhat sad gaze. "Look, doing justice is good. That's why we joined the police. But good taken to extremes turns bad.

That's what I've learned over the years. And, also, something else. That justice is not just a matter of content. Most of all, it's a matter of form. So if you don't respect the forms of justice it's the same as not respecting justice. You understand, don't you?" Melchor doesn't say anything. Deputy Inspector Barrera smiles tolerantly. "Well, one day you will. But remember what I've said, Marín, absolute justice can be the most absolute injustice."

"Fucking Barrera," Sergeant Blai grunts, as soon as they're far enough away from the deputy inspector's office. "He's gone philosophical on us."

"Barrera's right," Salom says, turning to Melchor. "You've been very lucky."

"That's for sure," Blai backs him up. "I've seen more than one guy get the book thrown at him for much less than that. Let's hope you've learned your fucking lesson once and for all, *españolazo*. OK, are we going for coffee?"

Over the following weeks, while Olga rereads *Les Misérables* to him in the evenings, as she did years ago, when she was pregnant with Cosette, Melchor tries to forget the Adell case. To his surprise, he manages it, partly because it is no longer spoken of in Terra Alta and no longer appears in the media all over the country, but mostly because a new case absorbs all his interest.

Shortly after the incident at Gráficas Adell, Melchor and Salom begin investigating a forced-entry burglary in a house in Le Pobla de Massaluca. Two days later they receive a similar report, this time a farmhouse near Arnes. Melchor and Salom don't take long to put the two cases together, as much for the criminals' way of operating, at night and breaking the locks, as for their objective: both the homes were summer or weekend places, and both were empty when they were ransacked. That same week they believe their hypothesis is confirmed when news arrives from the Móra d'Ebre station that a break-in with a similar MO has just been committed in Flix, north of Ribera d'Ebre, and in the following two days they receive similar reports from Prat de Comte and Vinebre. By then all the alarm bells have gone off in the station. Sergeant Blai has five of his men working on the case and has taken personal command of the investigation, an investigation that concludes a short time later, when, thanks to a tip-off from a bartender at a brothel near Ascó, they arrest a group of very young Georgians, three men and a woman, in an apartment on the outskirts of Móra d'Ebre.

They still have the Georgian gang in the cells at the station, trying to determine the crimes they've committed before they put them in front of a judge, when Melchor starts thinking about the Adells again.

It happens one Sunday morning in the Pujol pastry shop, in plaza Farola, in the centre of Gandesa. Melchor is choosing a dessert with Cosette at the counter when Daniel Silva, Gráficas Adell's finance manager, appears at his side. At forty-three he's the youngest of the company's executives, a handsome man, married with three children. He lives in the countryside near Bot and has spent his entire working life at Gráficas Adell. They've only met once before, when Melchor interrogated Silva in his office the same morning he interviewed Grau and the rest of the company managers, but they both remember and say hello. Then Silva crouches down to talk to Cosette, who hides behind her father's legs, spying on the stranger with a mixture of embarrassment, curiosity and flirtatiousness. While Melchor orders a cream-filled ring cake and the baker's assistant wraps it, Silva stands up and asks if there's any news on the Adell case.

"None," Melchor says. "And at the company?"

"None there either," Silva says. "At least for now."

Melchor raises his brows. Relaxed, Silva smiles: his teeth are very white, his skin bronzed, and he's dressed with informal Sunday elegance, clearly glad to be free of the obligatory suit and tie.

"Well, you know how things are," he says, half-closing his eyes in an expression of ironic malice. "The king dies and war breaks out."

"War?"

"Between Grau and Ferrer," Silva clarifies. "Nobody thinks Ferrer will resign himself to not having a significant role in the company, and nobody thinks Grau will allow himself to be amicably pushed aside. An opportunity has arrived for each of them, sooner than anyone expected, and neither of them is going to waste it. In any case, hostilities won't get under way until Rosa Adell starts to show signs of life and her mourning is over. Autumn should be interesting."

The assistant hands Melchor his cake, wrapped in the bakery's paper and tied with a blue ribbon; Melchor pays and Silva says goodbye, taking his place at the counter.

Father and daughter leave the shop and start walking home, but they're still in plaza Farola when Melchor tells the little girl that he forgot something; they turn around and arrive back at the pastry shop just as Silva is coming out.

"Sorry," Melchor says. "Have you got a moment?"

Silva's expression of surprise changes in a second to a willingness to please.

"Of course," he says.

So as not to block the way, they move to one side of the door. Melchor holds the wrapped cake in one hand and Cosette by the other; Silva, too, has both hands full: one with a tray wrapped in paper, the other with a plastic bag with a baguette sticking out of it. The late summer sun falls directly on the plaza and bodywork shimmers as cars circumnavigate the Farola roundabout.

"The last time you saw Adell," Melchor begins, not knowing where to begin. "I mean the dinner at their house. I heard that there was talk about the Mexican subsidiary."

"It's true," Silva says; perhaps anticipatinging a long conversation, he puts the bread bag between his feet and holds the tray with his other hand. "Recently we'd been talking a lot about that."

"I've also heard that Adell wanted to close the subsidiary," Melchor says. "And that Grau and Ferrer disagreed but that that night Ferrer changed his mind." Silva nods. "Were you surprised by that change?"

"Of course."

"Papá, can we go?" the little girl pleads, tugging on her father's hand.

"Just a moment, Cosette."

"How could we not be surprised?" Silva says, no longer paying any attention to the little girl. "Ferrer had been backing Grau for months on the matter, ever since Adell began to talk of closing the Mexican factory. And now, all of a sudden, after his last trip to Puebla, wham, just like that it was over. Of course it was a surprise. You have to know that for Ferrer the Puebla factory is not just the Puebla factory."

"What do you mean?"

"Ferrer had other projects in Mexico, for a long time he's been saying that we have to diversify, that if you're not growing you're shrinking and that Mexico was the ideal country for growth. Several times he had proposed that we get into the communications business, it seems he'd made friends in Mexican radio and television."

233

"And what did Adell say about all that?"

"You can imagine," Silva says. "He didn't want to hear anything about it, he thought it was his son-in-law's typical bullshit. And then, overnight, Ferrer turns around and takes the boss' side. How could we not have been surprised?"

"Why do you think he changed his mind?"

"Honestly, I don't know. Maybe he did it to piss Grau off. It's possible he realised his father-in-law was right, or maybe he was fed up with locking horns with him, since he was as stubborn as an ox. Who knows?"

"I heard that Ferrer seemed nervous around that time."

"Ferrer's always nervous. That man was born nervous and he'll die nervous. But yeah, it's possible he was more nervous than usual at that time."

"Do you think it had to do with that business?"

"It's possible. After all, Mexico had been really important to him. He had a lot more freedom of movement over there than he had here, he must have felt like some sort of viceroy. We'll see what happens now."

Cosette tugs Melchor's hand again.

"Yes, we're going now," Silva reassures her, ruffling her hair and picking up the bag with the bread. "I have to get going too, they're waiting for me at home." Turning to Melchor, he adds: "If you want, we can talk some other day."

"Just one more thing," Melchor says. "Why didn't you tell me this when we talked in your office?"

Although they are standing in the shade, Silva blinks several times, as if the sun is bothering him.

"You didn't ask," he says.

The next day, Melchor goes over the investigation into the Adell case in secret; specifically, he rereads the statements from everyone who was at the dinner the night before the murder, as well as those of all the people who were at the Adells' house that night. He also calls Botet, the personnel manager of Gráficas Adell, and arranges to meet him the following week at a restaurant called Can Lluís in El Pinell de Brai. Several days before that meeting is to take place, when he is having a coffee with Salom in the station canteen, the corporal tells him to be careful with what he's doing. The two men look at each other and, since he knows it's futile to pretend he doesn't know what he means, Melchor asks him how he found out.

"This is Terra Alta, kid," Salom says in a light-hearted tone, almost joking, although Melchor knows him well enough to realise he is really angry. "You don't seem to understand that everyone eventually knows everything here. Besides, have you forgotten that you leave digital fingerprints every time you open up investigation files? Make sure nobody finds out, especially Barrera. You don't want to get Blai and me in trouble."

"Don't worry—"

"Well, if you don't want me to worry, you'll fucking drop this matter once and for all," Salom cuts him off, gulps down his coffee, chucks the cup angrily into the bin and mutters on his way out of the canteen: "Let's hope you don't finally force me to do what I don't want to do, shithead."

Salom's warning has an effect: convinced that the corporal found out from Silva that he had begun to investigate the Adell case on his own again, Melchor phones Botet to cancel their meeting, and for a few days tries again to forget about the Adells. He only half-manages it. One evening, when he's getting ready to go and pick up Cosette from the house of a school friend, Elisa Climent, he gets a call from the station to say that Olga has been in an accident.

"What happened?" Melchor asks.

"I don't know, they just called," the duty officer says. "Apparently she was hit by a car. An ambulance is taking her to the Móra d'Ebre hospital. You should go there."

Driving as fast as he can, his legs weak and his heart in his throat, Melchor phones Elisa Climent's mother to tell her what's happened and to ask if Cosette can stay there until he can come and pick her up. The woman says that's fine, tells him not to worry, and fifteen minutes later, Melchor parks in front of the hospital.

Two patrolmen are waiting for him at the entrance, and tell him that Olga has been transferred from the emergency ward to an operating theatre. As they walk with him down a long corridor and up two sets of stairs, they tell him what they've been able to find out: at 8 p.m., just after Olga had closed the library, a car knocked her down on avenida Catalunya as she was walking home, and the driver had fled the scene. There are four witnesses to the accident: a couple of high school students, the driver of a van and an old lady. They all say the car mounted the pavement and was black, but none of them can say what make of car it was and none of them got the number plate.

When they reach the surgical ward, a nurse opens the doors and comes out; after Melchor says who he is, she tells him that Olga needs to have emergency surgery.

"Why? What's wrong? What are they going to do?" he asks.

"Wait here a moment," the nurse says. "The doctor will explain."

A few minutes later the doctor appears. He is a swarthy, plump young man, his body protected by a green gown, his head by an equally green cap and his hands by white gloves. Speaking in a Colombian accent, he explains to Melchor that Olga arrived at the hospital unconscious and that she remains unconscious, that she has a fractured cranium and they have to operate immediately because her condition is serious.

"Do you mean she's going to die?"

"I mean what I said," the doctor says.

Melchor stares at the man as if the earth is about to collide with the sun and the doctor were the only person capable of averting the catastrophe.

"Save her," Melchor begs.

"I'll do what I can."

Melchor spends the following hours sitting in the operating theatre's waiting room beside translucent glass doors through which doctors and nurses come and go. Behind him, some oblong windows overlook an interior courtyard filled with houseplants and lit by bare light bulbs. Every once in a while, Melchor's colleagues show up; Salom and Blai are the first to arrive. At around eleven-thirty, when Melchor has been there for more than two hours, waiting for news of the surgery, Deputy Inspector Barrera appears. He greets him with a pat on the shoulder, asks him how his wife's doing and what happened. Since Melchor is slow to respond (in fact, he's barely noticed the deputy inspector's presence: he hasn't even stood up to greet him, hasn't even looked at him), it is Blai who tells him that there's been an accident.

"It wasn't an accident," Melchor interrupts him.

Barrera has heard very well what he said, but says: "What?"

"It wasn't an accident," he says, lifting his head, looking the deputy inspector in the eye and standing up. "The car mounted the pavement and ran her down, all four witnesses agree. That's not an accident. And you and I both know it."

At that moment there are five people in the waiting room, all colleagues of Melchor, but the silence that follows is as solid as a block of steel.

"You're worried, Marín," Deputy Inspector Barrera says, forcing some warmth into his voice. "And tired. I understand how you feel. But you shouldn't worry, your wife has just had a bump, everything will be fine. Whether it was an accident or not, we'll find whoever's done this, and they will pay for it. I promise you that. I'll make sure of it."

Melchor shakes his head back and forth.

"No," he says. "I'll make sure of it."

"It's better for us to do it," Deputy Inspector Barrera insists gently. "Precisely because she's your wife." In silence, he steps forward and takes him by the arm. "You should go outside to clear your head. You can't do anything here. Come on, I'll go with you."

"Take your hands off me."

"Calm down, Melchor," Salom joins in, stepping between him and Barrera.

Only at this instant does Melchor notice that the doctor has just come through the door to the operating theatre and is right in front of him, behind the wall his colleagues have formed; like the nurse who is accompanying him, he is no longer wearing the green cap or gloves, but he still has on the gown. Melchor doesn't know how long he's been there – he doesn't know if he's just come into the room or if he's heard his last exchange with the deputy inspector – but he knows what he's going to say as soon as the wall parts, the man walks towards him and he can see his eyes up close.

"I'm so sorry," the doctor says. "There was nothing we could do."

He embarks on an explanation, but, try as he might, Melchor is incapable of understanding it: he understands the words one at a time, but he doesn't understand what they mean all together, as if he's lost the capacity to relate them to each other. Then he even stops listening to the words, because the only thing that fills his head is Olga's voice reading to him, just a few days ago, a fragment of *Les Misérables*: "All that can ever happen to her has happened. She has endured all, borne all, experienced all, suffered all, lost all, wept for all. She is resigned, with that resignation that resembles indifference as death resembles sleep. She fears nothing now. [. . .] It is a mistake to imagine that man can exhaust his destiny, or can reach the bottom of anything whatever. [. . .] He who knows that, sees all shadow." But at that moment Melchor sees nothing.

The hours after Olga's death are confused, or that's how Melchor will always remember them. At 5 a.m. on the same night, he is arrested in a brothel on the outskirts of Móra d'Ebre. He is completely drunk, he has smashed up the place, has fought with several customers, with the two managers and with the patrolmen who arrest him not knowing who he is and lock him up in the cells of the local station, from which Salom collects him the next morning and, asking no questions, takes him home, puts him in the shower, gives him clean clothes and accompanies him to the Gandesa funeral home.

From that moment on Melchor does not lose control of himself again and, with absolute coldness, he copes with the details of the burial and funeral, which takes place that very afternoon and is attended by neighbours and colleagues who all have the impression that he has handled the tragedy with admirable serenity and strength of character. Once he has buried Olga, Melchor calls Domingo Vivales, tells him what has happened and asks if he can look after Cosette for a while.

"Of course," Vivales says. "Bring me the girl whenever you want."

239

Melchor says it would be better to hand her over halfway to Barcelona. Vivales agrees and they arrange to meet at noon the next day at a service station on the motorway called El Mèdol, a short distance from the turn-off to Terra Alta. That night, at home, Melchor barely sleeps, but he drinks a lot, trying to numb himself to a pain that is beyond pain and a sense of guilt that is beyond guilt, and the next morning he goes to pick up Cosette from Elisa Climent's house. Almost the first thing he tells her, after putting her in her car seat in the back and buckling her in, while driving towards Barcelona, is that her mother has died. Cosette stares at him in the rear-view mirror; Melchor tries to explain the meaning of what he has just said.

"So we're not going to see Mamá?" the little girl says.

"No," Melchor says. "From now on it'll just be you and me."

Intrigued and surprised, but not crying, Cosette begins to ask questions and for the rest of the trip Melchor answers them or does his best to answer them.

Vivales is not yet at the service station when they arrive, so they go into the cafeteria and Melchor orders a glass of chocolate milk and a whisky with ice. While he's waiting to pay for them, the girl discovers an indoor playground. There is a games table and two plastic slides, and Cosette goes up and down them. Melchor watches her from a table nearby, taking sips of whisky and trying to focus all his attention on his daughter, who occasionally comes over to the table to take a drink and then returns to the slides, her lips stained with chocolate. A slightly older boy enters the play area a few minutes later, and a short time after that Vivales arrives. When she sees him, Cosette jumps off the slide and leaps into his arms. The little girl and the lawyer talk, or rather the lawyer asks questions and the girl responds. Until she gets tired of answering, takes another gulp of chocolate milk and runs back to the play area.

"Does she know?" Vivales says.

"Of course."

The lawyer sits down at the table. He looks depressed. He hasn't shaved or combed his hair, but he's wearing a clean shirt and an unstained suit; as usual, his tie is loose. At that distance, Melchor gets a whiff of dried sweat, like a gust of bad breath, and he wonders if Vivales has showered, whether he hadn't slept that night either. The two men remain silent for a few seconds.

"I don't know what to say."

"Don't say anything," Melchor says. "What do you want to drink?"

"Nothing," the lawyer says, noticing Melchor's whisky. "Do they know anything more?"

Melchor shakes his head and takes a long sip of whisky.

"I don't think drinking is going to help you much," Vivales mutters. "Speaking from experience."

"Have you come to give me a hand or a sermon?"

The other man starts, as if he's been suddenly woken up. Then he shakes his head with a grim expression on his face, and announces as he stands up: "I think I'll have a shot too."

He comes back from the bar with a cup of coffee and a whisky, and the two of them start to talk about Cosette. Melchor gives Vivales some instructions and Vivales asks Melchor some questions.

"Well," the lawyer says when they finish exchanging information about the little girl, "now what do you plan to do?"

They've ordered two more whiskies, one in a large glass with ice and the other in a short glass without. Melchor drinks half of his in one gulp, and doesn't ponder his reply. "I'm going back to Terra Alta to find out who killed Olga."

"Are you sure she was killed?"

"Completely sure."

"What do your colleagues think?"

"Nothing."

"Nothing?"

"I'm not interested in what they think."

Now it's Vivales who nods, savouring his whisky as his large mouth sags into an incredulous grimace. For a moment Melchor and he look out, through the window, at the parking lot where they've just left their cars and beyond, beside the motorway, the petrol station with its red pumps, its red roof held up by grey columns and red and white CEPSA panel, all bathed in a greyish light on the cloudy windless day.

"If that's really what you want to do, you're going to need help," the lawyer says, turning back to Melchor. "Let me make a suggestion. The three of us will drive to Barcelona and leave the girl with some friends. They're totally trustworthy. You'll like them. Then we'll come back here and look for the people who killed Olga. Between us we'll find them."

"You don't understand," Melchor says. "These people are dangerous."

"No matter," Vivales says. "I've got a gun. I know how to fire it."

Melchor looks at Vivales, uncomprehending: for the umpteenth time he wonders if this big, cynical, scruffy swindler might be his father; for the first time he feels like hugging him.

"Oh, really?" he hears himself say. "Where did you learn? At a fairground target booth?"

The sarcasm alleviates his pain momentarily, and the two men scrutinise each other for eternal seconds. Hating himself, Melchor holds back an apology.

"It's better if Cosette stays with you," he says. "She'll feel more comfortable with you. And I'll worry less."

242

Vivales accepts Melchor's argument without protest; then he takes a key out of his trouser pocket and hands it over.

"This is for my place," he says. "Just in case. Do you need any money?"

"Not at the moment. But if I do, I'll ask you." He finishes the rest of his whisky and says: "OK, I've got to get going."

The first thing Melchor does when he gets back to Terra Alta is empty his house, putting all his family's belongings into storage and keeping only what is absolutely necessary. The next morning he rents an apartment in Vilalba dels Arcs, a cheap flat furnished with a table, two folding chairs, a microwave and a mattress, and devotes himself to investigating Olga's death day and night. He reverts to carrying his pistol in his shoulder holster everywhere he goes, as when he first arrived in Terra Alta, but he doesn't return to the station and, although he gets several calls from Salom and from Sergeant Blai, he doesn't answer them. He is absolutely certain that Olga's death is linked to the Adell case, or more precisely to his insistence on investigating the Adell case, but for now he concentrates on the first and leaves the second for the future, also convinced that the solution to the first is the solution to the second.

He interrogates the four witnesses to the hit-and-run, none of whom remember any more than they remembered when they were first interviewed, in other words, that the car that killed Olga mounted the pavement where she was walking home, on the avenida Catalunya, and that it was black. That done, Melchor starts going into all the bars, shops and even the apartments and private houses in the area, interrogating everyone in the hope of finding more witnesses, someone who remembers some revealing or unusual detail, a car driving too fast or making a strange movement, or anything. He still hasn't found anything when he recognises Salom one night standing outside the entrance to the building where he's living, under the yellow light of a street lamp. Melchor observes him for a few seconds from a distance; then he approaches and, in greeting, says: "What are you doing here?"

The corporal answers this question with another question: "Could we talk for a minute?"

Looking distrustfully at his colleague, Melchor takes out his keys, but as he gets ready to open the door, he says: "We'd better leave it for another day."

Grabbing his arm, Salom pulls Melchor back and hisses in his ear: "What's got into you?"

"My wife's been killed," Melchor says. "That's what's got into me."

Salom does not let go of his arm. Only the edge of the circle of light from the street lamp separates the two men, who can hear each other's breathing. Around them, the town is almost completely dark and silent.

"I loved Olga too," Salom reminds him. "And I also want to find her killers. Let me help you."

"If you want to help me, get out of here and leave me alone."

"Don't be pig-headed," he says. "You're not going to be able to do anything on your own."

Melchor takes his colleague's hand off his arm, speaks between clenched teeth ("We'll see about that") and unlocks the door. Before it closes behind him, the corporal says his name again; Melchor turns around.

"There's news," Salom says.

As soon as he walks into the flat, followed by the corporal, Melchor flips a switch and a single light bulb hanging from the ceiling dimly illuminates a rectangle of bare walls, with

244

a window framing the night and the floor littered with pizza boxes, beer cans and empty or half-empty whisky bottles. At one end, also on the floor, is a bare mattress around which are piled various items of clothing, and at the other end a table with a computer, an adjustable table lamp and two chairs. The air smells of uneaten food, stale and damp.

Melchor sits down at the table, turns on the lamp, boots up the computer and, while he waits to be able to use it, empties an open beer in one swallow and throws the can on the floor. Standing amid that dirty desolation, Salom says: "And Cosette?"

"Away. In a safe place."

"You don't even trust me?"

Melchor finally gets into his email, which contains various routine messages from the station but none from any of the people he'd been interrogating in relation to Olga's death and to whom he had given his email address in case they remembered anything. He deletes the messages from the station without opening them, turns to Salom and, without even asking him to sit down, says: "So, what's the news?"

Fiddling with his beard, the corporal looks around him to see what he's already seen, or rather so that Melchor sees him seeing it, and says:

"Shouldn't you clean up a bit here?"

"That's none of your business."

Salom looks as though he's thinking Melchor's not wrong, but then he takes the other chair and sits down facing him.

"You're angry with the world," he says. "Just like when you first arrived here. I understand, you have every right to be. But if you think it through, we all do. Besides, it's not going to get you anywhere. It's not the world that took Olga away from you. It was the car that ran her over. And the bad luck that she hit her head on the edge of the kerb when she fell and fractured her skull."

"Bad luck has nothing to do with this."

"Bad luck has everything to do with it," Salom says. "But it doesn't matter. We're trying to find out who hit her and so are you. Don't you think we'd have a better chance of finding them if we were working together?"

Melchor looks at Salom with fury before turning his gaze to the yellowish darkness of the window. Then, without a word, he stands up, leaves the room and comes back a few seconds later with a bottle of whisky and two paper cups. He fills them, passes one to Salom, sits back down across from him, takes a swallow and says: "What have you found out?"

Salom sniffs the whisky, sips it and sets it back down on the table, beside the computer, open to the first page of Melchor's in-box.

"That you're probably right," the corporal says. "That it wasn't an accident."

"I already knew that."

"Yes, but what you don't know is that it may have to do with Islamists."

Melchor opens his eyes as wide as plates.

"What?"

"We're not sure," Salom points out. "It's just a theory. But it's a reasonable theory. It's got out that you were the one who killed the terrorists in Cambrils – people know that. Too many. And what happened to Olga could have been done by one cell, not even anyone well trained. Just sympathisers, people who know what you did, kids who don't have the balls to set up a proper cell and organise an attack, but who might do something like this."

"But then they would have gone after me."

246

"That's what they did, Melchor: when they go after you, they go after those closest to you. Besides, if they're not well trained and radicalised, they might be afraid to attack you directly. After all, they know what you're capable of. It's possible they didn't even mean to kill Olga, just to send you a message, let you know they'd found you, scare you. Just that things went the way they did."

With the paper cup of whisky in his hand, Melchor tries to take Salom's words on board. He has another sip and says: "Strikes me as incredible."

"Well, it's not. We've been going over it for a couple of days now, we've talked to Commissioner Fuster and his people and . . ."

"The last time I spoke to Fuster he told me the danger was past."

"Yes, at first they thought it was odd, but not impossible. Now, they don't even think it's odd. Have you had the feeling you're being watched?"

"No."

"And maybe they're not watching you. Or maybe they are. It's possible they got scared by what happened and went into hiding, hoping we'd forget about it. I don't know, like I said, it's just a possibility. But you'd better be alert."

Salom stands up. Melchor remains seated, still shaken by this news.

"Barrera says you should take as long as you need," the corporal says. "That you don't have to rush back to the station. And that, if you want to leave Terra Alta, you only have to ask. They'll find you another posting."

Melchor stares at Salom, nods vaguely and empties his cup in one swallow. Then he thinks of Vivales, and immediately knows why, suddenly aware of the self-destructive rage he turns on those who treat him best: the lawyer, who has backed him unconditionally since his mother died, or even before, and the corporal, who has not only been his mentor and the most generous and loyal colleague he's found in Terra Alta, but also – he only realises this now – the best friend he's ever had. Trapped in a filthy cesspool of self-pity, for a moment he wonders if he ever mistreated Olga the way he's now mistreating them.

"Can I ask you a favour?" the corporal says. Melchor says nothing, but sets the empty cup down on the table and stands up. "If you find out anything, tell us. Believe me, we're doing everything we can to resolve this case. Not for you, for all of us."

Melchor holds back an urge to cry and nods again.

"People are waiting for you at the station," Salom adds, before leaving. "Come back soon."

That night Melchor sleeps badly and briefly, as he has since Olga's death, and at dawn he wakes curled up on the mattress on the living room floor, naked, cold and with a headache, while a rhetorical question posed by Jean Valjean at the beginning of *Les Misérables* that he hasn't been able to stop asking himself since Olga died drums through his mind – "Can destiny then be malignant like an intelligent being, and become monstrous like the human heart?". And he thinks the same thing he's thought every morning upon waking since then: that he hasn't found the men who killed his mother, but he will find the ones who killed his wife.

A cone of bone-coloured light shines through the window and pallidly illuminates the living room: the dirty clothes strewn on the floor, the leftover food and drink, the two chairs, the table and the computer on the table still switched on. Melchor curls up even tighter, wrapping his hands around his tucked-up knees, and stays that way for a while, coiled in on himself like a caterpillar, remembering his conversation with Salom. He thinks again that he has been ungrateful to the corporal. He thinks Salom is right. He thinks what he's been doing since Olga's death is senseless: his irrational certainty that Olga's death is linked to the Adell case and his insistence on investigating the Adell case are senseless, investigating Olga's death on his own and without the help of his colleagues who want to help is senseless, having left his house, having moved into this flat that more and more resembles a garbage dump, and having moved Cosette away from Terra Alta thinking she was in danger there, is senseless. None of this makes any sense, or so he suddenly thinks, curled up on the mattress on the floor, as if everything he's done since Olga's death was nothing but a way to punish himself for her death, punish himself and punish those around him, as if they were all guilty of what happened.

Melchor uncurls, sits up on the mattress, rubs his eyes, his nose, his forehead. Then he stands up, puts on a T-shirt and a pair of underpants, and walks to the bathroom. Facing a wall mirror with its edges eaten away by rust, he asks himself, almost unable to recognise himself in the broken and ravaged face that studies him from the glass – jutting cheekbones, red eyes, a week's stubble – if the corporal is also right to think that Islamists killed Olga. It could be so, he thinks. He doesn't have the feeling that anybody's been following him, neither before nor after Olga's death, but it could be so. And, as implausible as it might seem to him, nor can he rule out that Olga might have been hit by accident. In any case, he should go back to the station that very morning, get up to date on the inquiries his colleagues have made, join the investigation. That's what he thinks. Later, while he showers and shaves, he thinks maybe he shouldn't, that perhaps he should leave the investigation in the hands of his colleagues: after all, having spent so many years searching in vain for his mother's murderers, maybe he should admit that what they taught him at the police academy was true and that a relative of a victim is also a victim and lacks the necessary distance, objectivity and dispassion to pursue the culprits. Besides, he's lost two of the women in his life, but the third remains. Maybe he should forget this matter entirely, accept Deputy Inspector Barrera's offer, request a transfer and move with Cosette. There's no sense in staying in Terra Alta either, he thinks, no sense in clinging to this poor, isolated, inhospitable place: thanks to Olga, Terra Alta had become his home, but now that Olga is gone, Terra Alta means nothing to him. He has to keep going, he tells himself in the mirror, freshly shaved and showered, recognising himself again. I have to start over, he also says.

As he tells himself these things, he feels a stab of hunger and remembers he hasn't eaten for almost twenty-four hours. He is on the point of leaving the house in search of a decent breakfast when, just as he is about to turn off the computer, he notices two new messages in his in-box. The subject heading of one of them immediately catches his eye: "The answer". The content of the message grabs his attention even more, consisting of a single sentence: "The answer to your question is in the investigation."

A shiver runs down his spine. Who has written this? Why have they written it? Is it meant to be taken seriously or is it a joke? The e-mail is not signed, and the Hotmail address it's been sent from means nothing to him. Melchor deduces that the question the message alludes to concerns Olga's death; also, that the answer to that question is to be found in the Adell case file. What else could it refer to? And supposing that the answer is to be found there, where should he look for it? In which of the hundreds, maybe thousands of documents it contains? Melchor tells himself that he should respond to the sender, ask for more precise information, try to verify if this unexpected clue, which unexpectedly links Olga's death to the Adell case again, is really a clue or not; but he doesn't because he has a hunch that if the author of the email message hasn't explained more, it's because they don't want to, and that, whether this clue is trustworthy or not, he should follow it to the end.

His first impulse is to dial Salom's number, but he calls Blai instead and they arrange to meet at eleven in the Trinos Bar in Vilalba dels Arcs.

Two hours later, when he arrives at the Trinos, the sergeant is already there, sitting waiting for him in a corner with a cup of coffee in front of him. Melchor orders a coffee too and sits down opposite Blai.

"How are you?" the sergeant asks.

"Fine."

Blai continues putting questions to him for a few minutes and he continues answering, not always with lies. The owner brings him his coffee and, when he's drunk it, Melchor says: "I have to ask you for two favours." Blai opens his arms as if to say: Name them. "I want to reread the Adell case file one more time." The sergeant's body tenses up and his face darkens. Before he can protest, Melchor says: "Stay calm. I haven't lost my mind. I think the key to Olga's death is in that investigation."

"In the Adell case?" The sergeant is surprised.

"Yes. And if I find the key to Olga's death, I'll find the key to the Adell murders."

"How do you know?"

"I don't know. I suspect it. To be sure, I need to get back into the case file."

Blai moves his shaved head from side to side. It is burnished by the honeyed morning light shining into this corner of the café through a window with frosted panes.

"You're going to get yourself into trouble again," he warns him, lounging back in his seat.

"Not if you lend me a hand," Melchor says.

Blai straightens up, his body tenses again and his gaze turns suspicious.

"I can't get back into that investigation with my password," Melchor explains. "I've already been caught delving into the Adell case when I wasn't supposed to; besides, I'm sure my access has been restricted. But, when Gomà provisionally closed the case, didn't he open the investigation to you?"

"Didn't I tell you he would?" Sergeant Blai says, relaxing again and smiling sarcastically. "Well, he did, the bastard. It was his way of getting the deaths off his books and handing them over to me, his way of saying: here are all the facts, reopen the case if you've got what it takes, let's see if you can solve it after all your strutting . . ." He stops mid-sentence; the smile has vanished from his lips. "Hey, you're not thinking of using my password?"

"How else am I going to get in?"

"Don't fuck with me, *españolazo*."

"Don't worry, they won't know. If someone does detect the virtual fingerprint, they'll think you've been looking into the investigation, which you are authorised to do. Nobody needs to know it was me, nobody even needs to know I've been to the station. Ideally, in fact, you'd help me access the files without anyone seeing me, and the sooner the better – the next time you're on a weekend night shift, for example. If we went in through the garage in the early hours and left before the morning shift started, nobody would even know I was there, not even the duty officer at the front desk."

Looking alternately at Melchor and two locals chatting with the owner at the bar, Sergeant Blai hesitates.

"Trust me," Melchor says. "And just think how you'll be able to rub Gomà's nose in it if we solve the Adell case."

Blai agrees without much conviction. The two locals at the bar pay for their drinks and leave.

"What's the second favour?" the sergeant asks.

Melchor takes out a folded piece of paper and hands it to Blai, who unfolds it: the paper contains a copy of the e-mail he received that morning with the message deleted.

"Find out who this e-mail address belongs to," Melchor says. "Or where it was written. Whatever."

The sergeant folds the paper, puts it in his pocket.

"It could take a while," he says.

"And the other?" Melchor asks. "Can I count on you?"

"Why don't you ask Salom?"

"Because I already owe him too many favours. And because you owe me one, a big fat one." Melchor pauses, looking at Sergeant Blai levelly. "Remember? You scratch my back, I'll scratch yours."

Just as Melchor planned, at ten o'clock on Friday night he and Blai enter the station through the garage, without anyone seeing Melchor, who is lying down on the back seat. They both go up to the first floor and Melchor shuts himself up in his office, where he spends the rest of the night immersing himself again in the Adell case, while, in the office next door, the sergeant works through a backlog of reports, naps, goes downstairs to get coffees from the machine and leaves the station a couple of times, first at the request of a couple of patrolmen who have a drunk to deal with, the second just before dawn, to get a breath of air.

As for Melchor, he doesn't know precisely what he's looking for in the case files, but, possessed by an unfounded optimism, he's sure he'll find it. Nevertheless, after hours of navigating through a sea of reports and evidence that he remembers with varying degrees of precision (after all, some of them he'd written himself), he is left with no choice but to give up. This happens shortly before six-thirty in the morning. Sergeant Blai has gone out again, but he must be about to return because the morning shift starts at seven and they should be leaving. Discouraged, unsure what to do, afraid that he's let himself be swept up again by a false hunch, Melchor checks his e-mail in hopes of finding a second message from his anonymous informant; he does not find one, and at that moment he is assaulted by the suspicion that has been prowling around his mind several times during the night: that the investigation he should be looking into might not be that of the Adell case. So, he opens the message and clicks reply and writes: "Is the answer in the Adell investigation?" He rereads the e-mail several times, sends it and, while he is waiting for a reply, Sergeant Blai bursts into the office.

"Have you found anything?"

Melchor shakes his head.

"I was afraid not," Sergeant Blai says, and stifling a yawn, adds: "Well, shut that computer down and let's go get some sleep."

When he gets home, Melchor again checks his e-mail: nothing. Unable to sleep he spends the morning compulsively checking it, surfing the web and talking to Cosette and Vivales on the phone. At about three he goes out to eat some lunch and when he gets back falls asleep in front of the computer, his head on his forearms. When he wakes up night is falling, and almost the first thing he sees is that a message has arrived in his in-box in reply to the one he'd sent at dawn. It says simply: "Check the fingerprints." Without a second's hesitation, he calls Blai and convinces him to repeat last night's trick ("It's the last time," he says. "I give you my word.") This time he restricts his search to the fingerprints collected in the Adells' house during the hours following the murder. He looks through all the photographic enlargements they'd made of them and establishes that all the fingerprints identified belonged to people who were in the house on the day before the crimes: Señor and Señora Adell, the Romanian maid, Jenica Arba, and María Fernanda Zambrano, the Ecuadorian cook. Then he decides also to review the enlarged photographs of the unidentified prints, but they all turn out to be unrecognisable, too blurry. Now in desperation he decides to go through the originals of the photographs, even though he's aware that, in principle, it's almost impossible to identify a fingerprint from the original photograph; he looks them over one by one, comparing each original with its enlargement, until all at once he notices an anomaly: one of the originals, a print found in the security room, seems clearer than the enlargement reflects.

Surprised, he decides to go to the lab and make a new enlargement from the same original. The operation takes him quite a while, but the result is a much better enlargement than the first, so much so that it is impossible to believe that its terrible quality was the result of clumsiness or chance. In any case, now, thanks to that new enlargement, it is possible to identify the print, and, almost running, sure that he has found what he was looking for or the thread that could lead to what he was looking for, Melchor returns to his computer, compares this print with the ones stored in the investigation and discovers that it does not match those of the Adells, the Romanian maid or the Ecuadorian cook. Then he compares the print with those of the managers of Gráficas Adell and rules out Botet, Silva and Arjona, but his heart misses a beat when he gets to those of Albert Ferrer, because, after double-checking, he concludes that they are identical to the one he has just found.

Trying to contain his elation, he stands up, walks to his office, and thinks about it. What he has discovered demonstrates that Ferrer was in the security control room hours or days before the Adells' murder, and that he could very well have been the one who switched off the alarms and security cameras, which, hours or days later, allowed the executioners to enter. This means that Ferrer has lied, or at least hidden the fact, and consequently is, almost certainly, somehow involved in the murder of the Adells. Also in Olga's death? It could be, he thinks. What is beyond doubt is something else, he also thinks, and that is that someone on the inside tried to neutralise that decisive piece of evidence. No: the terrible quality of the enlargement of the fingerprint cannot be the result of clumsiness or chance; it can only be the result of the guilty will of someone who did not want that print to be identified. That person knew they couldn't eliminate a piece of evidence that had already been documented, because to do so would betray them, and they decided to hide it behind a smudged enlargement in which Ferrer's fingerprint would be unrecognisable, in the hope that nobody would think to look back at the original. He immediately understood that this had to have happened in the first few hours following the triple homicide, and that the person who could have done it most easily – perhaps the only person who could have done it – is the one who collated the evidence in the Adells' house. Sirvent, he thinks.

Dazzled by the discovery he has made, Melchor turns off the computer, leaves the station as fast as possible and, while he's walking to where he left his car, phones Sirvent, who says he's just gone to bed, but who, pressed by Melchor, agrees to see him.

"What's going on?" he asks, alarmed.

"Give me twenty minutes and I'll tell you," he says.

Twenty minutes later, Melchor parks at the entrance to a semi-detached house on the outskirts of Móra d'Ebre. Sirvent is waiting for him, sitting on a low garden wall, beside the wrought-iron gate, wearing tracksuit trousers, a grey jumper and felt slippers. It is a clear November night, the moon almost full and the sky filled with stars. A lamp hanging above the lintel shines on the door to his house.

Sirvent stands up and starts walking towards Melchor, but, before he can say hello, Melchor grabs him by the throat.

"You were the one who smudged the enlargement, weren't you, you bastard?"

Sirvent begins to protest, but Melchor cuts him short by telling him what he's just discovered: without letting go of his colleague, he tells him that Albert Ferrer was in the security control room in the Adells' house shortly before the night the couple and their maid were murdered and that in the Adell case file there is a fingerprint that proves this; explains that this revealing fingerprint, which proves Ferrer's involvement in the murder, was hidden by an intentionally blurred enlargement, so nobody would notice it, and the only one who could have made that enlargement was him, the forensics officer in charge of collating all the evidence found at the crime scene and sending it to Sergeant Pires to be included in the case file.

"It wasn't me," Sirvent groans, after processing at top speed all the facts that Melchor, who still has him gripped by the throat, has revealed. "It was Salom."

Melchor looks at him as if he hasn't understood.

"What?"

"I'm telling you it was Salom, for fuck's sake," Sirvent sputters. "It could only have been him."

Stupefied, Melchor lets go of his colleague, who coughs, doubled over, then straightens up while Melchor demands that he explain.

"It could only have been Salom," Sirvent repeats, still rubbing his throat. "Gomà put me in charge of collating the evidence, that's true. But remember that day there was evidence all over the place, we were swamped with work and Salom offered to help. He has experience as a forensics officer, he was on the case, and he outranks me . . . Besides, he told us that Gomà had ordered him to give us a hand. I don't suppose he made that up, as you can understand, it didn't even occur to me to question it. So he was there at the house with us almost all Sunday afternoon and evening."

"It's true." Melchor nods, more to himself than to Sirvent, while he searches his memory in astonishment. "He offered to help you and Gomà accepted. Then I offered to help him, but he didn't want me to, he didn't want anyone overseeing his work. That night he was at the station very late, working on the evidence you were sending in. And the next morning . . ."

"Of course," Sirvent insists energetically. "On Sunday Salom ended up taking charge of getting the evidence together and sending it to Pires. And then, the next day, he continued supervising it all. He'd started doing it and it was best if he finished the job. And I was busy gathering evidence in the Adells' house, but Salom collated it at the station and sent it to Pires. Nobody else. I'm telling you, the only one who could have done that enlargement was him."

Melchor is still trying to take his colleague's explanations on board and work out how far they went when his mobile rings and breaks the nocturnal silence of that suburban street down which, since he arrived, not a single car has driven. Bewildered, unable to believe what he has discovered, he lets the mobile ring several times, but he sees it is the sergeant calling and answers.

"Do you want to tell me where you've got to?" Blai says. "I've just heard you were seen rushing out of the station as if you were going to put out a fire. Didn't we agree that nobody should know you were here?"

"Sorry," Melchor says, unable to look away from his colleague. "I'm in Móra d'Ebre, with Sirvent."

"With who?"

"Sirvent," Melchor says. "I'll tell you about it later."

"Have you found something?"

"I think . . ." Melchor hesitates, blinks, then finishes his sentence: "I think so. I think I now know who killed the Adells." After a pause, he adds: "And Olga."

"You're shitting me, *españolazo*."

"Stay at the station," Melchor says. "You'll soon have the first of them."

Melchor says goodbye to Sirvent without a word of apology and gets in his car. As he drives back to Gandesa, his brain is churning, trying to reconstruct what happened five months ago, at the end of another Sunday night shift like this one, when he was advised there were several bodies at the Adells' house, and, by the time he parks in front of Salom's apartment, he's sure he's identified almost all the pieces of the Adell case puzzle, and that they almost all fit.

His flat is in a modern three-storey building, near the courthouse. Melchor buzzes the intercom and Salom takes a while to answer, but, when his colleague asks him to open up, he opens the street door without any questions, and a little while later Melchor sees him, in pyjamas and bathrobe, framed in a doorway.

"You take the biscuit, man," Salom welcomes him, smiling sleepily, as he leans out into the corridor. "You've been turning down my dinner invitations for four years and now you show up unannounced at dawn. Do you know what time it is?"

Melchor's reply is to punch him, knocking him into a hall table with a noise of metal, wood and breaking glass.

"What the fuck . . . ?" Salom stammers incredulous, slumped on the floor. "Are you drunk or what?"

Melchor closes the door behind him, kicks the corporal in the stomach and in the face, drags him into the dining room and throws him on the sofa.

"Do you know something?" he says, in a tone of genuine curiosity. "The last time I saw you I thought you were the best friend I ever had, and now I think you're the biggest bastard that's ever looked me in the eye. What do you reckon?"

Salom squirms on the sofa, groaning and trying to sit up, clutching his stomach as if fearing his guts might spill out onto the carpet. There is no longer any trace of sleep on his face, nor of a smile. He has lost his glasses and a stream of blood coming from his nose splashes his moustache and beard.

"I don't know what you're talking about, Melchor," he finally manages to say.

"I'm talking about Olga, asshole. Were you driving the car that killed her? Or was your friend Ferrer driving?"

"I still don't know what you're talking about," Salom says. "Please, calm down. And, think what you're saying, how could you think I could kill Olga?"

Melchor punches him twice more, this time in the ribs. The corporal seems resigned to the beating, or maybe there is nothing he can do to prevent it.

"If you keep playing dumb I'll beat you to death," Melchor threatens him. Then he picks up a chair, brings it over to Salom and sits on it backwards, his arms resting on the back. "Tell me something, do you know what I'm talking about when I say I've just found the enlargement of the fingerprints Ferrer left in the Adells' security room? Do you remember that, since you couldn't get rid of them, as the forensics officers had already indexed them, you made the enlargements blurry so nobody would be able to identify them, trusting that nobody would think to compare them with the original photograph? Does that ring any bells? Well, does it? At first I thought it was Sirvent, but I just talked to him and it's impossible, of course. That day it was you who took charge of getting all the prints together and sending them to Pires. That's why you offered your help to Gomà and the forensics team, to protect your buddy, to cover up any errors he might have made, and that's why you didn't want me to help you, you wanted to work alone, of course, you didn't want any witnesses. That's why later you became the family's spokesperson, so all the information would pass through you, so nothing would get past you. And, of course, it was also you who told Ferrer when we bugged his phone, right? You wouldn't want him to have any imprudent telephone conversations or say something stupid, would you? And, by the way, wasn't it kind of you to get me the keys to Gráficas Adell, you've always been such a generous friend, you've always been there to lend a hand and get me out of trouble, haven't you? I bet it was you who convinced Ferrer to give you the keys to Gráficas Adell so that he could catch me in Grau's office. It was a way to get me off the case for good, wasn't it? But I wouldn't leave it so then you had to go after Olga, didn't you, you motherfucker?"

While Melchor, beside himself, waves his arsenal of incriminating evidence and reasonable conjecture, Salom has managed to sit up on the sofa and compose himself to some extent. As well as his glasses, he's lost his slippers and the belt of his robe, several buttons have popped off his pyjama top and part of his chest and belly are visible. His body is still and he's in pain, and he has an exhausted, stunned expression on his face.

"Do you really think there's any way out?" Melchor says, pointing an accusatory finger at him. "Don't you realise you're in the shit over your head? You tampered with evidence that proved Ferrer is at the very least an accomplice in the murder of the Adells. How do you explain that? Don't you realise that blurry enlargement points to you? Don't you see you've got no way out?"

Salom remains silent, his gaze fixed darkly on the tile floor. Broken, still panting, he seems to be thinking.

"Am I going to have to keep punching you?" Melchor says. "Don't you think I deserve to know the truth after what's happened? In any case, you're going to have to confess . . ."

"I had nothing to do with what happened to Olga," Salom mumbles at last.

For a few long seconds the two men stare at each other in silence, as if bewitched, but then the corporal looks away and Melchor keeps watching him, searching the unrecognisable face in front of him – hair a mess, beard bloody, eyes naked and lost – for the colleague he's spent half his life with for the past four years, his mentor in Terra Alta, his best friend. Salom gestures towards the front hall and says, in a dull voice:

"Bring me my glasses, please."

Melchor gets them and, instead of sitting down again, stands in front of him. In the dining room the only sound now is Salom's heavy breathing and the relentless ticking of a clock.

"I had nothing to do with what happened to Olga," the

262

corporal repeats grudgingly, while he tries to cover his chest and belly with his pyjama top and dressing gown. "When Albert found out you were still investigating, he got hysterical, he was afraid you were going to discover something, said you had to be stopped no matter how. I tried to calm him down, but I couldn't. Albert just wanted to scare you, send you a warning, but in the end it went wrong."

"Who did it?"

"He paid some guys to do it. That's what he told me."

"The same ones who killed the Adells?"

"No, I don't think so, they were real professionals. But I don't know. I was just trying to help a friend. Nothing more. I would have done the same for you."

"Are you crazy? You helped kill three people!"

"That's not true, I just tried to keep a friend out of jail. He'd already decided to kill his father-in-law. He would have killed him no matter what."

"Why?"

"Why what?"

"Why did he decide to kill his father-in-law?"

"Why else? Because Adell had spent twenty years swearing at him, fucking up his life like he fucked up all those around him. And because, to top it all, he'd decided to leave half his fortune to Opus Dei."

"What?"

"Adell kept it secret, not even his daughter knew, but he was about to do it. There are Opus Dei people who know, of course, but don't expect them to tell you. They're specialists in those sorts of tricks . . . That's what made Albert decide. The old man had spent a lifetime messing up his family and now that he was going to die he was going to fuck them over once and for all. A nasty piece of work."

"And because he was a nasty piece of work, you helped Ferrer to kill him."

"I didn't help to kill him. I just helped him not get caught. Or I tried."

"Go to hell."

Exasperated, Melchor looks away from Salom and, fighting with his disgust and rage, realises that the corporal is not lying about one thing: this is the first time he's ever been in his home. He looks around that impersonal dining room, furnished without taste or design: a humdrum imitation leather sofa, an ordinary table, several bland chairs and a graceless sideboard, with a few random books, an old television set and an old alarm clock. The only personal or hospitable touch, in the midst of the insipid greyness, comes from several photos of his wife and daughters, which stand on a shelf in front of him. One of them catches Melchor's attention. It is a family photograph in a silver frame, undoubtedly from a summer holiday: Salom is in the centre of the image, surrounded by his three girls, and the group seems to be just coming from the beach: they're all wearing swimsuits and T-shirts and flip-flops, and at their feet are beach bags, folding chairs and a parasol. Salom, young and clean-shaven, but already wearing old-fashioned glasses, is holding in his right hand the hand of Claudia, who can't be more than six or seven, while his left arm is around his wife's shoulder, and he's kissing her on the cheek while she holds Mireia's hand and smiles radiantly at the camera. Unwillingly, Melchor wonders how long before Salom's wife died that photograph was taken, if the cancer that killed her was already gnawing away at her from within; willingly, he wonders how Salom can live in that flat on the outskirts, like a newcomer to town rather than the born-and-bred Gandesan he is, he wonders where his wife and family's furniture and memorabilia

264

are, what Salom was doing with his tasteless and taciturn widower's life, surviving in that flat – a solitary man who hates solitude – while he was enjoying the happiest stage of his life with Olga and Cosette. He looks away from the photo and meets the eyes of the corporal, who is watching him.

"I don't understand how you could have done something like this," Melchor begins again. "How could you . . . ?"

He falls silent all of a sudden, paralysed by something he's just seen in Salom's gaze, and, in a flash of lucidity, while his memory plays back a conversation he had with the corporal and his two daughters on the day he and Olga got married, at the wedding reception – a conversation that now seems like a mere link in a series of conversations, or a repetition or an echo of many other conversations – he believes he understands it all, as if it were written in the corporal's eyes with infinite silent eloquence, and he feels that he is being dragged by a wave of sorrow that does not dilute his rage and his disgust, but joins them. He is on the verge of asking: "How much did your friend pay you to help him?" But Salom gets ahead of him:

"Are you really going to turn me in?"

The question hangs in the air between them.

"What will you gain from turning me in, apart from ruining my life?" the corporal asks again. "Give bait to the journalists so they can continue convincing people that the police are full of undesirables and that it's right they pay us shit and treat us like dogs? Or do you think by turning me in you'll get justice for an old son of a bitch who everyone hated and who had already lived the life he had to live?"

"You're forgetting about his wife and maid," Melchor says, sticking to the last question. "And you're forgetting about Olga."

"And I'm telling you again I had nothing to do with that,"

the corporal says. "Olga was my friend, I would have done anything I could to prevent what happened from happening. I didn't have anything to do with the other women either, I didn't know they were going to be killed too, and I assure you I had no idea that the old folks were going to be tortured like that. When I saw that, I was as horrified as you were. Albert says it was the guys he'd hired, that he just opened the door for them that night . . . I don't know. I don't know who they were. I had nothing to do with them. What I do know is that, even if you turn me in, nothing's going to bring Olga back, but my daughters are going to lose their father after having already lost their mother, and you're going to lose your best friend, the only one who has busted his arse for you when you needed it. Is that not true?"

Melchor stares at Salom, not knowing how to answer. This inability adds discouragement to his disgust, his rage and his sorrow.

"Enough talk," he says, making an effort to pull himself together. "Get dressed. We have to go."

"Where?"

"To the station. Blai's expecting you. I want you to tell him what you've just told me. He'll know what to do with you and with Ferrer."

After a moment of incomprehension, or of doubt, Salom lets his head fall forward till his double chin is resting on his chest and, for several seconds both men remain silent, hearing only the clock's ticking. Melchor notices something he hadn't spotted until then: that on the crown of the corporal's head a hairless circle is spreading out, like a monastic tonsure. To his surprise, when Salom raises his head again there is a vague smile, somewhere between sarcastic and sardonic, playing on his lips.

266

"Aren't you going to go and find Albert?" he says. The pause seems to have reanimated him, brought him back his composure. "Are you really going to waste the opportunity to beat the shit out of him, as you did me? Of course, you could also kill him. You're good at that too."

Again Melchor doesn't know what to say, and again he thinks that, despite having spent so much time with the corporal on a daily basis for the last four years, he barely knows him; then he's overcome by deep exhaustion, as if, once the fury that was driving him was extinguished, all the sadness, desolation and fatigue of the recent days had come crashing down on him.

"You think you're better than me, don't you?" Salom says, without abandoning his half-smile and vindictive, challenging tone. "Well, you're not. I may have made a mistake, but you're something else, Melchor. Do you want to know what you are?"

Melchor does not want to know, does not want the corporal to tell him what he thinks he knows, but he still cannot bring himself to answer Salom's questions.

"You're a murderer," Salom answers himself. "That's what you are. You can see it in your face, in your eyes. I noticed the first time I saw you. Tell me something: you enjoyed killing those kids, didn't you? Those four terrorists in Cambrils, I mean. You liked it, didn't you? Tell me the truth, go on. You can tell me. Did you enjoy it or not?" He pauses: his voice has become sinuous and warm, confidential. "That's what you are, don't kid yourself. You were born like that and that's how you'll die. People don't change. And neither will you. That's why you don't want to go and find Ferrer: because you know you'll kill him. Isn't that right?" The smile on the corporal's face is now a full smile, almost wild, shameless. "No, Melchor, you're no better than me, even if you appear to be now. You're worse. Much worse. And you know it, don't you?"

Melchor nods, as if he really did know it, and wonders if the other man is right. Then he feels like punching him. Then, for the second time in recent days, he feels like crying. Then he says: "Just get dressed, please."

Salom takes a moment longer before giving in, but finally, slowly and reluctantly, he stands up, walks to his bedroom and gets dressed. Minutes later, the two men get into Melchor's car and drive wordlessly from Salom's house to the police station.

Despite it being a Saturday night, the streets of Gandesa are almost deserted, and they meet hardly any other cars on avenida de Catalunya. Melchor makes an effort not to think of anything, but he doesn't manage it: he thinks of what Salom has just said to him, he thinks about Salom's daughters, he thinks about Cosette, he thinks about the four years he's spent in Terra Alta, he thinks about Javert.

When he parks in front of the station, he is still thinking of the police inspector from *Les Misérables*, and at that moment he makes out Sergeant Blai through the glass wall of the foyer, a brilliant rectangular prism like an illuminated aquarium in the middle of the night, which everyone in the station calls the Fishtank. When he sees the vehicle in the street, Sergeant Blai makes as if to come out, but in the end he stays inside, watching them. Melchor points to the sergeant and says: "He's waiting for you."

Salom turns to face him. In the faint light from the dashboard, Melchor sees the dried blood in the sticky curls of his moustache and beard, but most of all he sees that his earlier expression of security has evaporated, devoured by a cowering helplessness, by an asphyxiating anguish, by a speck of agonised, terminal hope.

"Can we really not settle this, Melchor?" he asks. "We still

have time. We could tell Blai it was all a joke, or a misunder-
standing. We could tell him we had a fight. Whatever."

Melchor shakes his head.

"He wouldn't believe it. Besides, Sirvent knows too. I told
you I just spoke to him."

"Of course, he'll believe it," Salom says. "And so will Sirvent." He pauses and implores: "Please. I ask you for the sake
of our friendship. I ask for the sake of our daughters."

Melchor sighs. For a couple of seconds, with his gaze fixed
on the darkness of the wasteland that stretches out in front
of them, he at last manages to think of nothing or to think
only that he's thinking nothing. Then he gestures towards the
entrance hall with an almost imperceptible nod and says without rage, without disgust and without sorrow: "Get out."

Salom does not beg again, nor does he protest, although he
takes his time getting out. Melchor hears him step down from
the car, but he doesn't see him do so; nor does he see him walk
the few metres to the station or go through the door that Sergeant Blai opens for him, doesn't even see him talking to the
sergeant in the artificial brightness of the foyer. The only thing
he sees, when he looks back at the station, is Blai on the other
side of the glass, facing him with his arms open in a questioning
gesture. Then he accelerates away.

4

Years later, when Melchor remembered his first months in Terra Alta, he would always think they were the happiest of his life.

The day he returned *The Tin Drum*, the novel by Günter Grass, to the library, Olga was waiting for him behind the counter with a smile of complicity.

"That's that," she said in greeting. "I finished reading it."

There was no need to say that she meant *Les Misérables*. The library had just opened and the dazzling light of that blustery morning was pouring in through the glass facade. For a while they talked about the novel without anyone bothering them, taking words out of each other's mouths, Olga sitting behind the counter and Melchor leaning on it with the copy of the Günter Grass novel beside him. They talked about Jean Valjean and Monsieur Madeleine, about Javert, Fantine, Cosette and Marius, about Monsieur and Madame Thénardier, about Gavroche, Fauchelevent and the young revolutionaries led by Enjolras, about the battlefield at Waterloo and the barricades in Paris. At a certain moment, Olga tells Melchor again what she had said over the past few weeks every time he asked her if she'd finished reading the novel: that it was odd. Melchor again asked her why.

"It's sentimental, melodramatic, moralistic," Olga said. "In other words, it's everything I detest. But I couldn't stop reading it. There's the strange thing. It seemed, more than the novels I do like, to resemble reality, which I don't like."

"It also resembles reality in another way," Melchor endorsed her verdict. "In that it's enormous. At least that's the impression I get every time I reread it. That everything is in there." He paused and, with what he himself judged a total lack of modesty, added: "But most of all I have the impression it's talking about me."

"All novels talk about us," she said. "Isn't that what your friend meant?"

"What friend?"

"The one who told you that half the novel comes from the author and the other half from us."

"Yes, but with *Les Misérables* it's different."

Melchor tried to explain why it was different, but he failed. He was rescued from his failure by the day's first library users: an old couple who were returning a book and DVD and who were interested in an event that was taking place in the auditorium that evening.

"I didn't know you organised book launches," Melchor said when they were alone again.

"Not as many as I'd like," Olga said. "I also organise book clubs. You should join one. You'd like it. It's just what we're doing now, talking to people about what we read and . . ."

"Thanks," Melchor interrupted her. "I prefer to talk to you."

Olga smiled again, this time as if she were facing a teenager who was trying to seduce her and who didn't stand the slightest chance of success. With a sort of melancholy fondness she said: "Yeah. The problem is that I get paid to run the library, not to talk about books." She sighed, picked up *The Tin Drum*, asked: "Do you want to return it?"

Melchor said yes and waited in vain for Olga to ask, as she always did, what he'd thought of the book he'd just read. While she processed the return, Melchor pointed to the Grass novel.

"I liked this one too," he said. "But now I'd like you to recommend a twentieth-century novel that doesn't seem like one from the nineteenth."

As if Olga felt Melchor was trying to put her to the test (or as if she'd been waiting for this request for weeks), without thinking twice she walked over to the back shelves with her little bird or child steps and came straight back with a book by Georges Perec, *Life: A User's Manual*.

"It's ten times as long as *The Stranger*," Melchor said, perplexed.

"Yes," Olga said contentedly. "Almost as long as *Les Misérables*."

"A bit of respect, please," Melchor retorted. "*Les Misérables* is twice as long."

Olga laughed. Melchor looked avidly at the web of lines that bloomed around the edges of her lips, picked up the book and sat down beside the big window overlooking the gravel courtyard.

He spent the morning there, reading Perec's novel, and at one-thirty, just before the library closed, he asked Olga to the bar in the plaza for an aperitif.

"Thanks, but I don't have time," Olga said. "But I live nearby, though, and I'm going that way. You too, right?"

They left the library together and walked together towards the old part of town. Winter was about to arrive in Terra Alta, and a cold wind swept the streets of Gandesa and cleansed the brilliant blue sky of clouds. They talked more about *Les*

Misérables, but when they reached the Farola roundabout, as the north wind furiously shook the branches of the palm tree that stood in its centre, and they crossed it, heading for the plaza, Melchor managed to divert the conversation to Olga's job. She told him that hers was the biggest library in Terra Alta and explained that she ran it with the help of one other librarian, Llúcia, who usually worked in the afternoons (just as she usually worked in the mornings), and that, although in theory Llúcia was in charge of looking after the library users and she was supposed to be in charge of the management, in practice they both shared the work as much as they could. She said that what she most enjoyed, though, apart from organising readings, poetry workshops and book clubs, was ordering books and travelling to book fairs to buy them.

They had reached the shelter of the plaza, where the wind blew less intensely. Melchor asked her why she had chosen to be a librarian. She stopped and looked at him as if nobody had ever asked her that question before; wrapped up in her coat, she held her dishevelled hair back with one hand.

"I don't know," she admitted. "I think because I like order. Why did you join the police?"

Melchor didn't need to think about his reply.

"Because of *Les Misérables*."

"But the police inspector is the bad guy of *Les Misérables*!"

"That's not true," Melchor answered, with absolute conviction. "Javert is a false bad guy."

For several minutes he tried to convince Olga that Javert was not what he seemed. Olga listened without contradicting him.

"He's a false bad guy," Melchor said again emphatically. "Don't you realise? And the false bad guys are the real good guys."

"If that's the case, there must also be false good guys," Olga said.

"Of course," Melchor said. "They're the real bad guys."

They were sitting on a stone bench under a mulberry tree with bare branches, the yellow leaves of which swirled around in the middle of the plaza, agitated by the wind. In front of them, on the terrace of the bar where Melchor spent many mornings reading, and where he often had lunch or dinner, only one table was occupied by two locals who, like them, fought off the cold wind with the warmth of the sun. Olga, who had greeted several people along the way, waved to a woman who walked past the bench. They talked about Terra Alta. Then Melchor asked her to tell him about her years in Barcelona.

"How do you know I lived in Barcelona?" Olga said.

"Salom told me."

"What else did Salom tell you?"

"Nothing."

"You're a terrible liar, you know? Especially for a policeman."

Melchor tried to defend himself, half-joking and half-serious, but Olga wouldn't let him and he again had the feeling that she was treating him like a teenager, which didn't bother him. Olga talked about Salom, about Salom's wife and daughters; as she did so she ran a distracted finger along a notch in the rough edge of the bench, a smooth and deep cleft like a scar in the stone. Then, belatedly answering Melchor's question, she spoke of her years in Barcelona, and asked him if he missed the city. Melchor was quick to say no.

"Well, except for one thing."

"What's that?"

"The noise."

Olga looked at him again. Melchor thought she was the most beautiful woman he had ever known.

"I'm serious," he said. "Without noise I can't get to sleep, at first I couldn't sleep a wink. Thank goodness, I found some sleeping pills. But sometimes the silence still wakes me up in the middle of the night."

"Shhh," whispered Olga, holding the index finger of her left hand to her lips and taking Melchor's hand in her right.

As they listened to the silence, the plaza seemed to fill with noises: the sound of cars going round the Farola roundabout behind them, the moaning of the wind in the bare branches of the mulberry, and the murmur of dry leaves gathering and scattering in little whirls in front of them. Then a group of little girls burst into the plaza, shouting and running around the fountain. They laughed at their failure. Olga let go of Melchor's hand and stared at the seam in the polished stone that became a notch at the edge of the bench, stroking it again. They remained silent for a few seconds. Not knowing why, Melchor thought of his mother.

"Do you know what this is?" Olga asked, pointing to the notch and looking up at Melchor. "During the war Franco's African soldiers used to sharpen their bayonets here. My father saw them do it."

In his thoughts, Melchor's mother was replaced by the pensioners playing dominoes in the Terra Alta and by a handful of Republican soldiers who had miraculously survived their own suicidal courage eighty years ago near the chapel of Santa Magdalena del Pinell.

"Your father fought in the war?"

"No," Olga answered. "He was just a child. But when he was old he talked about it a lot."

Melchor began to smile.

"It seems that here in Terra Alta the old folks never stop talking about the war," he said. "A colleague told me the other day that it's as if nothing has happened here in the last eighty years."

"It may well be true," Olga said. "Here, sooner or later, everything gets explained by the war." She watched the little girls for a moment; they were now playing hide-and-seek. The wind had died down, or was no longer reaching the plaza, the centre of which was carpeted in fallen mulberry leaves. "Anyway, what people are really talking about, if you pay attention, is not the war. It's the Battle of the Ebro. They're two different things. The battle lasted four months, the war lasted three years. The battle was a horror, but it had a certain dignity, it was fought by people from all over the world, it's in the history books and we even dedicate memorials to it. But the rest of the war was simply a horror, an unmitigated horror. And what really scarred us was the war, not the Battle of the Ebro." She looked down again, still touching the groove made by the old iron of bayonets: it seemed as though her fingers were reading everything she was saying in the smooth stone. "The battle only left visible wounds," she went on, as if she were no longer talking to Melchor but to herself. "The trenches, the ruins, the hills filled with shrapnel, all those things the tourists like so much. But the real wounds are the ones nobody sees. The ones people carry around in secret. Those are the ones that explain everything, but nobody talks about those ones. And, who knows, maybe it's good that that's the way it is."

A gust of wind ruffled her hair again. The terrace of the bar had emptied, but the little girls were still playing hide-and-seek.

"Well," Olga sighed, standing up. "I'd better get going. Llúcia's not in this week and I've got to open the library for the afternoon."

Melchor stood up too.

"Can we go out tomorrow?"

She looked at him again as if he were a teenager.

"I can't tomorrow," she said.

Melchor persisted: he suggested meeting on Wednesday, Thursday. Olga claimed or invented excuse after excuse, but finally gave in.

"OK, we'll meet on Friday." She pointed at the tables of the bar, on the other side of the plaza. "Over there at eight?"

At eight, when he arrived at the bar, the Gandesa town plaza was teeming with people come from all over Terra Alta to start their weekend there. Night had fallen quite a bit earlier and the wrought-iron street lamps here and there illuminated the area with a diffuse light, but the temperature was pleasant. Rowdy customers packed the terrace as well as the interior of the bar, and the waiters, sweaty and busy, circulated among them with trays raised high, trying in vain to serve all their requests.

Melchor took the first available table. He was wearing new clothes – trousers, jacket and shirt bought the previous day in a shop that a colleague had recommended in Móra d'Ebre – and he had put on a tie; although he hadn't arranged to meet Olga for dinner, he was planning to invite her to dinner. The waiter who served him knew him and teased him about his outfit; Melchor smiled politely, ordered a Coca-Cola, and the waiter brought it with unexpected speed. There were motorcycles coming and going around the plaza with the roar of exhaust pipes, and a gale of dance music blasted from a sports car parked in front of the bar, surrounded by young people. In the groups around Melchor people talked, shouted, laughed, jumped up and danced to the syncopated rhythm of the music, holding beer bottles, cocktails and cigarettes; every once in a while, someone would notice Melchor, sitting in the middle of the hubbub, alone with his Coke, and would stare or smile or elbow whoever was next to them. Melchor would smile at anyone who smiled at him, enjoying the spring-like night in the middle of autumn, the crowd and the music, waiting patiently.

Olga showed up shortly before nine, when Melchor had ordered his second Coke and some of the groups had begun to leave the plaza.

"Sorry I'm late," she said. "I had to send off a list of books. Today was the deadline for the funding application."

Melchor noticed that she had not dressed for a date.

"Don't worry," he said, hiding his disappointment. "I just got here."

Olga looked Melchor up and down and exclaimed: "Wow! Don't you look smart."

He took it as a compliment and offered her a chair. She seemed tired; looking around her for a moment, she registered without enthusiasm the revelry still reigning on the terrace.

"If you want we could go somewhere else," he proposed.

Olga responded by grabbing the arm of a passing waiter and ordering a vodka and orange.

"What for?" she said. She sat down beside Melchor. "In half an hour there'll be nobody left here."

By ten, the plaza was more or less abandoned, and inside the bar and on the terrace there were only a few remnants of that festive crowd: a small group, a few isolated couples or regulars watching television, drinking beer and nibbling at tapas. By then they'd had time to talk about this, that and the other: they'd talked about *Les Misérables* and about *Life: A User's Manual* ("You were right," Melchor said. "This one doesn't seem like a nineteenth-century novel written in the twentieth.

It's more like a whole bunch of nineteenth-century novels stuck into one from the twentieth"), about Olga's family, who she'd lost touch with after the death of her father, and about Melchor's family, which he'd lied about; he'd also lied about why he was in Terra Alta, although not about the fact that, as far as he knew, his posting in the region was only temporary.

Olga was now on her second vodka and orange and Melchor on his third Coke.

"Do you never drink alcohol?"

"No."

"I thought all policemen drank."

"I've already drunk all I needed to drink."

By her third vodka and orange, Olga was, he realised, quite intoxicated. She'd smoked a couple of cigarettes – one she'd cadged from a waiter, the other from another customer – and started asking Melchor about his love life. He felt obliged to ask her in turn.

"I'm sure Salom told you everything."

Melchor denied it.

"You're still a shitty liar, you know."

She laughed, choked on the smoke, coughed. Then she took another sip of her vodka and orange and squinted at the empty plaza, lit by the street lamps.

"Tell me something, Melchor?" she said. "Do you like Terra Alta?"

"I love it."

Olga greeted his reply with a sceptical expression and a drag on her cigarette. Melchor thought she was going to accuse him of lying again.

"I used to detest it," she said. "Now it's not that I like it. It's just that I don't know if I could live anywhere else." She fell silent, still looking at the plaza; the smoke from her cigarette floated straight up towards the sky. Withdrawn, shaking her head, after a couple of seconds she murmured: "Men." Then she turned towards Melchor, smiled blurrily, and continued with a vaguely defiant air: "Do you really want me to tell you about my love life?"

Melchor kept quiet.

"It makes me laugh to call it that," Olga said. "My love life. Do you want to know the truth? The truth is I've had a few men, but they all turned out to be big disappointments. All of them. They didn't love me. I gave them everything, but they gave me nothing. Nothing at all. They couldn't even give me a child." She smoked and blew out the smoke without inhaling. "What do you think? You don't need to say anything. A disaster. That's the truth. A fucking disaster. Tell me, what do you think?"

Melchor kept watching her but didn't answer straight away.

"I wouldn't leave you," he said at last.

Olga's eyes opened wide. For a moment Melchor thought she was going to burst out laughing; the next moment he thought the opposite: that she'd stopped looking at him as if he were a teenager, that for the first time she was looking at him as she would at a man. With her voice hoarse with alcohol, almost with rage, Olga said: "You're not my boyfriend, *poli*."

"No," Melchor said. "But prepare yourself, because I will be."

He did not invite Olga to dinner: at around ten-thirty he had to take her home, where he helped her to vomit into the toilet, put on her pyjamas and get into bed. He stayed with her until she fell asleep, and then he left. Olga phoned him at noon on

Saturday. She said Salom had given her his number and that she had a horrific hangover, and she apologised for the spectacle of the previous night. That's what she called it: a spectacle.

"I'm sorry," she apologised again. "I'm not used to drinking."

To make it up to him, to thank him for his patience with her, Olga invited him to lunch the next day. Melchor accepted. Years later, whenever he remembered those first happy months in Terra Alta, he tried to remember exactly what happened during that lunch. He never managed it. All he remembered was that, before even finishing the meal, he and Olga were in bed. They spent the afternoon and night there, and did not separate until, on Monday, Melchor got up very early and went to work at the station.

From that moment on his life began to revolve exclusively around Olga. If he had to work the evening shift, he spent the mornings in the library with Olga; if he had to work the morning shift, he spent the afternoons at Olga's house (as long as Olga wasn't working) or in the library (if Olga had to work). The rest of the time he was also with Olga: if he could, he had breakfast, lunch and dinner with Olga, went shopping with Olga and slept with Olga. He also read with Olga, who taught him the pleasure of reading aloud and being read to.

They finished reading *Life: A User's Manual* together and, when they got to the end, they decided by mutual consent, to alternate reading nineteenth-century novels – including those written in the twentieth century – with twentieth-century novels – including those that held nineteenth-century novels within them. During their first two weekends, they barely left Olga's house: they spent the mornings, afternoons and nights making love, sleeping, eating and reading the Perec novel to each other. On the third weekend, they drove to Valderrobres (or Vall-de-roures), had lunch there and walked around the old part of town for the afternoon and browsed in a bookshop called Serret, where they bought several books. They drove back to Gandesa after dark, and they'd just left Calaceite when Melchor suggested they move in together. Olga, who was driving with her glasses on, turned her head towards him for a moment and, in the semi-darkness of the car, her eyes gave off an ambiguous glint.

"You're mad, *poli*," she replied. "You want your colleagues to put me in jail for the perversion of minors?"

"I'm serious."

"Me too."

"Everyone in town knows we're going out together."

"I don't care what everyone in town knows, going out together is one thing, living together is something else. No way," Olga said. "What we've got is really lovely, all of it, but it won't last. Do you know how old I am?"

"No," he lied. "And I don't care."

"Well, I do. I'm old enough to be your mother, don't you understand? In four days you'll be tired of me and . . ."

"I'm not going to get tired of you."

"Of course you are. You'll get tired and look for a girl your own age, which is what you should have done from the start, instead of getting involved with an old lady. Look, Melchor, listen to me: let's not complicate things, let's just enjoy this as long as it lasts and then be friends. OK? Meanwhile, each in his own house and God in all of them, as my father used to say. So, please don't bring up the subject again."

They didn't talk about it again. And, although everyone in town knew that he and Olga were going out together, because they saw them together everywhere (in the street, in the shops, in the cafés, in the library, especially in the library), everyone acted as if they didn't know or as if there was no difference between knowing and not knowing. The only one who couldn't act as if he didn't know was Salom, who dropped Melchor off at the library several times, and sometimes went to pick him up from there. One afternoon, after the three of them had had coffee at the bar on the plaza, the corporal said to Melchor as the two policemen walked to their car: "What have you given Olga? I've never seen her like that."

"Like how?"

"So content."

Melchor laughed inside, but just said: "I thought you were going to tell me off."

"Tell you off, why?"

"For going out with a woman fifteen years older than me."

Salom laughed out loud.

"I'm not your father, kid," he reminded him. "And I wouldn't tell you off if I were. Quite the contrary."

They had parked the car in front of the Town Hall. They got in and, as the corporal was about to pull out, he seemed to hesitate.

"Will you let me tell you something?" he said. "It's about Olga."

It was a flash of intuition: his instinct warned him that, no matter what Salom said about her, it could only disturb his happiness. Besides, who was the corporal to meddle in his affairs? So he said: "Better not tell me anything. I already know enough about Olga."

But years later, when he often remembered those first months in Terra Alta as the happiest time of his life, Melchor would not only admire himself for letting prudence overrule curiosity that afternoon. He would also often wonder if his instinct had not betrayed him, if he hadn't made a mistake letting himself be dominated by the fear of losing Olga, if it might not have been better if Salom had told him what he wanted to tell him, and if he had listened.

One Thursday afternoon, while he was shopping with Olga in the Coviran supermarket, on the avenida de Aragón, Melchor took a call from Deputy Inspector Barrera, who told him that the following day Commissioner Fuster, from the Information division, was coming to see him at the station, and told him to be at his office at noon.

"Who was that?" Olga asked.

"Nobody," Melchor said, guessing what Fuster wanted to talk about. "Just work stuff."

He was not wrong. At noon the following day, when he walked into the deputy inspector's office, the two commanding officers were waiting for him. Melchor had not seen Fuster since the day when, in a building attached to the Mossos d'Esquadra general headquarters, in Sabadell, the commissioner had laid out the plan he'd come up with to protect Melchor from possible Islamist reprisals after his intervention in the Cambrils attack. Now, with more vitality and confidence than Melchor remembered, the commissioner was asking about the time he'd spent in Terra Alta and, after receiving several monosyllabic responses from Melchor, got down to business, not without first losing himself in a confusing prologue about how important Melchor continued to be to the force, the pride they took in him and the absolute priority they placed on his personal safety, all that interspersed with some excuse for not having been in touch with him in the intervening months.

Sitting beside Fuster, Barrera, in his too tight uniform, simply listened to the commissioner with his hands clasped over his potbelly, occasionally smoothing his moustache while nodding

284

in approval every once in a while. Fuster reminded Melchor that almost nine months had passed since the Cambrils attack and assured him that during that time they had been more attentive than ever to the movements of suspected terrorist cells and any possible suspects entering or leaving the country, working always in concert with the National Police and the Guardia Civil. He explained that they'd arrived at the conclusion that the terrorist cell that had carried out the attacks in Barcelona and Cambrils, trained and recruited in Ripoll by an imam who died just before the attacks while handling explosives in a house in Alcanar, was an isolated organisation, with no links to any other terrorists: they knew this because they had thoroughly investigated several trips the imam had taken to the city of Vilvoorde, a focal point of Islamism in Belgium, where he tried and failed to get a job at a mosque, and three trips by various terrorists to Paris, where they tried to get into contact with members of Islamic State, also in vain; similarly futile had been the arrests undertaken by the Moroccan police of relatives and people close to the terrorists: there was not the slightest indication that any of their acolytes were directed by or in contact with other terrorists. When he reached this point, Fuster declared that, by the express desire of the chief of police, he had come down there to give him the good news in person.

"We think you can go home," the commissioner announced, his fingertips drumming on the edge of the table around which the three of them were seated. "It goes without saying that we can't guarantee your safety one hundred per cent, because you know that's impossible. But we are reasonably sure that your identity has not been leaked beyond the force, that nobody is looking for you and that, at least for now, you are not in danger."

Fuster waited expectantly for Melchor's reaction, but the reaction did not come. Disconcerted, he turned to Deputy Inspector Barrera: the two commanders looked at each other for a moment and then back at Melchor.

"It's over," Fuster said, lifting his hands off the table and opening his arms, as if he thought Melchor might not have understood his words and was making an effort to translate them into gestures. "The danger is past. Goodbye Terra Alta. You can come back: civilisation awaits."

Melchor still did not react.

"You don't seem very enthusiastic about the news," the commissioner said.

"I didn't think it would come so soon," Melchor said.

"What did you expect?" Fuster said, smiling, stroking his goatee. "That we were going to reward you by leaving you in the lurch down here in the back of beyond? Is that how you think we repay our heroes? Is that the opinion you have of the force?" Turning back to Deputy Inspector Barrera, he explained: "Before sending him here we promised the situation would go on no longer than necessary and that . . ." He suddenly stopped, perhaps detecting something odd on the deputy inspector's face. "Don't get me wrong, Barrera, I didn't mean that Terra Alta is a bad post. Quite the opposite: if one is born here or has a family or is looking for peace and quiet, it couldn't be better. What I meant was that it doesn't seem like the best posting for a lad like him, with his record and his whole future before him."

"You don't have to apologise," the deputy inspector reassured him. "Things are what they are, and this is the back of beyond. Take it from me, I've spent half my life here. But I've only got four years left. As soon as I retire, I'll be leaving."

"Do I have a choice?" Melchor asked.

"Choice?" Fuster said. "You mean can you choose a different posting? Of course, they have authorised me very precisely to propose—"

"I mean, can I stay here?" Melchor said.

"Here? In Terra Alta?"

Melchor nodded. Fuster couldn't believe what he was hearing. He turned back to the deputy inspector again, whose moustache arched in a contemptuous sneer.

"I don't have any problem with it," he said. "Four years, I'm telling you. I won't be around much longer anyway . . ."

Barrera didn't finish his sentence. Fuster blinked once, twice, three times; then looked back at Melchor.

"Are you sure?"

"No," he admitted. "But I'd like some time to think about it."

The request opened a silence during which Fuster's fingertips started to drum on the edge of the table again.

"Alright," he resolved, exchanging the drumming for one resolute knock. "Take as much time as you need." He stood up and extended his hand. "When you've decided, let us know."

"Well, sooner or later it had to happen," Olga said that night, as soon as Melchor started to tell her about his interview with Commissioner Fuster and Deputy Inspector Barrera. They were in her kitchen. She had stopped preparing dinner, taken off her apron and collapsed into a chair. "So, when do you go back to Barcelona?"

"I didn't say I'm going back," he said. "I said they have suggested I go back. It's different. Besides, I'm sure I could choose another post."

"Are you going back or not?" Olga insisted without looking at him: she had a hard expression and her lips were tense.

"I don't know. It depends. I've asked for time to think it over."

"Depends on what?"

"Do you want me to tell you the truth?"

"Of course."

"It depends on you."

"And what does that mean?"

"It means that, if you want to come with me, we'll go. If not, I'll stay."

"Don't talk nonsense."

"I'm not talking nonsense. I don't want to argue."

"You are talking nonsense. You have to live your life. You're a child. You can't be depending on a woman of my age. I told you: this was just for a while. We both knew it, nobody . . ."

Melchor didn't understand the rest of the sentence. Olga's expression softened, her features trembled, her lips pursed. Melchor tried to touch her cheek, but she pushed his hand away.

"I am going to live my life," Melchor said. "But I want to live it with you."

"You're still a terrible liar," Olga said. "And you're still talking nonsense. My work is here. I have no plans to move. I told you that too."

"Then I'll stay."

"If you stay, you'll regret it."

"I won't regret it."

"Of course you'll regret it. Sooner or later you'll regret it. And you'll blame me. And everything will go to hell."

"I won't regret it. Please don't cry."

Melchor caressed her wet cheek, an ear, her hair. This time Olga didn't resist; she just wrung her hands in her lap.

"Don't cry," Melchor said. "Everything's fine. Nothing's going wrong."

"Of course it is. It's the same old thing. Everything's gone to hell."

"Nothing's wrong. Believe me."

Melchor again asked her to stop crying, assured her that he loved her, explained that he wanted to live with her, promised her they wouldn't be separated. Olga kept her eyes glued to the floor, as if unable to look Melchor in the face; thick tears rolled down her cheeks, her neck, disappeared under her shirt.

"You don't understand, Melchor," she sobbed. "I am forty years old. My life was a mess, a roller coaster of hopes and disappointments. Until, finally, after my father's death, I came to terms with it. I was alone, I had nothing, but I had found a balance, I was living well in my own way. And then you showed up and . . . Shit. I'm an idiot. I started to have hopes again. I knew this would end badly, it couldn't end any other way, but I did nothing to avoid it." Olga looked up at Melchor: her eyes were flooded with tears. "But you can. Please, don't make things worse," she begged. "Call Barcelona and tell them you'll go back. Please."

The next morning, Melchor called Commissioner Fuster and told him he was staying in Terra Alta.

Two days later he left his apartment on the Bot road and moved into Olga's house, in the old part of town, very close to plaza de la Iglesia. He didn't tell anybody, not even Salom; nor Vivales, who still called him once in a while from Barcelona ("Everything under control, kid?"), nor Carmen Lucas, who was still writing him e-mails from El Llano de Molina. There was no reason to do so. In fact, the change of residence didn't appear to make a big difference to Melchor's life, except that sharing a house with Olga stopped him from being quite so linked to her workplace to the point that in recent months some patrons had taken him for a librarian. With good reason: more than once he opened or closed the library because Olga couldn't, on another occasion he took her place because she had to go to a book fair in Barcelona, and, although he always roundly refused to join the book clubs Olga organised, because he maintained that his only book club was her, he soon helped her to improve or make possible certain events at the library: when the school holidays began in June, he took charge of the library-lido service, and for several weeks in a row, from twelve to two, or three to six, depending on the shift he was working at the station, he took a cart-load of books and magazines to the municipal swimming pool so the children and teenagers could read there; he was also soon involved in the book launches, and ended up taking care of all the catering for them: he reserved a table at the restaurant where Olga, once the event was finished, would take the speakers out for dinner, he bought wine, crisps and nuts, he set up the folding chairs in the auditorium, arranged the refreshments on the tables and, at the end of the presentation, helped to serve them, which, when this news reached the station, earned him the nickname "The Waiter" for several weeks.

That Melchor's life didn't appear to have changed didn't mean it hadn't changed in reality. The transformation had started a while earlier, although only now did he become aware of it. The first symptom of this radical change, or at least the first he managed to recognise, was the disappearance of his chronic insomnia: shortly after moving in with Olga, Melchor noticed from one day to the next that the silence of Terra Alta had stopped keeping him awake. He gave up the sleeping pills and began to sleep better than he ever had, six, seven or even eight hours straight every night, like a log. Still, it was only when Olga began to read *Les Misérables* to him that he knew without a shadow of a doubt that he was no longer the same man who had arrived in Terra Alta the year before.

It was at the beginning of that summer, once they were already in the habit of reading aloud to each other and spent several hours doing so every night before going to sleep (sometimes they even did it in the daytime). When Melchor first read *Les Misérables* he was still a teenager, locked up in the Quatres Camins prison and, like Monseigneur Myriel, felt that the world was an illness, but unlike that benevolent bishop who had turned Jean Valjean into Monsieur Madeleine and believed that the world's illness had a cure and that cure was God, Melchor held on to the certainty that he inhabited a world without God and that this world's illness was incurable; now, however, so many years later, while Olga read the beginning of the novel to him in the Terra Alta nights, sitting on their shared bed, with her glasses on and legs crossed, Melchor thought he understood that his fury, his solitude and his teenage pain had disorientated him, that at least for him the illness of the world had a cure and that cure was Olga's love. The first few times he read *Les Misérables*, when, especially after his mother's death, his orphan's resentment and desolation transfigured the novel into a living or philosophical guide, into an oracular or wise book or an object of reflection to turn round and round like a kaleidoscope, Melchor admired Javert above all the other heroes that populated it – his integrity, his scorn for evil, his sense of justice – but he had also felt, like Jean Valjean, that his life was a war, that in that war he was the vanquished and he had no weapons to defend himself other than hatred, nor any other fuel to feed on; now, so many years later, having searched tirelessly for his mother's murderers and resigned himself to that crime going unpunished, he still admired Javert, he still believed in what he believed in and still felt that he was the secret hero of *Les Misérables*, but as soon as Olga began to read the novel to him he realised he no longer identified with Jean Valjean, that he no longer felt at war with the world, that thanks to Olga's love he had signed a peace treaty with it and was no longer vanquished. As for his hatred, one night Melchor interrupted Olga as she had just begun to read the passage in which, still very near the beginning of the book, the miserable Jean Valjean reappears in the novel behind the mask of the prosperous Monsieur Madeleine, converted into the benefactor of Montreuil-sur-Mer (and very soon to be its mayor); while Olga scrutinised him from over the rim of her glasses, he confessed that Monsieur Madeleine had always struck him as an unbelievable character, that it seemed implausible to him that he didn't hate those who had unjustly incarcerated him and destroyed his youth, his whole life, that he couldn't believe that he didn't even hate Javert, the righteous police inspector who hounds and harasses him until the end.

"Well, he does seem believable to me," Olga said, after looking thoughtful for a moment. She took her glasses off and put the open book down on top of the sheets. "And do you know why?"

"Why?"

"Because the difference between Jean Valjean and Monsieur Madeleine is not that one is bad and the other good, but that Jean Valjean is a stupid young man and Monsieur Madeleine is an intelligent old man. And hating is not very intelligent, don't you think?"

The argument surprised Melchor, who judged it to be flimsy, although he only managed to counteract it with another, which, as soon as it was out of his mouth, seemed flimsier still.

"I think hatred is a respectable feeling."

"Well, I don't," Olga said. "Hating someone is like drinking a glass of poison in order to kill the person you hate."

Years later, when he began to think that those first months in Terra Alta had been the happiest time of his life, Melchor would often remember that conversation with Olga. He would remember it for itself and for something that happened the next morning that he would also remember frequently when he thought about those happy months. It all started just after a routine meeting had ended in Sergeant Blai's office, when he discovered three missed messages from Olga. He called her and asked if something was wrong. Olga answered in an urgent, choked voice: she said yes, added that she was at home and that he should come straight there. And then said it again: "Please, Melchor, come straight home."

He had never made quicker time on the kilometre between his work and home. He flew down the stairs and through the corridors of the station, across the wasteland that surrounded it and through the winding streets of the town, a swarm of dark thoughts besieged his head, but by the time he opened the door he only had one name in mind: Luciano Barón. He found Olga sitting at the kitchen table, with a herbal tea in front of her, untouched. The tranquillity of the scene did not calm him. Sweating and panting, he asked what had happened. She stood up; Melchor thought she looked a bit pale, too serious. He repeated his question.

"I'm pregnant."

Melchor stood open-mouthed. He had prepared for everything, but not for that. He only managed to say: "How do you know?"

Olga explained that, although her period was several weeks late, she hadn't wanted to alarm him, and that morning she'd gone to a pharmacy, taken a pregnancy test and the result was positive. Then she'd gone to the Gandesa health centre, where she'd been examined by a doctor.

"I'm two months gone."

Standing in front of her, Melchor was still paralysed by a mixture of relief and surprise; he had a lump in his throat, but he didn't know that it was joy.

"Aren't you going to say anything?"

Melchor didn't know what to say.

"Tell me you love me," Olga said. "Tell me you want to have a baby."

"I love you," Melchor repeated. "I want to have a baby."

There was a silence.

"Really?" she said.

Melchor heard himself say something he'd never said before: "I swear on my mother's grave."

Olga didn't smile, didn't lose her serious expression: she took two steps towards him and wrapped her arms around his neck.

"Come here, *poli*," she said. "I'm going to screw your brains out."

That very night, Melchor proposed. Olga refused: said they were fine the way they were, that people who love each other don't need to sign a piece of paper to live together. Since he didn't want to argue with her, Melchor didn't tell her what he thought of that rationalisation; he simply insisted they get married, said she knew more than he did about books, but he knew more than she did about laws, proved to her that, according to the law, it was best for them to get married, for the baby, for her and especially for him, and he assured her that he would feel much calmer if they did. Olga's resistance didn't survive breakfast.

They were married a month later, at the end of July, when they'd just learned the baby would be a girl.

"We'll call her Cosette," Olga said when she found out. "Like Jean Valjean's daughter."

Preparations for the wedding were so absorbing that they had to suspend their reading of *Les Misérables*. The ceremony was held in Gandesa Town Hall, officiated by a councilman and witnessed by Salom and Carmen Lucas, who had driven up from El Llano de Molina the previous night with Pepe; Vivales also attended the ceremony, and Salom's daughters, who that summer were working at a cooperative vineyard in Batea. The lawyer cried his eyes out during the ceremony – "What can I say, Pepe," he apologised to Carmen Lucas' husband, who'd just met him the night before and was making an effort to console him. "Deep down I'm a sentimental fool" – and, once the ceremony was over, Olga and Melchor took everyone to dinner at the Hotel Piqué.

Melchor would also recall that banquet many years later, of course, when he was no longer as happy as he had been in those early months in Terra Alta, although he would only clearly remember three things.

The first was that, without him having asked nor her having warned him in advance, Carmen Lucas spent the meal lying to Olga about his mother, and about the relationship she'd had with his mother, inventing a biography for her where reality mingled with fiction, while Pepe peppered Vivales with questions about his job as a criminal lawyer and asked him to translate or explain things the waiters and other diners said in Catalan.

The second was that, when dessert was served, all Melchor's colleagues burst into the bar, except for Feliu, who was on the night shift that weekend.

"Congratulations, *españolazo*!" Sergeant Blai squeezed him in his arms, on the verge of tears. "I told you the women in Terra Alta were the best."

"My condolences," Martínez said, hugging him. "My father always said that this marriage thing is like a castle under siege: the ones outside want to get in and the ones inside want to get out."

"Christ almighty, Melchor!" Sirvent was horrified. "You can't even stop drinking Coke on your own wedding day?"

"That Sirvent doesn't know anything," Corominas mocked him, patting Melchor on the shoulder. "Don't you worry, man: Coke's good for the *titola*."

"The *titola*?" Pepe enquired, turning to Vivales.

"The prick, my dear Pepe," answered the lawyer, as red as a tomato, one arm around the shoulders of his new friend and the other holding a snifter of Jameson Black Barrel. "The goddamn prick."

But what Melchor would remember most often years later was a conversation he had at the beginning of the dinner with Claudia and Mireia, Salom's daughters, with whom he'd barely crossed paths before. Both, in reply to his questions, told him about their studies in Barcelona and their summer jobs at the Batea cooperative, and at one point Claudia, the elder, mentioned that she was looking for a part-time job for next term.

"It's crazy," Salom interrupted with unexpected bitterness, and Melchor realised it wasn't the first time the father and his daughter had argued about this matter. "Hard enough as it is to pass a course when you spend all your time studying; imagine working and studying at the same time."

He felt obliged to back up his friend. Mireia supported Claudia.

"You're right," she said to Melchor, although he knew Mireia was talking to her father. "But do you know how much it costs us to live in Barcelona?"

The sisters started reeling off expenses, interrupting and

correcting each other, until, unhappy with the turn the conversation had taken, Salom put the brakes on.

"Of course," he said, adopting a different tone, somewhere between festive and sarcastic, but also addressing Melchor. "Both of them want to do master's degrees and doctorates and all that stuff that young people do these days, and they want to do it in Boston or I don't know where. What do you reckon? But there's no reason to worry. When that time comes the people of this country will have started to pay the police what we deserve for saving their bacon in an emergency and I can give these two swots what they deserve, right, Melchor? Anyway, kid, if you're going to carry on having babies you can start getting ready for . . ."

"For what?" Olga put the brakes on him in turn, pointing to Salom's daughters while whispering in Melchor's ear: she had barely had a drop to drink, but her eyes were shining as if she were drunk. "Careful with these two beauties. Either one of you touch my groom, I'll kill you. Took me long enough to catch him."

They didn't go away on a honeymoon. Before the wedding they'd bandied the possibility about, but in the end decided to stay home with the fridge full of food and drink, devoted exclusively to feeling how their daughter was growing in Olga's womb, to making love and reading *Les Misérables*. They picked up the novel where they'd left off, just before the end of Book One, and almost the first thing Olga read were words that for a moment Melchor thought she'd invented, because he didn't remember ever having read them before: "Fate abruptly brought together, and wedded with its resistless power, these two shattered lives, dissimilar in years, but similar in sorrow. The one, indeed, was the complement of the other. [. . .] To meet was to find one another." He didn't say anything, but the next day, while Olga was reading a fragment from the beginning of the second volume to him, a similar feeling suddenly hit him. "Had anybody said to him: 'Do you desire anything better?' he would have answered: 'No.' Had God said to him: 'Do you desire heaven?' He would have answered: 'I should be the loser.'" Melchor stopped Olga and asked her to reread what she'd just read. They had just made love, they'd lost track of time and were sitting naked on the floor in the hall, backs against the wall, facing each other.

"You see?" Melchor said, once Olga had finished rereading the passage. "This book is about me."

She took off her glasses and shook her head slowly.

"Not anymore, *poli*," she said. "Now it's about us."

5

The interrogations of Salom and Ferrer are held in Tortosa and last the regulation three days. Melchor takes no part in them. Deputy Inspector Gomà presides in person, assisted by Sergeant Pires and Sergeant Blai. Officially, he is the one who solved the murders by discovering the defective enlargement of Ferrer's fingerprint while consulting the Adell file for another case, and quickly unmasked Salom with the help of Melchor and Sirvent.

"Gomà's made a tit of himself," Blai tells Melchor, who he keeps regularly informed of how the interrogations are going. "He's desperately trying to spin it, but you can't polish a turd. And you know something, *españolazo*? You were right about everything."

During the interrogations, Ferrer confesses that he planned the murder of Francisco Adell. That he decided to get rid of him when he discovered that his father-in-law was going to deprive his family of half his fortune by bequeathing it to Opus Dei (a decision of which the directors of Opus Dei have since disclaimed all knowledge and indeed denied emphatically). That he hired some Mexican hit men in the city of Puebla to carry out the murder, two professionals who stayed barely twenty-four hours in Spain, disappearing back to their own country once the job was done. That he asked Corporal Salom for help and in exchange promised to pay him four hundred thousand euros. That it was Salom who designed the operation and in part directed or advised or protected it, who chose the day it should be carried out, and who instructed him that on the evening before, during the weekly dinner the Gráficas Adell management always had at the Adells' country house, he should switch off the security cameras, and how and when he should do so. That it was he, Ferrer, who on the night of the murder, after having dinner with his wife and two younger daughters and having watched television for a while with his wife, left his house, while in theory he was in his studio listening to music as he usually did on Saturday nights until late, and drove to his in-laws' house, opened the door for the hit men, left them there to carry out their work, and returned to his studio, having only been out for forty-five minutes, an hour at most. That he didn't know that the hit men were going to torture his in-laws. That the atrocity was not part of the deal, and, like the murder of his mother-in-law and the Romanian maid, had been the idea, exclusively, of those men, and that he didn't know why they had done it, although he understood that they had killed his mother-in-law and the maid in order not to leave any witnesses. What was part of the plan, however (or at least the plan between him and Salom, because it had been his idea), was that he should take his wife's car to his in-laws' house that night, a vehicle equipped with Continental tyres, just like those on Josep Grau's car, and drive up to the house to leave tyre tracks in front of the door, because Salom considered Grau the perfect scapegoat, and during the investigation steered suspicion towards him whenever he could. And that it had also been Salom who had kept him informed about the progress of the investigation at every stage and had fixed the only error he'd made – leaving a fingerprint in the security room when he deactivated the alarms and cameras on the Friday before the murder – and who had warned him of the police tap on his phone and facilitated Melchor's break-in at Gráficas Adell, so Ferrer could catch him on the premises. That he had hired someone to scare Olga and dissuade Melchor once and for all from investigating the Adell case, but the scare turned into a lethal hit-and-run, a confession which a short time later Ferrer is forced to admit is false, or at least partially false, when Sergeant Blai discovers by chance that, the morning after Olga was hit by the car, Ferrer had taken a black Volkswagen he had rented the evening before in Tortosa to a garage in Amposta, to get them to fix the bodywork, which had been dented.

For his part, Salom confirms in general terms Ferrer's confession, although he qualifies various points. He affirms, for example, that he tried everything to dissuade him from his plan of ending his father-in-law's life, but that, when he was unable to do so, he chose to advise and protect his friend, to keep him from getting caught. Furthermore, he denies that he was the architect of the operation, though not that he guarded it or gave advice. He also denies that he had any contact with the hit men Ferrer hired, or the slightest inkling that they planned to torture the Adells, which he also doesn't believe his friend had any knowledge of either, and has no idea what to attribute it to. And he maintains that he did everything he could to try to placate Ferrer's anxiety provoked by Melchor's stubbornness in continuing to investigate the Adell case, and that he found out that Olga had been knocked down by a car, to his horror, only after it had already happened.

This is essentially the substance of Salom's and Ferrer's depositions, a tale that in the judgment of Deputy Inspector

Gomà as well as Sergeants Pires and Blai leaves only a few loose ends, which perhaps the judge can tie up in the course of the trial, though no-one believes they'll be able to resolve the main ones: who the hit men were who Ferrer hired, how or through whom he contacted them (questions Salom has no answers for and Ferrer only vague or abstract or unlikely ones) and why were they so merciless to the Adells.

The arrest of Ferrer and Salom revives the Adell case in the media, which exploits it tenaciously and turns Sergeant Blai into the hero of the moment. When the news becomes public, Vivales calls Melchor, discusses the matter with him and asks if the danger has passed.

"Everything under control?"

"I'm not sure," Melchor says. "Can you keep Cosette for a few more days?"

"As many as you want," the lawyer assures him. "The kid is like God here."

One day later, Melchor asks for an interview with Deputy Inspector Barrera, who receives him in his office that very afternoon as if there had never been any unpleasantness between them. They talk about the resolution of the Adell case (although they tiptoe over Salom's arrest) and Barrera asks about Melchor's personal situation and promises to start to take steps to find him a post in another station.

"Do you have any preference?" he asks obligingly.

"None. All I want is to get away from here as soon as possible."

It's true. Since Olga's death, he feels that Terra Alta is no longer his home. And, although he went back to work at the station after Salom was arrested and tried to resume his interrupted routine, he soon realised that it was impossible, because the relationship with his colleagues cannot now be what it used

302

to be: with Olga dead and Salom in prison awaiting trial, with Sergeant Blai absent as well, abducted by the media and the judicial consequences of the resurrection of the Adell case, Melchor is again everyone's centre of attention, more or less as he was at Nou Barris after the Islamist attack in Cambrils, except worse, because now he is not the hero but the villain or the victim and must bear silent reproaches for having denounced a colleague and compassionate looks for having lost his wife. Giving up alcohol again doesn't improve things; the only thing that improves them is the prospect of leaving Terra Alta and going to live somewhere else with Cosette. Apart from that, Melchor is certain (with a certainty that deeply disturbs him, but which he shares with no-one) that in reality the Adell case is not altogether resolved, or that it has been falsely resolved. One week after Salom and Ferrer are arrested, Sergeant Blai returns to the station and, after bragging to his subordinates about his media adventures ("This fame thing is more annoying than it seems, lads"), he asks Melchor to come to his office.

"You'll never guess what I've found out," he says.

"What?"

"That Gomà has left his wife and moved in with Pires. Didn't I tell you those two had something going on? What I didn't know was that he was the lapdog, not her. Lately life brings nothing but surprises, eh?"

"I thought you were going to tell me you'd done me the second favour I asked you for."

"What favour was that?"

Melchor reminds him of the e-mail address he gave him so he could find out whose it was.

"Fuck me, you're right!" Sergeant Blai exclaims, clutching his bald head. "What with all the TV and the piss-taking, it had quite slipped my mind. I sent the address to headquarters and they told me it's impossible to know who opened the account, but they're sure the message was sent to you from an account in Mexico City. Is that any use to you?"

The information was of no use, except to heighten the unease that was eating away at him. One day, driving past the turn-off that leads to the dirt road up to Rosa Adell's house, just before Corbera d'Ebre if you are coming on the road from Gandesa, Melchor gives in to temptation and takes it; but, when he arrives at the front door and is about to ring the bell, he decides that it's too early to talk to the Adells' daughter and that she must still be in a state of shock over her husband's arrest, charged with her parents' murder, so he turns around and leaves. Another day he is on the verge of calling Josep Grau to talk about Gráficas Adell's Mexican subsidiary, but there too at the last minute he stops himself. That very night everything changes. Shortly after eleven, having finished his shift, when he's just parked his car in front of his apartment in Vilalba dels Arcs and has taken out his keys to open the door to the building, Melchor notices a sudden movement behind him and, before he can turn around or get a hand on his gun, he feels a blow to his head and a jab in his neck at the same time.

He regains consciousness half an hour later, sitting in the back seat of a car with tinted windows driving on a motorway at cruising speed. He has an acidic taste in his mouth, his head hurts, his hands and feet are bound with rope and his mobile phone and pistol have been taken away. Four silent men are travelling with him, one on either side of him and two in front, all wearing suits and ties. Melchor exchanges a glance with the driver in the rear-view mirror and comprehends that it would be pointless to ask who they are or where they are taking him, but a few minutes later, when he sees a sign announcing the exit for Vilafranca del Penedès, he realises they are driving towards

Barcelona. Overwhelmed by sorrow, by a sort of bittersweet sensation of defeat, he tells himself he will never see Cosette again; he also tells himself that he has found his destiny and that he will finally know the truth and, with an unexpected contentment (because he knows that Cosette is safe and that Vivales will take care of her), he prepares to die.

They pass Sant Sadurní d'Anoia, Sant Andreu de la Barca, Pallejà, Sant Boi de Llobregat and, just past El Prat de Llobregat, enter Barcelona on the coastal ring road. The bright lights of the night-time city dazzle him, he recognises the streets clogged with traffic, the pavements teeming with people, and is astonished that it took him four years of hardly ever leaving Terra Alta to turn into something he never imagined he'd be: a country bumpkin. They advance parallel to the sea, the dense gloom of which he catches glimpses of here and there in the darkness of the night. They pass the cemetery of Montjuïc and after a while they take exit 22 in the direction of Puerto Olímpico. At that moment, the man who is sitting on his left unties the ropes (first the one around his ankles, then around his wrists) while the man on his right digs the silencer of a pistol into his ribs and, when the car parks at the entrance to the Hotel Arts, among the jumble of taxis, private cars and limousines, says the only sentence Melchor has heard spoken on the whole trip:

"Now you're going to behave like a good boy and everything will go as smooth as silk. Got it?"

Surrounded by the four men and spurred on by the barrels of their guns, he enters the lobby of the Hotel Arts, waits for the lift, gets into it and rides up to the twenty-first floor. The group gets out of the lift, walks down an empty corridor and enters a room. More than a room, it is a suite, or perhaps an apartment, which at first looks to Melchor to be vacant although it is not, as he discovers after crossing a room in which a nurse is listlessly watching television. Then he passes through a darkened bedroom and advances down another hallway, the end of which seems to open into another room in deep shadow. He has not yet entered when he hears a male voice.

"Come in, Señor Marín. Forgive me for not standing up. The infirmities of old age, you know."

The man is lying on an ottoman, with a blanket pulled up to his waist and the illuminated cityscape behind him, on the other side of a huge window. Beside him is a nurse, and on his right a small table, beyond that an armchair and then a standard lamp that casts a soft ochre light; on his left, on the floor, is a stack of books. The man sits up a little with some difficulty and motions to Melchor that he should sit in the chair, while the nurse helps him arrange a cushion under his lower back.

"Sit down, please," the man says. "Make yourself comfortable. What would you like to drink?" he asks, pointing to a low table, where Melchor can see, beside the remote control for the television, a bowl of fruit, a plate of biscuits, a teapot and two cups, a bottle of water, glasses. "Take what you like. If you would like something special, please ask. I want you to feel at ease. You don't know how sorry I am to have had you brought here in this way, but I didn't think there was any other. I hope you'll be able to forgive me. Have my men treated you well?"

While he's talking to Melchor, the stranger gives a signal to the nurse and bodyguards to withdraw. They all obey, except for one bodyguard, who remains, stationed on the threshold, almost invisible in the darkness of the hallway. Melchor sits in the armchair and looks at the man. He is in his eighties at least, and speaks Spanish with a Mexican accent, gesticulating with arthritic hands that emerge from some sort of grey shirt or nightshirt; in the dim lamplight, he seems small and compact, with a patrician air, blue eyes, waxy skin, bald head and a constellation of liver spots.

"You will be wondering who I am and why I had you brought here," the old man says, with his hands clasped under his swollen chest, which rises and falls with the laborious rhythm of his breathing. "By the way, may I call you Melchor? It's a curious name. Who gave it to you?"

"My mother," he says.

"And do you know why she gave it to you?"

"She said that the first time she saw me I looked like one of the Magi."

The old man laughs with deep worn-out laughter. The laughter of a killer or a dying man, Melchor thinks.

"How sweet, your mamá." The old man adjusts the cushion at his back. "But, listen, aren't you going to eat anything? You won't have had any dinner, you must be hungry. Come on, eat something." Maybe to set an example for his guest, he pulls a grape off the stem and puts it in his mouth: a sunken mouth with wrinkled lips. "What were we talking about?" he says as he chews unenthusiastically. "Oh, yes. I was saying that you must be wondering who I am and why I've brought you here. Though I imagine you already have an idea."

"More or less," Melchor says.

With an expression of distaste, the old man takes a mess of seeds and skin from his mouth, leaves it on a plate and wipes his fingers with a linen napkin.

"Tell me, what idea have you formed?"

"That it's something to do with the Adell case."

"And what else?"

"That you were the one who sent the e-mail messages that helped me to solve it."

"Very good!" the old man says with approval, setting the

napkin down on the little table, turning towards Melchor, applauding silently, almost smiling. "I knew you were a very smart boy."

Melchor hears himself add: "And that you're planning to kill me."

"Oh, no, please, don't be melodramatic. How could you think that?" the old man says as he stops applauding and his shadow of a smile vanishes. "I am not a violent person. Actually, I hate violence. If you knew me, you'd know that. And speaking of knowing, I'm going to ask you a slightly more difficult question, especially for a Spaniard. Do you know who Daniel Armengol is?"

Melchor thinks the name sounds vaguely familiar, but after a few seconds says: "No."

"You see?" The old man clicks his tongue. "That's what you Spaniards are like. You've never paid attention to what happens in Mexico, as if my country were a little bit of shit, when the truth is that it's much better than your own, even if I say so myself." He pauses before announcing: "I am Daniel Armengol. And, believe me, in Mexico even the little squirts have heard of me. Which is terrible for a man in my position, between you and me: people with power, the less well known they are, the better. And I, at least in Mexico, have power. Too much, according to my enemies, who allege that I have the power to install and remove presidents. They exaggerate, of course. You know that enemies always overestimate a person, that's why we don't have to pay much attention to them, just enough to be able to get rid of them when the opportunity presents itself. But, as to what we're doing here, I'm going to tell you what I have to do with the Adell case. Are you comfortable? Are you sure you don't want to eat something? It's a bit of a long story. At least let me pour you some tea."

Before Armengol can move, the bodyguard in the hallway approaches, picks up the teapot, fills his cup and then Melchor's; the old man lets him do this, and picks up a biscuit and nibbles on it. As for Melchor, he is calmer now, less anxious: the welcome Armengol has offered him and the chime of truth that rings through what he says has imbued him with confidence, and he no longer believes he's in danger, at least not while he is with his host. That's why now the feeling that overwhelms him is not the resigned fatalism that filled him during the car journey, nor the vigilant amazement that has kept him in suspense since he arrived in that room, but curiosity. His head no longer hurts where the bodyguard hit him, the injection they used to put him to sleep has worn off and his eyes have adjusted to the semi-darkness created by the lamplight and the brightness of the urban sky from the window.

"I met Albert Ferrer four or five years ago, at a reception held by President Peña Nieto at the National Palace," Armengol finally begins, taking a trembling sip of tea. He speaks with a slow, husky voice accustomed to giving orders, his gaze fixed on the blank television screen, which hangs on the wall in front of him. Once he has poured the tea, the bodyguard withdraws to the hallway again, where Melchor can just make out the rounded tips of his shoes shifting constantly on the carpet, like a pair of little patent-leather creatures.

"Peña Nieto is a fool, but, once he was in power, he never stopped asking me for favours, and I was incapable of denying him. It's one of the many disadvantages of being a patriot, you know. That day the president asked me to attend a reception for Spanish businessmen interested in Mexico, most of whom had already invested in the country and who needed to be seduced to invest more and to collaborate with Mexican businesses. One of those things. I don't know who introduced me to Ferrer, but I remember very clearly that he was introduced to me as the managing director of Gráficas Adell, an important Catalan graphic arts company that had founded a subsidiary in Puebla. That's what I was told. 'Oh,' I said to Ferrer, shaking his hand. 'I knew a man called Adell many years ago in Spain.' 'You don't say,' Ferrer replied. 'Yes,' I said. 'He was Catalan, from Terra Alta, on the border with Aragón, I don't know if you know the area.' Ferrer told me that of course he knew it, he was from there, Gráficas Adell had started and still had its headquarters there, and that he wasn't surprised that I'd met someone called Adell from Terra Alta, because it was quite a common surname in the region. Then we started to join the dots and in the end it turned out that the Adell I knew was his father-in-law, the owner of Gráficas Adell."

"And how did you know him?"

"Ferrer asked me the same thing, and do you know how I would have liked to answer him?" Armengol pauses, as if leaving room for Melchor's reply, which does not come. "By laughing. But laughing with a huge guffaw, the kind that echoes around the Palace like thunder and makes everyone turn and look to see, wondering whether to appear scandalised or complicit . . . Believe me, I would have loved to reply like that. But I couldn't, all I could say was something like, 'Oh, that's a long story, I'll tell you some other time.' Then we chatted for a while about his company, the company's projects, a bit of everything. Ferrer knew who I was, or at least he'd heard of me, I told you people know who I am as soon as they set foot in Mexico, so I suppose he was a bit impressed at having met me in person. I don't know why I say 'I suppose' when I know for sure, I knew it as soon as I shook his hand, you know what Ferrer's like, he is transparent, he doesn't know how to deceive, his social climber's smile gives him away, another fool like President

310

Peña Nieto, worse than Peña Nieto, the most manipulable man in the world, because nobody is easier to manipulate than a social climber." Armengol nibbles another biscuit, or perhaps the same one as before, picks up his teacup again and takes another sip. "That was all for that day," he continues, setting the cup back down on the table. "He gave me his card, someone gave him mine and I urged him to come and see me whenever he wanted. I was very insistent, enough for him to understand that I wasn't just saying it, and after a while he came to see me. He took longer than I expected, but he did. Of course, if he hadn't, I would have sought him out. But I preferred him to come to me, the last thing I wanted was for him to notice anything odd."

Armengol says that, while waiting for Ferrer's call, he was amassing information about Francisco Adell, about Gráficas Adell, about Ferrer himself, and that he gradually came to realise that the chance encounter was more than a little miracle: it was destiny winking at him. Only then did he decide to carry out a project that for decades had been haunting him like a recurring dream, and which he'd never known whether he could or even wanted to carry out.

"Anyone might say that I was waiting for Fate to decide," Armengol mumbles. "Anyway, an opportunity like that only comes around once in a lifetime, and I decided to take advantage of it."

He pauses, sighs – his breathing is still troubled and laboured – and leans back on the ottoman. Melchor picks up his cup of tea and takes a sip: it's lukewarm, but it agrees with him.

"I don't know what excuse Ferrer made to ask me for the first meeting," Armengol goes on, "but I do remember that I told him to come to Mexico City, and that I invited him to lunch in my office. From that day on I began, how shall I put it, I began to seduce him. I'm not going to deceive you: it was very

311

easy." Armengol turns to Melchor, who at that moment realises that his pale eyes are green, and feline. "Do you like poetry?"

Melchor finds the question disconcerting, mostly because it reminds him of Olga, or rather reminds him that, for the first time since Olga died, he has spent several hours not thinking about her, and he understands that he is already being unfaithful to her, that he has already begun to forget her.

"No, of course not," Armengol answers for him, as if correcting himself. "You prefer novels, right? That's what I've been told. I get bored by novels, I confess. I never understand why I should read about things that haven't happened when I can read about things that really have. That's what poetry is, what really happens. 'That last infirmity of noble mind.' That's how Milton described vanity. What do you think? Even the best men have their grain of vanity. Which means the worse the man the more vanity he has, and the worst, like Ferrer, are nothing but vanity. So that's the flank I attacked."

Armengol says he did so with care, taking his time, because he was aware that, if he went too quickly, he could frighten his prey and ruin the operation. To begin with, they saw each other a couple of times in his office in the capital and he did a few favours for Ferrer, things of little significance: solved a couple of bureaucratic problems for him, hired an advertising company for him on advantageous terms, put him in contact with influential people. In this way he gained his trust and made him believe that he considered him worthwhile, a young man with a future, someone with whom he was anxious to strengthen ties and do business.

"You know Ferrer a little." Armengol smiles again, and his hands flutter in his lap, before alighting there again. "Imagine how he felt. Nobody in his own company had ever paid the slightest attention to him, he'd always been a puppet, the boss'

312

son-in-law, a guy who's only there because of his connections. And suddenly someone like me is seeking him out, making friends with him and flattering him. Son of a bitch, he puffed up like a turkey."

Armengol and Ferrer began to meet for lunch or dinner every time the latter travelled to Mexico, usually in Mexico City, but the old man occasionally travelled to Puebla to see him. After a while their relationship moved from purely professional onto a more personal level, or that's what Armengol made Ferrer believe: a father–son relationship, or master and disciple. That was when Armengol gave it all he had. From the beginning he'd known that Ferrer's relationship with Adell was either so-so or outright bad, that not only did Adell not respect him, but he belittled and humiliated him, and he applied himself to setting the young man against his father-in-law: he told him wicked things he'd done (real or invented), told him he didn't understand how Adell could refuse to recognise his talent unless he envied him, he made him see that his father-in-law was not only a gutless despot but also an antiquated and egocentric businessman who was putting obstacles in the way of Ferrer's professional career, frustrating his expectations and annihilating him as a person, he put it into his head that Gráficas Adell should just be a starting point for him, he must not remain stranded inside a worthy but modest company without prospects, he had to start thinking big, insinuated that the two of them were in a position to embark on great projects together, confessed that he had plans to expand his business into Spain and told him he had thought Ferrer could be his man in that country.

"Anyway," Armengol sums up, "as well as inciting him against Adell, I filled his head with delusions of grandeur – I got him drunk. Or he got himself drunk. To top it all, I had some luck: in spite of the favours I did for him, the Puebla subsidiary was struggling and beginning to lose money; Adell was considering closing it and that led him into even more confrontations with Ferrer."

At this point Armengol falls silent again, his gaze fixed on the television screen, as if his mind has gone blank. His chest continues rising and falling to the laboured rhythm of his breathing.

"I heard about that," Melchor says, to encourage him to continue. "It seems in recent times they were always arguing about the subsidiary in Puebla."

"Of course," Armengol says, returning from his reverie. "Ferrer didn't want it closed for anything in the world, the other Latin-American subsidiaries also interested him, but this one was the jewel in his crown and nobody controlled him over here. Besides, I had convinced him that it should be his springboard into other businesses in Mexico. All this, as I say, embittered him even further against his father-in-law, and eventually our lunches together were devoted exclusively to ranting and raving against Adell, sometimes I even pretended to defend him so Ferrer could let off steam and attack him with more venom, it's a trick I've learned over the years, if you know someone's got an enemy and you want to incite them against that enemy, defend him a little, speak well of him. Never fails. And, well, while I was priming Ferrer as if he were a bomb, I looked for a way to make him explode. As you know, I soon found it."

"Opus Dei."

"Quite so." Armengol swivels in the ottoman to applaud him soundlessly again, this time with a wider smile. "You'll agree with me that you Spaniards are horrible people," he says as he settles down again. "They spend their lives committing heinous acts, worse and worse, and in the end, instead of facing up to the consequences of their actions like men, they get frightened and beg the priests to forgive them and send them to heaven. How cowardly, damn it, how disgraceful! But, anyway, since I know very well what you lot are like, I wasn't surprised to find out that a heartless soul like Adell had converted into an Opus Holy Joe. As soon as I found out, I saw the heavens open, and when I realised Ferrer was ripe, I told him I had it from a reliable source that Adell was planning to leave half his fortune to Opus."

"And it wasn't true?"

"Well, I don't know. It's plausible, don't you think? There are people who are so afraid of death that they are capable of believing any old foolishness they're told about it. Adell was one of those, no question, and rightly so: if I had done the things he'd done, right now I'd be terrified. Although it doesn't matter if it's true or not, the important thing is that Ferrer believed it. From then on, everything was easy."

"Do you mean you convinced him to murder his father-in-law?"

"Bullseye again," Armengol says, this time without applause, without even a smile. "If he didn't want to lose half his wife's inheritance, what choice did he have? And, do me a favour, credit where credit's due: I was the one who convinced him and also the one who organised it all. Or do you think an idiot like Ferrer could have done what he did all by himself? I encouraged him, I lent him the guts he didn't have and made him understand that killing his father-in-law would be much easier than he thought, that he wasn't going to run any risks and he'd barely have to lift a finger, because I would do all the crucial things."

"For example, hire the murderers."

"For example. Two specialists who did their work well and left no traces. In my country we have a few of those."

"Was it also your idea to get Salom involved?"

"You mean your colleague?"

"Yes."

"Ah, no, that was Ferrer's. And I have to admit it was a good idea, though I don't understand how it occurred to him. One day, when he'd already decided to kill his father-in-law, he told me that he had a good friend in the police, who would most likely be involved in the investigation, because he was stationed in Terra Alta and knew the family and I don't know what else. It must have seemed to him like buying an insurance policy, an airbag or something like that, in case we made any mistakes, and it struck me as not a bad idea. After all, I had just as much interest as he did in it all working out and them not getting caught. And, if it hadn't been for you, it would all have worked out fine. In fact, the last time I saw Ferrer, in Mexico City, the investigation had been closed and we drank a toast to how easy it had all been and how well it had turned out. That was the day Ferrer told me his friend had covered up his only mistake by blurring the enlargement of the fingerprint he'd left in his in-laws' house – you can't imagine how proud he was to have had the idea all by himself of getting the corporal involved, how he boasted . . . But you kept digging and digging, and Ferrer got nervous and screwed the whole thing up."

At that moment the nurse who had been with the old man when Melchor arrived interrupts them. "It's time, Don Daniel," she says. Armengol looks at her, but, when she and the bodyguard from the hallway take a step towards him, the old man stops them with a gesture. Slowly, he takes off the blanket that covers him from the waist down and, with a moan, leans forward until he's sitting upright.

316

Melchor then sees his whole body. In spite of the nightshirt that disguises his shape, it's obvious that he is much more heavily built than he appears to be when reclining on the ottoman and that, under his Roman emperor's bust of a head and his abbot's double chin, he still has a powerful trunk, strong arms and rough hands. From the waist down, however, his appearance is that of a fragile, diminished man: the nightshirt reveals a pair of pale, sickly and pointed knees, and feet so small they look incapable of supporting his great frame. A plastic catheter sticks out from below the nightshirt and leads to a bag that lies at his feet, full of a dark liquid. Seeing him like that, voluminous and precarious, panting, Melchor is certain for the first time that the man is seriously ill.

"I want you to know that I am very sorry about the death of your wife," Armengol says. "That was also entirely Ferrer's doing, not mine."

The two men stare at each other for a couple of seconds during which Melchor perceives a faint foetid odour of medicine and putrefaction. The old man says, "You believe me, right?"

Melchor doesn't think the old man is lying to him, but says:

"What I'm wondering is why you sent me those e-mails. Why you're telling me all this. And why you were so keen to kill Francisco Adell."

"Ah," Armengol says, as if he had been waiting for Melchor's questions. "That is the best part of my story, my friend." Encouraged by the old man, the nurse and bodyguard help him to stand up and, almost carrying him, take him out of the room as he adds: "Be kind enough to wait a few minutes, Melchor. I'll be back."

Alone – not even watched by the little patent-leather creatures on the fitted carpet of the hallway – Melchor stands up and stretches his legs while looking around the room. Beside the television there is a desk, and on top of the desk a jug with a bouquet of fresh flowers; in the corner beside a somewhat cubist still life stands a telescope mounted on a tripod pointing towards the window. Melchor looks through it at his city stretching out before him like a black expanse studded with fireflies and familiar presences: to his right, the Glòries Tower, shaped like a suppository, its skin covered in illuminated blue and red scales; in front of him the open seam of calle Marina, which ends at the Sagrada Familia; to his left the solid shadow of the Ciutadella; and beyond, the Collserola mountains, with the darkened fairground at the top of Tibidabo, like the gloomy skeleton of a gigantic spaceship grounded on the horizon. Melchor stays for a while, spellbound by the spectacle and thinking of Cosette sleeping down there, warm, tiny, soft, fluttering and protected, thinking he'll see her again soon and that, even though he might meet his fate that very night, it won't be what he was imagining when he was travelling here in a car hours earlier, sure that this was the end.

Armengol reappears, escorted by both nurses and one bodyguard, with the catheter and a fresh bag protruding from beneath his nightshirt, which is not the same one he was wearing before.

"I'm sorry to keep you waiting," he says, as lively as if they'd given him a shot of cortisone. "Have you eaten anything? Are you sleepy? I've always slept very little, but recently I've only been sleeping in very short spells. I hope you're like me, because now comes the most interesting part of my story."

With help, Armengol lies back down on the ottoman, arranges the cushion behind his back and covers his legs with the blanket. For his part, Melchor takes his seat again in the armchair beside him. The nurses leave, and Melchor senses that the bodyguard is no longer stationed in the hallway. Is

318

it because the old man is no longer distrustful of him and has given instructions not to keep watch over them? Or is it that he doesn't want anyone to hear the next part of his tale, not even a subordinate?

"Well, the time has come to tell you the truth," Armengol declares. "The truth is that I am not Mexican. I am Spanish. Don't misinterpret me, please. What I mean is that, although I am Mexican in my heart, and Mexico is my homeland and the country that has given me everything, I was born in Spain. Guess where? You can't guess. I'll tell you: in Terra Alta. In Bot, to be precise. That's how I know Francisco Adell, Francesc we called him in the village. After the war he Castilianised his name. He was from Bot, too, our families knew each other. His father was a day labourer who worked for the richest man in town, the owner of Ca Paladella; my papá had a grocery store. They were two humble families, although his was more humble than mine and, as far as I know, they'd always got along fine. Until the war came. I was born that very year, in '36, so I have no direct memories of it, they are all borrowed memories, things my uncles told me, or that I read in books. The thing is, the beginning of the war was terrible in Terra Alta. Although, more than the war, what they lived through there was the revolution, right? First the revolution and then the war. Two horrors, for want of one."

The first began in the summer, Armengol tells him. At the beginning of September a busload of Barcelona anarchists arrived in Terra Alta; the bus was painted black with white skulls on it, and its occupants began to kill people in cold blood. In a short time they had sown terror all over the region, and not just in our region: in lower Aragón as well, in Ribera d'Ebre, in the whole area. They burst into villages, talked to the local anarchists, asked for a list of right-wingers and killed them all.

"To give you an idea," the old man says, "in Gandesa, in a single night, they killed twenty-nine people. That was the famous Spanish revolution, at the beginning of the war: an authentic orgy of blood. Nice, eh? Oh, and then they say we Mexicans are violent. The truth is that, compared to you, we are a peaceful and compassionate people. But wait, here comes the good bit. Do you know what they told the Barcelona anarchists in Bot when they arrived in the village asking for a list of right-wing people? They told them not to worry, that they didn't need any outsiders to come and do the job for them, that they, the people of the village, had already done it."

They were not lying, Armengol went on. In the first days of the war the local Republicans executed twelve or thirteen people a kilometre outside Corbera d'Ebre, along a straight stretch of the road that Melchor must have driven a thousand times, the old man imagines, and where until recently a cross commemorated the murders. Among those twelve or thirteen people, neighbours of the criminals, was Francisco Adell's father. It is not known for certain why they killed him: perhaps because he was as faithful as a dog to his boss and, since they didn't find his boss, they killed him instead; perhaps because he was Catholic and went to Mass on Sundays; perhaps because someone wanted to take revenge.

"There are people who forget that the war was that as well," the old man says. "A valve for alleviating hatreds, quarrels and resentment accumulated over years."

Armengol clears his throat, stretches out a hand towards the table and a bodyguard immediately appears and pours him some water, then, at the old man's request, takes away the teapot, fruit bowl and the plate of biscuits. When the old man takes a sip of water, Melchor notices his hand is shaking again.

"Adell was almost ten years older than me, so he must've

been nine or ten when his father was killed," the old man goes on, leaving the glass on the cleared table and folding his hands in his lap. "I don't know if he was living in Bot then, but I do know he was there two years later when Franco's troops moved in, after the fall of the Aragón front, in the spring of '38. I was still living in the village, with my mamá. My papá, however, had fled. As far as I know, he hadn't done anything bad, he was a man of order and had not participated in the murders at the beginning of the war, he was just a member of Esquerra Republicana who had agreed to sit on the Town Council. But he was right to leave, because, when they returned to the village, the rebels held all the Republicans of the Town Council responsible for the murders, even though they knew very well that the decision about who to kill and who not to hadn't been made by the party committees. The problem was that they couldn't find anyone to hold responsible, because anyone who had any political or trade union links to the Republic had left, as had my father. They were afraid, believing that the Francoists were coming back to take revenge, and they were right."

Armengol falls silent. When he speaks again, his tale slows down yet more, and Melchor listens to it with the feeling that this is the first time the old man has told what he is telling and that he has to choose each word with the greatest care, like someone walking barefoot over broken glass.

"My papá spent the rest of the war in Barcelona, building air-raid shelters. And when the war ended, he went to France. He spent three years there, and we received the occasional letter from him, some of which I know almost by heart, my mamá taught me to read with them. Until he came home. It was a fatal error, and I'll never know why he made it. My aunt told me he couldn't live alone, that he missed me and my mamá, that he was dying to see us. That may be so, but I'm sure he was also influenced by Franco's propaganda, which said that Republicans who didn't have blood on their hands had nothing to fear, that they could come home without anyone bothering them. My papá must have believed that lie, and that was his undoing." He pauses, this time for longer, staying as still as Melchor. "I remember very well the day he came home, because I was six years old and because it was the happiest day of my life . . . Don't worry, I won't tell you, other people's happiness is irritating, and besides, I've told it to myself so many times. But I do want to tell you about another day, another scene on another day, I mean. I didn't witness it. I was told, or I put it together from phrases and comments I heard whispered here and there, I've never had it completely clear, perhaps because for years I didn't want it to be clear, or because I was afraid to establish the truth of it, and when I tried to do so it was too late. But I do know the essential bits."

The essential bits, the old man assures him in a voice that, while still hoarse, has turned so icy that at times it makes Melchor's blood run cold, are what follows.

One day his father and his mother were walking arm in arm in the village plaza. It was a Sunday, the plaza was full and his father had just returned to Bot after four years in exile. All of a sudden, someone shouted his name, and a boy began making his way through the crowd, or the crowd opened to let him pass; when he reached the couple, the boy raised the pistol he was clutching in one hand, pronounced a few words that nobody understood or that everybody instantly wanted to forget, and fired a shot into Armengol's father's head. Then, standing beside the body lying on the ground, he shot him twice more. All this happened in front of the whole village, without anyone moving a muscle to stop it, as if they were all paralysed with fear, or as if it weren't a murder but a ceremony.

322

"And I ask you," Armengol says, looking Melchor in the eye through the darkness. "I bet you can't guess the name of the boy who killed my papá."

The answer is so obvious that Melchor does not say it.

"Of course it was him," the old man says. "And do you know why Adell killed my papá like that, like an animal? What am I saying, like an animal? Much worse than an animal, animals aren't treated so badly. Do you know what crime he had committed? He was the only member of the Republican Town Council who returned after the war. What do you think of that?"

Armengol says that his father's body stayed in the plaza for hours, just as he'd fallen, his shattered head surrounded by an increasingly large puddle of blood. Nobody dared to approach until, after speaking to the mayor, Armengol's uncle took a wagon, loaded him onto it and buried him in an empty field. The old man did have memories of that day. What he most remembers was the silence. The silence in his house, the silence in the village. The silence of his family crying silently, as if one of their members had just committed an atrocious crime, a crime that had brought guilt and shame upon them for ever.

"That's the impression I had," Armengol confesses. "Everyone was crying, but they cried without a sound. All except my mamá, who was beside herself and wouldn't stop murmuring my father's name while caressing my head . . . The next day my uncle went to see the mayor again and then the priest, they dug up my papá and buried him in the cemetery, just my uncles, my cousins, my mamá and me. And two or three days later, after selling our house and our shop and my uncles' house as fast as possible, we got on the train and we left."

Armengol pauses again, sighs, and the noise of air being taken into and then expelled from his lungs seems to grate on the intense quiet of the room. Melchor thinks that, since he started to talk about the war, about his father and his mother, the old man's voice has not trembled once, and at that moment he remembers Olga sitting beside him on a bench in the plaza in Gandesa, not long after they'd first met, telling him about the war, telling him: "But the real wounds are other wounds. The ones nobody sees. The ones people carry in secret. Those are the ones that explain everything."

"Since that day I have not been back to Bot," Armengol says. "Not to Bot nor anywhere in Terra Alta. The rest you can probably imagine."

Shortly after they left Terra Alta, his mother was admitted to a psychiatric clinic in Tarragona and, since his uncles couldn't support him, he was sent to an orphanage. His mother died of tuberculosis a year and a half later. Around that time a friend of his uncle's wrote from France to say that the boss of the factory where he worked could offer him a job; his uncle accepted the offer without a second thought, but, instead of leaving just with his family, he took Daniel out of the orphanage and took him with them, as if he were their third child. They lived in France for a while, and when the world war ended they set sail for Mexico.

"I had just turned ten when we landed in the port of Veracruz," Armengol recalls. "And there another story began. But, tell me, can you now imagine what I felt the day I was introduced to Ferrer at President Peña Nieto's reception and learned that he was the son-in-law of Francisco Adell? No, you can't. Nobody can. Although you can more than most people, can't you?" Melchor knows or guesses what the old man is referring to, but says nothing. "Look, when I left Spain I was only a little kid, but I swore I would never again set foot in this country that had killed my parents. I hated Adell with all my heart and soul,

324

and I hated Spain. I kept my oath, I did not return to Spain. This is the first time I've come back. I concentrated on hating this country, but most of all I concentrated on hating Adell, until I had almost converted him into something abstract, not a flesh and blood man, but the incarnation of evil. Do you know what it's like to hate someone like that for more than seventy years?"

"I think so," Melchor says, remembering Olga. "More or less like drinking a glass of poison thinking it will kill the person you hate."

The old man turns towards Melchor, who glimpses a sparkle of triumph in his eyes.

"You see?" he says. "I knew you would understand me. That's how it is: hatred poisons us down to the marrow. And that's why I tried not to hate. To stop hating. Believe me, I did what I could. Forget the whole thing and act as if nothing had happened is what I tried to do. As if Adell didn't exist and hadn't killed my papá and driven my mamá mad and destroyed my life. As if neither he nor Terra Alta nor Spain existed. And do you know what? Sometimes I managed it. There were days when I didn't wake up thinking of Adell and Terra Alta, days when I got up with a prodigious lightness and everything flowed with a painless buoyancy, as if I were drugged, until I suddenly remembered, and the habitual weight returned, the habitual anguish and pain. There were days, hours like that. Hours without hatred. Few, but some, and more and more as I grew old and all this seemed to be left behind and disappear into the past, just as dreams disappear in our waking hours. But it was an illusion, of course. At the last moment Ferrer made his appearance and suddenly it all came back, whole and true, as if it had never left. And then I understood that, since I couldn't stop hating Adell, it would be best to get rid of him, to stop poisoning myself, I realised that was the only way to free myself of him and to die peacefully, by killing Adell and by making him suffer as he died, no matter how much he suffered it would be a tiny part of how much he had made me suffer, to avenge my papá and my mamá so they could finally rest in peace, so many years after they died."

"That's why you had them torture Adell and his wife."

"That's right," Armengol says with a soft singsong emphasis, sweetly, while Melchor remembers his first impression before the tortured corpses of the Adells had been that the slaughter had been the result of a ritual, and he says to himself that perhaps he was not so wrong after all. "So that at least at the end he might have an idea, an inkling, of what my life has been like. It's fair, don't you think? And, if not, tell me, what would you have done if you'd found your mamá's murderers, after searching for them for so long?"

"You have done a very thorough check on me."

"More than you can imagine. But you haven't answered my question."

"You're forgetting that not only have guilty people died, that, because of you, innocent people have also died. Among them, my wife."

"I'm not forgetting. I had nothing to do with that. I told you and I'll repeat it. Deep down, not even Ferrer is entirely responsible, after all he didn't do it on purpose, there was no cruelty or viciousness in what he did, he just wanted to scare you and your wife. It was a foolish act by a foolish man . . . I'm not trying to make excuses, but that's how it is and you know it. That's why you didn't take revenge on Ferrer as you would have on your mamá's murderers, that's why you preferred to let him be judged in court, the same with your friend the corporal. In any case, what happened to your wife was not right, by any stretch, and if I wanted to talk to you it's in part because of that, because I thought it was wrong, to be able to tell you I thought it was wrong. And I'm sorry. I had a wife too, you know? And two sons. I know what it's like to have a family. Now they're all dead, I'm the only one left, but I haven't forgotten . . . and I'll tell you something else, I'm also sorry about Adell's wife and the maid. I am not a violent person, I told you that too, I detest violence, but Adell's wife had to be made to suffer, it was necessary so that Adell would suffer, so that he would watch her suffer and understand what I have suffered. And the maid . . . let's say she was collateral damage, you can't make an omelette without breaking eggs, anyway, forgive the clichés, I think I'm starting to get tired from talking so much, I'm getting sleepy. What I mean is that I wanted to see you to apologise, because I felt you deserved an explanation. That's all. And also because I thought you'd understand me. I wasn't wrong, was I?"

Melchor is sure he has understood the old man, but he refuses to give him the satisfaction of telling him so, perhaps because by this hour of the morning he feels too close to him, and that proximity perturbs him. As if he now has the answer he has been looking for, or as if, deep down, he didn't really need it, Armengol stretches a little on the ottoman and puts the cushion that was behind his back under his neck.

"Would you mind switching off the light?" he says, pointing to the standard lamp. "It's too bright, it's bothering me a little."

Melchor switches off the lamp and the light in the room is reduced to the night outside that shines in through the window, so the shadows engulf the old man's body.

"Well, that's all I had to tell you," he says. "I hope it's made up for the trouble of the journey."

Again, Melchor declines to answer; but, after a few seconds

during which he hears only the increasingly tired breathing of his interlocutor, he speaks again: "Tell me one thing: Aren't you afraid Ferrer will inform against you? He may already have done so, but he may also do so during the trial."

"Oh, the trial." Armengol sighs. "How long do you think I have? You know the Spanish justice system better than I do. With a bit of luck, by the time the trial rolls around I'll no longer be here and there won't be any point in Ferrer informing on me. Not to mention that he might be wary of doing so, after seeing what happened to his in-laws. Perhaps that's why he hasn't informed on me yet, don't you think?"

"Could be," Melchor says, sufficiently confident of the situation to add: "Of course, I could also inform on you, if you let me leave. Don't forget I'm a policeman."

Melchor's hypothesis paints a white streak across the shadowed face of Armengol: it is his smile.

"I hadn't forgotten," he says. "And yes, what you say is right, of course, but I'm prepared to run that risk. And, by the way, what's this 'if I let you leave'? You're not obliged to be here, Melchor, I already told you I couldn't think of any other way to talk to you, and I apologised for the inconvenience. Although, now that you've brought up the subject, clear up a doubt for me. Are you sure you'd be believed if you walked out of here and turned me in? Think it over. What proof do you have? Who's going to testify against me? Ferrer? The hit men I hired? Where are those gentlemen? And another thing, do you think there's anyone left in Bot, or in all of Terra Alta, who remembers that Adell killed my father? Nobody arrested him or tried him! That crime happened more than seventy years ago! And there's no trace of it! Look for my father's name on the cenotaphs and war memorials of Terra Alta, and then come and tell me. Do you really think anyone's going to believe your story?" The white streak has disappeared from the old man's face, obliterated by the darkness again. "In any case, I am going to leave it to your judgment. But if you do want to, I'd recommend you do it soon, if you want to make sure I'm still here."

"You're planning to return to Mexico so soon?"

Armengol answers with a sort of grunt, which soon fades; his breathing is still grating on the silence.

"Do you know something?" he says, his voice growing quieter and more laboured. "A few days ago, when I came to the conclusion that you deserved the truth and made the decision to help you resolve the Adell case, I thought Spain was a bad place to live, but a good place to die. In my case, the best. Or perhaps the only place. So I decided the time had come to break the oath I swore when I left. And here I am, after so many years. I arrived yesterday. I've barely been out of this room yet, I still haven't been to Terra Alta, I didn't want to do that until I'd spoken with you. But, if I feel up to it, tomorrow I'll go to Bot. And, if not, I'll still go: after all, I came here without the permission of my doctors. Fucking doctors, those people want us to stay alive longer than we should . . . So, tomorrow I'll return to Terra Alta. I'll have a look around my village. I'll see how it all is, the streets, the houses, the countryside, the people. I'll see what's left of my memories. I'll look for my parents' shop, the house where we lived, the cemetery where they both lie. I'll stay a few days down there, we'll see how many, I've rented a farm. It will be strange, but . . . After that I'll be able to rest in peace, just like my papá and mamá, now that Adell has died the way he deserved to die, now that justice has been done and the hatred has finally ended. I don't know how much time I've got left, but probably not much, that's why I said if you want to inform on me, you should do it as soon as possible. Maybe it's fair that I should pay for what I've done. I don't know. You decide. You're a smart kid, I'll go along with whatever you decide, I'm too tired now to make decisions like that."

Armengol's voice dies down into an unintelligible murmur. Then Melchor hears him again: "May I ask you one last favour?"

Melchor says yes.

"Keep me company for a while, if you don't mind," the old man says. "Just a short while. When you get tired, leave. It's been a pleasure to chat with you. Now I'm tired, I need to rest."

Armengol's voice fades again into a muttering, and soon his regular breathing reveals that he has fallen asleep. Melchor stays still, sitting there in the armchair beside him, as if he were not watching over the sleep of an old man he just met, but that of a sick child or a close relative, with the old man's words resounding in his head and the Barcelona night shimmering on the other side of the glass, feeling an increasingly pleasant heaviness in his eyelids and an increasingly deep serenity in his limbs, with no desire to leave that suite to which he'd ascended as one ascends a scaffold, slipping towards the mental maelstrom of a sublime slumber in the centre of which spins the blurry certainty that he will see Cosette again and that, even though Olga won't be there, Terra Alta is still his home, that poor, rocky, inhospitable, temporary losers' place is the home that Olga has left him, the only homeland he knows and that knows him, that this is his true destiny.

He sleeps. He wakes. He wakes up straight away (or that's the impression he has), bewildered and anxious, not knowing where he is, although he comes back to reality when he sees the old man sleeping face up on his ottoman, inhaling and exhaling noisily. Beyond the window, dawn is beginning to bathe the city in an ashen light.

Melchor gets up, looks at Armengol for one last time trying to retain a final image of him – the senatorial skull, the wrinkled sealed eyelids, the fleshless cheeks and lips, the disdainful mouth, the aquiline profile, the hands crossed on his chest, rising and falling with the rhythm of his breathing – then walks down the empty corridor and crosses a bedroom with nobody in it. In the next room the two nurses and three bodyguards are in conversation, and greet his appearance without surprise. One of the nurses asks if Señor Armengol is still asleep. Melchor says yes, then asks the bodyguards for his mobile phone and pistol, and one of them returns them to him. For a moment he wonders whether to ask the nurses about the old man's health, what illness he's suffering from, how long he has to live; for an instant he wonders whether to leave him a message.

But he does neither one thing nor the other. He leaves the suite, takes the lift down to the lobby, walks out onto the street and, when he's about to get in a taxi, changes his mind and starts to walk in the direction of the port. He needs to clear his head, needs to put his thoughts in order, needs to decide. He walks quickly, breathing fresh, cool, damp dawn air and, before the ramp that leads down to the docks, he turns right on the promenade and carries on walking parallel to the beach. Does he need to decide, he wonders. Is it not all decided? The old man in whose company he just passed the night is at the very least responsible for the deaths of three people; he conceived the Adell murders and directed them from the shadows, he was the brains behind the operation, he impelled Ferrer to plan the murders, he hired the murderers and could identify them, he should pay for those deaths at least as much as Ferrer and Salom should, if not more. Armengol was right about one thing, Melchor continues thinking: he and his murdered father deserved justice, and they did not get it; but, by taking justice into his own hands, the old man lost the right that he'd had, because justice is form, as Deputy Inspector Barrera had told him, and he didn't respect it, and because, as Barrera had also told him, sometimes absolute justice can be the most absolute injustice. So, although it would probably not be easy to demonstrate Armengol's responsibility for the Adell case, he should not for that reason fail to report it or pursue him. What is there to decide, then, he asks himself once more. Is it not obvious he has to arrest the old man? No, he answers. Because while Armengol is not right, at the same time he is: it's true that he took justice into his own hands, but also that there was no other way to get it; it's true that he did not respect the forms of justice, but also true that it would have been impossible to get justice by respecting them. Is that sufficient reason not to punish him, he wonders again. And also, should his crime go unpunished for that reason? And also, had Armengol not wanted to tell him his story precisely to gain his indulgence, so someone able to understand what had happened would absolve him? And also, did this indulgence not make him complicit in the Adell case, and even in Olga's death?

Melchor leaves the promenade and walks down to the sea. A soft breeze is blowing and the horizon line is a reddish colour. An indecisive light illuminates the beach while he walks across it towards the water. When he gets to the edge he sits on the sand and stays there for a while, abstracted, hearing the sound of the waves, feeling the breeze on his face and watching the breaking day move across the sky. He hears barking and sees a dog and its owner in the distance. Then he sees another dog. Then he takes off his clothes and walks into the sea. To fight off the cold, he swims hard against the swell, diving under the surface over and over again. Now far from shore, where the waves are gentler, he turns on his back, and floats on the water with his eyes closed and his mind blank, feeling the weight of sleep on his eyelids and hearing the deep sound of the sea while letting himself be rocked by the waves. After a while he dives down again and swims strongly, this time parallel to the shore, and, between strokes, he suddenly realises that he must choose between two contradictory truths, between two equally fair reasons, and that impossible decision and the freezing water remind him of a scene from *Les Misérables*, actually one of the last scenes of the book, the moment when Javert, stunned after Jean Valjean rescues him from the barricade at Chanvrerie and refuses to execute him as he gave his word to do, allows the fugitive from justice he has been pursuing for years to escape, unable to arrest him, and thus betrays the rectilinear idea that sustains his life: Javert resigns himself to not fulfilling his duty as a police officer by letting Jean Valjean go, he chooses his own rules over and above the common rules, private justice over public justice, natural right over formal right, God's law over the law of men, and that unexpected decision, which dynamites his stoniest convictions, leaves him perplexed and defenceless, bereft of certainties, and plunges him into an icy desperation that drives him to throw himself into the blind waters of the Seine. Melchor knows that, even though now he must choose, as Javert had to, between two discordant truths, between two equally valid reasons, on this occasion he is not going to imitate him, he is not going to give in and let the water flood his lungs, in Terra Alta he has found certainties that Javert never even dreamed of, the certainty of Olga's love and Cosette's love, which is all that remains of Olga's love, and suddenly, for the first time in his life, Javert seems like a distant and alien character to him, his behaviour absurd, tragically ridiculous. And, as he keeps swimming and the waves keep breaking against his body, Melchor feels immeasurable compassion for Javert, infinite pity, as if he hadn't drowned in the Seine, but is drowning there, in that precise moment, inside him, vanishing into the water like the ghost of his absent father. Then Melchor stops swimming and floats in the sea, panting and looking at the beach, tinged gold by the first rays of morning sun, with the strip of sand ever busier, until he notices an anomalous sensation, as if he were melting inside, and he suddenly realises he is crying, hot, salty tears run down his cheeks and dissolve in the cold, salty seawater. Melchor cries as he did not cry on the day he heard his mother had been murdered or the day he learned that Olga had died, he cries as if he's crying for all the times he didn't cry and as if he's just learned to cry, there in the Barcelona sea, on that autumn dawn, after a night spent awake at the side of an old man who, just before dying, will fulfil his destiny by returning to his real home, his poor, inhospitable, stony and inclement lost homeland, returning to Terra Alta. And, when Melchor finally stops crying, or he thinks he's stopped crying, he dives underwater again, deep down, as if he wanted to cleanse himself of the tears, and when he breaches the surface he starts swimming again parallel to the shore, to the spot where he left his clothes, and from there he walks out of the sea and sits on the sand until the sun and the breeze dry his skin. Then he gets dressed and crosses the strip of sand again and walks up the promenade and hails a taxi.

The taxi drops him off minutes later in front of Domingo Vivales' place, an old building on calle Mallorca. Melchor opens the wrought-iron door using the key the lawyer gave him, and takes the wooden lift up to the fifth floor. As he's trying to open the door to Vivales' flat, someone behind him orders: "Put your hands in the air and don't move."

Melchor obeys. In the Sunday morning calm of the landing, he hears stealthy footsteps approaching and feels a hand take his pistol out of his shoulder holster, a moment he takes advantage of to drive his elbow into the face of his assailant, who falls to the floor with a cry of pain that seems to echo through the whole building. Melchor grabs the man by the neck, lifts him up and is about to rupture his testicles with a kick when the voice of Vivales stops him.

"Wait, Melchor!" he shouts. "Don't hit him!"

Melchor turns round: accompanied by a fat man in pyjama bottoms and a vest, Vivales has appeared at the door of his flat, in an unbuttoned shirt and a pair of boxer shorts that reach his knees. The lawyer has a pistol in his hand; the fat man, a baseball bat.

"Everything's under control, Manel," Vivales adds, talking to the man Melchor is gripping by the neck. "This is the little girl's father."

Melchor looks perplexed, observes his victim who looks back at him, his eyes still popping out of his head in terror, and, when he finally seems to understand, lets him go. The man collapses on the floor and the fat man rushes to his aid.

"Are you alright, Manel?" he asks.

"Can somebody tell me what's going on here?" Melchor says.

"Nothing," Vivales says. "These two are friends of mine. We did our military service together. Manel Puig and Chicho Campà. I asked them to help me protect Cosette. There are two others. We've been doing shifts these past days."

"You're going to go home with a black eye," Campà warns Puig, who is still sitting on the floor. "Your wife's going to think you've had one hell of a night."

"Shit, what a wallop he gave me," Puig mumbles, his hand over his eye.

Melchor starts to apologise, but Puig interrupts him.

"Not at all, kid," he says. "Occupational hazard. But, don't you worry, as long as I'm here, not even God will touch that child."

"Shut the fuck up, Rambo," Campà scolds him, helping him up. "What a mess you've made of guard duty. If Lieutenant Herruzo caught you, he'd knock your fucking block off."

At that moment the other door off the landing half-opens, footsteps are heard in the stairwell and a man's voice warns that he is going to call the police; almost at the same time, Cosette appears on the threshold of Vivales' flat, barefoot, in her nightgown and rubbing her eyes with the back of her hand.

"Papá?"

Melchor scoops up his daughter in his arms and, followed by Puig and Campà, walks into the flat while Vivales stays outside, arguing with his neighbours at the top of his lungs and threatening to sue them for public nuisance. When the commotion in the stairwell dies down and the lawyer comes back inside, Melchor is getting Cosette dressed in her bedroom. Father and daughter talk about the days the little girl has spent there.

"She's behaved very well," the lawyer says from the doorway.

Puig and Campà lean their heads in behind him.

"She's a great girl," Campà says.

"And very brave," Puig chimes in, holding a bag of ice to his injured eye.

Vivales asks Melchor what he's doing in Barcelona, and is everything under control in Terra Alta, and Melchor says yes and adds that he'll fill him in later. When Cosette is dressed, Melchor puts the rest of her clothes in a holdall.

"Are you leaving?" Vivales asks. "You're not even going to stay and have breakfast with us?"

Melchor says no, adding that they're in a hurry because they have to catch a bus.

"Where are you going?" the lawyer asks.

Melchor knows better than ever where he's going, but he stares at the lawyer for a moment, looks at his messy hair, his bad-tempered face, his truck driver's build, his drinker's belly and his skinny white legs, looking at him he suddenly remembers all the illusory or spectral fathers that troubled his childhood nights in his mother's flat, there in the neighbourhood of Sant Roc – the man who strode down the hallway with proprietorial steps and the one who tiptoed, trying to go unnoticed, the one who coughed and sputtered like a dying man or an impenitent smoker, the one who sobbed inconsolably behind a partition wall, the one who told ghost stories and the one who left at dawn wearing his long leather jacket – and although he is unable to put Vivales' face to any of those strangers, for the second time in his life he feels like hugging him. But he does not hug him: he just says goodbye to him and his two friends, while he takes his daughter by the hand and the holdall in the other. Vivales asks again where they're going.

"Home," Melchor says. "To Terra Alta."

Author's Note

I must thank Juan Francisco Campo, María Deanta, Jaume Escudé, Jordi Gracia, Miguel Ángel Hernández, Carlos Sobrino, Cinta Roldán and David Trueba for their help. Also the Mossos d'Esquadra of Terra Alta, without whom this book would have been impossible, because they opened wide the doors of their station and put themselves at my disposal; and in particular Deputy Inspector Antoni Burgés, Sergeant Jordi Escola and Agent Antoni Jiménez, and especially Sergeant Jordi López and Corporal Joaquim Rípodas, who, as well as patiently answering all my questions, were kind enough to read the manuscript of this book and share extremely useful observations with me. I must also thank Antoni Cortés, Terra Alta's best ambassador possible, who can't stand anyone thanking him.

JAVIER CERCAS is a novelist, short-story writer and columnist for *El País*, whose books include *Soldiers of Salamis* (which was awarded the Independent Foreign Fiction Prize among many other prizes and sold more than a million copies worldwide), *The Tenant & The Motive* (the latter now a film directed by Manuel Martín Cuenca), *The Speed of Light* (short-listed for the 2008 IMPAC Award), *The Anatomy of a Moment* (winner of Spain's National Narrative Prize), *Outlaws* (short-listed for the 2016 Dublin International Literary Award) and, most recently, *The Impostor* (winner of the European Book Prize) and, most recently, *Lord of All the Dead* (winner of the Prix André Malraux). In 2015 he was the Weidenfeld Professor of Comparative Literature at St Anne's College, Oxford, and a book based on the lectures he gave there is published under the title *The Blind Spot: An Essay on the Novel*. His books have been translated into more than thirty languages.

ANNE MCLEAN has translated Latin American and Spanish novels, stories, memoirs and other writings by many authors including Héctor Abad, Julio Cortázar, Gabriel García Márquez and Enrique Vila-Matas. She has twice won the *Independent* Foreign Fiction Prize, with Javier Cercas for *Soldiers of Salamis* and with Evelio Rosero for *The Armies*. She shared the 2014 International IMPAC Dublin Literary Award with Juan Gabriel Vásquez for his novel *The Sound of Things Falling* and in 2016 and 2004 won the Premio Valle Inclán for her translations of *Outlaws* and *Soldiers of Salamis* by Javier Cercas. In 2012 Spain awarded her a Cruz de Ofi cial of the Order of Civil Merit.